CLEAR
BLUE SKY

CLEAR
BLUE SKY

A NOVEL

F. P. LIONE

Revell
Grand Rapids, Michigan

© 2007 by F. P. Lione

Published by Fleming H. Revell
a division of Baker Publishing Group
P.O. Box 6287, Grand Rapids, MI 49516-6287
www.revellbooks.com

Printed in the United States of America

Library of Congress Cataloging-in-Publication Data
Lione, F. P., 1962–
    Clear blue sky : a novel / F. P. Lione.
      p. cm.
    ISBN 10: 0-8007-1886-0 (pbk.)
    ISBN 978-0-8007-1886-2 (pbk.)
    1. Police—New York (State)—New York—Fiction. 2. Cavalucci, Tony (Fictitious character)—Fiction. 3. New York (N.Y.)—Fiction. [1. September 11 Terrorist Attacks, 2001—Fiction.] I. Title.
    PS3612.I58C57 2007
    813'.6—dc22
                                          2007006533

This book is dedicated to Jesus,
who calls us friends.

Greater love has no man than this,
that he lay down his life for his friends.

PROLOGUE

In New York City, September is a beautiful month. The summer humidity is gone, and the skies are warm and clear. It's also the time of street festivals throughout the five boroughs of the city. Neighborhoods in Queens, Brooklyn, the Bronx, and Staten Island close off their streets, and people bring their picnic tables and grills out from the backyard for block parties. We sit and schmooze with neighbors we'll argue over parking spots with for the rest of the year and talk about who died, who moved, who got arrested, and how bad the neighborhood's getting. We also have the San Gennaro feast, with the annual procession of the statue of the patron saint of Naples paraded through the streets of Little Italy, and the smell of sausage and peppers, zeppoli, and cannolli from the street vendors fills the air. Labor Day starts it off with the West Indian Day parade on Eastern Parkway in Brooklyn.

September 11, 2001, was a beautiful clear day with a soft wind blowing from the north. It was also the electoral primaries in New York City. With new term restrictions, there was a mass exodus of a lot of the incumbent locals, and the new blood wasn't impressing any of us. The last thing we needed was another mayor who hated cops and handed the streets back to the perps.

But all of this was forgotten at 8:46 that morning when American Airlines flight 11 slammed into the North Tower of the World Trade Center and began the darkest day New York City has ever seen. This forever changed not only our skyline but also the lives of everyone in our city. And the soft winds that blew that day were of smoke and fire and death.

1

My name is Tony Cavalucci, and this is my eleventh year as a New York City cop. I've spent most of my career working midnights in a sector car in Times Square. My precinct is in Midtown Manhattan, in a detached, brown brick building off 9th Avenue that enhances the gloominess of the mostly commercial, litter- and graffiti-filled block.

I came here six months out of the Academy at twenty-two years old, and I've worked patrol here ever since. I was hoping to be "out of the bag," as we call it, and in the plainclothes Anti-Crime Unit before the end of the year. That move would eventually take me from Anti-Crime to Robbery in Progress—or RIP, as we call it—with my silver shield, and then on to the Precinct Detective Unit with my gold shield.

It was September 2, the Sunday before Labor Day, and even though it was 70 degrees outside, it was hot in the precinct. It would take a couple of weeks for the cooler air to make its way inside, and I was already starting to sweat under my vest. I was standing by the radio room with a cup of coffee, waiting for my partner, Joe Fiore, to come up from the locker room. I had a couple of minutes before roll call to shoot the breeze with Vince Puletti, the old-timer who runs the radio room. He was standing at the open door, with the ancient cassette radio on the battered metal desk tuned to the oldies station. He was listening to either Norm N. Nite or Cousin Brucie;

I couldn't tell with the static. The wire hanger wrapped in foil that he'd stuck in the spot where the antenna snapped off wasn't helping, and I wondered how he could listen to it that way.

Vince has at least thirty years on. He's big and beefy and won't give the time of day to any cop with less than five years on. He's bald except for the band of hair around the back of his head and has hands like sledgehammers. He reminds me of the bulldog on the *Tom and Jerry* cartoons; all he needs is a spike collar around his neck. He smokes two packs of Marlboros a day, has high blood pressure, and is so big in the gut he can't see his shoes anymore. He's been having some stomach problems lately, but it obviously isn't affecting his weight. He puts the max into his deferred comp and spends most of his time watching his investments and hoping he can retire without having to work another job.

"How's it goin', Vince?" I asked, shaking his hand.

"Ah, can't complain," he said, grabbing his belt and hoisting up his pants over his stomach like he always does. They slid right back down, so I don't know why he bothers.

John Quinn from the four to twelve handed Vince his radio and said, "I'm outta here."

"Have a good one," Vince called after him and stuck the radio into one of the chargers mounted on the wall behind him. I watched the charger lights go from red to yellow to green and back to red to show the battery was charging.

We heard the front door open, and we both turned to look as one of the new rookies came in. He stopped in front of the flags stationed just inside the door, saluted, and headed toward the stairwell to go upstairs.

"Is it that time again already?" I asked.

"Yeah, we got the rookies coming in tonight," he said, shaking his head. "Sorriest bunch I've seen yet."

Vince was talking about the brand-new rookies, the ones that have been writing summonses in their field training units since they got out of the Academy in July. Tonight would be their first roll call with the squad.

I've known Vince for almost eleven years, and every year when the new rookies come in he says they're the worst cops he's ever seen and how if this is all we got, the department is going down the tubes.

"Joe Fiore." Vince smiled past me as my partner came upstairs from the locker room.

"Hey, Vince. Hey, buddy," Fiore said, shaking our hands.

I started working with Fiore last June when my partner John Conte blew out his knee and needed surgery. Sergeant Hanrahan put me with Fiore, saying there was a lot I could learn from him. Fiore only had a couple more years on the job than me, so I didn't know what the boss was talking about. Looking back, he was right. There was a lot I could learn from Fiore, but it wasn't about police work. When I met him I was depressed from just breaking up with someone I'd been seeing for a few years, I was in the bar more than I was home, and I was toying with the idea of eating my gun. Fiore stood by me when I crashed and brought me into his family and his church. He also introduced me to Michele Dugan, the woman I'll be marrying this November. I've changed a lot this year, and when I get up in the morning and look in the mirror I'm not disgusted with what I see there anymore. I'm probably closer to Fiore than I am to my own brother. To be honest, he's the best friend I've ever had.

"Ready for tomorrow?" Fiore asked me, smiling.

"If I didn't need the money, I'd be home eating hot dogs," I said.

"You guys working the West Indian Day parade?" Vince asked, shaking his head. "You're outta your mind. You couldn't get me to work that on a bet."

Before Vince could go off on a tirade about the parade, Joe and I made our way over to the muster room, where roll call is held. The room is about thirty feet long by thirty feet wide with a wall of gated windows on one side. The other walls have crime stats, bios of wanted perps, and precinct club news that nobody reads. I saw a hand truck full of boxes taped shut. There must have been a sting operation on the four to twelve, and the boxes were taped shut to give the property clerk something to do in the morning. There were also two bicycles with evidence voucher sheets stapled around the handlebars leaning against the desk. The windows were open to let in some of the cool air and exhaust fumes, and I could detect the faint smell of urine, since the windows face the alley between the buildings.

The room was buzzing as we waited for Sergeant Hanrahan to give the attention to the roll call order. Hanrahan is a good boss. He's been my sergeant for a lot of years now, and except when he put me with Joe, I've never had a problem with him. He's in his late thirties, about six feet tall, with dark hair and deep blue eyes. He has some gray in his hair, but he's got a baby face, so it doesn't age him.

"The color of the day is white," Hanrahan said, giving the citywide color plainclothes cops use to identify themselves as police and keep them from getting shot if they're stopped by uniformed officers and reach for their badges.

Hanrahan went through his usual spiel, going from the color of the day right into the sectors.

"Garcia."

"Here."

"Davis."

"Here."

"Adam-Boy, 1886, five o'clock meal," which designated their sector, the number of the patrol car they'd be driving, and their meal hour.

"McGovern."

"Here."

"O'Brien"

"Here, boss."

"Charlie-Frank, 1883, four o'clock meal."

O'Brien was recently back from a stint in the pension section after an off-duty domestic incident involving his wife and the guy she was sleeping with. She claimed he threatened to shoot her and let off a round in the house. He was cleared of discharging his weapon a while ago, and last week he was cleared of the death threat and finally allowed back to work.

Sergeant Hanrahan went through David-George, which is me and Joe, and Eddie-Henry, which is Rooney and Connelly.

Midtown is divided up into sectors. The sectors in my command include the Garment District, 34th Street, Port Authority, Penn Station, Grand Central Station, Madison Square Garden, Times Square, the Empire State Building, and 42nd Street between 7th and 8th avenues, which all the old-timers call the Deuce.

When he finished up the sectors and got to the foot posts, there were a couple of new names, one of them being Nick Romano's replacement. Nick worked with us until last spring when he went over to FDNY.

"Snout?" Hanrahan said it like a question, and it came out with a choke.

"Here," a female answered, and we all swung our eyes toward her. She was tall and skinny, with curly dark blond hair and the fair skin and smattering of freckles that pegged her as Irish.

"Look at the Snout on her," Rooney called out.

A couple of snorts went up around the room as Hanrahan shook his head and said, "Robbery post 4." He gave Bruno Galotti robbery post 5 and called out two more new names. One of them was Walsh, a massive, dopey looking blond-haired guy. His upper body was huge, and his biceps were straining against the sleeves of his uniform.

"Here," Walsh boomed, his voice deep and thick.

I looked over at him and thought, *He's exactly what you want with you when it all hits the fan and you need some muscle.*

"We've got a new interim order about tasering emotionally disturbed persons," Hanrahan said, looking at a piece of paper on the podium. "There was an incident up in the Bronx where an EDP had soaked himself with gasoline earlier, and when the taser hit him he lit up like a Roman candle." He looked around the room. "So if you have an EDP who looks wet or you smell gasoline, let me or one of the sergeants know so we don't have a repeat of this occurrence."

This kind of thing happens sometimes. We try to lock up an EDP, and they're so psycho they wind up getting hurt. A lot of times we can't get close enough to them to know if they smell like gasoline or if they're soaking wet before they get tasered. It's not like we have time to ask them, or like they're willing to cooperate with us, but we end up looking bad anyway.

Hanrahan finally wrapped it up with, "You new guys"—he looked around the room at the rookies—"make sure you don't walk up together to your foot posts. Try to stay separate." They used to tell us this in the Academy. A group of rookies is an easy target, and someone who hates cops enough would get more bang for his buck with a bunch of rookies if he was looking to hurt us.

"Cavalucci, Fiore, Connelly, Rooney, and Davis, see me after the roll call," Hanrahan said as he grabbed his papers off the podium. As we approached him he said, "Make sure you're back at the house by 7:20 so we can be on the road by 7:30," which was the time we would leave the precinct to head out to the West Indian Day parade in Brooklyn.

"You working the detail, boss?" Rooney asked. "You must really need the money."

"I got four kids in Catholic school, my oldest is in high school," Hanrahan said. "Five grand a year just for her tuition."

"You should move to Long Island," Joe said. "You could send your kids to public school and save money on tuition."

"Yeah, and pay ten grand a year in taxes. No thanks, I'll stay in Queens," Hanrahan said, walking toward the desk to give Lieutenant Coughlin the sectors so he could call them in to Central.

"Central" stands for central communications, the familiar unknown voices that transmit our jobs from the 911 operators. The Central operators each work one division made up of three commands. When 911 gets a call, they dispatch it to Central, who then transmits to us.

When we went back over to the radio room, Vince was scowling at a baby-faced rookie standing over by the desk talking to Lieutenant Coughlin from the midnights.

The rookie he was watching now, a kid named Perez, made the mistake of letting Vince overhear him telling a couple of his buddies to stay away from the old-timers 'cause they'll get you in trouble. Vince was standing with his arms folded and a scowl on his face, staring the kid down, which is mild compared to what he used to do.

"What's the matter, Vince?" I asked as he glared at Perez.

Vince pointed over at the desk and said, "Look at this meatball." He was shaking his head in disgust.

Perez had come out of the back by the cells with a couple of EMS guys and a perp in a wheelchair wearing a Bronx party hat—a blood-stained, gauze-wrapped turban—from having his head busted.

"What's the collar for?" the lou was asking Perez.

"Past assault," Perez said.

"Past assault? Past assault? Pass the pepper, you moron!" Vince yelled. "It's assault in the past!"

Perez got red in the face when everyone around us started laughing. "He tossed a bottle into a crowd of people outside a bar on 8th Avenue. They caught up with him at the light on 44th Street. Officers Alvarez and Rivera locked up the two guys that hit him."

I saw the corner of the lou's mouth twitch a little. We call Alvarez and Rivera Rice and Beans, but Perez wasn't chummy enough to call them that.

"Is he going to the hospital?" the lou asked.

"Yeah," Perez said with a nod, looking nervously at Vince.

Vince stared at him until he went out the front doors of the precinct. Terri Marks was working the desk. She's half in love with Fiore and was looking at him sideways through her black-eyelined silver blue eyes.

"So when are you gonna leave your wife for me?" she asked.

"It's never gonna happen, Terr," Joe said with a smile.

I shook my head and laughed. We go through this just about every night. Terri's divorced, no kids, with the wear and tear of eighteen years on the job. Vince says she was beautiful once, before the years and the booze got the best of her. For all her show about wanting Fiore to fool around with her, I have the feeling she'd be disappointed if he did.

We grabbed our radios and Bruno Galotti and went out to our RMP. We grabbed the copy of the *Daily News* that Rice and Beans had left in the car from the four to twelve and threw our hats on the backseat. The car was pretty clean. Before I met Fiore I used to lose it and throw all the trash out onto the street if someone left my car dirty. Now I usually clean it out without saying anything, but a couple of times I got mad enough to dump the garbage outside their locker.

We drove to the corner of 9th Avenue and threw Bruno out of the car to get us coffee and the *Post*. I used to throw Nick Romano out of the car to get our coffee, but since he went over to the fire department, Bruno's all I got to boss around. He's not as much fun as Nick. He never argues with me.

Mike Rooney pulled his RMP up behind us. Rooney's the clown of our squad. He's a big Irishman who's built like a linebacker and drinks like a fish. He's got a mop of brown hair, blue eyes, and a big belly laugh. He's a good cop and probably would be a lot further up the ranks if he could shut his mouth and watch the drinking. He's the kind of guy they're talking about when they say, "God invented alcohol so the Irish wouldn't rule the earth."

He started singing, "When the moon hits your eye like a big pizza pie, that's amore," over the patrol car's PA system. I shook my head and ignored him. He was always calling me, Joe, and Bruno dagos and greaseballs. Bruno takes offense at any kind of slur against Italians. He was born in Brooklyn, but his parents were off the boat and they speak Italian at home. He's not too bright, and when he got the flag of Italy tattooed on his arm he got the colors backwards and wound up with Portugal or something.

While Joe and I are loyal Italians, stuff like that doesn't bother us. My fiancée, Michele, is only half Italian, and my grandmother says when I have kids I'll dilute the Italian blood. The way I see it, if I dilute the blood my son won't look like a goombah and my daughter won't have hair on her upper lip.

Bruno, Joe, and I all look Italian. Joe is a couple of inches taller than me, about six foot. He has dark wavy hair and brown eyes, but his skin is lighter. Bruno and I both have thick black hair and olive skin. Bruno has big brown eyes and a gullible look that reminds me of Baby Huey. My eyes are light, almost hazel, but I still look like I should be wearing six gold chains and looking for the hood ornament to my caddy.

"Did Geri drop your change again?" I asked Bruno when he got back in the car and handed Joe and me our coffee.

"Yeah," he said. "I think she does it on purpose."

"Nothing gets past you, Bruno," I said.

Geri works midnights at the deli and is always sexually harassing the cops in one way or another. She drops our change so we have to bend over and get it and find her smiling when we stand back up. She has a couple of perverted T-shirts about calling 911 and says a lot of raunchy things about handcuffs and nightsticks. Joe and I pretty much ignore her, but her and Rooney hit it off, and I was sure he'd be in there for the next ten minutes joking back and forth with her.

"Why is Vince always like that to the rookies?" Bruno asked as we drove up 8th Avenue.

"That's nothing," I said. "You should have seen what he was like when I came on."

"It's like he loves to humiliate us," Bruno said.

"Be glad that's all he does," I said. "Remember when the rookies were coming out of the Academy with 9mm's and the old-timers still had the .38's?"

"I think that was before my time," Bruno said.

"I remember it," Fiore threw in. "The old-timers had to qualify, and these guys were coming out of the Academy with them. I was working out in Queens then, and I remember a lot of the old-timers not wanting to use the Glock."

"Exactly," I said. "And Vince took a real dislike to one of the gung-ho rookies. The rookie was standing at attention in the front of the roll call with a couple of his Academy buddies, and Vince stood behind him. Vince had taken the bullets out of his .38 Smith & Wesson and started dry firing the gun next to the rookie's ear—click, click, click—slowly and methodically.

"The rookies were looking at each other, wondering if the old-timer was psycho enough to shoot them in the back. The sarge at the time was also an old-timer who was amused by the whole thing.

He stopped and said, 'Alright, cut it out now,' but he laughed when he said it. The rookies looked at each other again, shocked that the sarge didn't blast Vince. The sarge gave them a wicked smile, and I watched the color drain from their faces. When the sarge went back to the roll call, Vince started dry firing in rapid succession—click click, click—and by the time he hit the sixth round, one of the rookies fainted dead on the floor."

As I drove past 40th Street I saw the group of rookies, including Snout, walking together up 8th Avenue. Bruno waved to them, but they didn't see him. They looked more promising now that they disobeyed a direct order from the boss. It's the ones like Perez who do everything they're told that you gotta watch.

I pulled over at 44th and 8th to let Bruno out.

"Pick me up for my meal?" he asked.

"No problem, Bruno," I said, thinking of Nick, who used to ask me the same thing every night.

I started to pull away from the curb, when Central came over the radio with, "I got a job in the South. A female is being harassed by a group of people and a man on a horse at four-five and eight."

I gave Fiore a "What's this?" look and saw Galotti on the sidewalk fumbling with his radio. "Robbery post 5. I'll take that job," he said.

Snout came over the air with, "Uh, robbery 4 . . . robbery post 4. I'll respond to that too."

Central came back with "Which job are you responding to, robbery post 4?" Central likes to mess with the rookies too.

"Uh, the horse job."

Someone yelled, "Rookie!" and horse snorts and neighs started coming over the air.

"Robbery post 4, that's at four-five and eight." I could hear the smile in Central's voice. Then all the rookies chimed in.

"Robbery 3 to Central."

"Go ahead, robbery 3."

"I'm gonna go to four-five and eight also."

Robbery 7 cut off robbery 3. "I'm going too."

Central cut in with, "Units, you're cutting each other off."

"We better go over there to help them out," Joe said.

"This should be interesting," I said. I love working midnights. People are always nuttier when the sun goes down.

Joe waved Bruno over, and he got back in the car. I threw the lights on as I approached 45th Street. On the east side of 45th and 8th we saw a guy on a horse standing a little south of 45th Street near the curb.

I pulled up next to the horse, just past the entrance to the Milford Plaza. I saw two guys, one with a camera, laughing while a Park Avenue–looking female talked on a cell phone while staring them down.

The horse was big and brown, with a black mane and tail. It started doing a little nervous dance, I guess from the turret lights. The tail swished, the ears came up and back, and it jerked its head up and back every time the red light on the turret swung around.

There was a hot dog cart on the corner where a vendor wearing a white sweatshirt with a blue apron over it was selling Sabretts to the theater crowd. It was late for him to be out, but the line was three deep as people stopped to get a hot dog and see what was going on. About ten feet down from the cart, a table was set up where a guy was selling framed prints of different spots around the city.

We walked toward the small crowd that had gathered, and the cameraman walked over to the guy on the horse and pointed his camera lens down at the street. He pulled his headset off, and it hung around his neck.

"Officer, I called you," the female on the cell said. She had dark hair and blue eyes, was maybe in her midthirties, and wore a black dress and pearls. Looked like money.

"What happened?" I asked.

"I was coming from the theater," she said, pointing up toward Schubert Alley, "and these men approached me and started asking me questions. When I wouldn't answer their questions they started yelling and cursing at—"

"Officer, we have a permit," one of them cut her off with his British accent. "We're documentary filmmakers."

I guess he was the mouthpiece, because he held up his hand to one of the other guys who started walking over. I didn't like him already.

"Excuse me, I was talking," the woman said, staring at him. "As I was saying"—she looked at me—"when I told him not to curse at me, he pushed me."

"He pushed you? Give me the permit." Joe glared at him. He took the permit and press card and as he was reading asked, "What's with the horse?"

"People see the horse, and they stop to talk and pet it. It gives us an opportunity to interview them, uh, question them." The mouthpiece said it like Joe was too stupid to understand what *interview* meant. He was tall, over six foot, with blue eyes and dark hair. He was the best looking one out of the group, confident, and used to getting his way.

"I did not stop to talk to you or pet your horse!" the female said, raising her voice.

"What are you doing here?" Joe asked him.

"We're just interviewing people randomly," he said, a smile pasted on his face.

"About what?" Joe wasn't smiling.

"The city nightlife in Times Square."

"So why is she telling me you're cursing at her?" I threw in.

He hesitated. "We weren't. We were just asking questions, and she got mad."

"What kind of questions?" I asked.

"Do you feel safe walking the streets at night?" he said with a shrug.

The female cut in. "I told him I wasn't interested in answering his questions, and he asked if I worked in a peep show, what kind of sex I liked." She added some other stuff that they said that was pretty gross. She wasn't the type to approach from that angle. They were probably just mad that she blew them off, so they started mouthing off. I guess they didn't expect her to call us.

"Officer, she doesn't know what she's talking about," the mouth-piece said, dismissing her.

I looked over at her. She was upset enough to call us, and I didn't think she was lying. I looked back at them. There were four of them: one with the camera, one on the horse, a female, and the guy talking to me. The female was holding a tripod and had what looked to be a camera bag slung over her shoulder. They were trying hard to look artsy, unshaved, and shabby in their designer clothes. Instead, they reminded me of the squatters down in Alphabet City, where they move into abandoned buildings acting like they own the place.

I heard the jingling of cuffs and the clanging of nightsticks as the stampede of rookies came running up behind me.

"You got a permit for that horse?" We all turned, speechless, to see Walsh, the muscle-head rookie, stomping toward the guy on the horse.

"Whoa, hold on there, tiger," I said, grabbing his arm. "You only need a permit for a horse and carriage, not a horse."

"Really?" Walsh asked, cementing the public's theory in general that cops are stupid. I was glad he didn't start scratching his head.

"Yeah," I said. "It's the same thing as riding a bike. You just have to obey the traffic laws."

The rookies gathered around us, still out of breath from running up 8th Avenue.

"Okay, here's what we're gonna do," I said. "Show us the tape when you were interviewing her." I pointed to the female in the black dress. "If nobody was harassing her, you can go on with what you were doing."

"You're not allowed to see this tape. It's protected under the First Amendment. I know my rights," the mouthpiece said as he shook his head at me like I was too stupid for him to talk to. I hear people talk about their rights all the time, but it's much more annoying with a British accent.

"You're an American citizen?" Joe asked, a lot nicer than I would have.

I smiled at his blank look, but he regrouped quickly enough and said, "I have a permit."

"I don't know, Joe," I said to Fiore. "You think documentary filmmakers get diplomatic immunity?"

Joe smiled at him. "Maybe you can call over to the UN and see if they can help you out with that."

"Buddy, come here," I called to the guy with the camera. "And you, John Wayne"—I pointed to the one on the horse—"off the horse."

They looked at each other.

"Today," I said.

He got off the horse, still holding the reins as the cameraman walked over to me.

"I know my rights," the mouthpiece said, getting louder.

"Listen," I said. "We can straighten this all out and avoid going back to the precinct if you let us watch the tape." I turned back to the cameraman. "Now show us the tape."

He lifted up the camera for me to look at, and the mouthpiece jumped in front of him. "I told you, you can't see the tape. I have a permit. I know my rights."

"I know your rights too," I said, half yelling. "And that camera is investigatory evidence, the only evidence we have of what happened." The louder I got, the more he backed down.

"Now, you have two choices," I continued. "One"—I counted off on my fingers—"you can show me the tape, or two, Officer Galotti here is gonna lock you up and let a judge decide whether or not we can see it."

Galotti gave me a blank look and then nodded his head.

"That's right," Galotti said, reaching for his cuffs. I saw the other rookies reach for theirs and move in closer, itching for a collar that didn't involve force or gunshots.

"You don't have a permit to harass people," I said. "Let us look at the tape. If you didn't do anything wrong, you can leave."

The female in the black dress was looking pretty smug, so I knew there was something on the tape they didn't want us to see.

I heard Fiore get on the radio, "South David to Central."

"Go ahead, South David."

"Can you have the sergeant respond to four-five and eight, non-emergency."

"10-4."

"This camera is worth over a hundred thousand dollars!" the mouthpiece was yelling. "It's not ours, it's the production company's. You can't take it!"

About three minutes later Sergeant Hanrahan pulled behind my RMP, and him and his driver, Noreen, got out of the car. Noreen put her hat on over her hair, which was falling out of the clip on top of her head.

"What's going on?" Hanrahan asked.

Joe pulled him to the side. He turned his back to us while he filled

24

in the sarge, talking low so as not to incite anyone. Hanrahan was nodding, and every once in a while he would look over at one of them and nod.

The mouthpiece was still in my face. The cameraman was next to him, and the guy with the horse and the female stood by the street. The female was short, with a mop of curly brown hair. She started to pet the horse's neck, talking quietly to it.

"Okay, this is what we're gonna do to clear this up," Hanrahan said loudly, walking back toward us. "Either we see the film, or we lock you all up and take the camera."

"No!" the mouthpiece said, shaking his head. "I know my rights— you can't take the camera."

"Wrong," Hanrahan said and turned to us. "Joe, grab the camera." He pointed to the cameraman and the mouthpiece. "Tony, Bruno, lock them up." He spotted Snout with the other rookies and gave her a "Come here" signal. "Snout, grab the female." Then he got on the radio and had Rooney and Connelly respond to take the complainant back to the precinct.

The complainant smiled. "That's fine with me." She looked at her watch. "Will I be long?"

"Shouldn't be," I said, shaking my head.

She looked at the mouthpiece and said, "It's worth it."

I said, "C'mon, get up against the car," as Joe took the camera and placed it on the sidewalk.

As I put the mouthpiece on the hood of the RMP, he said, "You can't do this! I know my rights."

"Just show them the tape!" This was from the curly-haired female that Snout was cuffing. He gave her a look that told me we were gonna lock them up anyway once we saw it.

"Bruno, you gotta lock him up too," Joe said, nodding toward the guy with the horse.

25

Once we got the four of them handcuffed and spread-eagle against the RMP, I said, "Now, this is New York City nightlife. You want me to get this on tape for your documentary? We'll even pass the peep show on the way down to the precinct if you want." I guess they didn't think that was funny, and none of them said another word.

"What do we do with the horse?" Bruno asked Hanrahan.

"I'll ride it," Walsh jumped in.

When you're a rookie you always volunteer to do stuff like this. As time goes on you learn to shut your mouth and let the new schmuck take it.

"You know how to ride a horse?" Hanrahan asked, skeptical.

"Sure," Walsh said with a shrug. "How hard could it be?"

Hanrahan looked at Joe and me. "Either of you know how to ride a horse?"

We both shook our heads no.

"Boss, I got it," Walsh said. "I've ridden before."

"I don't think pony rides at the zoo count," I said.

Hanrahan smiled and shrugged his shoulders. "Let him ride it."

Walsh got on the horse, putting his left foot in the stirrup and hopping off his right foot to propel himself over. As he grabbed the saddle, the horse started to turn in a circle.

"I gotta see this," Hanrahan said, shaking his head.

As Walsh pulled the reins to the right, the horse started going the other way in a circle. Walsh tried to nudge it forward with his knee and actually said "Giddyap," but the thing wouldn't go forward. He gave it a small kick in the side, and the horse took off. He pulled back the reins and said "Whoa," and the horse stopped and started to walk backwards.

"Anybody else know how to ride a horse?" Hanrahan called over to the rookies and got a bunch of blank looks. He looked over at Walsh, who was now kicking the horse in both sides, sending it into a full gallop and almost flipping himself backwards. We heard the screech of tires as a cab entering the crosswalk at 45th Street almost picked off Walsh and the horse. The guy that'd been riding him started to move toward Walsh, but I grabbed him. "Nothing's gonna happen," I said.

Once the light changed, Walsh made it across 8th Avenue okay, heading west on 45th Street.

"We'll follow him to make sure he doesn't kill himself on the way back," Joe said.

Hanrahan nodded, his eyes still on Walsh.

We put the horseman and the cameraman in our car and the female and the mouthpiece in the sergeant's car with Snout. Bruno got in the car with us and radioed Central.

"Robbery post 5 to Central."

"Go ahead, robbery post 5."

"I got four under and a horse at four-five and eight."

"That's zero zero twenty hours, robbery post 5."

"10-4."

2

On the way back to the precinct the radio was bombarded with "Hi-yo Silver," "There's a new sheriff in town," and "Algebra, this is no place for you!" from *The Little Rascals*. Then I heard the clip-clop of horse hooves being tapped on the dashboards of the RMPs to the theme song of *Bonanza* while someone sang "Happy Trails." Cops always do this stuff. It breaks up the monotony of the job.

We followed Walsh as he went down 9th Avenue on the horse. Except for almost getting whacked by the cabbie on 45th Street and going back and forth between a trot and a full stop, he didn't do too bad.

The perp that had been riding the horse looked nervous seeing Walsh ride him, and I saw him wince every time Walsh came to a corner and pulled back on the reins to stop the horse.

"Relax," I said to him. "Nothing's gonna happen to the horse."

"He has no idea how to ride a horse," he said in his snotty British accent.

I had no idea what one of those blue-blooded fox-hunt types looked like, but I didn't think he was it. He was right about Walsh though—he had no idea how to ride a horse.

Walsh waited on the horse by the front steps of the precinct while we parked the car. When we walked up with the cameraman and the horseman in cuffs, he asked, "What should I do with him? Should I just tie him up out here?"

"Tie him up in the side yard where peddlers keep the vendor carts," I said. The last thing we needed was someone stealing the horse and Walsh losing five vacation days. I could hear Central calling us with reports of someone riding the horse through the Lincoln Tunnel.

"Can I check on him?" the horseman asked, nodding toward the side yard where Walsh was taking the horse.

"You can, but he might not recognize you with the cuffs on," I said.

"You're not as funny as you think," he said.

"Sure I am." I smiled and grabbed his elbow. I walked him over and let him take a look at the horse before we went inside.

Lieutenant Coughlin was at the front desk when we came in.

"Whaddaya got?" he asked, looking at whatever he was writing.

"I got four under for harassment," Bruno said.

Coughlin peered over the top of his eyeglasses, "Where's the horse?" obviously having heard Bruno's transmission earlier.

"He's in the side yard," I said.

"Is he tied up?"

"We tied him to the dumpster in case he wants to graze," I said, watching Coughlin's mouth twitch. "And if he fertilizes the alleyway, it won't smell any different."

The sarge came in with the mouthpiece and the female. The mouthpiece looked mad, and the female looked humiliated. Her face was blotchy as if she'd been crying. Rooney and Connelly followed with the complainant, who was still on her cell phone, probably calling her lawyer.

Joe went behind the desk and grabbed the block of wood shaped like a .38 that held the keys to the gun lockers. He took my, Bruno's, and his guns and put them in the lockers behind the desk.

"Terr, can you buzz us in and come in the back?" Joe called as we stood in front of the gate leading to the back by the cells.

"Right now, with everyone watching? I knew you'd come around, baby." She beamed at Joe. "Does anyone have a breath mint?" she yelled to the room.

"I need you to search the female, Terr," Joe said seriously.

"Anything for you," she said, smiling, as Joe shook his head.

The female looked horrified. I guess she forgot you get searched when you're arrested. The four perps were looking at the "Stop! No firearms beyond this point" sign, and I saw them reading the other signs posted around the door on white eight-by-ten-inch pieces of paper. Their eyes got big when they saw the "No weapons beyond this point," "All prisoners must be handcuffed when entering this area," "All prisoners must be handcuffed when leaving this area," and "Authorized personnel only" signs and an extra "No weapons beyond this point" sign in case you didn't see it the first time.

They do this so a prisoner can't go for your gun in the close quarters of the cells. I've heard stories where this has happened and cops have gotten shot, but it's never happened here.

We walked them past the fingerprinting machine, and I saw the perps eyeing the "Bad guys are watching" sign that has a picture of a guy that always reminds me of the Hamburglar. We took them back to the holding pen/arrest-processing room. We process the arrest in the room with the prisoners so we can watch them and make sure they don't hurt other prisoners or themselves.

It's a small room, about fifteen feet by fifteen feet. To the immediate right are the height markings for mug shots. Next is the pen with the anchored bench with metal loops for handcuffs, and then outside the pen are two benches for the female prisoners. There's a wall of gated windows and a desk where the cops sit and do the paperwork.

The room was filled with the stink of feet and the sound of snores coming from the cell. I spotted Walter the drunk passed out on the bench in the cell. Everyone knows Walter. He's homeless and drinks up on 8th Avenue and 42nd Street. We're always locking him up for spitting at the tourists who won't give him any money when he's panhandling.

Walter was dressed for winter even though it was 70 degrees outside. He wore a blue wool cap, an aqua-colored plaid jacket, and fleece pants with a hole in the knee. His worn laceless sneakers were lying on the floor haphazardly, and he wore dingy gray socks that were white once and would probably stick to the wall if you slapped them up against it.

Terri Marks took the female into the stairwell to toss her while Joe stood within earshot of her, watching us.

Galotti and I tossed the other three, taking their wallets, cigarettes, lighters, and keys. I wanted to give them the full experience of their arrest, so I took their belts and shoelaces in case they tried to hang themselves. I let them keep their cash. If they'd had a lot of money on them, I would have vouchered it, but none of them had more than sixty bucks.

We put the three males in the cell and watched their faces as the gate clanged shut and the two bolts slid home. This is my favorite part of the arrest, when all arrogance is gone and reality sets in.

"Can I have a cigarette?" the mouthpiece asked, not so loud now.

"Nope. This is a smoke-free environment," I said, lighting a cigarette with his lighter.

You're not supposed to smoke, but we usually let the perps smoke unless, like this guy, they have no respect for cops. Then we use their lighters and make them breathe secondhand smoke.

I saw Joe smirk and shake his head, and for some reason I remembered that I haven't been in church for two weeks. I collared up the last two weekends, trying to save as much money as I can before I get married. I guess it's beginning to show, 'cause I find myself cursing more, losing my temper easier, and letting my Bible collect dust on the floor next to my bed. I told myself that once November came I'd be in church every Sunday again.

Since Walter was asleep on the bench, there was only room for one of the three male perps to sit. The cameraman sat next to Walter's feet, but the smell hit him, and he moved to the floor and leaned up against the metal bars of the cell. The other two were standing, and the female was cuffed to the bench outside the cell with her head down, looking at the floor.

Joe and I left Bruno to process the arrest. We went back out and got our guns out of the lockers behind the desk. Hanrahan was talking to the lou when we came out.

"What are you gonna do with them?" Joe asked the lou.

"Since the camera recorded the event, it's considered investigatory evidence. We'll give it to the DA and let them figure it out." He shrugged. "It's aggravated harassment, we'll ACD them." (ACD is basically a misdemeanor with a court appearance. They also wouldn't get back their camera worth a hundred grand without the assistant district attorney's okay. This would inconvenience them and make them think twice about playing games again.)

Joe and I went back out to the RMP and drove down to 9th Avenue and over to 34th Street to take a look at our sector. We patrol our sector by driving east to west from 9th Avenue to 5th Avenue and north to south from 34th Street to 40th Street. This gives us a look at the whole thing, which we wouldn't get just driving the avenues like some cops do. Since it was Labor Day weekend, the city was pretty quiet. It was the last weekend for the beachgoers to hit the Jersey Shore or Long Island, and for the first time since Memorial Day I didn't have to battle the Sunday night traffic while driving in to work.

I stopped for coffee at the Sunrise Deli on the corner of 40th and 7th and drove over to the parking lot on 37th Street just off 8th Avenue while we waited for a job.

Joe and I each took a paper. He took the *Daily News* and I took the *Post*. The only thing the papers seemed to be talking about these days was the mayoral election. I scanned an article about Herman Badillo, Mike Bloomberg's opponent in the Republican primary. He was complaining that Bloomberg was upping his charity giving here in the city, trying to buy New Yorkers. I didn't want to hear it. As far as I'm concerned, they're all full of it.

I went over to the sports section. Giuliani was making a last-minute deal to build new stadiums for the Mets and the Yankees before he left the mayor's office. He's a big Yankee fan, so I was surprised that he included the Mets in it. He called it a win-win deal. Since there's no such thing, I was immediately suspicious, and as I got further into the article I saw why. The deal was between the city and the owners of the two New York ball clubs. The deal was valued at $1.6 billion. The teams would split the cost, and our taxes wouldn't go up—like that would ever happen. Then it said that it was a nonbinding agreement and the new incoming mayor didn't have to go through with it. I'd bet money we'll never see the new stadiums.

"How'd it go with Vinny?" Joe asked.

"Huh?" I asked, still reading.

"Vinny, the bachelor party, what'd he say when you talked to him?"

I looked over at him. "Oh." I shook my head. "I must be outta my mind with the whole wedding thing. If it was up to me, I'd elope, but Michele won't do it."

"What happened?" He chuckled.

"I had a fight with him. He's insisting on throwing me a bachelor party the way he wants it. I told him forget it, I'm not going. Then my father jumps in and goes off on me, screaming about the wedding and how I'm so selfish—"

"I thought he wasn't talking to you."

"He wasn't talking, he was yelling," I said. "Vinny called me this morning and asked me to meet him at Grandma's for dinner so we could talk. I used to go every Sunday; now I only go if I have to. My father was there, and aside from him yelling at me for being selfish, he didn't say a word."

Joe knows enough about my family that nothing they do surprises him much anymore. He comes from a nice stable family, and I wonder if a lot of this isn't entertainment for him. When I started working with him I still lived with my brother, Vinny, in the house we grew up in. My parents had both moved out, leaving me and Vinny to renovate the three-bedroom colonial in Shore Acres on Staten Island. Occasionally my sister, Denise, would move back in, usually in the summer because the house sat right on the water, on the Narrows of New York Bay.

My mother was an alcoholic up until last summer when she went into rehab and has been sober ever since. Ironically, it was the same time I went on the wagon, but unlike me, she never fell off. I hit a bar last Christmas and tossed back a couple after a brawl with my family, but it didn't do much damage. My mother's doing good, and this summer she started going to school for nursing at a community college in Pennsylvania where she lives.

The argument Joe and I were talking about was about my and Vinny's weddings. Vinny got engaged last Fourth of July and picked October for his wedding. I got engaged in February and picked November for my wedding, and the whole family is in an uproar.

The uproar is more over the fact that they don't like my fiancée because she's not Catholic and has a little six-year-old son, Stevie. She's never been married and opted to keep the baby when the father wanted nothing to do with the whole thing.

Vinny and I are each other's best men and have to throw each other bachelor parties. Since I've been walking with God I don't want the strippers and the prostitutes, but Vinny does. Vinny's fiancée, Christie, doesn't seem to mind him having one last wild night, and everyone seems to feel Michele should feel the same way. But she doesn't, she's furious. So now I'm stuck in the middle and everyone is mad at me.

"What I don't understand is why Vinny is mad at you for not having what he wants at your bachelor party," Fiore said. "It's your night. It should be what you want."

"Yeah, well, I could have gotten away with it if we could do the fishing trip, but it's too late in the season for it. I told Vinny to make it this weekend, when I was going out fishing anyway with a bunch of guys from the precinct. I told him we'd get a bigger boat and take everyone out, but he wouldn't hear of it. He's not even talking to me," I said miserably.

I don't remember Vinny ever not talking to me, and I didn't know how to handle it. He's the peacemaker in the family, which makes things worse. It's like they think if Vinny's mad at someone, that person must be wrong because Vinny's never mad at anyone.

"Your family is so manipulative," Joe said.

I almost argued with him, but he was right. They do this stuff all the time. Before I met Joe I never noticed this stuff, or if I did I just drank until I didn't notice it anymore. My parents divorced years ago when my father had a thing on the side with his current wife, Marie, a man-eating shark who lives to make all of us miserable. Last spring Denise found out Marie's been fooling around on my father with a detective she works with at the 5th precinct. She works as a civilian there, and like my father, this guy is a lot older than her. I guess she bagged him the same way she bagged my father, with her youth and cleavage. We had a blowout when I told my father she was fooling

35

around on him. He called me a liar, and he hasn't spoken to me since. I've been keeping my distance from the family, making excuses why I can't go to my grandmother's house for dinner, which is where the family usually meets.

Last year when I stopped drinking and started going to church it was like the family spun off its axis and realigned, and I'm not sure where we are.

Whenever I'm there I understand why people fall off the wagon and go back to drinking. The hardest times I have not drinking are when I'm with them.

"And Michele isn't helping anything. She says if there's prostitutes at my bachelor party she won't marry me," I added.

"Can you blame her?" Joe said.

I looked over at him. If it was anyone else they would have said she was wrong. But Fiore is different—Captain America, I call him. He always does what he thinks is right, and nobody ever gives him any grief over it. When I try to do what's right I get reamed from every angle.

"I understand where she's coming from, Joe, but she's the one that wanted the wedding. She knows how my family is, and she should have expected this," I said.

He smirked. "So you're saying it's her fault?"

"No, I'm saying she's not the one that has to deal with them. And Vinny has a point. Up until the time I met her I would have wanted exactly what he's planning, and now all of a sudden I change the rules," I said and got out of the car to light a cigarette.

"What do you want to do, Tony? Do you want to start off your marriage making your brother happy or making your wife happy? Because Vinny won't compromise what he wants for you," Joe said, stepping out of the car with me.

He had a point. Vinny didn't care what I thought or how upset

Michele would be about it. He wanted to throw me a wild party that would go down in the history books. At first he wanted it to be one big party for the both of us, a weekend in Atlantic City with about thirty guys with lots of drinking, gambling, strippers, and hookers. I knew I couldn't do that, and I told him I just wanted to go out to dinner with him, my father, Joe, and a couple of friends, and I'd throw him the party he wanted. We first talked about it when we were at my grandmother's apartment for my birthday in June. When Michele realized what kind of party Vinny was having, we had the biggest fight we ever had. She wanted to know what would be at the party, and I said I didn't know, and she lost it, saying that I was lying to her and if this was the kind of stuff I did, she didn't think I would be a good role model for Stevie, whether or not he ever found out about it.

"Since you're so smart, what would you do?" I asked Joe, raising my voice a little. It was easy for him. His family wasn't like mine. He also didn't live his life one way and then wake up one day and change everything like I did. My family doesn't understand me anymore, and they feel I'm being influenced by Joe and Michele, which I guess is true.

"Tony, I can't tell you what to do," he said quietly, but I could hear the laugh in his voice.

"I know that, Joe. I'm asking what you would do if you were me."

He thought for a minute. "I'd tell Vinny that we were going out to dinner like you want and if anyone didn't like it they could stay home," he said with a shrug.

"What about his party?" This was the one I was having trouble with.

"I'd pay for him to have the party he wants like you said you would, but I wouldn't go. If he gets mad, he gets mad, but that's not your problem."

"I don't know, Joe. I'm so stressed out about this. My grandmother told me the family is calling her asking why I'm not getting married in a Catholic church. She said some of them might not come because of it." I took my last drag and flicked my cigarette toward the back of the parking lot.

"I think Granny's got her own agenda," Joe said, looking at me as we got back in the car. "She wants to get rid of Michele and Stevie and have you back just the way you were."

Sometimes I feel like my family, my blood, are on one side, pulling me back, and God, Joe, Michele, and Stevie are on the other side, pulling me forward, and I'm in the middle wondering if I'm gonna lose a limb if I go in either direction. Things have changed so much over the past year. It's like my family is uncomfortable around me now, and even when they don't say a word, I know they don't approve of me. They liked me better when I was drinking and fighting and sleeping around.

On the other side of that is Michele, who knows they don't like her and doesn't see that changing. "It's like they have this little club, Tony," she said once. "And they let me know right from the beginning that I'm never getting in. And Stevie's too young to understand it right now, but someday he will. And what will we tell him? That it's because he's your stepson that he's not good enough? I never want him to feel that kind of rejection."

Neither did I, but I was hoping that as long as he didn't feel it from me that it wouldn't matter what they thought.

Since I didn't want to talk about my family anymore, I switched the radio over to the Brooklyn citywide channel to see how the night detail was going at the West Indian Day parade. There was a lot of chatter on the radio, and I could already hear the chaos.

"Shots fired on Utica Avenue . . ."

"I need a bus forthwith . . ."

"Suspect running northbound on Utica Avenue toward Lincoln Place . . ."

"This is Lieutenant Robinson, dispatch Brooklyn North task force to Utica Avenue and Eastern Parkway . . ."

"It's starting already," I said.

"I hate this detail," Joe said, closing his eyes.

"You ever work the detail the night before?" I asked.

"Once. Never again," he said.

I felt the same way. While the big parade isn't until Labor Day, there's a lot of buildup into it. The morning of the parade there's a predawn celebration, so things are cooking all night.

The whole thing started back in the 1940s up in Harlem when someone got a permit to close off Lenox Avenue for the parade. It's supposed to be a Lenten celebration, but for some reason it's held on Labor Day. It was held there up until 1961 when a band marcher bashed a spectator over the head with his steel drum that he wore around his neck. Apparently, the guy tried to take his instrument and he knocked him in the head with it, and next thing you know, bottles and bricks are flying. Ten people were arrested, and that was the end of it. A couple of years later another rock fight broke out and the permit was revoked.

They moved it to Brooklyn after that in the form of block parties in Crown Heights. Then in 1971 another parade permit was given to hold the parade on Eastern Parkway and parade eastbound to the Grand Army Plaza through Crown Heights and Flatbush.

Brooklyn has the largest West Indian community outside the Caribbean, and the parade draws close to two million people. It's a wild party with lots of steel drums and reggae music with calypso and other dancers. Some of the costumes are colorful and provocative, while others are ghoulish and devilish, freaky stuff. It evolved from a nineteenth-century festival for freeing the slaves.

In recent years the parade has become dangerous. There's so many stabbings and shootings in the course of a few hours that it's almost impossible to keep it under control. Things are thrown out of buildings at the crowds and at the cops. Gang colors are worn, and shootings erupt out of nowhere, with innocent bystanders catching bullets.

Two years ago when I was still with my ex-girlfriend Kim I worked the night detail. I thought I'd be working at one of the mobile command centers, but I wound up getting a foot post in one of the residential areas.

I was with three other cops from my precinct, all East Long Islanders looking to make some overtime. We wound up being separated into foot posts on different blocks. When we got there and the place looked like a war zone with the litter and the haze of smoke in the air, one of the cops broke out in hives. The litter was worse than the Fourth of July—that's all paper from the fireworks. Plus everything else, there were bottles, garbage, and boxes, and the smell of incense, pot, and barbeque was making us nauseous. We worked the midnight, but it could have been the middle of the day with the amount of street traffic, music playing, and people partying outside.

For the most part the West Indians are nice people. It's the punks, the Brooklyn boys starting trouble over "Who dissed me?" "You lookin' at me?" and "Who looked at my girl?" Crap like that.

My post was in front of a four-story building. The people in the building were nice enough. A group of about six kids between fifteen and eighteen were saying, "Hey, officer," and "Can we get ya something?" I told them to pick me up a soda, which they did. It was in a can, so I knew they didn't poison me. I shook their hands and told them not to do any smoking in front of me and we'd be okay.

There was this one female trying to get me to go into her apartment with her. She would come in and out of her apartment during the course of the night asking if she could "get me anyting" and offering me food and drinks. She looked sultry in a banana yellow halter dress with a matching headband. Her accent sounded exotic, and I remember her catching me watching her as she walked up toward Eastern Parkway. At about 6:30 that morning when I was about dead on my feet, she came walking up again. She smiled and said, "Come on inside, officer, take a break. Take your shoes off. You must be tired." When I hesitated she said, "I'll make you breakfast, maybe some chocolate cake?" Her eyebrows went up with the question.

"Sorry, I can't leave my post," I said, trying to sound serious but sounding like something out of *Dragnet* instead. She laughed and shrugged, swaying suggestively as she walked inside.

I switched back to channel 9 on the radio and went back to reading the paper. I heard Joe start to snore and got out of the car to smoke another cigarette, wondering if I'd ever be able to quit. I seemed to average between one and three days without smoking before I found myself so agitated that I went back to it. I finally decided to wait until after the wedding, when all the stress died down, before I even attempted it again.

At about 2:30 Central came over with an alarm. "South David."

"South David," Fiore said automatically, bringing the radio to his mouth with his eyes still closed.

"There's a 10-11 at 4 West 38th Street."

"Do you have a premise name and floor number?" he asked, getting the alarm info with his eyes open now.

"Goldman's Jewelers, suite 1215."

"10-4," Fiore said, sticking the heels of his hands into his eye sockets.

I put the car in drive and drove the wrong way down to 9th Avenue when Central came back with, "South David, I'm getting multiple alarms for this job, and Holmes Security is responding."

A single alarm can go off for a lot of different reasons, but multiple alarms mean someone is running through the place.

"This should break up the night," Joe said as I floored it.

I had the turret lights on as I drove eastbound on 38th Street. I heard the other sectors come over the radio:

"South Sergeant responding."

"South Henry responding."

"South Adam responding."

Burglary, robbery, and grand larceny are big crimes in Midtown because of all the commercial establishments. The fact that it was a three-day weekend made it prime for someone to hit. On a long weekend someone can set off an alarm on Friday and sit on it until Sunday. The security people will respond on Friday and see nothing out of place and figure it's a false alarm. They hit it again on Saturday with the same results, and by Sunday we don't come back. Then they hit at 3:00 in the morning on Sunday, drilling into the safe from the floor above or below it, and no one is due back in the building until Tuesday.

Other times they can overcome the alarm system using telephone wires and a box. The alarm system sends a beacon through the phone lines to the security office. When the line is cut, the beacon isn't sent and the alarm is set off. When they overcome the system, they'll connect their homemade box to the phone lines. The box will send a false beacon to the security office, letting everyone at the security office think everything's okay. Then they have three days to empty the place at any time.

At 7th Avenue I heard South Sergeant and South Adam radio Central that they were 84, and I wondered where they were that they got there before us.

When I hit 6th Avenue I shut the lights off, just in case anyone was watching for us.

Rooney and Connelly pulled up with Joe and me in front of the twenty-story yellow brick building. The scaffolding that had been in front of it all summer when they resurfaced the building was gone, giving the front a new look. There was no activity outside the building, and someone had stuck a nightstick in the door to keep it open for us.

The elevators were to our right, and Sarge, Noreen, Garcia, Davis, and an old-timer from Holmes Security were already inside holding the elevator door for us.

Rooney and Connelly stepped in, and I told the sarge Joe and I would cover the stairs. Across from the elevators was the door to the stairwell. When we stepped inside the stairwell doors there was a five-by-five-foot foyer with an arched doorway that led to the staircase. I stepped through the vestibule to the staircase and saw that the stairs went down to the basement and to the upper floors of the building. It was actually an outside staircase that had been closed in at some point. There were windows on each landing, and we could hear street noises as we entered the stairwell.

The place had a musty smell of urine, and it always amazes me that people will urinate in any stairwell. We see it in office buildings, apartment buildings, you name it. It's disgusting. How hard can it be to find a bathroom or go outside to relieve yourself?

We turned our radios all the way down so that if we got a blast from Central anyone in the stairwell wouldn't hear it. I was a little taken aback by the street noise and tried to filter it out to see what else I could hear. There was the hum of the overhead fluorescent lights as they flickered, but other than that there was nothing.

As we started to move toward the steps we heard the sound of muted footsteps a couple of floors up. The stairs were cement, and we were hearing a softer thud rather than the hollow sound you get from the metal ones.

Joe pointed up the stairs, and we backed up into the vestibule past the arched doorway because it looked like we were gonna run into whoever was on their way down.

As the footsteps got louder, we pulled out our guns. I moved to one side of the archway, and Joe moved to the other. From there we couldn't see the second-floor landing, and we wouldn't be able to see whoever it was until they were on us.

I once heard an old-timer say that the job was 90 percent boredom and 10 percent terror, and for some reason that flashed through my mind now.

I heard the footsteps getting closer, and while I couldn't tell how many people it was, I knew it was more than one. I felt my heart start pounding and a flash of heat as I started to sweat. I heard what sounded like metal scraping, and I was thinking they were dropping their tools.

Our guns were punched out in front of us. We didn't know if they'd come down with guns or what. We heard the movement, but it didn't seem to be coming any closer.

I thought maybe they got down the stairs and were behind the arched doorway and were behind the wall from us, but when I leaned into the stairwell there was nobody there.

As I stepped back I looked at Joe and shrugged. He shrugged back and gave me a "Where are they?" look. I grabbed my radio and called the sarge.

"South David to South Sergeant," I said keeping my voice low.

"South Sergeant."

"Boss, there's movement in the stairwell."

"Where?"

"I thought they were coming down to the first floor, but they must have stopped up on the second or third floor. We're gonna go up and investigate it," I said.

44

"10-4."

As I approached the stairs I looked up into the upper floors and saw nothing but empty handrails. I had my gun pointed upwards toward the second floor with Joe backing me up.

We kept hearing outside noises: cars, horns, the squeal of brakes. I heard a bus on 5th Avenue as I reached the first landing between the floors. I saw a window at the second-floor landing and realized that was where the street noise was coming from. As we approached the second-floor landing my eyes and gun were focused on the third floor to see if anyone was above us.

I looked out the window and saw that two of the four bars that covered it were cut on the bottom and bent out. I pointed to the window to show Joe and pointed to my eyes and up to the third floor to let Joe know to watch it.

Joe went up the stairs toward the third floor as I reached for the second-floor stairwell door. It had a "No Reentry" sign with a "#2" above it, but I gave it a pull anyway. It was locked, which I figured it would be because we hadn't heard a door open or close.

I went back over to the window and started pushing on the bars that were cut. They didn't budge. I could tell the cuts were new. There was no rust on them, and I could see tiny metal filings, which would have been blown away by the wind if they'd been there any length of time.

Joe came back down and said quietly, "The door's locked, no reentry on the third floor."

"They must've used a pry bar to bend the bars enough to get through, but I don't see one laying around. We're not gonna be able to follow them through the window," I said as I tried to push back and forth on the bars, showing that they wouldn't move.

Then we heard Hanrahan tell Central we had a confirmed burglary. My pulse kicked up a little. I can't help it. I love this stuff.

3

I looked out into the alley behind the building. There was some light coming from the building but not enough to see what was down there. Joe and I pointed our flashlights out the window, but all we saw was garbage and the heating and air conditioning units from the buildings. Then we heard glass breaking in the alley on the 38th Street side, and Joe got on the radio.

"South David to South Sergeant."

"Go ahead, South David."

"Sarge, I think they're in the alleyway right now. We can't get in there from here, and we can't see where they're at."

"See if you can find an entrance into the alley. I'll send South Eddie down."

We heard him tell Central to have the K-9 unit respond, and then Rooney radioed us. "South David on the air?"

"Go ahead," Fiore said.

"Where do you want us to search?"

"Mike, go over to 38th Street and see if there's any activity on the street there."

I remembered a parking lot on 37th Street that would give us access to the alley behind the building and got on the radio again to

Rooney so in case something happened back there someone would know where we were.

"Mike, we're going in through the parking lot on 37th to check behind the buildings."

"10-4."

Joe and I walked westbound on 37th Street, looking for anyone sitting in a car with an engine running, anyone walking on the street or coming out of one of the buildings.

I didn't think anyone would be jumping roofs. They came far enough downstairs to put them at street level.

There were a couple of things they could do right now. They could gain access to one of the buildings and hole up until the next day. If they rented a place they would stay there or exit out one of the buildings to a waiting car. I didn't think they'd hit the 6th Avenue subway. They usually plan this kind of thing right and have radios to communicate to a driver in a waiting car or have a backup place if they need to hide.

When we got to the parking lot, which is about a quarter of the block off 5th Avenue, I saw three cars parked westbound on the north side of 37th Street. You can park on the street here after 7:00 p.m., and as I got closer I saw the TLC plates of two black Lincoln livery cabs.

As we walked up on them I heard the engines running and looked inside. The first guy was reading an Arabic newspaper, oblivious to us. The driver of the second car looked over as we walked past. He had a guilty look, but that could have been for anything—worried about being summonsed, using someone else's cab, you name it. He was watching a mini TV perched on his dashboard and plugged in to the cigarette lighter. Both drivers looked like they were from Pakistan or Bangladesh or somewhere in the Mideast like most New York cabbies.

I wrote both the plate numbers down and moved to the third car, a black Mercedes CL500 that was unoccupied. The owner was probably in the club across the street, an upscale dark redbrick building with green marble accent. I know it's a good club because we never get calls there. There's a huge smoked glass window in the place that no one's ever been thrown through.

Central came over the radio with "South Sergeant on the air?"

"Go ahead, Central," I heard Sarge reply.

"There are no K-9 units available."

"10-4."

"I guess Dog Man took Shane to the beach for the weekend," I said to Joe. Dog Man is what we call our K-9 cop.

"You'd think he'd be in on a long weekend," Joe said. "This is when they always hit."

Without the dog to track the scent of these guys, they'd be even harder to find.

Joe and I went into the parking lot and saw that the light in the back of the lot by the alley was out, leaving the whole back area in darkness.

As we walked back there we saw that the bulb was burned out rather than that someone had smashed it. The lot had been closed since 7:00 p.m., and the workers were gone. Any cars left there after 7:00 are on their own. There were no cars in there. People are too afraid of having the cars broken into. Plus, the overnight charge is ridiculous. At the back of the lot were the black-framed metal lifts used to stack the cars when the place gets packed. To the right of the lifts was a fifteen-foot pit that we'd have to go through to get into the alley behind the building. I have no idea what it's for, except that it's the bottom of what used to be an old outside stairwell that was removed and not filled in when they built the lot.

It was so dark back there, even with the flashlights. I couldn't see the bottom of the pit clearly, but I was guessing it was filled with stagnant water, garbage, and rats. To our left was a metal link fence that ran the length of the back of the parking lot, along the edge of the pit.

We saw a walkway with handrails on the other side of the pit, running along the back of the building across from us. There was a two-foot cement ledge that we could shimmy across while holding on to the fence, or we could climb through the pit.

"Take the ledge," Joe said, reading my mind.

"Definitely. I'm not walking through that."

I stepped onto the ledge, pulling back hard on the fence to make sure it didn't pull away from the poles and we'd fall in the pit anyway. It seemed like it'd hold us, and I faced the fence and sidestepped my way along it. When I got to the middle between the poles, there was some slack in the fence and it pulled away.

"Whoa," I said as the fence rattled.

"You okay there, buddy?" Joe asked.

"Yeah, just make sure you don't pull on the fence when you're in the middle."

When we got to the other end I walked on top of the cement wall of the pit to get to the walkway. The further we got from the parking lot, the darker it became. I had my flashlight out, and I tried to listen for noises, but all I heard were the cycling HVACs. When we got to the end of the walkway we had to walk up a couple of steps to a platform that crossed us over to the other side of the alleyway.

There was a maze of metal walkways, stairs, and fire escapes. It was hard to hear anything with the sound of the air-conditioning units, and we were trying to sift through the drone of noises for footsteps, talking, or the crackling of footsteps on garbage.

We spent about fifteen minutes back there with our flashlights, looking for the broken window from the glass we heard break earlier.

There were hundreds of windows and doorways, and unless something was broken, we were wasting our time back there.

"South David on the air?" We heard Rooney's voice.

"Go ahead," Joe said.

"There's nothing going on over here. You want us to come over and help you canvass?"

Joe looked at me and gave me a "Nah" face and shook his head. "No, we're gonna wrap it up here. Meet us back at the premise," he said.

"10-4," Rooney said.

We walked back up to 5th Avenue and over to 38th Street. Rooney was smoking a cigarette, talking to Connelly, Garcia, and Davis.

"So, Tony, I hope you and Joe are ready to do some real fishing on Sunday," Rooney said as we walked up.

"Joe, did you hear what happened to Garcia last year when he went out fishing with us?" Rooney smiled, taking a drag.

"No, I must have missed that one," Joe said.

"Oh, here we go," Garcia said, shaking his head.

"It was hysterical!" Rooney barked out a laugh.

"Hysterical? You almost killed me!" Garcia yelled.

"We did not. Don't blame me that you spent the whole trip puking over the side of the boat." Rooney laughed.

"Do you know what he did?" Garcia half yelled at me, furious.

"No," I said.

"Rooney invites me out with him, Connelly, McGovern, and O'Brien. When we left Montauk the weather was bad. I didn't think we'd be able to fish, but the captain said it was supposed to clear up. They started pounding down beers before we left the dock. The boat was rocking, and I started feeling sick—"

Rooney cut him off. "You left a chum trail of puke."

"Shut up, Mike," Garcia said. "I put one of those motion sickness patches behind my ear and laid down on one of the benches next to the captain's chair to sleep it off until I felt better. When I was sleeping Rooney took the box of patches and put them all over my arms and legs!" Garcia was raising his voice now.

"He . . ." Rooney cracked up. "He . . ." Rooney was laughing so hard he couldn't get the words out. "We hear this little 'Help me.'" Rooney started coughing now. "It sounded like . . ." Rooney's eyes were tearing, and he couldn't finish the sentence. "It sounded like a kitten mewing. I look over at him and he's got . . ." He coughed again. "He's got drool dripping from his mouth, and his eyes are rolling back in his head. His whole body looked like it was novocained, with his mouth opening and closing like a guppy."

"I had to go to the bathroom and I couldn't move," Garcia yelled at Rooney.

"You were fine," Rooney said, waving him away. "We took the patches off and you were up in half an hour."

"Yeah, I was bouncing off the walls trying to make it to the bathroom. Do you know what it's like trying to pee when you can't stand up straight? I was slamming into the walls while the boat rocked. I peed all over myself and the walls."

We were howling now, and Garcia said, "It's not funny, he could have killed me. You're nuts going fishing with him. He's a psycho. If you find yourself in the bottom of the ocean from one of his stunts, don't blame me."

This Sunday, me, Joe, and Nick Romano are going tuna fishing off Montauk Point. Mike Rooney, McGovern, and Bruno Galotti from our squad are also going. I've never fished with Rooney before, but like most things with him, I'm sure it'll be memorable.

We went inside the building and took the elevator up to the twelfth floor. As we stepped off I saw the camera up on the wall, the lens set on the elevator. I saw the stairwell door, its bar lock still in place, with the bottom half of the door flapping. It looked like someone had cut off a section of the door and kicked the rest of it in.

We followed the hallway to Goldman's Jewelers and entered the receptionist area.

"Sarge?" I called out.

"Back here," he said from somewhere in the back.

We walked past the tables where the jewelers work and down to the end of a long hallway with offices on both sides. There was nothing posh about the office—gray carpet, old furniture, probably ten million in diamonds in the safe.

We walked past the safe and saw they had attempted to access it. There was a saw with a circular diamond tip blade on the floor.

It was a custom-built safe made of concrete and steel. The first layer was Sheetrock, then concrete, then steel. They had cut through the Sheetrock and concrete and must have gotten scared off as they were cutting through the steel.

The tools were brand-new—a pry bar, a sledgehammer, a saw, and a flashlight.

Hanrahan was in the back office with the Holmes security guard and Lieutenant Farrell. They had a VCR set up and were rewinding the tape when we came in. It was from the camera facing the elevator, and we watched the hallway and the stairwell door. In one frame the hallway was empty, and in the next frame the four guys came out from underneath the cut stairwell door wearing masks and gloves.

The first guy came out of the door and held the bottom up for the others, looking up and down the hallway as he was holding it. The second guy was wearing a backpack and holding the sledgehammer. The third guy was also wearing a backpack, but he was talking into a walkie-talkie. The last guy was big, almost on his stomach coming through the door. He got up, slapped the guy who was holding the door on the shoulder, and pointed toward the premise for him to follow. They were all looking around the hallway as they walked and disappeared from the camera's view. Approximately four minutes later we saw the four of them running like the tape was in fast forward.

The first guy held the door again as the other three dove underneath it. Thirty seconds later we saw Hanrahan and Noreen step off the elevator with South Adam and South Eddie behind them.

"Wow," Joe said.

"Yeah, thirty seconds later we would have had them," I said.

In all the years I've been here this is the closest I've gotten to grabbing something like this. There were a few burglaries where I've gotten there not long after the fact, like the Harper brothers that usually hit the garment district. We know a lot about them—that they usually hit on a long weekend like this and that they access from the roof or the fire escape—and we've never caught them.

"Somebody definitely warned them," Hanrahan said, looking at Farrell, who was clicking his unlit pipe against his teeth.

Lieutenant Farrell's the guy that handles the burglaries. He's an old war dog who looks like Santa Claus and smokes a pipe. He's about sixty years old, with more than thirty-five years on the job. They'll be making him retire in a couple of years, which, believe me, is a shame. He's one of the most brilliant cops I've ever met. He used to be a drinking partner of mine, and he's been to the farm to dry out a time or two. He's got no family. His wife left him long ago with two kids he probably wasn't fit to raise. They're all screwed up now. His daughter married an abusive guy, and his son battles with drugs. But he's good at catching burglars, and he was so intent on the tape he didn't realize we were in the room.

"Hey, Lou." I smiled at him as he rewound it.

"Tony!" He shook my hand, happy to see me. "I hear you're getting married." I sent him an invitation, but I guess he didn't want to say that in case anyone else in the room wasn't invited.

53

"Yeah, it's coming up soon," I said.

"I'm surprised you're marrying an Irish girl," he said with a smirk.

"Half Irish, half Italian," I said.

"Half Irish, half ashamed," Rooney cut in. My family says half Italian, half ashamed.

I could see him eyeing me up, and I knew it was to see if I was drinking again. He gave me a nod, like he realized I was sober, but he did it in a way like he wished I were drinking again. Not because he wants me to get hurt, but so we could hang out like old times. Sometimes when I see him I miss drinking. I miss the connection we had over good scotch, stories about the job, and cigarette smoke.

"So what do you think?" I nodded toward the VCR.

"They knew the layout, they knew exactly where the safe was and what was in it. Maybe they know one of the employees or they bought jewelry here to scope the place out." His eyes went back to the tape. "What happened downstairs?" he asked me.

I gave him the spiel about them jumping out the second-floor window, us hearing glass breaking, and the license plates of the three cars parked on 37th Street. "I never thought they'd go out the second-floor window," I said, wishing I had realized it.

"Maybe you're better off," Farrell said, chewing on his pipe. "These guys were serious."

I knew what he meant. I've seen burglary tapes where the perps had machine guns strapped around them, and you knew they had no plans to let us lock them up.

"Collect the tools," Farrell said. "We'll dust them for fingerprints. Maybe we'll get lucky with the batteries from the flashlight. Holmes'll get in touch with the owner so he can lie to us about what's in the safe."

The owners don't tell anybody, not even the cops, what's in the safe unless it's broken into. Then they'll jack up whatever's in there for the insurance.

Joe and I collected the tools and loaded them in the RMP. It was still dark outside as we made our way back to the precinct. The streets were still pretty quiet and the air nice and cool.

Joe vouchered the tools while I filled out what I could on the complaint report. We finished up around 5:30.

Hanrahan and Farrell came back with the videotape from the premise and were talking to Terri Marks over by the desk.

"Boss, we're gonna go downstairs for our meal," Joe said. We'd skip the food and catch an hour's sleep we'd need later for the parade.

"Go ahead," Hanrahan said, looking exhausted himself. "If I need ya's out I'll call."

"Thanks, boss," I said as we headed downstairs to the lounge.

The lounge where we take our meal is supposed to be for precinct club members only. For the twenty bucks a year we pay in dues we get to sleep in the lounge, shine our shoes with the shoe-polishing machine in the muster room, and go to different functions like ski trips and picnics even though we have to pay extra for them.

There are four tables put together in the middle of the room with chairs around them to sit and eat. Cushioned benches are built into the walls on the outer perimeter, and there's a TV perched on a stand across from someone's old couch that they donated to the room. The TV has cable, which the club also pays for.

There's an old moldy refrigerator that stinks so bad we try not to open the door 'cause the room will stink for hours afterwards. You can't put your food in it or it'll absorb the smell. Someone put a sign on the fridge that says, "Your mother doesn't work here, clean up after yourself," but the thing is still filthy. On top of the fridge is an ancient food-splattered microwave that you have to stick a matchbook in to keep the door closed.

55

The lounge was dark and quiet. The only light was from the TV with the sound muted off. Joe and I took off our shirts, vests, and gun belts and passed out on one of the benches.

◆

Joe's watch beeped twice, and we finally dragged ourselves up at 7:15. I used the bathroom, washed my face, and brushed my teeth before heading upstairs. Joe was moving slower than me this morning and grunted as he walked past me into the bathroom.

The sun was shining when I went upstairs, and I could already feel the heat in the air. I went across the street to the deli and got Joe and me coffee and ham, egg, and cheese on a roll. I bought an extra pack of cigarettes; I knew the prices would be jacked up in Brooklyn to accommodate the parade.

Joe, Rooney, and Connelly were standing on the front steps outside the precinct when I walked up.

"I'm not looking forward to this one," Rooney said, shaking his head. "Why did I do this?"

"So we could pay for our tuna trip on Sunday," Joe said.

"That's right," Rooney said, then added, "Does this mean you're gonna miss church?"

"Yup," Joe said.

"Won't you get in trouble with the big guy for that?" Rooney raised his eyebrows and pointed his thumb toward the sky.

"Absolutely not," Joe said like Rooney was nuts. "And don't call him the big guy, it's disrespectful. What's the matter with you, a nice Catholic boy like yourself? You should know better than to say something like that."

Now, if I woulda said something like that to Rooney, we'd have ended up fighting about it, but he never yells at Joe.

"You're right, Joe, that was disrespectful." Rooney nodded and looked down. "I'm sorry. I just always thought it was a sin to miss Mass," he said with a shrug.

"It's not a sin, Mike, but like I told Tony, if you're only going because you're afraid God's gonna punish you, you're going for the wrong reasons anyway. I don't like to miss church, and I don't do it very often. But the Lord likes fishing, and he'll be there with us." Joe smiled.

"You're gonna need the Lord to keep up with me," Rooney said arrogantly.

"I always need the Lord, Mike," Joe said.

"You think you can catch more fish than me?" Rooney asked, obviously doubting it.

"Yup," Joe said confidently.

"Ya wanna bet?" Rooney asked, taking a step closer to Joe.

Joe paused. "Sure. I'll tell you what. If I catch more fish than you, you come to church with me next Sunday."

Rooney seemed to be thinking it over, then said, "Okay, but if I catch more fish than you, you buy me lunch for a week."

"Deal," Joe said as they shook on it.

I don't know what Joe was thinking. Not that I didn't trust God, I was just surprised Joe would use him in a bet. Plus, tuna fishing isn't like fishing off a pier. The chances that none of us would catch anything were always there.

We were taking two vans over to the parade, one with Hanrahan and the other with Sergeant Bishop, the administrative sergeant who most of us hate. He's a real player, shady and personable with the brass, which makes him dangerous. Rooney went across the street for coffee, and then he, Connelly, Joe, and I went to sit in one of the vans to wait for Hanrahan and Noreen. Walsh and Snout got in the van. I guess we didn't have enough cops to work the detail and they were asking everyone to work the overtime. Snout and Walsh were stupid enough to take it this time, but I doubted they'd be looking for it next year.

A couple of the day tour cops got in the van. They looked raring to go, while us midnight cops looked rumpled and exhausted. When Noreen got behind the wheel, Rooney yelled, "I would have jumped in the driver's seat if I knew Noreen was driving."

"Mike, you're probably not even van qualified," Noreen said, adjusting the rearview mirror so she could look at him.

"Like that would matter," Rooney said.

I saw Noreen smirk and gun the van in reverse, sloshing Rooney's coffee on his shirt.

Rooney jumped up and tried to hold his coffee out in front of him when Noreen gunned it in drive and pulled out onto 35th Street, sloshing it on his pants leg.

"You stupid, friggin'—" he started yelling.

"How do you like my driving now, Mike?" Noreen smiled at him in the rearview mirror.

"Come on, I'm soaked. What's wrong with you?" He shook his head as he flicked the coffee off his hand and glared at the back of Noreen's head.

We took the West Side Highway to Canal Street and went over the Manhattan Bridge. The bridge connects the Bowery and Canal Street in Chinatown to Flatbush Avenue in downtown Brooklyn. We took the Flatbush Avenue exit and turned onto Eastern Parkway.

The parade is less than ten miles from our precinct, and we made it there in about twenty minutes. If this were rush hour on a day other than a holiday, it'd be a nightmare.

Noreen said, "We're here," as she parked the van near the corner of Eastern Parkway and Underhill Avenue. There was a mix of vans and RMPs from different precincts around the city, all packed in together. We were on the east side of Prospect Park, the crappy side. There were "No Parking Today" signs posted on telephone poles up and down

Eastern Parkway, and the barriers that would be used later were still in piles on the corners of Eastern Parkway and the side streets.

We were close to the end of the parade, about two blocks before the Grand Army Plaza. The parade starts at Utica Avenue and runs along Eastern Parkway till it hits Grand Army Plaza and finally wraps it up.

Vendors were setting up on the sidewalks, with grills and tables to sell Caribbean food. I saw a vendor setting up a grill advertising Italian sausage, which I thought was strange, as the only Italians here would be cops. Then I remembered working here as a rookie and paying eight bucks for a sausage on a roll.

I lit a cigarette as a barrier truck rolled by and dropped a bunch of barriers near Washington Avenue. There were about eighty cops standing with us, some with their hats on, some holding them. Everyone was talking, and I could hear bits and pieces of conversation.

"I'm working up in the four-four now . . ."

"Transferred to Street Crime . . ."

"His wife left him last year, he was depressed . . ."

What I heard most was, "How'd you get stuck on this detail?"

It was 7:55, and we were supposed to muster up at 8:00, but nobody moved. We finished our cigarettes and finished talking. Why give the city any more time than we had to?

An inspector was talking to a couple of captains. They huddled together in their white shirts for about ten minutes before calling the sergeants over. They talked for about ten minutes more before a lieutenant said, "I want everybody in groups of five, starting with the 1st precinct."

He pointed to an area near the corner of Underhill and then pointed to individual spots and said, "5th, 6th, 7th, 9th," all the way down. We were after the 10th, with the 17th precinct next to us, and since our command was the largest, we took almost four lines.

The lieutenant, whose collar brass said the 5th precinct, started counting by five. When he got to the 7th precinct he saw a line of four next to a line of six and barked out, "Listen, slide down and stay in lines of five!"

Cops get scared they're gonna get separated from their commands, so they try to stay in the line with their precinct even if it messes up the count.

Once they had us lined up, the sergeants and lieutenants were briefed by the captains. The sergeants were given their roster sheets, which would give them eight cops each, and information on the location of their posts.

Hanrahan's face was red as he came back over with Sergeant Bishop. Bishop was trying to talk to him, but Hanrahan walked past him, shaking his head as he waved Bishop away.

We huddled around Hanrahan as he read off his roster sheet, and while we wanted to say, "Pick me, don't leave me with Bishop," we kept our mouths shut and hoped we got to stay with him. Noreen didn't huddle with us. She's Hanrahan's driver, so she knew he'd pick her. He also picked me, Joe, Rooney, Connelly, Alvarez, who we call Rice, who came in on his RDO to get the overtime, along with Snout and Walsh, the only rookies in our group.

Bishop took his guys, or his angels, as we call them. Bishop's first name is Charlie, and we call all the suck-ups that work for him Charlie's angels. I was surprised they would work something like this. They're usually working at the house or the cushy details. They walked us over to our post at Underhill Road, which runs between Eastern Parkway and Lincoln Place.

The two groups of cops stood together, and Bishop addressed us first. Then I realized why Hanrahan was so mad, and I asked myself like I always do why I bother to work something like this.

4

Sergeant Bishop put on his best politician's face without the smile as he addressed us.

"As you know, there's a No Drinking Enforcement at parades in New York City. Being that this is a residential neighborhood, it will be difficult to enforce." He looked at each of us before he went on. "Anyone can go into their house or into a bar and come back out onto the street after drinking. We will not be issuing urination, drinking in public, marijuana smoking, or possession summonses. If paint or powder is thrown at you, you are not to retaliate. There's been problems in the community with our increased presence in the area. This year the department has increased the number of officers present to four thousand." He shot Hanrahan a look and said, "We don't want this escalating into an incident with bad press for the department."

Yeah, it's a big conspiracy. Us cops have nothing better to do than come down here on Labor Day and harass the parade goers. I love how this always gets twisted around to the cops.

"You finished?" Hanrahan barked at Bishop.

Bishop looked hard at Hanrahan before he nodded.

"Good. My guys, listen up." Hanrahan gave a "Come here" gesture with his hands, and we moved in closer.

"Sergeant Bishop and his squad can get hit with as much paint and powder and bottles as they want," Hanrahan continued, his face hard. "If you get hit with *anything* and need to defend yourself, use your nightstick. Then we'll take whoever hit you over to Kings County Hospital if we need to. We are here to make sure everyone enjoys the parade, not to be assaulted for doing our job."

"You got it, boss," Rooney said, nodding and glaring at Bishop.

This is why cops hate this detail; none of the rules apply here. I never understand why the permit isn't revoked, and the only reason is the city is afraid of backlash with the press. If this crap was going on at the St. Paddy's Day parade, they would have shut it down long ago.

"We'll be taking the south side of Lincoln Place," Hanrahan said, looking at his roster. "Sergeant Bishop will be taking the north side. Split up into twos every hundred feet up the street."

We were closer to Eastern Parkway, more where the action is. While the barriers were along Eastern Parkway, there were none here because we weren't in the direct line of the parade.

We were in a residential and mom-and-pop-type commercial area. At the beginning of the block there were dry cleaners, Jamaican delis, restaurants, and a place that advertised live chickens and goats. Most of the gates were still down on the stores, graffitied in the urban scrawl that I can never understand. The stores gave way to brownstones toward the middle of the block, with big stairs and black wrought-iron handrails. The brownstones are beautiful and probably worth a million bucks a piece.

It was now 9:00, and the block was still quiet enough to hear the birds chirping. Joe and I grabbed our post, the first one off the corner.

My cell phone rang about 9:30, and I saw Michele's number on the display.

"Hey," I said.

"Hey yourself," she said, as I tried to place her mood. It's not that she's moody, but this bachelor party thing was showing me a whole other side of her, a side with claws and fangs.

"Where are you?" she asked.

"Flatbush, we're over by Eastern Parkway, near the end of the parade."

"Did it start yet?"

"No, it'll start in about an hour, but it takes a while for it to get down to this end," I said. "What are you up to?"

"I just finished wrapping the favors," she said. "They came out nice."

We're getting married at one of the restaurants on the North Fork of Long Island in November. Since it's a Sunday, an afternoon, and the off season, we were able to afford it. For the favors Michele picked out sets of glass candleholders with candles that smell like vanilla. There's three candleholders, with one that says Faith, and the other two say Hope and Love. She loved them, and I could care less what the favors were, so it was fine with me. We had an unspoken deal going—Michele was making all the arrangements for the wedding, and I was working all the overtime to pay for it.

"So how'd it go with your brother last night?" She asked it nice enough, but here's where it could get ugly.

"Pretty much how you'd expect. He's not talking to me. My father screamed at me, says I'm selfish—"

"I thought he wasn't talking to you," she cut in.

"He was screaming, not talking," I said dryly.

"Let me get this straight," she said. "Your father screamed at you and your brother's not talking to you because you won't have a bachelor party with strippers and hookers?"

I felt my head start to pound behind my eyes. "Michele, I can't talk about this right now—"

63

"They are so controlling and manipulative," she said, raising her voice.

"You knew all this when you had to have this wedding," I shot back.

"So now it's my fault? I deserve this for wanting to have a wedding like any normal person? If this is what they're doing and it's just the wedding, what will they be doing once we're married?" she yelled.

"Don't worry, I'm sure by the time we're married no one will be talking to us anyway and you'll be happy," I yelled back and caught Joe in the corner of my eye trying to look like he couldn't hear me.

"What I don't understand, Tony, is why you're mad at me. Why aren't you mad at them?"

"I'm not mad at you. I expect them to give me a hard time, I don't expect it from you," I said tiredly.

"I'm giving you a hard time because I don't want my fiancé messing with some hooker the week before I get married?" She was in her teacher mode, sounding like she was talking to a ten-year-old or an idiot. "And I won't let you do this to me behind my back, Tony. I won't marry someone who would do that to me. If I marry you and find out down the road that you did that to me, I'll leave you."

"That's not what—"

"Tony," she cut me off, her voice rising. "I don't care what Vinny or your father think. It is of no interest to me whatsoever. I don't care if I don't fit into their view of what a woman and a marriage should be. I won't allow you to go off on some wild binge before you're married because of some barbaric notion that you deserve one last night of freedom before being shackled to a wife."

"Are you finished?" I half yelled.

"Probably not," she said calmly. I gotta admit I admired her for sticking up for herself. She never gets riled, and she's sexy as anything when she's mad. Maybe it's the Italian in me. I like a good fight.

"You had your say, so let me talk now," I said, calm. "I'll go out to dinner with whoever wants to go for my party, and I'll pay for the party Vinny wants and stay home," I said, catching Joe's smirk as his eyebrows went up.

"Really?" She sounded happy now, and I gave Joe a thumbs-up and mouthed "Thanks."

"I'm so glad, Tony. That was really bothering me," she said, and I could hear the relief in her voice. "I don't like the whole bachelor party thing. It's not right to do something like that right before a marriage, it cheapens it. I also think if a lot of women knew that their husbands were with a prostitute before they got married, they wouldn't marry them."

"Good, I'm glad you feel better," I said, trying to change the subject. "Let me call you back tonight when I get back to the precinct," I said. She got all mushy then, saying I love you and promising me something pretty interesting on our honeymoon that made me forget that I'd have to tell Vinny I wouldn't be there for his night of depravity.

I hit END and shut the phone off. If I leave it on in my pocket, a lot of times I dial myself and wind up with twenty minutes of muffled conversation. Then I have to listen to the whole thing before I can delete it.

"Thanks, Joe," I said. "She sounds better now about the bachelor party. Now I just have to tell Vinny, but I know it's gonna be a problem."

"Tony, this isn't just about him. And he has no right to manipulate you into doing what he wants just because he'll be mad about it. Let him be mad. Someone in your family is always mad about something." Sometimes Joe and Michele sound so much alike it's scary.

"That's what Michele said, that they're controlling and manipulative and if they're doing this now it'll be worse once we're married," I said.

"Not if you take care of it now."

I took off my hat and lit a cigarette. It was getting hot already, and if I left my hat on I'd end up with just the tip of my nose sunburned. The streets were still pretty quiet. A few older people walked by. I guess the partiers from last night were still sleeping it off. Joe started saying good morning to the people that walked by. I could see they were taken aback by it. They're used to our bored indifference, and I guess they were suspicious of Joe's friendliness. An older woman was strolling by, and Joe smiled and said good morning with a nod.

"Well, good morning, officer," she said with her West Indian accent, beaming.

"What are you doing?" I asked Joe once she passed.

"I'm trying to make nice with the public," he said.

"Why? They'll think we're an easy target and start throwing bottles at us," I said.

"No, they won't. You should try it," he said.

I shook my head and took a drag off my cigarette.

"Weren't you paying attention at roll call last week?" Joe asked. "You were supposed to memorize that blue card Santiago gave out."

I pulled out my wallet and fished through it to find the blue plastic card. Last week Santiago, the training officer, gave these out at roll call. It read like *The Idiot's Guide to Addressing the Public*, and we keep finding them in the garbage cans all over the precinct. I looked it over to see if it said anything about saying hello to people as they walked by.

Address and introduce yourself to members of the public during the course of your duties as appropriate.

66

I didn't think standing on our post meant we had to say hello to everyone who walked past us, so I moved on.

Use terms such as "Mr.," "Ms.," "sir," or "ma'am," "hello," and "thank you."
Refer to teenagers as "young lady" or "young man."

If we started saying "Hello, sir, lady, ma'am" to everyone who walked by, they'd be tying up merchants and cleaning out their stores while we addressed the public, so I knew this was useless too.

Respect each individual, his or her cultural identity, customs, and beliefs.

Nope, nothing about saying hello.

Evaluate carefully every situation that leads to contact with the public and conduct yourself in a professional manner.

Nope.

Explain to the public in a courteous, professional demeanor the reason for your interaction with them and apologize for any inconvenience.

"So now when we lock up a perp we have to apologize for the inconvenience?" I asked, incredulous. "Who was the moron that thought these up?"

"It doesn't say that," Joe said with a laugh.

"Yes, it does, read it." I showed him the card, my finger pointing to the line near the end.

He shrugged. "There's nothing wrong with a little community policing. Hey, good morning," he said as he smiled at an older man walking his dog.

"Mornin', officer," the guy said, smiling at him.

The next guy to walk past was a Rastafarian.

"Good morning," Joe said, smiling again.

"Morning, mon," he said to Joe. He had the Bob Marley look and walked with a laid-back kind of bop. His braids were caught up in a red, yellow, and green Rasta hat.

"How are you today? Looking forward to the parade?" Joe asked.

"Yeah, and how is it witchyou?" he asked, nodding with his whole body.

"Good, thanks," Joe said.

The Rastas are generally mellow. I don't know if they're smoking weed or if that's just their way, but they're usually pretty friendly.

"Come on, the next one's yours," Joe said.

The only reason I said hello to the next person walking by was to shut Joe up. It was a heavyset woman who looked to be in her fifties. She was dressed in a pink polyester housedress and orthopedic shoes. I could hear her pantyhose scratching from ten feet away. She looked mean as anything and was sweating and gasping for breath in the morning heat.

"Good morning, you're looking nice today," I said with a smile as she passed me.

She stopped and looked back at me and spit on the ground next to my foot, mumbling as she walked away.

I heard Joe choke on a laugh, and I said, "Ya see? She spit at me."

"She spit on the ground, Tony. Maybe she had a bad experience with a cop," Joe said, still laughing.

"And this is my fault?" I pointed to myself.

I didn't say good morning to anyone else, but Fiore was saying hello to everyone who walked by. About 10:00 a freaky-looking guy stoned out of his mind and covered in ashes shuffled past us. He had short-cropped kinky hair and was wearing only a pair of cutoff jeans and sneakers with no socks. The whites of his bloodshot eyes were more pronounced because of the ashes, and as he passed us, all we could do was stare.

"What are the ashes for?" Joe asked me. "I see it every time I'm here."

"I don't know, Joe," I said. "But I noticed you didn't say hello to him, and according to rule four on your blue card, not saying hello because he's stoned out and covered in ash is disrespecting his cultural identity, customs, and beliefs."

The day was heating up, and I could feel my arms and face getting sunburned, and my T-shirt was already soaked in sweat under my vest. Joe and I watched as some yo-yo in a white Gilligan hat and red shorts urinated in a doorway next to the entrance to a deli about twenty feet from us.

"Check this out," I said to Joe, nodding over at the doorway.

"Is he kidding me?" Joe said. "We're standing right here."

We walked toward him as people in the deli looked over at him with disgusted looks on their faces. He was actually humming when we walked up, and I pulled out my nightstick and poked him in the back.

"Hey!" I said.

He spun around like he was gonna hit me, and his eyes got big when he realized I was a cop.

"What do you think you're doing?" I yelled.

"Officer, I really had to go," he said as he fixed himself.

The owner of the store flew out the door, dressed in a white apron, looking like someone you shouldn't mess with.

"My customers are complaining that someone is out here relieving themselves," he said. Actually, that's nothing like what he said, but I'm editing here.

"Can you get a bucket of bleach water?" I asked the owner before he killed the guy. "He's really sorry and would like to clean this up for you."

"Come on," Gilligan complained. "People do this all the time. It's so hot out here it's already dry."

"We're not smelling this all day," Joe said. "You made the mess, you clean it up."

The owner came back with the bucket of bleach water, a scrub brush, and some paper towels. We stood there and watched Gilligan scrub it and then dump the rest of the water to rinse it off.

We might not have been able to summons him, but he'll think twice before taking a whiz outside again.

Hanrahan came over to sign our books about 10:30.

"Rooney and Connelly took the van over to the seven-one," he said. "They're having their annual barbeque, you pay five bucks to eat all day. They got a nice spread set up. When Rooney gets back with the van, you two can head over. Do you know where it is?"

"Yeah, we've been there before," Joe said.

The seven-one throws a barbeque every Labor Day and makes a fortune off all the cops working the parade.

At 11:00 Rooney and Connelly relieved us, and we walked up to the corner of Eastern Parkway holding our hats in our hands.

A lieutenant was directing traffic in the intersection while a couple of cops moved some of the barriers around to let police vehicles through. He looked up, staring at us. We knew it was because our hats were off. Not wearing our hats is a minor violation and could cost us part of our overtime, but a bus passed by, and Joe and I looked at each other and smiled. By the time the bus cleared the lieutenant, our hats were on and we were fit for duty. The lou gave us a "Who you kidding" look and said, "Officers, aren't you supposed to have your hats on?" as we crossed the street.

"Boss, we made sure we respected you by putting our hats on," Joe said diplomatically.

"How would you like to be standing in the intersection directing traffic with me?" the lou threatened.

"Is that why you're here, Lou?" I asked. "You didn't have your hat on?"

He actually turned red trying not to laugh, like he couldn't believe I had the nerve to say that. Joe cut him off quick with, "Lou, we've been up all night working a midnight before we came here."

"Get out of here," he said as we crossed the street.

We picked up the van on the other side of Eastern Parkway and drove eastbound to Washington Avenue and turned onto Empire Boulevard. The precinct was packed, and I wound up parking in a bus stop halfway down the block.

We could smell the barbeque as we walked up to the front of the precinct. We went around to the courtyard on the side of the building and saw a line of about twenty people.

"Is this the line to pay?" I asked the cop in front of me, whose collar brass showed he was from the sixty-one precinct.

"I hope so, I'd hate to think it's the line for the bathroom," he said.

The Crown Heights precinct is in a residential and commercial area with lower- to middle-income families in central Brooklyn. The area is made up of blacks, West Indians, and Lubavitch Hasidim and is home of the famous riots of the 1990s.

They call the seven-one Fort Surrender because years ago the Hasids stormed the precinct and managed to take it over. They stormed it once when I was here as a rookie, during my field training unit out of the Academy, but they didn't get control of it that day.

It took Joe and me about ten minutes to get up to the cash box and pay our five bucks. They gave us raffle tickets that said PAID on them

71

so we could come back later and eat if we wanted to. The pay line went directly into the food line, and we picked up dishes and plastic forks at the head of the food table. They had two huge rusted steel grills going, and we both grabbed a hamburger and hot dog before piling on potato salad and corn on the cob. There were trays of olives and pickles. They had those big dill pickles, the kind we used to get out of the barrels when we were kids. They don't keep them in the barrels anymore. They found out the rats loved the pickles too and the barrels were easy for them to get into.

There was no place to sit, so we leaned up against the bumper of an RMP. I heard someone call "Tony," and I saw Andy DeLuca, a Highway cop I knew from Staten Island, walking over toward us. He worked at the South for about a year before he went over to Highway.

"Hey, buddy," I said. "This is my partner, Joe Fiore. Joe, Andy DeLuca."

They shook hands, and Andy filled me in. He just had a baby, twins actually, since his wife was on fertility drugs. I wondered for the thousandth time why people who have kids think the rest of us want to hear about childbirth. I can see a rotted dead body and not lose my lunch, but talk about placenta and umbilical cords and I break out in a sweat.

"How's Tommy doing?" I asked, talking about his brother-in-law Tommy Pagano. "I saw him down at court. He said you were getting him in Highway," I said.

"Yeah, I got him in Highway. And the moron couldn't pass the motorcycle test," he said, shaking his head. "Unbelievable."

"I thought he knew how to ride," I said.

"He does. Go figure. Oh"—he laughed—"remember Danny King who worked at the South with us?"

"Yeah, I heard he made boss and is working out in Queens," I said.

"He's here today. He told me he got drafted over to IAB before he went to Queens. He was saying that 90 percent of the allegations in Patrol Borough Manhattan South were from the South."

Allegations are civilian complaints against cops. Since we have the largest command, it makes sense that we'd have the most complaints. Plus, given the nature of our job, how happy could we be making people?

We talked and chewed. I told Andy to say hello to Tommy for me and that I was getting married.

"To that same girl, the hot-looking one that worked on Wall Street?" I couldn't tell if he looked impressed or surprised.

"Nah," I said. "Someone else I met, a schoolteacher from Long Island."

Joe and I finished eating, said good-bye to Andy, and drove back to our post.

As we parked the van we could see the sky was dark to the west of us. I guess a storm was coming in from Jersey. We could already hear the rumble of thunder in the distance.

We relieved Rooney and Connelly off our post, and they moved back down to their spot near the corner. The wind was starting to blow, kicking up dust, plastic bags, and garbage. It felt nice and cool even though it was gritty. We could actually see the rain as it came in toward us in fat drops along the pavement. Joe and I stood under the deli's awning as it was flapping around with the wind. People were holding stuff over their heads trying not to get soaked. Some ran under the awning with us, and we all squashed ourselves against the building. The rain was torrential, running down along the curbs into the sewers.

I pulled down my vest to let some of the heat out while the spray hit my face and arms. It rained for about fifteen minutes, and within a half hour the skies were clear again. Steam was coming off the pavement as it dried, and the air was thick and muggy. You don't get that damp woods smell in New York, you get the damp dumpster smell.

If anything, it got hotter after that, and the streets were starting to fill up as the parade got closer to us.

"Did you listen to the tape I gave you?" Joe asked.

"How was I gonna listen to it? You just gave it to me yesterday," I said.

"I gave you one last week," he said.

Since I hadn't been to church in a few weeks, Joe had been bringing me tapes of the services. I didn't know you could do that at church, but Joe gets tapes of the sermons and listens to them in his car. I had started to listen to the one he gave me last week, but I felt too much like it was talking to me, so I shut it off.

"Is the tape supposed to be a dig?" I asked.

"Not at all, Tony," he said seriously. "I just thought it lined up with what's going on with you right now. I know you need money for the wedding, but just remember it's important for you to be in church. Did you understand what it was saying?"

"Basically what it said was that the reason David got in trouble with what's-her-name was because he was somewhere he wasn't supposed to be," I said.

"Yeah. It said it was the time of the year when the kings went out to war, where David normally would have been."

"Instead of peeping on some female taking a bath," I said.

He started to say something but then said, "Yeah, pretty much."

"Don't worry, Joe. I won't be looking in anyone's windows while I'm working overtime," I said.

"Tony, that's not what I meant. What Pastor John is saying is that when we consistently keep our mind on God it keeps us on the right path and not vulnerable to whatever could take us off track. He was also saying that the same way we feed our body food to keep it strong, we need to feed our spirit God's Word to keep it strong."

"I know what you're saying. And to be honest, I feel the difference from when I'm in church every week and reading the Bible. I just want to get enough money put away for the wedding and the honeymoon and not come back broke," I said.

"You and Michele are fine financially. You both work full-time. You said you pretty much had the wedding paid for, and I'm sure you could collar up on other days and be able to go to church on Sunday," he pointed out.

"Once I'm living on Long Island I plan to go on Wednesday and Sunday," I said. "I also don't want to be working overtime for a while once I'm married. Christmas is six weeks after the wedding, and I don't want to be killing myself. I want to have it all paid for so I can be home and enjoy it."

"I understand that, but this week Pastor was talking about how we don't know what we're gonna need to be strong for. Like right now the thing with Vinny and the family. You need to build yourself up before taking on something like that. Or we might get into something at work that we need to be focused for."

"I'll listen to it," I said, meaning it. "I'll throw it in on my way home later. Maybe it'll keep me awake while I'm driving."

The parade was making its way down this end now, and we could see the floats on Eastern Parkway. It was a colorful parade with a lot of reds and yellows. I could see a group of females in exotic yellow headdresses and costumes that just covered the essentials as they danced their way along the street. Some of the floats carried steel drum players, and there was a lot of reggae and calypso music.

We could tell the crowd wasn't intimidated by our presence there. I saw people drinking and smoking in the doorways and on their front steps, daring us to say something.

The cops were gearing up now, and Joe and I moved toward the corner to a cluster of cops. We were standing with our hands on our belt buckles or leaning over the barricades as our eyes scanned the area around us. Cops were talking about some of the stuff that had gone on already. Eight people had already been shot, some when someone shot into the crowd with an automatic weapon. Most of the injured people were hit in the legs and torso. There were other sporadic shootings, one with a fatal shot to the head. We saw clusters of gang colors as we watched the crowd, not the parade. We were looking for pickpockets, weapons, aggressive behavior, EDPs, or deviants like this one guy Joe and I spotted standing behind a group of teenage girls.

They looked about fifteen or sixteen and oblivious to how provocative they looked in their short shorts and bathing suit tops with their thong underwear showing at the waistband.

The first few years I was a cop, this kind of thing would really annoy me. How could these girls come out dressed like this? Where were their fathers? When they dress this way the psychos and perverts are gonna bother them. Now I just accept the fact that people dress this way hoping to get noticed, but it's usually the wrong kind of attention.

The guy was maneuvering himself behind them, pretending to watch the parade and looking over their shoulders down their tops. He was wearing a short-sleeved white shirt that rode past his hips over cutoff jeans. As the crowd pushed closer to the street to see a float go by, he pressed himself against one of the females. She looked behind her, but he was looking past her at the float as if he had nothing to do with whatever had touched her.

As one of the steel bands passed by on a float, he started dancing up against her like a dog when it's got hold of your leg.

The female looked horrified and froze with fear. Joe and I pushed through the crowd as he grabbed her and held himself against her. When we were just about there we saw that he had exposed himself. "Look at this fruit loop," I said as a couple of onlookers grabbed the guy and started throwing him a beating.

"Alright, alright, we got him," Joe said as we grabbed his arms. "We got him!" Joe yelled as one guy threw an extra punch.

"Did you see what he did?" the puncher yelled.

"We saw him, stop hitting him," Joe said, yelling over top of the PA system on the float.

The humper was a skell and looked to be about forty years old. Other cops were there now, gathering around us while we cuffed him with the plastic cuffs issued at the detail. When we're at details where we know there'll be a lot of arrests, they give out these white hard plastic cuffs, almost like the plastic zip ties you'd use on a garbage bag. The cuffs are strong enough to restrain someone until you get them to a holding pen.

The crowd was watching us now. They hadn't seen what the perv did to the girl; they only saw a bunch of cops cuffing someone who looked like he was just watching the parade. Their eyes were suspicious and hostile as they stopped and watched us, which ticked me off.

"In case you can't tell by the uniforms," I said loudly, looking around, "we're police officers. The reason for our interaction with you today is because this lowlife"—I pointed to the perv in cuffs—"sexually assaulted that female over there." I pointed to the female, who was crying now. "I apologize for any inconvenience this may cause, and I hope the rest of you enjoy the parade. Have a nice day."

Joe was choking on a laugh.

"How's that for community policing?" I asked him.

He shook his head. "You're a piece of work," he said.

"Who's looking?" I asked the cops standing with us. I didn't want the collar, as this was already overtime for me. I was exhausted and wanted to go home and sleep.

"I'll take it," a cop from the six-oh said, which was fine with me.

As the parade neared the end of Eastern Parkway the crowd was the biggest, with people twenty to thirty deep along the curbs and grass and all the way up the sidewalk to the storefronts. It's not like New Year's Eve, when the businesses are boarded up. The merchants here were all open, making a fortune.

It had gotten too congested at the Grand Army Plaza for the big finale, and Hanrahan called us all to the corner of Underhill and Eastern Parkway, where a captain was standing.

There were a bunch of cops holding rolls of orange mesh fencing, the kind they use during road construction. The captain was listening intensely to the radio, not talking to anyone as we filed in. He called over the sergeants and lieutenants, and Joe and I were close enough to hear him trying to tell them over the noise that they wanted to reroute part of the parade. He said when a certain vehicle hit the corner they would redirect it up Underhill Avenue. I saw Hanrahan's face fill with a mixture of dread and disbelief and wondered what was up. Hanrahan and Sergeant Bishop called us in to tell us the deal.

"Boss, we don't have any barricades on this block," Joe said.

"They're gonna have cops holding the orange mesh for the first twenty feet, after that they're using us as a human barricade," Hanrahan said, not meeting our eyes.

"Are you kidding me?" I yelled, sickened. "We can't write a summons for drinking in public and we're gonna keep the crowd from rushing the float?" It wasn't only stupid, it was dangerous.

"I know what you're saying, Tony," Hanrahan said. "I want you to stay close together and keep an eye on each other."

"Boss, this is a bad move," Rooney said, furious. "This isn't gonna work."

I saw Joe put his head down, I thought to compose himself, and then I realized he was praying. I added my own prayer for help, along with an apology for not being in church lately.

It turned out that the float in question had a well-known rapper on it. The guy has a huge following. The brass didn't want this particular float adding to the pandemonium at Grand Army Plaza where the parade ends.

The cops unrolled the orange mesh and held it where the float would turn the corner and up another ten feet.

"Get everyone outta the street," the captain yelled. "Then line 'em up on either side."

Once we cleared the street, Hanrahan and Bishop put between twenty-five and thirty of us on each side of the street. I had Joe on one side of me and Rooney on the other, which was a good place to be if something went down. Rooney may be a dope and annoying as anything, but he's a good cop and he'd have our backs.

"If the crowd breaks through let them go, we're not getting trampled," Rooney said.

We both nodded.

We could hear the float before it came into the intersection. It was on the bed of a huge eighteen-wheeler. The speakers that were set up throughout the float were so loud I could feel my eardrums vibrate. The rapper was shirtless, showing off his washboard and gold chains. He was wearing sunglasses and holding the microphone with lots of swagger as he bopped and danced up against the female singers in their black leather bikini tops and shorts.

The float stopped in the middle of the intersection as if to wait for the thousands of people who came in on a wave after it.

"This is the float that's gonna turn," Hanrahan said.

"Oh no," Joe said as he watched the sea of people heading for us. Rooney said something else.

The cops with the orange fencing ran across Eastern Parkway and blocked it off.

"This is insane," I said. "Look at these people."

"We shouldn't do this," Rooney said, shaking his head. "This is not good."

The captain walked over to the cab of the float and pointed down our street, telling the driver to move this way. As the driver turned and passed the corner the float stopped again. There was a sea of people now rushing toward the float, psyched out of their minds at the rapper.

The rapper bent down and picked up a bottle of Heineken, and they went wild as he saluted them with it.

"Let's give it up for the cops," he yelled and guzzled the beer as the crowd went wild.

I'd like to think that he meant it and wasn't trying to get us all killed, but considering the liquor ban, I doubted it. He started rapping again as the float moved forward, and people were now running from Eastern Parkway, following the float toward us.

As the float came up on us I saw that the wheels were almost as big as me. If we got pushed back into them, we'd be crushed. I started thinking that if the crowd rushed me, I'd spin them around and toss them to the side and work my way into the crowd away from the wheels. The float probably wouldn't stop any quicker for a cop than it would for a bystander, and I didn't want anyone to get hurt.

"If they rush us, jump up on the float or you'll go under the wheels," Rooney yelled.

I could picture Rooney trying to haul his 230-pound rear end onto that float. He'd probably fall off attempting to heave himself over and go under the wheels anyway.

The crowd was close enough on us now that I could feel the heat coming off them. They were young, most of them in their early twenties. The guys were shirtless and sweating, stinking of booze. And the females—although the clothes were minimal, the hair and makeup was done up.

It was frenzied now, and I felt a shift in the atmosphere as the rapper passed behind me. The sound was so loud it obliterated everything around us, and while we could see the animated faces, they made no sound. Fists were pumped in the air, and mouths were moving while all eyes were mesmerized on the float.

We were trying to keep the crowd back, but they were pushing in on us. As the crowd looked past me, up at the float, I saw a kid, maybe about ten years old, struggling to keep from getting crushed in the crowd. He was big for his age, but I could tell he was young. I wondered why the kid was here and who in their right mind would leave him alone in a crowd like this.

I don't know what happened behind me, but the crowd roared, and I saw the fear on the kid's face right before he went down. I started screaming, "Watch the kid!" as I pushed people out of the way to get to him.

No one heard what I said, and I saw the eyes of the crowd swing toward me, and I knew it was gonna get ugly. I saw their anger, like I was challenging them, and I pointed to the kid on the ground. A couple of people realized what happened and started pushing everyone out of the way to grab the kid. Once we got him up we pushed back the crowd and pulled him out of there, and it was almost like it broke the spell.

I went to step back next to Joe and Rooney, and the next thing I knew, the crowd overtook us. I panicked a little realizing I couldn't see Joe or Rooney, and I started to pray, *Lord, help me here. I don't want anyone getting killed, especially not a kid.*

People spilled from the sidewalks, filling the street in a matter of seconds. They reached the float as it passed, running after it as it went down the street. I saw one of the cops holding the mesh get knocked on the ground as everyone scrambled to put the barriers back up and close off the block.

Once the barriers were in place it stopped the stream of pedestrians onto the block while the rest of them ran after the truck. I heard someone yell, "They're calling us on the radio to get back to the corner of Eastern Parkway."

They didn't have to tell me twice. My hands were shaking as I lit a cigarette, and I was sweating so much my clothes were sticking to me. I spotted Joe and Rooney at the corner, sweating and looking like they just cheated death.

Rooney started screaming at the captain, "That was the most asinine thing I've ever seen. You could have gotten us killed! Who's the moron that thought this up?"

The cops were so angry, ranting about how we could've gotten killed. The captain and Sergeant Bishop didn't say anything, but I could see Hanrahan was fuming.

Walsh and Snout, who I hadn't seen since this morning, looked scared out of their minds. I smiled at them and said, "Welcome to the NYPD," as I took a drag off my cigarette. "You're alive, you'll get to sign out at the end of the day."

"Aren't you glad you signed up?" Joe asked them.

Walsh looked shell-shocked as he said, "I can't believe that I'm at a parade where I'm almost killed and they tell me not to summons anybody."

"You'll get used to it," I said.

Rooney went on to say that the brass had no testosterone-producing body parts.

"No, seriously," Walsh said. "Why didn't we lock up that rapper? He was guzzling that beer, inciting the crowd."

"If we locked up that rapper," Joe said. "There would have been a riot."

Walsh and Snout wouldn't be back next year. The way it works is you work the detail and it winds up being a day like today. Then you stay away for a few years until you forget how bad it is and you sign up again.

The parade was winding down, and we opened the streets again to pedestrians but not cars. We were all exhausted, legs aching, full of sweat and grime. At about 4:00 they mustered up another group of cops to take over for us. We climbed back into the van at 4:30, and I immediately fell asleep to the sound of Rooney complaining about the captain.

We got back to the precinct at 5:00, and I went down to the locker room to change and was back upstairs to sign out in ten minutes. We were getting travel time until 6:00, and I wanted to be home by then.

"What time are we meeting tomorrow?" Joe asked, looking exhausted.

Joe and I were working a day tour tomorrow. We had to qualify at the range up in the Bronx, and we wanted to get there early so we could be in the first relay and get out early.

"How about six fifteen?"

"Sounds good," he said, shaking my hand. "I'll see you then."

My steering wheel was hot to the touch when I got in my truck. I rolled the windows down and blasted the air conditioner to cool it off. There was no traffic on the West Side Highway as I headed downtown, just long shadows of the buildings in the afternoon sun. It was one of those weird days, a Monday that felt like a Sunday.

The roads were clear. The day was nice enough to keep everyone at the beach, but by 9:00 tonight it'd be bumper-to-bumper coming in from the Jersey Shore.

I took Father Capodanno Boulevard home, watching families pack up their coolers and blankets in the parking lots along the beach.

I live in a basement apartment in Grant City, a block up from the beach. It's a dead-end street with access to Miller Field, the old airfield that is now used by the Parks Department. It's quiet there, except on Saturday and Sunday mornings when the sounds of whistles and soccer games can be heard from a mile away.

I moved there a year ago last month when my family home was sold. The sale of the house was the last round of my parents' long divorce battle. They had a verbal agreement that my mother would keep the house, which was worth half a million bucks, and my father would keep his pension, which was worth double that. In the end my father screwed her and had the house sold out from under her anyway.

My landlord, Alfonse, was in the backyard grilling sausage with one hand and holding a glass of wine in the other.

"Tony!" he said with a smile. "You look exhausted. You work today?"

"Yeah, I worked the parade in Brooklyn," I said.

"What parade?"

"The West Indian Day." I said it like a question.

"Never heard of it," he said.

Most people haven't unless they're from the area. Plus, he's Italian, so unless it's the San Gennaro feast he can't relate. Alfonse must be about seventy. He came to America from Sicily about fifty years ago and still makes his own wine and sopressata. He has a huge garden with figs and a grape arbor, and I've been eating beefsteak tomatoes for a month now.

"Hey, Julia," I said to Alfonse's wife.

She's pretty in an old-world Italian kind of way. She has short black hair and big brown eyes and always wears a dress. Even today barbequing in her backyard she had on a white shirt and pink floral skirt.

"Did you eat?" she asked.

"Nah, I'm good," I said.

"Don't be ridiculous," she said, already putting together a plate for me.

I sighed and put my bag down next to the picnic table. I might as well sit and eat to save myself the ten minutes we'd argue until she talked me into it.

She sliced some Italian bread and took a sausage link off the grill. She made me a sandwich and topped it with sautéed peppers and onions. She threw some tomato and red onion salad, grilled chicken on a skewer, and a skewer of grilled zucchini, tomato, yellow pepper, and carrots on the plate. Then she added some cold ravioli salad with sun-dried tomato and basil and set the plate down in front of me.

"Sandy stopped by," Julia said. "She left something by your door."

Sandy lives across the street with her two kids. In the spring her psycho soon-to-be ex-husband almost killed her. He beat her within an inch of her life one day and then came back the next day and stabbed her three times. Alfonse woke me up on both days to go over and help her, and the day her ex stabbed her I managed to hold him at bay while she crawled out of the house. She's so grateful it borders on pathetic. She makes me food, gives me vegetables out of her garden, and washes my truck while I'm sleeping. She also told everyone on the block what a hero I was, which, trust me, wound up working against me.

Now every time someone gets a parking ticket they want me to take care of it. They call me when the guy on the corner plays his music too loud, and last week they had me pulling an old lady with Alzheimer's off the cement divider on Father Capodanno Boulevard. Not that I wouldn't have helped her, but you call the cops for stuff like that.

"You're gonna be here on Saturday, right, Tony?" Alfonse said, talking about the block party. Everyone on the block chips in money for the rides and stuff, but we all do our own food.

"Yeah, I'm working the night before, so I'll catch a couple of hours' sleep first."

"Who did you invite? I have the two tables for the food and about twenty chairs. Let me know if you need more, and I'll have my brother bring some."

"Well, Michele and Stevie are coming. My partner Joe, his wife and three kids, his parents, my sister, my grandmother, and I don't know who else." I shrugged.

Half my family wasn't talking to me, so I didn't know who'd show up. Fiore's father said he hasn't been to a block party since he left Queens and moved to Long Island, so he's all excited about it.

"We got the slide and the moon walk," Alfonse said, talking about those inflatable rides that you rent. "We also got the pirate ship, the candy cart, and the face painters. The only thing we need is the fire trucks, and we thought you could call the firehouse up in New Dorp to make sure they're coming."

"Just get me the number, I'll give them a call," I said. I knew a couple of firemen there.

I finished my food and felt my eyes starting to close.

Alfonse smiled. "Go get some sleep."

"Yeah, I'm beat," I said. "The food was delicious, thanks."

I walked down the cement stairs to my apartment and found a brown shopping bag with a foil-covered plate outside the door. I unlocked the door, put the bag on the counter, and hit the PLAY button on my answering machine. I had four messages.

The first was Denise. "Mom's coming Saturday, but I want to talk to you about it first. Call me back." It beeped again, and I heard my grandmother's voice. "Tony, it's Grandma," she said in a clipped voice. "Call me back." The third call was a hang-up, and the fourth was from Michele asking me to call her when I got in.

I called her cell phone but got her voice mail. I called the house and told the answering machine that I got her voice mail on the cell and to call me when she got the message.

I took the plate from Sandy out of the bag and put it in my fridge without unwrapping it and sat down on the couch to watch the Yankees game. I was too tired to call anyone else back, and I would have read my Bible, but I knew I wouldn't be able to concentrate. I didn't have to think to watch the game. The Yanks had just wrapped up a three-game sweep with Boston and were beating the Blue Jays. I passed out after two minutes and woke up at midnight. I ignored the blinking light on my answering machine. I hadn't even heard the phone ring. I set my alarm for 4:45 and crawled into bed.

I showered, shaved, and was out of the house by 5:15. I stopped for coffee and an everything bagel with cream cheese on the corner of Clove Road and Hylan Boulevard. It was early enough that I didn't have to wait in line for twenty minutes, and the guy made a good bagel, soft and chewy, still warm from the oven. I finished the bagel, lit a cigarette, and drank my coffee with it.

The sun was still on the rise, sending streaks of pink and blue across the eastern sky. It was cooler today, probably in the sixties now that I would be out of uniform and wouldn't have to stand around in the heat all day.

I put the radio on 1010 WINS because, like every other New Yorker, I'm obsessed with traffic. After years of being stuck in it we know at least three alternate routes to anywhere around the city. 1010 WINS is the only place you can hear traffic reports from all five boroughs, upstate, Connecticut, Long Island, and Jersey. Six times an hour you get the skinny on East River Crossings; Hudson River Crossings; the bridges; the tunnels; inbound and outbound traffic; subway delays, including which lines are running, who had a track fire, and which lines are closed because someone got pushed onto the tracks; which alternate side of the street parking is in effect; and where there was an accident. I couldn't live without it.

The range where we qualify to shoot is in the Pelham Bay Park up in the Bronx. I took the Gowanus Expressway—or the "Don't Go on Us Expressway," as it's called. It's always crowded and the slowest way to get into Manhattan. I took the FDR to the Bruckner and took the Willis Avenue Bridge to City Island Road. Because it was early in rush hour, it took me less than an hour to get there.

The range is an old fenced-in compound. It's isolated by marsh but close enough to the bay that you can smell the salt water. It opened in 1960 and still uses the same life-size, two-dimensional target it used back then. The old-timers call him the thug. We just call him the bad guy. He reminds me of a gangster from the fifties, a cross between Ernest Borgnine and Rocky Graziano, which is who my father said they had in mind when they made him.

I pulled up to the gatehouse and let the old-timer check my ID. It was early enough that I got a parking spot near the front, next to Rooney's car.

I went around to the back of the cinder-block building and got in line to sign in. Rooney was in front of me, still bellyaching about the captain who used us as a human barricade at the parade yesterday. I shook my head. It was the last thing I heard him talking about yesterday and the first thing I hear him talking about today. Then he started yapping about what a great shot he is, how he always qualifies with a 100 and his groupings are always great. No wonder his wife is a stewardess. Who could live with him on a full-time basis?

The line was getting longer now, and I gave a "Hey, buddy" to Fiore, who was about three people behind me. He switched off with the guy behind me so we could shoot together. Further down the line I saw Walsh and Snout, along with Rice and Beans from the four to twelve.

I got up to the table, showed my ID, and filled out the paperwork to get my rounds. Since I use my Glock 9mm both on and off duty and I have a .38 for off duty, I would have to qualify with both and would need bullets for both.

I got into relay 2 and had the twenty-first shooter position, which meant I'd shoot first and then hear the lecture on how not to point our guns at anyone, not to scratch our heads with our guns, and not to turn and point our guns while we're looking around or being chased by a bee. The speaker also tells us that if we get hot brass from the bullet casings down our shirts to holster our guns, step back, and raise our hands instead of screaming and letting off rounds as we jump around while our skin blisters.

I reholstered my gun, got my bullets and paperwork, and waited for Joe and Rooney, and the three of us made our way over to the range.

5

The part of the range where we shoot is a cinder-block structure. It's painted red, with cement floors and a wooden overhang that ends at the twenty-five-yard mark. There are two range instructors who buzz you to shoot from a glass-enclosed booth. To the right are big metal drums filled with discharged shell casings.

Colored circles are painted on the cement floor—white, yellow, green, and red—with the corresponding number above on the overhang to coordinate with your target. Past the twenty-five-yard line is all grass, leading up to a sand dune. It was nice and quiet, and I could still hear the birds chirping and the drone of planes overhead, probably an air path from LaGuardia or Newark airport. Once we started shooting, we wouldn't hear anything.

Rooney and Joe were on either side of me. Joe and I had our three-dollar goggles, but Rooney brought top-of-the-line stuff. He wears a medal for all the times he got 100. They don't give it to you, you have to buy it yourself at the police uniform store. Rooney was going at it again about how great he is, and it was starting to get on my nerves. I always score between 98 and 100, and you don't see me beating on my chest.

The way they score you, you get two points for every shot inside your target line and lose two points for every shot outside your target line. They don't count the bullet holes in the targets because they're not gonna count fifty shots for each person, but they do check to see if you're outside the target.

We shot our fifty practice rounds and then went inside for the lecture. The instructor looked to be in his forties, with black hair and a black handlebar mustache. He wasn't Joe Combat, and he kept it interesting. Like every time we come here, he tells us that most gun battles with a perp are within seven to ten feet and last between ten and twelve seconds, which is why we shoot the most rounds at seven yards. He gave us the stats on why we do the least practice from twenty-five yards and why we don't carry a .44 Magnum like Dirty Harry. By the time you recoiled and shot again, you'd be hit with five or six rounds.

He gave us the basics: You point at the target. The target's blurry but your sight's clear. You don't anticipate the recoil when you shoot and jerk the gun or your next shot will be off. You squeeze the trigger and don't jerk your hand back. It's funny, you see these gang movies where they're shooting with the gun upside down. The first shot won't get you, but if it's automatic gunfire you'll eventually get hit with a couple of rounds.

It's not brain surgery, but some cops fail. You'd think if you're taking thirty shots at seven yards away, you'd get them all in the target and have sixty points right there. You only need a 70 to pass. If you fail they can either give you another shot at it or take your gun until you qualify. Once in a while you get an old-timer like Vince Puletti, who's been sitting in a radio room for twenty years and never shoots his gun and fails to qualify. A lot of times the instructors work with the old-timers to help them pass, because they don't want to see the old-timers humiliated.

We started off shooting for our qualifying round with five rounds at a target twenty-five yards away. Then we moved up and shot fifteen rounds at fifteen yards away, and then we shot thirty rounds at seven yards away.

"Three rounds in eight seconds," was announced over the loud-speaker, followed by a whistle to signal shooting. We fired three shots in eight seconds at our own pace. Boom-boom-boom. If you rush your shots, you'll miss the target.

When we shot off the first round and the whistle blew for us to stop, Rooney said, "Look at that, perfect as usual."

"Two shots in five seconds," the announcement came again with the whistle.

Rooney's shells were hitting me on my left shoulder, so I stepped over, hoping one didn't go down my shirt and burn me. Joe is left-handed, so as soon as I moved toward him I was getting hit on my right.

My goggles always fog up on me, so I pulled the valve out to let some air in, but it never helps. Rooney's goggles were clear as a bell as he smiled at my fogged ones, looking like an oversized bug. He was ready to swoop in and qualify with 100 percent.

We dropped our clips to reload. You aren't supposed to take your eyes off your target, being that if the target was real, he could charge you while you were reloading. Of course, Rooney looked down to reload, and I took the opportunity to fire a round in the left-hand corner outside his target.

Rooney came back up and fired off two rounds, and I saw him squinting where the bullet was off the target. I had to turn around not to laugh, and Joe put his head down with his shoulders shaking.

The next time Rooney looked down to reload, Joe put a round in the bottom of the right-hand corner outside of his target. We watched the shock on his face when he saw it, and Joe and I both cracked up.

"It's just not your day today, Mike. Looks like a 96," I said as Joe choked on a laugh.

"That's impossible," he said, still staring at his target.

We picked up our spent rounds while they marked our scores. We all qualified. Joe and I both scored 100, while Rooney said it was impossible that he got a 96. I figured we'd tell him about it on Sunday when we were fishing and he was wasted.

We skipped the lunch, mostly because I wasn't paying four bucks for food that looked like it was cooked over at Rikers. The inmates that worked cleaning up the range seemed okay. The guy that cooked the food looked like an ex-con to me, and let's be honest, we're cops and there's always the spit factor.

We cleaned our guns, got our qualifying sheets, and went to the bathroom to wash our hands.

We were out by 12:30. We were working a midnight, so we headed back to the precinct. No sense in driving all the way home just to come back later.

Traffic was a little heavy on the Bruckner. In another hour it would look like a parking lot. This was the first day back to school in New York City, and everyone was back from vacation. I beat the shocks on my truck as I slammed into a pothole every couple of feet. I once read that the two worst roads in the country were right here in New York City, the Bruckner and the Cross Bronx Expressway. Trust me, it's true.

I got to the precinct at 1:50. Rooney went over to the bar without bothering to ask me. It used to be that I'd hit the bar in between tours and souse myself up with Rooney. Now I go down to the lounge and watch reruns of *Law & Order* and *In the Heat of the Night*. It's not that I miss it, not like I used to. I just wish I could still do it once in a while. I knew the feeling would pass, it always does.

About 5:00, Rooney got back from the bar with a load on. He, Joe, and I walked over to the #1 Kitchen on 34th and 9th for some Chinese food. The place isn't filthy, and the food's pretty good. Walsh and Snout were sitting by the window when we walked in. Joe and I gave them a nod, but Rooney ignored them.

There were about six tables and chairs and then a second-floor dining room, I guess for the lunch crowd. Rooney was busting chops, ordering "flied lice, vely crunchy egg roll, and lotsa soup and dumpling" in a Chinese voice while keeping his face straight. The female behind the counter fired off in Chinese as she pulled a pencil out of a cup filled with rice and circled the items on the menu order form. "What you want?" she asked Joe and me as she pounded her fingers on the plastic-covered cash register. I got Hunan chicken, and Joe got chicken and broccoli, no MSG.

"Number 47," she yelled, tearing off the bottom of the menu and handing it to us.

When we finished our food Rooney handed out fortune cookies to each of us.

"Now," he said, smiling. "You gotta read your fortune but at the end of it add 'in bed.'"

"Why?" I asked.

"Because it's hysterical." He started laughing and then turned to Snout and Walsh. "Rookies, come 'ere, and bring your fortune cookies." He waved them over.

They scrambled over with their cookies in hand, happy Rooney was paying attention to them. Rooney looked like his blood pressure was up; he was red faced and sweating. I guess from the booze and salty food.

He told them what he'd told us, to read the fortune and add "in bed" at the end of it.

"You first," he said, throwing a nod at Walsh.

Walsh looked down at his fortune. "The good old days were once present too." He looked at us and added, "In bed."

"Now you." He nodded to Snout.

"Okay," she said, looking embarrassed. "You would make a good lawyer, in bed."

"Those suck," Rooney said, turning to Joe. "What does yours say?"

Joe looked at his fortune and smiled. "Where there's a will there's a way, in bed."

Rooney let out a laugh. "Now you, Tony."

I looked down at my fortune. "I like this," I said. "You will enjoy good health. You will be surrounded by luxury, in bed."

"Now you, Mike," I said.

He pulled the paper close to his face. "Our first love and last love is self-love, in bed."

We all cracked up at that. "That's not funny," he said.

"Yes, it is," Joe said, laughing.

We walked back to the precinct at 6:30. Joe went down to the lounge, and I stayed outside and called Michele because I couldn't get a signal down there.

"How was the range?" she asked.

"Good. I qualified, got 100."

"Good for you," she said. "How'd Joe do?"

"Same thing," I said. "What are you up to?"

"I'm just cleaning up after dinner and getting ready to sit down for the first time all day."

"How's Stevie? How'd he do for his first day of kindergarten?" It hit me then that I probably should have been there to see it.

"He was nervous. But I checked on him later on and he was fine," she said.

Michele lives in Manorville but works in Shirley, so she put Stevie in school with her. Joe told me the area isn't as good as Manorville, a little rough, but Michele is trying to transfer to the Eastport schools and put Stevie in school there.

I talked to her for a couple of minutes and went down to the lounge to pass out until my shift. Rooney was snoring loudly enough that Rice and Beans, who were taking their meal, threw a shoe at him.

◆

Joe's alarm went off at 10:00. We washed our faces, brushed our teeth, and went across the street to pick up coffee.

Geri was working the counter earlier than usual, and we saw that the store owner was there with her. A guy in a blue maintenance uniform brought a cup of coffee over to her and said, "Ger, is there something wrong with the coffee machine? I think the coffee's cold."

Geri lifted the lid off the cup and stuck her finger in it. "Nope, it's hot," she said, putting the lid back on and sucking the coffee off her finger.

The owner stopped counting the money in the register to look at her. "Did you just stick your finger in his coffee?"

"Yup," she said and smiled at him. "He wanted me to tell him if it was cold."

"You could give anyone a heart condition," the boss said, shaking his head. "Get yourself another coffee," he told the maintenance worker.

"That's alright. Geri's hands are clean." He smiled at her, and she stuck her bent index finger to her nose, pretending to pick.

"I could fire you for that," the boss said.

"But you won't, because if the customers found out you fired me, they wouldn't come in anymore." She laughed.

The funny thing is, it's true. She's obnoxious as anything, but everyone likes her. She puts up a tough front, but she's soft underneath it. One time I saw her make a sandwich and put her own money in the register. I figured the boss made her pay for her own food. Joe and I were still sitting outside drinking our coffee in the RMP, and we saw her go out and give the sandwich and a cup of coffee to a female skell who was sitting outside the deli. She smiled at the woman and gave her some of the cigarettes out of her pack before she went back inside the store.

"Hey, good lookings," she said to Joe and me. "You're early tonight."

"Yeah, we worked a day tour and slept through most of the four to twelve," Joe said.

"Does this mean you'll be back at 11:20 for more coffee?"

"You know it," Joe said. "But we'll probably send Bruno in."

"That's alright," she smiled. "He's not the sharpest knife in the drawer, but he's cute."

We went back to the precinct and stopped at the desk so Terri Marks could have her nightly shot at seducing Joe.

"Joe, did you see the new Victoria's Secret billboard on 34th Street?" she asked.

"Nope," he said. "Why?"

"I just bought the same underwear the model's wearing," she said.

"Ah, come on, Terr. Why'd you have to ruin it for me?" Vince yelled from the radio room. "Now I'm gonna picture you in the underwear."

"Very funny," Terri said, giving him a sneer.

Vince gave Joe and me a "Come here" signal.

"What's up, Vince?" I asked, shaking his hand.

"I heard the captain at the detail yesterday almost got you guys killed," he said quietly, his eyes scanning the room.

"I guess Rooney told you," Joe said.

Vince put his hands up. "I'm not saying who told me. You guys know if someone tells me something they can trust me with it."

Vince has the biggest mouth in the precinct—don't tell him anything.

"Look at this," Vince said with a nod toward Walsh, who was being approached by John Shea, an old-timer with about nineteen years on.

Unlike most old-timers, he's always asking the rookies to partner up with him. That's because anyone with any time on knows not to go near him. It's not that he's dangerous; he's a harmless guy. He's not a very good cop, and he's a drunk. He'd give you the shirt off his back, and has actually done that at times, coming back to the precinct missing articles of clothing after passing out in some of the seedier movie theaters on 8th Avenue.

He's bald and skinny, and his rumpled uniform hangs over the potbelly on his five-foot-ten-inch frame. He had to lean his head back to look up at Walsh, who had a confused look on his face. Walsh looked over at me with a "What do you think?" look, and I shook my head and looked away. I didn't want Shea to see me shaking my head. I liked him, but he really wasn't the kind of cop you learned from. I couldn't hear what Walsh said as he shook his head no while shaking Shea's hand. Shea was smiling at him, so I guess Walsh didn't hurt his feelings.

We talked to Vince until Hanrahan made his attention to the roll call announcement.

"The color of the day is orange," he said.

He gave out the sectors and foot posts, and we all turned to the sound of a nightstick clanging on the floor.

"Rookie!" Rooney yelled to Snout. "Give me ten push-ups!"

In the Academy if you dropped your nightstick you automatically had to do ten push-ups. This was to teach you not to play with your nightstick and to hold on to your weapons.

Snout dropped to the floor and started firing off push-ups, when everyone started laughing.

"Nice form," Garcia said.

When she realized what she was doing she got up, her face flaming red, and dusted herself off. I guess she forgot for a second she wasn't in the Academy anymore. She picked up her nightstick and hung it on her belt before lifting her chin up. She was smart enough not to say something to Rooney. I gotta say, her and Walsh were looking pretty promising.

"What's wrong with you, Mike?" Bruno asked Rooney.

"Shut up, Galotti, before I make you do push-ups," Rooney barked at him.

We finished roll call and got our radios, and the three of us walked out to the RMP.

It was a perfect night. Clear and cool, making the lights of the buildings around us stand out against the cloudless sky.

We stopped for coffee again, sending Bruno in this time. He came out without comment with a cardboard cup holder and three blueberry muffins. We drove up 8th Avenue and pulled over between 43rd and 44th to drink our coffee.

We watched an Irish guy who looked to be in his midfifties walking down 8th Avenue from 44th Street. He was probably coming from the Irish pub that I haven't been in since we locked up Santa Claus last Christmas. Santa had been drinking with the Grinch, and they wound up rolling around on the floor of the pub over a twenty-dollar bill that had disappeared off the bar.

The guy was drunk enough to be unsteady on his feet. A couple of skells were following him, eyeing him up for a quick roll.

"You okay there, buddy?" Joe asked him as he was passing the car.

"Yeah, officer," he said, looking behind him. "I just got out of the bar, and these guys are asking me for money."

He didn't realize that if we hadn't shown up, they'd be beating it out of him. Up close I could see blue eyes, a red nose, and gray hair with a little black tossed in there. He was dressed nicely enough in a short-sleeved collared shirt and beige pants.

The skells hung back now, stopping outside a gated storefront a couple of doors up, still watching him.

"Where are you going?" Joe asked.

I don't think he realized they were gonna roll him, more like they were annoying him.

He named a bar over on Lexington Avenue and started telling us that his brother-in-law and his niece were both cops.

"Where do they work?" I asked.

He told us their names and where they worked up in the Bronx, but it was no one we'd know.

"How are you getting over to the bar?" I asked him. He seemed like a nice guy, and I didn't want to see him get jumped once we drove away.

"I'll take the crosstown bus on 42nd Street," he said.

"Jump in the back," I said. "We'll take you over there." We had nothing going on yet anyway.

"You sure?"

"Yeah, come on," I said and hit the button to unlock the door.

"Thank you so much," he said as he got in, filling the car with the smell of booze.

"I love you guys," he said with emotion you'd only show when someone does you a favor while you're plastered. "You guys do a great job."

"No problem," Joe told him. "We want to make sure you get there okay."

I shot up 42nd Street over to Lexington and down to 40th. We dropped him off at another Irish bar that looked just like the last one.

"Here, I want to give you this," he said as he pulled out a roll of bills.

"No, buddy, we can't take that," I said.

"You saved me the trouble of waiting for a bus," he said.

"Really, it's okay," Joe said. "We can't take the money. We just wanted to make sure you got here."

He pushed a twenty-dollar bill through the screen into the front seat.

"Buddy, really we can't take this," I said, wondering for a second if we were being set up by IAB.

"No, officer, I want you to have it," he yelled as he ran into the bar.

"I'm not chasing him into the bar," I said.

"We'll just give it to the widows and orphans," Joe said, talking about the fund for the wives and children of slain cops. He wrote in his memo book that we received twenty bucks for the widows and orphans fund just in case we *were* being set up by the rats at internal affairs.

Technically, we're also not supposed to put anyone in the car without notifying Central, but we're not gonna call for something like this.

As I made the turn onto 39th Street and headed westbound, Central came over the air with, "South David."

"South David," Fiore answered.

"We have a possible robbery in progress, males with guns at 47 West 37th Street between five and six."

"Do you have a callback?" Fiore asked.

"There's no callback. Male caller states he believes there's a robbery going on in the building right now."

As we rushed down 5th Avenue Joe said, "Isn't there a geisha house there?"

"Yeah, halfway down on 37th Street."

Most of the brothels, or geisha houses, as we call them, are between 5th Avenue and 6th Avenue between 35th and 39th streets. They're Mob run, stocked with Asian girls, and closed down only to pop up again on a regular basis.

As we pulled up we saw South Adam's RMP there, and I heard Garcia tell Central they were 84, on the scene. Our sectors border at 5th Avenue. The east side of it is theirs, the west side of it is ours. When we dropped the drunk off we were in their sector.

Garcia and Davis jumped out of the car and had their guns pointed at a guy standing along the building line.

As we pulled the car up behind Adam's RMP Joe put "David 84" over the radio.

Garcia and Davis holstered their guns and started tossing the guy on the wall.

As we stepped out of the car four more guys came out of a doorway about ten feet from the perp Garcia and Davis had on the wall. Garcia and Davis didn't even see them.

"Watch these guys coming out the door," Joe yelled as he stayed behind the car door and punched out his gun. I crouched down behind the hood of the RMP with my gun punched out and yelled, "Get against the wall! Don't move!"

Joe and I charged at them with our guns up as they got on the wall pretty quick, looking panicked.

Something was up with these four, and we came up behind them with our guns still on them.

"Arms and legs out!" I yelled.

"Cover us while we toss them," Joe called to Davis, who was between us and Garcia. Garcia stayed with the first guy, with his gun on his hip and one eye on us and one eye on the perp.

All five of them were Hispanic, dressed for a night of robbery in long-sleeved, dark, nondescript clothes that covered their waistbands. They all wore plain dark baseball hats with no writing on them pulled down on their foreheads.

I still had my gun out when I reached around to check the waist of the first guy lined up. He was the tallest of the group, maybe five foot ten.

"Gun!" I yelled as I got to his waistband, and my heart started hammering in my chest. I don't know why it surprised me that he had a gun, but it did.

Joe had taken the last guy, and I heard him yell "Gun!" as the two guys in the middle started talking in Spanish. Both my guy and Joe's guy had knapsacks on their backs, and we pulled them off almost simultaneously and threw them away from us on the ground.

"*A lo major correnos?*" the second guy in said to the third guy.

"*Callate!*" Garcia yelled to them. "They're gonna run!" he said to Joe and me and then yelled to them again. "*No te Muevas!*" He switched back to English. "I'll shoot the first one of you that moves!"

Garcia cuffed his guy and had him kneel down with his hands on the wall.

I grabbed the butt of the gun of the guy I was tossing and took a step back with his gun in my hand, still pointing my gun at him. Davis had his gun out, covering us. He stood behind us with his gun drawn out and down a little, not pointing at us but ready to shoot.

"Get on your knees," I yelled to the first guy as I stuck the gun in my waistband. "Put your hands on the wall."

I surprised myself by remembering to pray right then, throwing up a "Lord, please help us here and don't let anybody get killed" prayer. I knew it wasn't much in the way of prayers, but it's new that I even think to pray in the middle of something like this.

I grabbed the second guy and went straight for his waistband and yelled "Gun!" again. He was one of the two talking in Spanish about

103

running, and I wouldn't take my eyes off him. I put the gun in my waistband, thinking *I'm running out of room here, and I can't toss these guys good kneeling on the floor like that.*

Just then Joe patted down his second guy and yelled "Gun!" again.

Once Joe and I had all the guns, we could search them better. They weren't talking now that they realized Garcia spoke Spanish. I guess English or Spanish we had them covered.

Joe and I walked back to where Davis was standing to secure the guns.

Three of the four guns were real. One was a .38 with a four-inch barrel, fully loaded with six rounds. I dumped the bullets in my hand and put them in the front left pocket of my uniform pants, and then I stuck the gun back in my waistband.

The second gun was a cheesy .380 semiautomatic. I took the clip out and stuck it in my right pocket and took the live round out of the chamber and stuck it with the clip.

Joe's guy had a two-inch .38. What we call a policeman's special, snub-nose five shot.

The last gun looked real but wound up being a cigarette lighter. "Let me see that," I said, pointing it at the ground and flicking the flame. I lit a cigarette and waited for my heart rate to slow down a little. I opened up one of the knapsacks. "Looky here," I said as I showed them the knapsack full of money.

Joe opened the second knapsack and said, "Videotapes," with a shrug.

Now that we had them all cuffed and on the ground, a guy came out of a black Lincoln across the street. He was about six foot one, 230 pounds, dressed in a suit jacket and pants with no tie. He had wise guy written all over him.

We were so engrossed with the five Hispanic guys we never saw him. He was looking pretty nervous, his eyes darting around like he expected someone to jump out at him.

"Can I help you?" Garcia asked, watching the guy's hands.

"I'm the one who called you," he said, nodding at the perps on the wall. He was sweating profusely, and I didn't think it was from his weight.

"And who are you?" Garcia asked suspiciously.

"I work upstairs," he said. He took a handkerchief out of his back pocket and mopped his forehead.

"Why'd you call?" I asked.

"I saw these guys going into the building."

"So what made you think they were gonna rob it?" This from Garcia. "Did they have guns out?

"No. There's been a group of guys robbing geisha houses," he said.

"How do you know that?" I asked.

This guy knew whatever was going on here. He was being evasive, which made us suspicious. He looked like a wise guy but acted like a coward, like he was afraid someone was gonna jump out and shoot him at any minute.

"I gotta go check upstairs," he said, turning.

"Whoa, whoa, whoa, get back here. Where upstairs?" Joe said, signaling him to come back.

"Third floor."

"You work in the geisha house?" I said, it dawning on me.

Geisha houses are Mob run. If he was running it and it was robbed on his watch, he'd have to answer for it.

He shrugged. "Yeah, I work there. I gotta get upstairs."

"Come on, I'll go with you," I said.

"I'm coming too," Joe said as he got on the radio and had Central have South Sergeant respond to 47 West 37th Street, nonemergency.

6

The geisha house was in a narrow, ten-story white brick building. The entrance led into a bronze-speckled marble-floored hallway to the elevator. There was a camera over the elevator, monitoring the front door.

"You have a gun on you?" I asked the goombah as we entered the building, thinking that might be why he was so nervous.

"No," he said, opening his suit jacket and turning around so we could look.

"What's your name?" Joe asked.

"Rocco Marracini," he said.

"You have some ID?"

He showed us his driver's license, and Joe started writing down his info.

"How did you know they were gonna rob the geisha house?" I asked him again, wondering what his involvement was in this.

"As a courtesy when a place is robbed, they call the others and warn them with a description."

"Kind of like an illegal community watch?" I asked him.

"Something like that," he said with a shrug as Joe handed him back his license. He looked like a bulldog but acted like a wuss.

The elevator was old, the kind that bounces when it starts and you can barely tell it's moving. There was a camera in the elevator in plain view, not hidden in the dome of a light, I guess so the madam could watch the clientele coming in.

"Where'd you call us from?" Joe asked.

"I was on my way home" — he held up his cell phone — "and when I crossed the street I saw them enter the building, and they fit the description of the guys that have been doing the robberies. One of them was standing out front."

Joe continued to press him. "How many altogether?"

"Five. Four on the inside and the lookout. I waited a couple of minutes and called upstairs to the madam. When she didn't answer I knew something was wrong. That's when I called you guys."

The elevator door opened, and there was a door right in front of us with a peephole. Behind us, above the elevator, was another camera so they could see who was at the door.

"Unlock the door," I said, hoping there wasn't a bloodbath on the other side.

His hands were shaking as he worked the lock, and he mopped his head again with his handkerchief.

"Step back," I said once he got it unlocked. "Let us go in first."

He stepped back, and I took my gun out and pushed the door open with my left hand, scanning the room, coming in low but not crouched in case anyone was in there.

The cool air from the air conditioning hit me as the door opened into the waiting room. There were three couches wrapping around the room with corner tables in between with lamps on them. There was a line of chairs to my right where clients picked their girls from, and to the left, behind the door, was a desk.

I counted two johns, four pros, and one madam, all with their mouths and legs duct taped. Their arms were taped behind their backs. One of the johns was shirtless, wearing pants and socks. The other was in his underwear and black dress socks. I guess they got robbed in the middle of a transaction.

The four Asian women looked to be in their twenties and were wearing various negligees, garter belts, and other prostitution-looking outfits. Their makeup was smeared, and some of them were still crying. The madam was yelling through her tape. She looked about sixty years old and was wearing black pants and one of those red short-sleeve tops that buttons at the neck that some Asian women wear.

I stepped in further and looked behind the door where the madam's desk was. The first room on the right was the office, and Joe and I walked through it while the cowardly wise guy started pulling the tape off the females.

The safe in the office was open and empty, and there were papers all over the place. We continued down the corridor to the rooms where business was conducted. They reminded me of a doctor's office except there were massage tables and soft lights.

The place smelled like perfume. It reminded me of the perfume girls wore in junior high school. I guess smells associated with the rush of puberty are right on the money with a lot of guys that pay for sex. They come here with that heated "I can't get sex off my mind" mentality.

All the rooms were empty, so we went back to the waiting room. At this point everyone's hands were free and they were pulling the tape off themselves.

The madam was talking a mile a minute in her broken English. She said the perps slapped her around to get her to open up the safe.

Just then Hanrahan came over the radio with, "South Sergeant to South David."

"Go ahead, South Sergeant."

"Is this confirmed?"

"Yeah, we're on the third floor."

"I'll be right up."

Joe and I started getting information from everyone in the room. The story was that while two of the perps were getting in the safe, the other two were ripping off the johns, taking three hundred bucks of one guy's pocket money, his watch, and his wedding ring. They pistol-whipped the john in his underwear because he wanted to put his clothes on, and he had a pretty nice bloody welt on the back of his head. It was nice to know how serious these guys were after we found the guns.

The story everyone in the waiting room was telling was that the four men came in and drew their guns. They grabbed the madam and two of the pros in the waiting room and put them on the floor. Three of them went into the back and dragged the two Johns and the other pros into the waiting room. When they got all of them out there, two took the madam into the office for the money in the safe. One of them kept the gun on them while another taped them up.

Hanrahan came in with Noreen. "Whaddaya got?" he asked, looking around the room.

Joe and I went through the whole spiel with him, and he got on the radio and called South Eddie to pull Walsh and Snout off of robbery posts 4 and 7 and bring them to this location.

We collected all the duct tape. It was evidence and probably had fingerprints on it. The perps hadn't bothered with gloves because the geisha house wouldn't have reported a robbery and chanced getting closed. If Rocco hadn't called and we hadn't walked up on it, they would have gotten away with it.

"Who are you?" Hanrahan asked Rocco.

"Rocco Marracini, I work here."

"How much was in the safe?" Hanrahan didn't bother with what kind of work Rocco did here, as the detectives would interview him later. Even though it was an illegal operation, it was still a robbery.

"I emptied the safe when we got the warning that the other geisha houses were being robbed."

Yeah, and laundered the money through car washes around the tristate area.

"How much was in the safe?" Hanrahan asked with less patience than he did last time.

I watched Rocco think for a second before he said, "About seventy-five hundred dollars."

I think it's anything over ten grand you have to report to the IRS.

"We're in the wrong business here, boss," I said as Hanrahan shook his head.

The boss knew I was joking. Between my Catholic school upbringing and my father drilling into my head that ill-gotten money is cursed, I couldn't work at something that wasn't honest. Despite our Italian heritage my father has an aversion to bent noses and taught us never to get in bed with mafiosos.

"When Walsh and Snout get here, send them up. Have Rooney and Connelly wait outside with you guys," Hanrahan told Joe and me as we were heading back downstairs.

When we got off the elevator we saw Rooney and Connelly outside with Walsh and Snout.

"They had guns?" Walsh asked, excited, when we opened the door.

"Three guns and a lighter," I said as Connelly started making kissing sounds like we were suck-ups to the bosses.

"Three guns is nothing," Rooney said.

"Better than the two vials and the crack pipe you called an 85 for last week," I said. His call for assistance forthwith had us flying through traffic for a crack pipe.

"He swung at me, Tony," Rooney snapped.

"He was waving the smoke from the crack pipe out of your face," I laughed.

Joe called Central to tell them we had five under.

"That's zero one ten hours," Central said.

Walsh and Snout went upstairs with the complainants while we separated the perps and put them in the four RMPs to take them back to the precinct.

Each of the other cars had one perp, and Joe and I had two, the lookout and the first guy I searched. We do this so they can't talk to each other and get their stories straight before we interview them.

The lookout mumbled something, and Joe turned around and said, "Listen, no talking," as he looked at each of them until they turned their faces to look out the window.

"You're looking, right?" Joe asked to see if I wanted the collar.

"Sure, I'll take it. Unless you want it," I asked.

"No, I know you're looking for OT," Joe replied.

This was a great collar—armed robbery, plus the inspector would have an intel report on the geisha house. The inspector would love me when he went to the COMSTAT meeting this month with good numbers for the brass.

At the precinct we stopped the five perps at the desk. Lieutenant Coughlin asked, "Whaddaya got?" even though he already knew.

"Five for robbery," I said.

"Any weapons?" he asked, all business.

"Three guns and a lighter."

"Make sure you do a pistol index card on the lighter and give Terri the numbers off the guns so she can run them through the computer."

"You got it, boss," I said.

111

"When you search them make sure you know which property is theirs and which isn't," he added.

"I might not know until the complainants ID the stuff taken off them," I said.

"Then put all the property on the pedigree sheets and you'll sort it out later."

"You got it, boss."

We searched them at the desk again, this time going through their pockets, counting their money, and getting their pertinent information, making sure all the items were with the correct perp. Sometimes perps won't give us their names, and in that case they go down as John Doe, but these guys knew they were screwed, so they were pretty compliant.

Joe left with a van to pick up the complainants at the geisha house, and Rooney, Connelly, Garcia, Davis, and I got the perps settled into the cells on the second tier. The second tier is over the parking lot and holds twenty cells, ten on each side, separated by a cinder-block wall. We separated them by eight cells and put the lookout in the holding pen in the arrest processing area. Garcia and Davis stayed with the four perps to make sure they didn't try to communicate with each other.

In a case like this there's a lot of work. The detectives get involved and do the interviews on both the perps and the complainants. They would watch the videotapes that filmed the whole robbery, so the perps wouldn't be able to get out of this.

Jack Sullivan and Eileen Toomey are the RIP, or Robbery in Progress, detectives. I've worked with both of them before. Eileen is Italian, married to an Irishman. Sullie is an Irishman, married to Jack Daniels and paying child support to two women. I liked them both, but Sullie was funnier.

Before we took the perps one by one into the squad room, we started with our boy Rocco.

Rocco's story was the same as what he told me before.

"What do you do, own and operate a geisha house?" Sullie asked him.

"No, I own a shoe store in downtown Brooklyn," Rocco said, seeming almost surprised that we thought he owned the geisha house.

"A shoe store? What do you sell, cement shoes?" Sullie asked.

"No, women's shoes imported from Italy. I run the shoe store, and I work at the geisha house four nights a week."

"What do you do at the geisha house?"

Rocco thought about it for a couple of seconds. "I make sure everything operates properly," he replied with a shrug. "I keep the books."

"Who owns the geisha house?" Sullie was writing as he talked.

"A corporation called Equinox."

"And who owns Equinox?"

Rocco shrugged. "I don't know."

"Stop playing games with me," Sullie snapped. "Who do I contact if I want to talk to someone over at Equinox?"

Rocco got amnesia after that, but he did remember his lawyer's phone number.

Next we brought in the first gunman and played the videotape for him.

"Hey, this guy looks just like you," Sullie said as we watched him duct tape the complainants. "Where'd you learn how to tape like that, the Boy Scouts?"

The perp had a "This can't be good" look on his face. We watched as one of them grabbed the madam and threw her and the two girls on the floor. The girls were crying, but the madam was snapping like a terrier. She'd been robbed before. Three guys went into the back and came out with the johns and the other two girls. The tape ended when they grabbed the madam and pulled her into the office. A minute later the tape went blank.

We went through the same thing with the four gunmen. The only one who tried to get out of it was the lookout.

"I had no idea they were gonna rob the place," he said, all innocent. "I thought they were going to get girls."

"Why didn't you go get girls?" Sullie asked. "Are you gay?"

"No way, I'm not gay," he said puffing his chest out a little.

"Are you saying there's something wrong with being gay?" Sullie got in his face.

"No!" His voice rose an octave. "I got no problem with it."

"So you're telling me your friends went up to buy some geisha and you stayed outside to lean against the building? Why didn't you go up and wait on one of the couches?"

"I didn't have any money," he said.

"Tony, did he have any money on him?" Sullie asked me but was looking at him.

"Sixty-seven bucks," I said.

"I'm sure you could've got something for sixty-seven bucks." Sullie looked at me and said it like a question.

I shook my head. "Probably not."

"Well, you could've gotten the complimentary beer."

Sullie hammered away at him for a while, but the guy didn't change his story. All five of them had records, with everything from larceny to robbery to assault and burglary. The lookout had been involved with a robbery before; I guess he's always the lookout.

Joe came in with the madam and stayed with the pros as we called them in one by one. The madam had to interpret for the girls. They all told pretty much the same story, making gun gestures and showing their hands taped behind their backs.

This was pretty cut and dried. The lineups would take time to set up; they probably wouldn't be ready until after 8:00 in the morning. We use cops, people off the streets, merchants in the area. We have a list of people we can grab from. Plus, there's a lot of Hispanic guys in the area, but it was five perps and we had to do separate lineups.

We spent the rest of the night doing the interviews and vouchering the guns, videotapes, jewelry, watches, money, pictures of injuries, and duct tape. We stopped about 4:00 when Sullie ordered out coffee and sandwiches from the deli across the street. He got Joe and Toomey turkey on a roll and roast beef and Muenster with spicy mustard for me and him.

We went down to the lounge to eat, and when I finished my sandwich I turned my cell phone on to check the messages. I usually don't check it until morning, but something was telling me to take a look. Sure enough, there was the envelope showing I had three new voice mails.

"Tony, it's Denise. Grandma's in the hospital. They took her by ambulance, I think to St. Vinny's. I don't know if it's a heart attack or what. Give me a call." The message was at 11:45 p.m.

"What's the matter?" Joe asked, staring at me.

"Denise said my grandmother got taken to the hospital, she might have had a heart attack."

He looked away as I accessed the second message, which was from my father.

"Tony, Grandma's in the emergency room at St. Vinny's. Get over here as soon as you can."

I deleted my father and answered the third one.

"I know this family isn't important to you anymore," Vinny's voice said, "but Grandma's in the hospital and it would be nice if you showed your face and at least let her think that you care."

"What is his problem?" I snapped.

"Who's that?" Joe asked.

"My brother, Vinny. He says my family's not important to me anymore and it would be nice if I showed my face at the hospital and at least pretend to care." I shook my head, angry and scared at the same time.

My mind started racing. What if Grandma died, what if this was all my fault because everyone was mad at me and the stress killed her? The last time Grandma was at the doctor he said she was fine, good cholesterol, good blood pressure.

"I'm sure she's fine," Joe said, sounding certain.

"How do you know that?" He looked funny, and I said, "Say what's on your mind."

"I have a feeling it might be a bid for attention." He shrugged. "You never fought with Vinny before, right?"

"Right," I said. "And?"

"Maybe this is something to make you come around to Grandma's way of thinking and make you realize all the trouble you're causing."

I didn't want to admit I had the feeling he might be right as I called information and got the number of the hospital.

I got through to the emergency room and identified myself as both a police officer and Anna Cavalucci's grandson. I heard talking, and a minute later my father got on the line.

"Dad, it's Tony," I said.

"Where've you been?" he half yelled.

"I'm at work, my cell phone is off. What happened?"

"Your grandmother started having chest pain, and it got bad enough around 7:30 that she called an ambulance—"

"Why didn't she call one of us?" I asked. "She could have gotten ahold of someone."

"She didn't want to bother anyone," he said.

"What'd the doctor say?"

"They're doing tests now. When can you get here?" He sounded impatient, like he wondered why I wasn't already there.

"I'm in the middle of an arrest, an armed robbery. I probably won't get there till this afternoon," I said.

I heard him sigh, and then he said, "Not for nothin', Tony, but you got your friggin' priorities all screwed up."

"Dad, it's my collar, you know I can't leave." I waited for him to answer me, and I said "Dad?" twice before I realized he'd hung up on me.

"He hung up on me," I told Joe, stunned the way you always are when someone hangs up on you. "Do you think it's serious enough that I should leave?"

"Call the ER back and talk to the doctor yourself," Joe said.

It took me about ten minutes to get the doctor. He told me Grandma's EKG was fine, her blood pressure was fine. He said they'd be doing some tests so they'd wait and see. I thanked him and hung up the phone, so aggravated at my father. He was a cop for twenty-two years. He knows you can't leave a robbery collar like that.

"Well?" Joe asked, eyebrows raised.

"He said so far she's fine, but they're gonna run some tests."

"That's good," he said.

"Joe, what are you seeing that I'm not seeing?" I asked, since I could tell by his face that he thought this was bogus.

He shrugged. "I don't know, Tony, your family seems to always have an emergency. It's like they feed on some kind of drama all the time, and if nothing's going on, they create it. Do you think your grandmother would play sick just to get everyone jumping?"

There was a time I would have said no, but now I wasn't so sure.

Joe was sitting on one of the benches, reading his devotional book, when I asked, "Can I see that when you're done?"

"Sure, take it," he said, handing it to me.

I felt him watching me as I read it, and I laughed out loud. The passage was from Judges 6:25–26. "Tear down your father's altar. . . . Build a proper kind of altar to the LORD." The devotional reading was the story of a man who never got a compliment from his father. His father thought it was unmanly to show affection, and this guy passed it on to his kids and did a lot of damage. He saw his kids doing the same thing to his grandchildren, and he wished he could change things. I didn't see what this had to do with the Scripture until it talked about how God told Gideon to tear down his father's altar and build a proper altar for God. It said that in the same way, we should tear down old habits and ways of communication and bless our children and honor God.

"This is true," I told Joe, handing the book back to him.

"So what's with you, Tony? Why you ducking church lately?"

"A lot of it is money, like I said. I guess the other part is that I don't feel as close to God as I did at first," I said. "I was getting a lot out of praying, but it's just not the same."

"Maybe it's time to come up a level," Joe said.

"What do you mean?"

"Our relationship with God is like anything else; it's supposed to grow with time. If you find that what worked then isn't working now, you need to go to the Word and find out why." He started thumbing through his Bible. "It says here in Hebrews 4:16, 'Let us then approach the throne of grace with confidence, so that we may receive mercy and find grace to help us in our time of need.' How do you interpret that? What does 'come boldly before the throne of grace' mean to you?"

I shrugged. "I don't know, I guess you take a deep breath, suck it up, and hope lightning doesn't hit you when you go in."

"Is that how you go into Michele's house?" he asked.

"No, of course not, it's my house too," I said.

"I would use your own father as an example, but I think you probably approach his house the same way you approach the throne room of God." He smiled. "You're comfortable with Michele's house because there's a place there for you, you belong there. The Bible tells us in Ephesians that God raised us up with Christ and seated us with him in the heavenly realms. That means we have a right to be there. You need to come up to that place in prayer."

"What do you mean?" Sometimes he gets so deep, this stuff flies over my head.

"Like, before you dedicated yourself to Christ, what kind of prayers did you pray?" he asked.

Usually it was the morning after and my head was hanging over a toilet bowl someplace I didn't remember getting to. I'd be begging God—*I'll never drink again. I'll never drink and drive again. Please don't let her be pregnant. I'm sorry, I didn't know she was married.*

"I don't know," I said, "just your basic I promise to be good if God would get me out of this."

"But you're different now. Your relationship to Jesus is different. Back then you were a sinner, without Christ. You were without hope and without the covenant you have with God. Jesus is our mediator, or our way to the Father. When he died for you, he saved you a seat in God's throne room. So when you go to the throne now it's as a son, and a son who's loved. In Matthew 6 Jesus gave us the Our Father and told us to pray like this. Not pray this, but pray *like* this." Joe's Italian, so he uses his hands a lot when he talks.

"'Our Father, who art in heaven' says a lot. Unfortunately, *father* means a lot of things to a lot of people. It doesn't mean the Father of love like God is; to a lot of people *father* conjures up memories of abuse and cruelty, so they can't relate to God as a loving father. 'Who art in heaven' makes people think of this mystical far away place. It's not, but it's where God's throne is, and for lack of a better way to explain it, it's where he does business. We approach God like children in the fact that we trust him, but we can go in there as grown men who are about our Father's business, just like Jesus was."

Joe stopped talking when the door to the lounge opened and Bruno Galotti came in and put a brown paper bag down on the table.

"Hey, Tony, Joe," he said, taking off his shoes and gun belt. "Jeetyet?" Which translates to "Did you eat yet?"

"Yeah, we got sandwiches from the deli," Joe said. "What about you?"

"No, but I brought in some homemade ravioli that my mother made. You want some?"

"Was it in the fridge?" I asked. I wasn't eating anything outta that fridge.

"No, I left it in the custodian's fridge, that one's clean," he said as he took out a big plastic bowl and popped it in the microwave.

"I'll have some," Joe said.

"I'll have a couple," I said. I wasn't really hungry, but I'm not about to pass up homemade ravioli that someone from Italy made.

These were the real deal, big and round like someone used a coffee cup to cut them. Some were cheese and some were spinach and cheese covered in a meat gravy. They were delicious.

We finished the ravioli, thanked Bruno, and passed out on the benches.

7

We were back upstairs at 5:30 to finish up the paperwork on the arrest. Joe went home at the regular time, and I stayed around for the ADA to call me. I went outside on the front steps of the precinct at 7:30 and called Michele.

"Hey, babe," I said when she picked up.

"Hi," she said, sounding hurried. "I have six minutes to talk. I'm starting to forget what you look like."

"Five ten, black hair, hazel eyes, two holes in my nose," I said.

She laughed. "Now I remember. Did you speak to your father?"

"Yeah, Grandma's in the hospital," I said.

"I know. Your father called here at 11:30 last night looking for you."

"What'd he say?"

"He was very nice, he said he was looking for you and that Grandma was having chest pain and if I heard from you to let you know she was at Vinny's, which I didn't get."

"He meant St. Vinny's, the hospital."

"So when will I see you?" she asked.

"I don't know, I'll try to get out there tomorrow or the next day. If not I'll see you Saturday."

"I miss you," she said. "Do you think I'll see you once in a while once we're married?"

"Definitely," I said. "That's why I'm working all the OT now, so I can stay home for a while."

Then she got all mushy—"I love you, can't wait till we're married"—which I love hearing, but I looked around hoping Rooney didn't hear me talking or I'd never hear the end of it.

The ADA called at 8:30. Her name was Rachel Katz, and I'd worked with her before. She was in the special prosecutors section and deals with only felony arrests like burglary, robbery, gun possession, and assault one.

"Good morning, Officer Cavalucci," she said. I could picture her with her big smile and brown frizzy hair. I could hear the chaos of the DA's office in the background, phones ringing, people talking, and computers clicking.

We went through it pretty easy. I gave her a brief scenario—we had five perps, four with guns (one of them a toy), and they robbed the geisha house. She wanted to make sure it was a felony and wasn't gonna get knocked down. She said she'd call me later for the whole deal after the lineups were done.

It took a while to get the lineups set up. We used a couple of Hispanic cops from the day tour in civilian clothes. We also have a list of merchants, a couple of skells that we throw a few bucks to, along with other people in the area that we call when we need to put a lineup together.

Sullie and I brought in the madam first. Sullie explained the lineup to her, telling her that there were going to be six people standing in line holding a number.

"They can't see you, but you can see them," he said.

"Okay, okay." She nodded as Sullie knocked on the block of wood covering the two-way mirror to alert the officer on other side of the wall that we were ready to begin. We heard a knock from the other side letting us know they were all in position.

"You ready?" Sullie asked.

She nodded, and he pulled the block of wood away from the window.

Whenever I'm at a lineup I picture all but the perp wearing police uniforms and pointing at the perp so the complainant will know who the bad guy is.

"Take your time," Sullie told her as she squinted. "Do you recognize anyone?"

She pointed at the window. "Number two."

"Number two?" Sullie looked at me.

"Yeah, number two, he customer," she said nodding rapidly.

"Listen, I don't care who's a customer," he said dryly. "Can you pick out anyone who robbed you last night?"

She scanned the rest of the line. "Number five, but number two, he customer."

"Was number two there last night?" Sullie asked her as he wrote down everything she said.

She shook her head. "No."

"Then we don't care about number two."

"Good thing it wasn't one of the cops who was a customer," Sullie said.

"You're not kidding," I said. It wouldn't be the first time.

The lookout wanted to lawyer up right before the lineup, but Sullie told him he wasn't waiting for a lawyer to do the lineup. We can let a lawyer be present for the lineup, but we don't have to wait for him to get here to do it.

We went through the lineups with the two johns and the other pros. I talked to Rachel Katz again and finished up around 2:30. I had changed into street clothes earlier, so I didn't have to go back down to the locker room before I signed out.

The day was warm and clear and felt about 75 degrees. My truck

123

was hot, and I kept the windows down and snorted exhaust until the air conditioner kicked in. I almost went downtown, but I saw there was no traffic heading into the Lincoln Tunnel and went through Jersey instead.

I rolled down my window and lit a cigarette as I came in to Staten Island over the Goethals Bridge and got hit with the smell of the dump. It's hard to describe the smell except that it smells like the dump. You have to be from Staten Island and surrounded by 2,200 acres of fifty years' worth of rotting garbage to understand what I mean. I read in the paper not too long ago that the pile of garbage at the dump is higher than the Statue of Liberty at 225 feet. The dump has also evolved into its own ecosystem with forests and tidal and freshwater wetlands. Apparently, the dump's in the path of the Atlantic flyway and the birds stop there every spring and fall as they migrate. They say you can see herons and other birds, but the only birds I ever see there are the seagulls screeching and circling like vultures on top of the mountain of garbage.

I got off at the Clove Road exit and took Bard Avenue over to the hospital. I parked in the visitor's lot and saw Denise and Nick Romano smoking outside the emergency room doors. Denise and Romano started going out after my engagement party in the spring. They knew each other before that; they used to hang out in the bowling alley together. After my party things got serious pretty quick, and the fact that she brought him to the hospital for a family crisis shows it's real serious.

"Nick Romano, long time no see," I said with a smile as I walked up. I actually felt a little choked up. I guess I missed him more than I realized.

"Hey, Tony." He shook my hand, then he hugged me and slapped me on the back.

"How you doin', buddy? How's FD?"

"Good," he said. "I'm loving it."

He looked better, happier, than I'd ever seen him.

"Good for you," I said.

"Hey, Denise." I kissed her cheek. "How's Grandma?"

"Loving being the center of attention," she said, rolling her eyes. "She's healthy as a horse. Thanks for calling me back the other day," she added sarcastically.

"When was that?" I asked. The last few days seemed to blur.

"It was Monday. I wanted to talk to you about Mom," Denise said.

"What about her?" I asked, bracing myself. My mother's been on the wagon for over a year, and I didn't want to hear that she was drinking again.

"She's been seeing someone, and I told her to bring him to the block party on Saturday."

"I'm going back inside," Nick said, probably thinking a fight was coming.

"You mean a boyfriend?" I asked.

"Just someone she's been seeing. His name is Ron, he's a great guy. I met him a couple of times, and he's crazy about Mom." She shrugged. "I'm hoping everyone will be happy for her, but she's nervous about introducing him to the family."

"Smart lady," I mumbled. "Where's she know him from, AA?"

"No, I think she goes to church with him," she said and paused. "He rides a Harley."

Denise sells Harleys for a living, so I could see how she'd think this was a good thing.

"What's he, a biker dude?" I pictured a hairy, fat slob riding my mother around on the back of a hog.

"No, Tony, he's a sweetheart. I think you'll really like him."

Just what I needed, my mother dating a sweetheart biker.

"Nick and I went up to see her last weekend, and he took us all to dinner," she said as she put her arm through mine. "Come on, I'll go with you to see Grandma. The doctor says she had an anxiety attack from stress, so it's all your fault."

"If it's an anxiety attack why is she still here?"

"They're waiting for the test results to make sure she didn't have some mini stroke or something."

The waiting room was filled with my relatives. Everyone was there—my father; his wife, Marie; my brother, Vinny; Christie, Vinny's fiancée; Aunt Rose, who's Grandma's sister, and her grandchildren (and my cousins) Paulie, Gino, and Little Gina. Even Frank Bruno, my father's partner from the police department, was there. They were competing with the volume of the TV anchored to the wall to hear each other.

I heard Aunt Rose yell to my father, "Vince, you're over fifty now, you should have it checked."

"Tony," Frank Bruno yelled. "Glad you made it."

"Hey, Frank," I said, shaking his hand.

I was surrounded then. Aunt Rose and little Gina each kissed a side of my face. "Don't worry, Tony," Aunt Rose said. "I said the rosary last night, and I went to church this morning and lit a candle."

Paulie got me in a bear hug, saying, "Grandma's gonna be fine."

My father got up and kissed my cheek, and so did Marie, which didn't surprise me given the circumstances.

Hospitals and funerals are very serious things in my family. In times of sickness and death all ill is forgotten and the family bonds. Nothing was said about my wedding, Vinny's bachelor party, or anything that would cause God to bring bad luck on my grandmother 'cause we weren't getting along.

Vinny was cool, but he stood up and gave me a hug, and Christie smiled sweetly like everything was just fine.

Talk was limited to family stuff, everyone's job, and the colonoscopy Aunt Rose had three weeks ago. She told us how she had to drink some pineapple-flavored drink and use suppositories and described a procedure that sounded like a sexual assault to me.

I jumped out of that conversation and asked Nick what he was doing over at FDNY. He'd finished training up at Randall's Island last month and was telling me about his first fire. He was a probee, a probationary firefighter, working at a firehouse in downtown Brooklyn.

"It was a chemical fire on 4th Avenue," he said, his face animated. "I wound up in the hospital having to get my blood oxygen levels checked. I fell asleep, and the next thing I know the department chaplain shows up. I'm thinking maybe this is worse than I thought and he's giving me last rites. I tell him, 'No disrespect, Father, but I don't think I'm ready to see you yet.' He laughed and told me it was just a courtesy, and then he tells me this joke about a lawyer going to heaven. It was pretty funny."

"What was the joke?" Marie smiled, eyeing Romano up like a piece of meat.

"What? Oh, it was saying that a priest and a lawyer took an elevator up to heaven. The priest steps off first, and St. Peter says, you know, 'Good job, welcome to heaven.'" He started turning red when he realized everyone was listening. "I'm not good at telling jokes," he said.

"No, we want to hear it," Marie urged, still smiling. "Come on," she insisted, making a circular motion with her hand.

"Okay. Anyway, the lawyer steps off the elevator, and a cheer goes up that rocks throughout all of heaven. The priest says, 'Why does he get a welcome like that?' and St. Peter says, 'He's a lawyer, we get so few of them.'"

He got a few good chuckles, and Marie cracked up. It was a cute joke, but it wasn't as funny as she was making it.

"I'm glad you're happy, Nick," I said. "I guess you don't miss the job."

"I miss the guys," he said seriously. "I didn't think I would, but I do. Even Rooney, but don't tell him I said that."

"Tony," Aunt Rose cut in. "What's this I hear you're having a block party Saturday? Why didn't you invite us?"

"I didn't think you'd want to come—"

"Of course we want to come! What should we bring?"

"Uh, whatever you want. We're just grilling—"

"Oh, Grandma Rose, make your potato salad with the dill," Little Gina said.

"I'll get some steaks," Paulie said, standing there in his velour track suit, cracking his knuckles. "I know a guy who delivers to the restaurants. I'll give him a call."

This went on and on. By the time they were done, six more people were added to the block party and we were having steaks, Aunt Rose's dill potato salad, Little Gina's eggplant parmigiano; Paulie's wife was making a tomato and onion salad with the tomatoes from the garden; and Gino was bringing wine.

I finally got to go inside and talk to Grandma. She looked pale and thin, swallowed up in the hospital bed.

"Tony," she said as I kissed her cheek.

"You okay, Grandma?"

"The doctor says I've been under too much stress."

"So I hear," I said.

"You have to make things right with your brother," she said, squeezing my hand.

"Don't worry about me and Vinny, everything's fine," I said, feeling like choking him.

"I hope so, Tony. Women come and go, but you only got one family." She squeezed my hand again, her bony knuckles digging into my fingers.

I had to force myself not to get sucked into telling her I'd do what Vinny wanted. I talked to the doctor, who told me she was fine and they'd be releasing her. I kissed Grandma and went back and said good-bye to everyone in the waiting room.

By the time I picked up a meatball hero and battled the traffic on the way to my apartment it was 5:00. I ate my sandwich and called Michele, telling her I was going to bed and I'd call her before I went to work. I set my clock for 9:30 and passed out as soon as I hit the pillow.

Ten seconds later my alarm went off, telling me it was 9:30. I pulled my alarm clock off the nightstand by the cord and hit the snooze button, too exhausted to lift my head off the pillow. A second later it went off again, and I got myself into the shower. I was still groggy when I left at 10:15, and I had to stop at the deli on Lincoln Avenue for a cup of coffee.

I talked to Michele on the ride in. She was exhausted and was waiting for me to call so she could go to sleep. Traffic was clear through to Midtown, and I was changed and in the muster room by 11:15.

"How's Granny?" Joe asked, handing me a cup of coffee that I didn't take. I'd rather drink the coffee at the deli; I only drink the precinct rotgut in emergencies.

"She's fine. The doctor said it was an anxiety attack, that she's under too much stress."

"Stress from you?" Joe smirked as he pinned his shield onto his uniform.

"That's what I'm hearing."

Walsh and Bruno came over to shake our hands, saying, "Great collar, guys," as Hanrahan called, "Attention to the roll call."

He gave out the color of the day (red) and the sectors and foot posts and ended the roll call with, "Good collar, Cavalucci, Fiore, Davis, and Garcia. Everyone did a great job, backed each other up, and apprehended five perps with four guns—"

"Three guns and a lighter," Rooney yelled. "They were cooping in the place, that's the only reason they got the collar."

Cooping is hiding out somewhere on your post but not on the street. If I was gonna coop somewhere, it wouldn't be a geisha house. You can get in too much trouble for that.

Hanrahan gave Joe and me notifications for the grand jury for Friday on the geisha house robbery. Normally we wouldn't go until next week, but apparently the madam was leaving the country on Monday for three weeks. This actually worked out better, since we'd be working a day tour on Friday and could sleep the night before the block party.

After roll call we grabbed Bruno and stopped at the corner for coffee.

"Just coffee, Tony?" Bruno asked.

I gave him two bucks. "Get me a buttered roll."

"Sounds good, me too," Joe said, reaching for more money.

"I got it," Bruno said, already heading into the deli.

He came out a couple of minutes later balancing the coffee. He handed me the coffee and pulled my buttered roll out of his pocket. I drove up to 44th and 8th and parked on the southeast corner while we had our coffee.

"Hey, Bruno, how's your girlfriend?" Joe asked him. "She's a nurse, right?"

"She's good. She's working twelve-hour shifts now, so she's off a lot."

"I'd rather work twelve-hour tours, wouldn't you?" I asked.

"Yup," Joe said.

"Definitely," Bruno said.

"I don't know why they don't let us do twelve-hour tours. We're here twelve hours half the time anyway," Joe said.

"Because we'd be happy then, and we'd have businesses on the side like the firemen and make enough money that we wouldn't have to be cops anymore," I said.

"Things any better with your girlfriend and your mother?" Joe asked. Bruno's mother hates his girlfriend.

"Not really," he said. "My mother slipped a couple of times and called Bianca 'Nicole.' Nicole is my old girlfriend," he explained. "Bianca says she does it on purpose, but my mother wouldn't do that."

"How long you seeing this girl?" Joe asked.

"Three years."

"Sounds like a Freudian slip," Joe said.

"What's that?" Bruno asked.

"Don't use big words, Joe," I said, shaking my head. "It'll only make it worse."

"Robbery post 5," Central came over the air.

"Robbery post 5," Bruno answered.

"We got a call for a pedestrian struck—43rd Street between 8th and 9th in front of 325. Bus is ten minutes out."

"10-4."

Joe got on the radio with, "South David on the back, we're right around the corner."

We went up 8th Avenue and made a left onto 43rd Street. There were stores closer to 9th Avenue, then a driveway for a parking garage, and then an apartment building and an office building next to each other.

We pulled up to the driveway, not blocking the entrance to the parking garage. There was a white Suburban parked just past the entrance to the garage, and a male in his early twenties was sitting on the ground, leaning up against the apartment building. A woman was crouched down next to him, talking to him and looking worried. A man who appeared to be in his midfifties was standing next to her, and he turned as we pulled up.

"What happened?" Bruno asked as the three of us got out of the car.

"My wife and I were at the theater. We went to see *The Producers*, and I wanted to take my car out of the lot and park it on the street so we could walk around the city a little."

This made sense, since the lot closes at midnight. I looked at the Suburban, noting the Jersey plates. They looked like money, and I pegged them as Bergen County.

"Where you from?" I asked.

"Maywood," he said.

Like I said, Bergen County.

"Did you hit him?" Bruno asked.

"I was backing the car up, I didn't see anyone around me, and when I pulled forward I heard a bang on the rear quarter panel, and this guy"—he pointed to the man sitting with his wife—"is laying on the ground screaming that his leg hurts. I never saw him, officer. I didn't even feel anything hit the car."

Joe walked over and crouched down next to where the guy was wincing and moaning.

"So what happened?" I called over to him.

"I was crossing the street . . ." He stopped and winced. "I noticed the guy was backing up and I thought he saw me, but he didn't stop. He hit me . . . Ahhh. I fell down." He grimaced and held his leg and said, "They won't even give me their name and address. I'm hurt . . . Ahhh. I can't work like this."

I could tell the husband was leery of giving this guy any information.

"Don't worry," Joe said. "We'll make sure you get their information, we just want to make sure you're okay. Where did you say it hurt?"

He pointed to his hip and the top of his leg.

He looked fine to me.

"Is everything okay?" an older man going into the apartment building stopped and asked.

"Everything's fine," Joe said.

"Ahhh," he said again a little louder.

I looked at Joe, and he smirked at me. How fast could this guy have been going if he was parking the car? I've been hit worse playing ball in the street. In fact, I remember getting my foot run over once and not even going home until I finished the game. I wasn't crying like this guy.

I heard someone call "Tony" behind me, and I turned to see the security guard for the office building next door.

"Hey, Louie," I said, shaking his hand. "What's going on?" Louie is short and Hispanic and has worked in this building for as long as I've been here.

He waved for me to come with him, and I followed him into the office building.

"Listen, Tony, he didn't get hit by that car," he said.

"How do you know, you see it?"

Louie smiled. "Yeah, I was watching it on the monitor."

"Where's the camera?"

"Under the awning," he said and pointed to it outside the door. "We put the camera in when we were getting threats for some of the shows the models were doing. They were wearing fur, and the animal activists were up in arms, protesting and making a lot of noise."

We went into the security office just past the front desk. Louie

133

stopped the tape that was filming and rewound it to where the white Suburban pulled out of the parking garage.

I saw our victim walking down the street and watching the couple as they started backing up. He stopped, still on the sidewalk, and looked up and down the street. He slammed the back of their car with his hand and lay down on the ground, flat as a board. Then he grabbed his hip and writhed in pain.

Typical hustle. Next he'd ask them for fifty bucks or tell them he'd sue their insurance company. But he didn't know Big Brother was watching and had caught the whole thing on tape.

"Lou, let me take the tape with me," I said.

"Go ahead," he said, pulling out another tape and sticking it in the machine.

I put the tape under my arm and walked back outside. Bruno was getting the information from the driver, and I saw Walsh and Snout were there. Walsh shows up at every job he's so gung ho. I thought he learned his lesson at the West Indian Day parade, but I see he's a little thick.

EMS was there, Burns and Foley were their names. Burns, the chubby female with the short, spiky black hair, was getting the victim on the gurney.

"Hey, hold up," I called to her, thinking this was gonna be good. She smiled. "You again, Tony?"

"How you doing?" I said as I smiled back.

"Doreen," she added for me.

"I knew that," I said. "Hey, you." I pointed to the guy on the gurney. "Get off of there."

Everyone turned to look at me, and I saw Joe trying not to look like he was smirking.

The victim stopped moaning long enough to say, "Huh? What?" I could see him thinking, *Is he on to me?*

"You heard me, get off the gurney," I repeated, jerking my thumb toward the sky.

He gave me a blank look.

I leaned in close to his face and spoke quietly to him so no one else could hear me. "You see the tape I have tucked under my arm?"

He looked at the tape and nodded.

"I just watched your whole scam. Now you have two choices. One"—I counted off on my thumb—"I can lock you up right now. Two"—I used my index finger—"you can apologize to these nice people and walk away. Now I'm gonna hold on to this tape, and if I ever see you pull this stunt again, I'm gonna charge you for this too."

Technically, I couldn't do that, but he got the message.

He looked embarrassed and panicky as he got off the gurney and started walking away.

"Hey! I said apologize to the nice people," I said.

"I'm sorry, I'm okay now," he said as he scurried out of there, looking back to see if I was coming after him.

"He was faking?" The wife looked shocked.

"I knew I didn't hit him," the husband said. "Was he trying to hustle us? Trying to get money from us?"

"I can't believe this," the wife went on.

"It's a miracle," Joe said.

"Amen," Bruno said, making the sign of the cross.

8

Joe got back on the radio and told Central there was no pedestrian struck, and EMS was notified at the scene, because it would take Bruno too long to figure all that out.

We left Bruno talking to Walsh and Snout as we started patrolling our sector.

"You didn't get to finish telling me that stuff on prayer this morning," I said. "About how I need to change the way I pray."

"Not change it, just develop in it. If you feel like it's a struggle to pray and you're not getting out of it what you used to, then God's probably drawing you into a different level."

"There's levels to this?"

"For lack of a better word, yeah," Joe said with a shrug. "It's like Gracie—we used to feed her, and now we put the food on her plate and she eats it herself. We still cut it up for her, but she's grown enough to put the food in her mouth herself."

Joe has three kids, Joshua, Joey, and his baby daughter, Gracie. I noticed that when he's trying to show me something, he uses them as an example. Either that or he thinks I'm as immature as they are.

"I hear what you're saying, and I understand what you meant about going into God's throne room as a son, but it's still hard for

136

me," I said. "When I'm praying I pray for Michele and Stevie and the family, and then I run out of things to say."

"I think, Tony, it has to get to the point where it's a back and forth type of thing. It's like we pray for the family, for God's protection and provision, and we're supposed to pray for the leaders of our country—"

"We are?" This was news to me.

"Yeah, it says in 1 Timothy 2, I think it's verses 1 and 2, to pray for kings and all in authority and expect to live a quiet and peaceable life," Joe said.

"Really, is that what you say? I pray for kings and all in authority and expect to live a quiet and peaceable life?"

"I pray for the president, his advisers, the Congress, the judges, that they make decisions based on God's Word. I ask for wisdom and godly council for them, and I ask God to remove those who oppose righteousness and replace them with people who will follow God," he said.

"I didn't know you could pray stuff like that," I said. "I figured the cards just fall where they're gonna fall and we have no control over that."

"Don't kid yourself, Tony, our prayers are powerful, and they can affect the whole world. Do you remember the story of Daniel?"

"I think so, the lion's den and the fiery furnace, right?"

"Right. Do you remember who was in control of Babylon at the time?"

"King Nebuka-somebody?" I was taking a guess here.

"No, not King Nebuchadnezzar. Daniel was."

"Daniel?"

"Yup. His prayers changed the whole nation at the time, and it's the same with us. We have authority in prayer, not our own authority, Jesus gave it to us. He gave us his name to use and all the authority that goes with it. When we pray for people and for our country, even our job, things change."

I was driving down 43rd Street and made a right onto 9th Avenue and headed south. There was a line of cabs lined up in the left lane under the overhang that runs the length of the back of Port Authority.

"I never thought of it that way," I said, noticing a cab pulling to the left along the curb like he was going to drop off his passengers on the corner.

Someone was hailing a cab halfway up the block, and the cab went to shoot up the block, I guess to drop his passengers there and pick up the fare. Another cab pulled out in front of him, cutting him off. He stopped short but not in time and rear-ended the other cab. He didn't hit it hard, just bumped it. I doubted there'd be any damage to either cab, but I threw my lights on and pulled up behind him.

Joe and I got out of the car and started walking over to him. When we got to the front of our car he put the cab in reverse and started backing up. We both stopped and automatically put our hands on our guns. He slammed the cab into gear and shot forward, clipping the back of the other cab as he took off down 9th Avenue.

The two passengers in the backseat looked back at us with their eyes wide as he drove away.

"Great," Joe said.

"It's probably stolen," I said as we scrambled back to the car. "Now we gotta chase this clown."

"South David to Central," Joe was on the radio. "We're following a yellow cab, possible stolen vehicle heading south on 9th Avenue from 40th Street." Joe gave the number of the cab and license plate; they're easy enough to read.

We took off after him, and as we passed 40th Street the lights turned red down 9th Avenue, but our cabbie was flying through them.

"Doesn't this idiot realize he's gonna get himself killed?" I asked Joe.

Joe stopped answering questions like this the first week we started working together. He was looking to the right; I looked to the left. When I slowed and whooped at each intersection he yelled "Good" when traffic was clear on his side, and I'd hit the gas.

We were keeping our eyes on the side streets and the cab and not telling Central that we were in pursuit of the cab. Technically, high-speed car chases are frowned upon, because they usually end up in accidents and possibly injured pedestrians or destroyed property.

Sure enough, when the cab got to 37th Street we heard the screech and bang as he got T-boned by a westbound cab crossing 9th Avenue, right by the entrance to the Lincoln Tunnel.

"Ya see," I yelled as the cab spun at impact.

"Alright, Tony," Joe said. "Just pray everyone's okay."

I did, but I found I couldn't focus trying to pray, drive, and keep my eye on the cab at the same time. Joe seemed to be fine with it, so I left the praying to him. We passed the hero store and the Italian deli run by the brothers who everyone says own stores next to each other and haven't talked to each other for thirty years. I wondered if Vinny and I would wind up like that.

The driver gunned the cab and went eastbound, the wrong way on 37th Street toward 8th Avenue.

"I guess he's not done yet," I said.

"It has to be stolen," Joe said. "Why else would he be taking off like that?"

We could see the passengers slamming on the glass partition that separated the front and back seats of the cab. We could hear the engine racing. After the hit it took I was surprised the cab was still moving.

The other sectors put over the radio:

"South Eddie going."

"South Adam on the back."

We were catching up to him now. About thirty feet before the corner of 8th Avenue he slammed on the brakes, forcing me to slam on the brakes and fishtail sideways.

I guess he couldn't open his door, 'cause he jumped out of the passenger side with the cab still in drive and fell on the ground. He looked at us and took off running. Joe and I bailed out of the RMP with Joe yelling on the radio, "Foot pursuit, Central, going toward 8th Avenue from 37th Street, jeans, black shirt, white sneakers!"

Yeah, the same thing a million other people in New York were wearing.

The cab was still rolling down the street when we caught up to it. I tried the door handles for the passengers, but they were locked. The two females were screaming, trying to get out of the car.

"You take him," Joe yelled, nodding toward the cabbie. He jumped into the cab through the passenger side door, and a second later, out of the corner of my eye, I saw the cab stop.

The cabbie was running south on 8th Avenue and turned right at 36th Street. I put over the radio, "Going west on 36th Street from 8th Avenue." Maybe he didn't realize he was running toward the back of the precinct.

When I came around 36th Street I didn't see him anywhere. I slowed to a walk, looking in doorways or an open building that he might have run into. I saw RMP lights coming down from the other side of 8th Avenue as either Eddie or Adam caught up with me.

As I passed a building on my right, I saw a guy lying curled up under an arched doorway. His collar was pulled up around his head, and his cheek was resting on his hands. He had his eyes closed like he was sleeping, and I thought, *Is he kidding me?* I ran over to him and put my hand on his chest and felt his heart pounding a mile a minute.

Yup, this was him.

I grabbed the back of his shirt and put him on the ground with my knee in his back.

"What? What's going on?" He tried to sound sleepy. Everyone's an actor today.

"Oh, cut the crap," I said as I took my cuffs out. "What do you think, I'm a moron?"

Okay I didn't say *crap*, I said the *S* word and was feeling guilty about it. Then I thought about what Joe says, that God forgives me if I ask him to, and I felt confused that I cursed and now I expected God to forgive me when I did something wrong. Then I got aggravated that I had all this crap in my head when I was trying to cuff this guy and was glad when Rooney and Connelly jumped out of the car and ran over to help me. Rooney jumped on the guy's back too in case he had thoughts of running again.

We pulled him up and got a look at him for the first time. He was skinny, stood maybe five foot nine, and had black hair and brown, almost black eyes and olive skin. He was a little banged up, but it didn't look serious.

"Call it off, Central," I said over the radio. "South David has one under at 305 West 36th Street."

"That's zero zero forty hours."

I gave him a fast toss up against the wall. I had Rooney take him back to the house for me, and Connelly and I walked back over to 37th Street. Joe had an ambulance there, Burns and Foley again.

"You guys having a good night?" Burns asked.

"Yeah, and we've only been out an hour," I said.

I walked back up to 37th and 9th to see the cab that T-boned them. The driver refused medical help; he said he was okay, just shaken up. I got his info and the info on his cab and gave him my name and the phone number of the precinct so he could get the number of the accident report. His cab company was over on 10th Avenue, and they were sending a tow truck to pick up the cab. Joe drove the stolen cab back to the precinct, and Connelly and I drove the RMP.

I stood outside on the front steps of the precinct smoking a cigarette, looking up at the red on the New Yorker Hotel, which is probably visible from space, while I waited for Joe to park the cab.

When we went inside, there was a blond female who looked forty or better talking to Terri Marks at the desk. She was tall and thin, not bad looking, dressed in a blue skirt and white blouse with a pair of black heeled sandals with stockings. The reason that I noticed this is because it drives Denise nuts. She says you *never* wear stockings with sandals, it's tacky. I don't know if it's tacky, I think it just defeats the purpose of wearing sandals. It's like the old Italians with the sandals with the black socks. Why bother?

This lady wasn't a skell, but something about her was off. She didn't have a New York accent, and I could tell she was educated. She was agitated with Terri and turned to me and Joe.

"Officers, please, can you help me?" She looked at both Joe and me but moved closer to Joe. "This officer refuses to take a complaint from me."

"What's this about?" Joe asked her, looking at Terri.

I guess we both thought Terri was just blowing someone off as usual.

"Someone is trying to kill me," she said, sounding completely sane.

"Who? Terri?" I asked, pointing at her.

"No—"

"She thinks the CIA is trying to kill her, Joe. I don't have time for this," Terri said, cutting her off and looking aggravated.

"Officer, I have all this information," the blonde said, walking over to three shopping bags lined up on the bench on the side of the desk. She pulled out a file folder and took a piece of paper out and handed it to Joe.

He looked at the page and said, "What is this from?"

"A woman was murdered in my building, and I was a witness. Since then there are people following me, my phone is tapped—"

"Lady, if the CIA wanted you dead, you'd be dead already," Terri said. "And how do you know they're CIA, anyway?"

She ignored Terri now, focusing all her attention on Joe and me.

Joe handed me the piece of paper, which was a witness report from Dr. Nancy Allen. She described people coming in and out of the apartment down the hall from her.

"You're a doctor?" I asked her.

"Yes."

"What kind of doctor?"

"I have a Ph.D. in philosophy. I'm a college professor." She named the school, nothing too impressive.

I've seen this before. I guess paranoid schizo is what they are, conspiracy theorists who crack after being traumatized by something. They're not completely out of their minds, and you usually have to listen to them for a couple of minutes until you realize they're making no sense. The paperwork they have is useless, usually fragments of different things that add up to nothing. It always makes me think of the Mel Gibson movie *Conspiracy Theory* and how he was actually right about a conspiracy. But these people are off their bird. There's never anything going on.

"You said you saw a lot of people going in and out of the apartment," Joe said. "Could this woman have been a prostitute, or could it have been drug related? Both of those things would bring a lot of traffic into the apartment."

"How long ago was this?" I asked, still reading the piece of paper.

"Three years ago," she said, her voice cracking a little like she was about to start crying.

"Three years ago?" Terri shook her head. "If the CIA can't kill *you* in three years, this country's in trouble."

"Okay, Terr," Joe said, a little impatient. "Let her talk a minute."

"What makes you think someone is trying to kill you?" Joe asked, sounding serious enough that I almost laughed.

"I told you, I get calls and no one talks. When I ask who it is, they hang up. There's a clicking sound every time I use my phone, like it's being tapped. People watch me outside my building, and I'm afraid to go outside."

As she blathered on, she seemed relieved that Joe was listening to her until he asked, "Do you take medication?"

"Oh, because I'm crazy, right?" she said, starting to cry. "Why won't anyone believe me?"

"I just thought maybe you took something for anxiety. I can see you're very afraid," Joe said soothingly.

"I can't take the pills, they're poison. That's what they want me to do, so they can keep me quiet."

Behind her Terri crossed her eyes and mouthed "Psycho" as she gave the universal sign, twirling her finger next to her head, that shows she's nuts.

To give him credit, Joe's face never changed. If I didn't know him better, I'd have thought he was talking to someone with all their marbles.

"Listen," Joe said quietly. "You're at a police station in the middle of the night reporting that the CIA wants to kill you. Writing a report that you saw people going in and out of an apartment doesn't explain to me why the CIA is trying to kill you."

"Because I know too much!" the woman said, exasperated. "Aren't you listening? They killed my neighbor, and they know that I know about it! Why won't anyone believe me?" she yelled.

Joe put his hand up. "It's not—"

"Oh, forget it!" she said and walked over to the bench and picked up her bags in quick, jerky motions and went out the front door.

Joe surprised me by following her out there. He called her and she turned around, and I saw him talking to her with his hands out.

Rooney came out from the back by the cells and said, "Lou, our perp is puking, saying his head hurts. Maybe he's got a concussion, he's got a nice knot on his head."

He got on the radio and told Central to have a bus respond to the South.

"What's the condition?" Central asked.

"I have a prisoner with a possible concussion," Rooney said.

"10-4," Central said, probably thinking we were playing piñata with the prisoner and cracked his head open.

I was exhausted from getting only a couple hours sleep, so I let Rooney take the collar.

I left Rooney with the paperwork for the arrest and went back out. The blonde was gone, and I saw Joe across the street heading into the deli.

I crossed the street and went in. Geri was there, yelling on the phone to someone.

"You're a nice guy, Bill, but you suck as a mechanic," she said as she closed her eyes and shook her head. "Don't touch anything. I appreciate it, but I'll get someone else to look at it." She hung up.

"Everything okay?" Joe asked her.

"No, it's not. This is what happens when your car dies and you let your neighbor work on it, then he makes it worse. I woulda been better off letting them rip me off at the gas station," she said. "He takes the car this afternoon, and it takes him until two o'clock in the morning to tell me, 'I don't know what you did, but it's bad.' No kidding." She waved her hand and started ringing us up. "I don't even wanna think about it."

"Where do you live?" Joe asked.

"Bay Ridge."

"Why do you work here?" Joe asked.

I didn't get it either. Why come into the city in the middle of the night if you don't have to.

"My brother-in-law owns the store and my sister's too lazy to work, so I help him out," she said.

"I didn't realize you were related to the owner," I said. "You two don't even get along."

"It's like a sexless marriage, Tony. We hate each other, we're just together for the money," she said, sounding like she meant it.

"I hope everything works out with your car, Ger," Joe said.

"Yeah, thanks," she said, sounding disgusted. "Have a good one."

Joe and I took our coffee and walked back to the RMP to drink it. The coffee was from the bottom of the pot and had that bitter, burnt taste to it. I drank about half of it and was pouring the rest of it out the window when we got a call from Central.

"South David."

"South David," Fiore answered.

"We got a call for a possible DOA on 39th Street between 8th and 9th in front of 331 West 39th."

"Oh, good," I said. "We went back out just in time for this."

"Central, is there a callback number?" Joe asked.

"No callback."

"10-4," Fiore said as I put the car in gear and drove down 9th Avenue.

146

9

I flew up 9th Avenue to 39th Street, whooping at the lights to get us over there. I was picturing a dead skell or a drunk not moving. I was looking in doorways on our way down from 8th Avenue, looking for feet sticking out. A guy was waving to us as we got about halfway down the block, and when we pulled up there was a dead dog lying on the sidewalk next to him.

"Easy, Tony," Joe said as I got out of the car.

"Did you call us?" I snapped at the guy standing with the dog.

"Yeah, I called," he said, all attitude.

"So where's the dead body?" I half yelled, pushing my shoulders up with my arms extended out.

"Right here," he said and looked down and pointed at the dog.

"It's a dead dog," I said, not looking at it.

The man just glared at me.

"South David to Central," I said into my radio.

"Go ahead, South David."

"Slow it down here, Central. There's no DOA," I said, shaking my head. "It's a dead dog."

I probably shouldn't have mentioned the dog, because now the radio was assaulted with barks and howling, someone was singing the theme from *Old Yeller*, and I heard Rooney say, "Zoinks, Shaggy, I'm dead. Scooby Dooooooo."

Central came over the air, saying, "No unauthorized transmissions over the air, please."

"You guys are sick," the guy said with contempt.

I turned to him. "We're sick? Hey, I don't need cops getting hurt because they're rushing here thinking someone's dead and it's actually a dead dog!" I yelled at him.

"I knew you wouldn't come for a dog!" he yelled. "I hear them on the radio, they think this is funny!"

Joe and I both lowered the volume on the radio so no one else was quoted in the *Post* tomorrow.

"Yes, we would have come for the dog," Joe cut in. "But we wouldn't have come flying over here thinking it's a person."

"It's just another dead dog to you," he said. "You don't care what happened to it."

"What am I, the ASPCA? You act like I killed the dog," I said, getting angrier by the minute.

I didn't like him already. He was young, maybe midtwenties, with a five o'clock shadow it probably took him three days to grow. His hair was messy, but you could tell he meant to make it look that way. He was wearing jeans and a gray T-shirt with an MTV logo and had a backpack hooked over his shoulders. He had that punk, antiestablishment attitude that probably only comes from money and privilege.

I could smell the burnt hair and flesh from the dog. It was about two feet from a light post that had the screws off and the plate missing on the bottom. A lot of times skells open up the bottom of the light post and hook up a stolen TV or a boom box. Frayed wires were sticking out the bottom of it, so I knew the dog had been electrocuted. He probably lifted his leg to take a leak and got blasted when he got

148

too close to the live wires. The dog had a handmade rope collar and a leash made from an old clothesline. It was a black mutt, bony and matted, probably belonged to a skell.

Joe took out his cell phone and dialed the precinct. "Terr, this is Joe." I saw him close his eyes and shake his head. "Listen, we got a dead dog here. Who takes care of picking up the . . . uh, who handles this kind of thing?" He paused. "Okay, good. We also got some exposed wires. I have to get in touch with Con Ed—" He stopped and listened. "Yeah, actually they're working up on 8th Avenue. Thanks, Terr, I appreciate it," he said and hung up.

I didn't think we'd need Animal Control, since the dog was dead. We use them and Emergency Service when some schmuck drug dealer that has too much money buys himself a tiger pup that grows up and mauls him and he winds up calling us from a locked room half bleeding to death. They come for rabid rats and dogs, and one time a couple of years ago there was a coyote loose in Central Park that the cops and park rangers wound up bagging with a tranquilizer gun.

"Okay," Joe said. "Terri's gonna notify Con Ed, but she said it might be quicker to flag them down if they're working in the area. We saw them up on 8th Avenue, so either you or I could go over and let them know. She'll also call Sanitation to pick up the dog." He turned to the kid and said, "Thanks for calling, we'll take it from here."

"I'm not leaving," the kid said, shaking his head. "Forget it. You think I don't know the minute I leave you'll toss him in the garbage pail."

"We wouldn't throw him in a garbage pail," Joe said, taken aback. "Why would you say that?"

"Sure you would, that's how you guys are."

You can't argue with these people, they're thickheaded.

"What's your problem?" I snapped, staring at him.

"I hate cops," he sneered.

149

"So leave, no one's keeping you here," I said with a shrug and a scowl.

"I'm staying for the dog. I could tell he was starving. He suffered enough already."

"And this is my problem?" I said, my voice rising. "If you were so concerned about the dog, why didn't you feed it?"

"Why do you hate cops so much?" Joe asked, always the diplomat. He should work for the UN.

"Who cares?" I said. "He's lucky I don't lock him up for falsely reporting an incident."

Joe gave me a "Tony, please" look. I waved him away and lit a cigarette. I was cranky and tired and in no mood for a bitter do-gooder who thought the cops were everyone's problem. These yo-yos think they know everything; let them try to run the city without us.

"So why do you hate cops?" Joe asked again.

"I think they're an infringement on people's basic human rights," he said angrily.

"Oh please with this crap," I said as I walked over to the RMP. "I'm going over to notify Con Ed."

I drove around the block and stopped where a Con Ed worker was feeding a hose into an open manhole. A compressor was going, so he couldn't hear me. He was looking down into the hole with a cigarette hanging out of his mouth and his Yankees hard hat turned backwards.

"Hey, buddy," I yelled over the noise.

"Hey, what's up?" he yelled.

"We got some exposed wires around the block, electrocuted a dog. You think you guys can take care of it?" I asked.

"Are you kidding? Take a number, get in line. We got hot spots all over the city. There's a number you call to report it. They'll send someone out eventually," he said, already looking back down into the manhole.

If we were uptown or in the Village, the press would be out here already and Con Ed would respond quick enough. Otherwise, all you'd see on the news was people crying while walking their mutts, saying what a tragedy it was.

When I got back, Joe was still standing there making nice with the liberal. I stood, leaning back against the RMP away from them while we waited for Sanitation. Since Sanitation was right over by the West Side Highway it shouldn't take too long, and sure enough, ten minutes later the truck came rumbling down 39th Street.

The Sanitation truck pulled up in front of the RMP, and an over-weight guy about fifty years old came out in his regulation greens and an orange and green Department of Sanitation T-shirt. He had on thick gloves and old work boots and was friendly enough.

"Hey, guys, what's going on?" he asked, pulling his right glove off to shake my and Joe's hands.

"Hey, San Man, sorry we had to call you out here. We got a dead dog." I pointed to the ground. "It must have hit the wires in the utility box of the light post and got shocked."

"Yeah, we see this with the dogs more in the winter. The salt and the snow corrodes the wires," he said, nodding toward the dog. "A lot of times it's the dog owners. The dogs seem to sense the electric current, and when they back away from it the owner pulls them on the leash and they wind up getting jolted. They should pay more attention when the dog is pulling away."

We went into it about the hot spots around the city. I've heard of sidewalk grates and manholes being electrified. In fact, I remember reading in the paper about someone rollerblading who fell on a live manhole cover and wound up getting the metal imprint of the cover seared into his skin.

San Man was telling us about a kid uptown that got electrocuted crossing the street by walking on the metal plates the city uses to cover the road while they're doing construction.

"Was there something live under there?" Joe asked.

"No, it was road construction," San Man said. "They call it stray voltage. It can be anywhere, not connected to anything. I guess it just latches on to the metal and zaps the next thing it hits."

Yeah, another thing to kill you in this city.

"So does the city do anything about it, or do they just let Con Ed murder all the dogs?" This from our cop-hating loudmouth.

"What's his problem?" San Man asked, pointing at him with his thumb.

"Please, we've been listening to this for twenty minutes," I said, waving him away. "He's gonna run for mayor and straighten us all out."

"The greatness of a nation and its moral progress can be judged by the way it treats its animals," the bigmouth recited.

"And this is my problem how?" I raised my eyebrows and put my hands out. "Now I'm responsible for all the dogs in America?"

"It's Mahatma Gandhi," he said. "You could learn a lot from him."

"Really, so could you. Maybe you should go on a hunger strike or something, get the city to do something about the way the poor dogs are treated," I said.

The truth is, I like dogs, and although it's not very often we see them running around Midtown Manhattan, we always help them when we do. I wouldn't tell this clown, but whenever I've seen one I've put the lights on and stopped traffic so the dog wouldn't get hit by a car. If the dog has a tag, we find the owner; if it doesn't, we take it back to the precinct to see if someone will take it. A lot of times a cop will take the dog home, and we only bring them to the ASPCA as a last resort, because we know they put the dogs to sleep.

San Man was rolling his eyes and shook our hands again, saying, "Alright, have a good one, guys." He shot the bigmouth a hard look and put one of his gloves on. He looked down at the dog and up at the bigmouth from the corner of his eye as he put the other glove on.

I knew Joe caught the look and knew what he was going to do. I saw Joe rub his forehead and mumble, "This guy's gonna freak."

"I know," I said, running my hand over my face.

We watched as the San Man walked over to the dog and started whistling. He picked the dog up and tossed it into the back of the truck. I heard an empty-sounding *gong* when the dog hit the metal. We tried to look busy with our memo books not looking up, knowing loudmouth was gonna lose it.

The bigmouth lost it and shrieked. He turned on Joe and me, calling us every name in the book while he was holding his head.

The San Man got back in the truck, and the bigmouth started chasing the truck as it pulled away, cursing as he ran, ineffectively swinging his backpack at the back of the truck.

It bothered me when the San Man threw the dog in there like that, but that's the way the city handles dogs they find on the street. I wasn't being callous here, there was nothing I could do. Trust me, if I could I'd give the dog a decent burial, but I had no place to bury him.

"Why are you playing with this guy?" Joe said, looking disappointed with me.

"Me? Play with him?" I asked, incredulous. "He started in with us before we even got here."

"He was upset about the dog," Joe said, like I didn't know.

"He was blaming us for the dog being dead," I said to Joe's blank face. "He made it seem like we did something to the dog, and the

153

dog's dying had nothing to do with us. He wasn't bothering you with all his 'I hate cops' crap?"

"No," Joe said.

"Well, we can't all be you, Joe," I said.

Sometimes it aggravates me that nothing bothers Joe. I'd love to see him lose it sometime so I can see what I look like. Then I'll stay calm like him and he can see how annoying it is.

"What?" I said when he kept staring at me. "I don't care if you think I'm wrong. It's people like him that want to take 'One nation under God' out of our pledge of allegiance and the Ten Commandments out of our courthouses."

"He doesn't know any better, Tony, or he wouldn't be doing that. And even though he's on the opposite side of things from God, God still loves him and wants him to know it," Joe said. Joe wasn't being pious or anything. He means this stuff.

"Those nearby. I get it," I said. "But I'm not there yet."

"You'll get there," he said, smirking.

"Shut up," I said.

One night Joe was telling me about the parable of the Good Samaritan, and he was talking about loving our neighbor, and I guess like the guy asking in the Bible, I thought it meant the people that lived next door to you. He said *neighbor* means "nearby," anyone that's near you. I'm selective a lot of the time about who's "nearby," and like tonight, it's only if I like them. It's funny; I can feel sorry for a skell quicker than I can work up any sympathy for some big-mouth liberal.

Joe called Terri back and had her call Con Ed for us. We waited there until we went in for our meal at 5:00 and passed out on the benches until Fiore's watch beeped at 5:55.

The rest of the night was quiet, and Joe and I signed out at 7:50. Since we were working a day tour tomorrow, I was driving out to

Long Island to see Michele and Stevie, and I'd head home tonight so I wouldn't have to battle rush-hour traffic from out east in the morning. Joe drove home with me instead of waiting for the train.

There was some crosstown traffic on 34th Street, and Joe fell asleep before we cleared the Queens Midtown Tunnel. The stretch of 495 coming out of the tunnel was lined with electronic screens and billboards, which I personally think slows traffic down for the first mile or so through Queens. The roads were clear on the Long Island Expressway once I got into Nassau County.

Joe woke up around exit 52 and asked, "What time should we be at your house on Saturday?"

"Whenever you get there," I said. "Is your dad driving out with you?"

"Yeah, he's psyched. He's been trying to start the block party tradition since he moved out to the Island, but everyone feels it's too much like Brooklyn," Joe said.

"So what's wrong with Brooklyn? That's what I don't get, all these people brag about how they're from Brooklyn, but once they move out of Brooklyn, they forget where they came from," I said.

A part of me didn't want to move to Long Island and lose the part of me that's from Staten Island. I like the house I'm moving to, but except for Michele and Stevie, I'm not sure I'll like living out there. I like living in a neighborhood, and once you move out of the city you don't have that.

"It's good we're working a day tour tomorrow. At least we'll get some sleep the night before," Joe said.

We also wouldn't be playing catch-up for Sunday when we went fishing.

"It should be fun now that my whole family's gonna be there," I said.

Fiore barked out a laugh.

Donna's minivan was gone when I dropped him off, so I didn't stop in to say hello to her.

"Have a good one, buddy," I said as I shook Joe's hand. "I'll see you tomorrow."

"Thanks, Tony," he said, still groggy.

I drove back to the LIE, enjoying how the traffic got less and less as I headed toward exit 70. I've never lived anywhere this quiet and rural. There are a lot of farms out here and a lake not too far from the house. One morning a few weeks ago a family of mallard ducks waddled right up to our house while I was sitting outside smoking a cigarette. I got so excited I made Stevie go inside and get a loaf of bread, and we started feeding them. We stayed a little ways away from them because when I tried to get closer they moved, almost as one, and shuffled away from me. A couple of days later they surprised me by coming back, and I fed them again.

I know they're just ducks, but you don't get much wildlife in Staten Island other than the rats, the pigeons, and the seagulls. I'm not saying we don't have ducks; we do. But not the mallards. We have the big honking white ones. They're in Wolf's Pond Park, down in Richmondtown, and a few other places, but they're mean ducks. The minute they see you have food, a pack of them swoops in and attacks you. They bite your hands and go after little kids trying to feed them; it's terrible.

The ducks weren't around when I pulled up. I grabbed my pack and surveyed the house. The addition we put on was done. We added a second story, putting in three bedrooms and two bathrooms. We bricked the bottom half of the house and put up cream-colored siding with green shutters on top. With the landscaping and brass light post it really looked nice. We spent a lot on the mailbox, almost 150 bucks. In Staten Island our mailman walks from house to house to deliver the mail, and the mailboxes are small. Out here the mailman drives up. We got a nice big post with a green mailbox that matches the shutters on the house.

When Michele bought the house her taxes were over four thousand dollars a year. When we put the addition on they shot up to seven thousand a year. By the time I retire I probably won't be able to afford to live here.

I put my key in my new twelve-hundred-dollar door and felt my blood boil when I saw a bunch of indentations in the wood at the bottom, just over the brass kick plate. The door was beautiful, oak and frosted glass that complemented the brick, and now it had marks all over the bottom of it.

"What is this?" I said out loud. "Are you kidding me?"

The marks weren't scuff marks. They were imbedded into the wood. I was glad that at that minute I remembered all the times my old man went berserk over something getting broken, and I calmed down. I couldn't picture Stevie purposely gouging the door, and I thought maybe Michele pushed it open with a pair of cockroach killer shoes, but that's what the kick plate is for. The door was solid oak, a hardwood; it shouldn't get marked up that easily.

Since Michelle was at work, I wouldn't be getting any answers about the door till she got home. I went upstairs to the bedroom first and put my gun in the safe in the closet so I wouldn't forget. I was tired, but I didn't want to sleep too much or I wouldn't be able to fall asleep tonight.

I went back downstairs to the kitchen and looked in the fridge. There was half an artichoke pie, still in the foil plate, wrapped in plastic. I could see the chunks of artichokes and salami mixed with eggs and cheese. I cut a piece and ate it cold. It didn't taste like my grandmother's; it had a bite to it, like maybe she used some jalapeno cheese. Plus, my grandmother makes hers with pepperoni, and it's a lot greasier. Personally, I like Michele's better.

I sat down at the table where Michele had her Bible open to 1 Corinthians 13. The love chapter. She was always reading it, and I could see notes she had written in the margins. "Love suffers long, puts up with, endures, and is patient and kind while enduring." The passage was highlighted in yellow and pink, and when it came to the part that says, "When I was a child," she had added, "When I was a child of love." She wrote, "Love overlooks faults and is slow to expose. It believes all things and is ever ready to believe the best of someone." Stuck in the page was a picture of me, her, and Stevie from the church picnic she dragged me to out on the North Shore last month. I picked up the picture and stared at it. Stevie was up on my shoulders. His nose was sunburned, and his cheeks were red from the game of touch football we played with Joe, his boys Josh and Joey, and a few other people. I was holding Stevie's ankles, and Michele was leaning up against the both of us. You could see the waters of the Long Island Sound behind us. We were smiling, looking relaxed and happy. I started thinking about that day, feeling guilty about that "Love is eager to believe the best of someone" part.

It hit me then that it was after that day I stopped wanting to go to church. I don't know if I felt like I didn't belong there because I was cynical and jaded or if I just know something when I see it.

What happened the day of the picnic was I had come back to our table to get a bottle of water out of the cooler after we played football. Fiore, Donna, Michele, and the kids were playing by the water. There was a group of people from the church standing together talking. Our pastor was there too, standing back from the group, and when I went to throw him a wave he had a funny look on his face. Even though I was in his line of vision, he didn't see me. His eyes were fixed on something behind me. The look bothered me, and I turned to see what he was looking at.

It was Nicole—I forget what her last name is—the woman who

sings in the choir. They call it a "worship team," and she's always singing the solos. To be honest, I don't like her. I mean, she sings great, but she's in love with herself, and no one but me seems to notice it. They're always sucking up to her. I remember one Sunday she sang some song, and Donna went up to her after the service, telling her how beautiful the song was and how great she sang it. She didn't answer Donna, just smiled at her and nodded. The smile was indulgent and condescending at the same time.

Anyway, when I saw Pastor looking at her, she was looking back, and something passed between them that made me raise my eyebrows.

I'm not saying that one look between two people means they're fooling around, but it looked like something was going on, and I remember it bothering me for the rest of the day. The following week when I went to church things sounded different to me. I noticed how many times during his sermon Pastor mentioned Nicole. Her voice, how God gave her such a beautiful gift and it was an honor to have her lead the worship. He talked about a recording project they were trying to put together. Then he started talking about the pressure that pastors are under and how good men of God are struggling. I remember looking over at the pastor's wife, but she had her head down. And my gut told me she knew something was up too.

Then Joe gave me the tapes about David and how he was supposed to go off to war and instead got in trouble with a woman. Give me a break. I felt like I was being spoon-fed, and to be honest, I was choking on it.

When I first started coming to the church, Pastor used to talk about his wife a lot. They had met in China on a missions trip, and he would say how he fell madly in love with her and how amazed he was that she spoke fluent English. It turns out she's Chinese from Brooklyn, not Chinese from China. They have two kids, a boy and a girl, who are fourteen and sixteen years old, with a mixture of Irish and Chinese features.

I didn't know what to make of the whole thing, and I've had an excuse not to go to church ever since. I haven't talked to Joe or Michele about it. They think the pastor is great. I felt guilty for thinking something was up, but I knew something was. Then I felt brainwashed, like maybe this God stuff isn't real and we're just programmed out there in the seats while the lead guy tells us what to think and do. And I guess the worse thing is if this guy, who's supposed to know God better than the rest of us, can't walk the straight and narrow, how was I gonna do it?

A hard, rapid hammering on the door interrupted my thinking, and I jumped up, ready to pound whoever it was that was blasting on my new front door that way. I stomped toward the door, and the knocking started again. The sound was sharp and fast, definitely not a knuckle knock.

"Hey!" I yelled as I whipped the door open. "Get outta here!" I screamed, scaring the group of ducks I was so happy about feeding last week.

The ducks waddled away from me across the lawn, making that warbled quacking sound as they went. I yelled after them, "What's wrong with you, pounding on the door like that? You dented it!" They stopped in the middle of the lawn, and I ran after them, yelling, "Don't let me see you around here again!" They waddled faster this time and shot across the street toward the lake.

I looked down at the door to see the damage. A few more divots were in the door, and I tried to think about what to put over the door in case they came back. I couldn't think of anything, so I went back inside.

As I closed the door I saw the yellow Post-it with Michele's neat print in bold black magic marker. "Do not feed the ducks!!!!"

"Yeah, now you tell me," I muttered.

I went upstairs and set the clock for 3:00 so I could shower before Michele and Stevie got home.

Since the alarm clock is on the other side of the room and I had to get up anyway to shut it off, I was actually up at 3:00 and not snoozing for eighteen minutes. I showered and put a pot of coffee on before Michele walked in the door at 3:45.

"Hey! Look who's here!" she said with a smile.

I leaned in and gave her a kiss just as Stevie yelled, "Tony!" and hurled himself at me.

"Hey, buddy," I said as I got him in a hug. "How was school?"

"It's good," he said, nodding seriously. "We get to play outside, and we get snacks, but we have to take a nap on our mats."

"I wish I got to take a nap," Michele said, looking tired and gorgeous in a black skirt and black-and-white shirt.

"I get to take a nap," I said.

"How could they make the police take a nap?" Stevie asked, scrunching up his face.

"It's all part of the job," I said.

"Are you hungry?" Michele asked.

"Starving," I growled, grabbing her and chomping on her neck. She laughed. "What are you in the mood for?"

I looked at her and raised my eyebrows.

"I mean for dinner," she said and smiled again.

"How about pizza? We'll grab a pie and relax tonight."

"Sounds good to me," she said.

I didn't like the pizzeria up on 111. A cop from my precinct, Giacomo, has a pizzeria in Yaphank, right off the expressway, that makes a good pie. I called and ordered a plain slice for Stevie and

161

a gavone for me and Michele. The gavone is basically a garbage pie with meatballs, pepperoni, sausage, peppers, mushrooms, and olives. The correct name in Italian is *cafone*, which is someone who is an embarrassment because they have no manners, someone who eats with their hands, hocks up spit, and passes gas in public. I guess, on a smaller scale, if you're eating a slice of pizza with this much garbage on it, your father would slap you in the back of the head and say, "Whatsamatter wit' you, eating like that? You gavone!" But you're only a gavone if you eat the whole pie. Plus, Michele eats it with a fork and knife, and I limit myself to four slices. She usually brings the leftovers to school with her and leaves it in the teachers' lounge, and they get eaten the next day.

Michele wanted to take a shower before dinner, so I took Stevie with me when I drove over to Yaphank to pick up the pie. If Giacomo was there I'd be stuck talking to him for a half hour while Stevie used up my quarters on the gumball machine. The machine was a pinball game, and when you lost you got your gumball. If you got enough points you got a bonus gumball, and more times than not, Stevie went home with his mouth blue, green, or whatever color from gum he stuck in his mouth. Once he got bored with the gumball, he'd get the slime stuff and throw it at me, laughing like crazy until it stuck to my face or arm or whatever he could hit.

Giacomo wasn't there, but his wife was. She was pregnant with their fourth kid and couldn't get close to the counter with her stomach sticking out in front of her. The other three kids were there, all boys who looked like mini Giacomo's. She gave me the pie and threw in some garlic knots for free. Stevie played two pinball games and whacked the slime against the back window of my truck the whole way home. There were smudges against the window where the slime stuff hit, and it didn't even bother me. As kids, if we ever did that to my father's car, he would've had a stroke. Actually, we wouldn't have done that to my father's car. We knew better.

We ate the pizza, or actually, Michele and I ate the pizza. Stevie pulled the cheese and the crust off and ate just the inside of his slice. The three of us stayed outside until the sun went down. Michele watered the lawn and the flowers, and Stevie and I played stoop ball with a pink Spalding ball I picked up in the city.

Stoop ball is played against cement steps, and you throw the ball against the steps on either a fly or a bounce. You get points if you catch it on a fly or a bounce, and you get a hundred points if you catch a line drive that could take your eye out if you missed it. Everyone has their own way of playing it, and Stevie was new at it, and he kept sending the ball out in every direction. It was quiet, not like where I live. The sounds are different out here in the country. Instead of sirens, people screaming, and horns honking, I heard the pop of the ball against the steps, the spray of the hose, and a million crickets. The lightning bugs were putting on a show, and the mosquitoes were eating me alive.

We went in about 8:30 and put Stevie in the tub. He fell asleep by 9:00, and Michele and I sat and watched a documentary on Elian Gonzalez. I never watched documentaries, and if the Yankees weren't off tonight we'd be watching the game. The show chronicled the whole story, the fishermen rescuing Elian a couple of miles off the coast of Fort Lauderdale, his mother and eleven others dying on the trip over, the fights in the appellate courts over custody and political asylum, Fidel Castro, the protests in Miami, and that famous scene with the soldiers in their green riot gear, gas masks, and automatic weapons as they stormed the house to take the kid who was hiding in the closet.

"I don't want to see this," I finally said. "It's depressing. Look at the kid's face, he's scared out of his mind," I said as I stretched.

"I know, there was no reason for that," Michele said.

That picture was so famous someone made it into an email with the faces of the soldiers changed to Bert and Ernie, Bill and Hillary, Arnold Schwarzenegger, and Spiderman. Then it was Michael Jackson holding Elian—that would scare any kid. There was another picture of Janet Reno with a blacked-out box in front of her like she was posing naked; it was ridiculous. Maybe it's just me, but if the kid went through all this crap to get here, let him stay. I know the father made a big thing about wanting to stay in Cuba at his press conferences, but I bet if the camera pulled back a little you'd see the rest of his family blindfolded with cigarettes in their mouths waiting for the firing squad to shoot them if he didn't say whatever Fidel's henchmen told them to.

"So are you ever coming back to church?" Michele asked as I hit the off button on the remote.

"Yeah," I said, not looking at her.

"What's bothering you?"

I shrugged.

"If you don't mind, Tony, I'd like to keep things honest between us right from the start," she said with half a smile.

I looked at her, thinking how beautiful she was. Not showy or made up. She looked the way she was, honest and open and probably too good for me not to tell the truth about why I haven't been there.

"The day of the picnic at the beach I saw something funny between pastor and the woman that sings at the church," I blurted out.

She didn't say anything at first, and then she nodded. "Oh."

"Oh? What's that supposed to mean?"

"I'm sorry, Tony," she said. "I don't know what to say."

"Is something up with them?" I asked, a little tight.

"I don't know."

"But something is?" I asked.

"I don't know. It's funny, Joe said something to Donna about it too. I think right now we should be praying and not judging or getting offended," she said. "We really don't know if anything is going on."

"Joe knows this, and he didn't tell me?" I asked, raising my voice.

"He didn't want this to throw you," she said.

But it was throwing me.

"Tony, this is exactly the kind of thing I mean," she said, managing to smile. "You're telling me you aren't going to church because you're working, and it's really about something else. That's not being honest."

"No, I guess it isn't," I said with a shrug.

"But you can still tell me, even if you're not sure. Whether you realize it or not, your decision not to go affected me and Stevie. I thought maybe you weren't as interested in serving God as you once were, and that's very important to me."

"But I wasn't 100 percent sure about it, and I didn't want to throw it out there. I don't wanna believe something's up with Pastor, but I think there is."

"That's the thing about being married. It's not just about you anymore, there's other people involved," she said. "I realized that when I had Stevie. Every decision I made affected him. I've been much more careful in my decisions since then."

Scary thought.

◆

I left about 10:30, cruising straight through the LIE, the Southern State, the Belt Parkway, and the Verrazano Bridge without any traffic. I stopped at the firehouse on Richmond road and talked to a couple of the firemen about showing up at the block party on Saturday with one of the trucks. The firemen are pretty good about it. They let the kids climb on the truck and teach them about fire safety. I told them to shoot for about 4:00, and as long as nothing else was going on, they'd try to be there.

I got home at 12:00, set my clock for 5:00, and passed out again without reading my Bible. Sooner or later I was going to have to face God about church, but for now I was just avoiding him. The funny thing was, he was still here all the time, whether I avoided him or not.

10

My alarm went off at 5:00 Friday morning, and I snoozed twice, finally getting out of bed at 5:18. I was showered, shaved, and on the road by 6:10. I cut up Sand Lane in South Beach and grabbed a bagel on McClean Avenue before getting on the bridge. It wasn't my favorite place for a bagel. The everythings were burnt, so I grabbed a plain with cream cheese that tasted stale. I ate half of it and wrapped the rest of it in the wax paper.

Traffic on the bridge was steady and moving, but as I got near the 92nd Street exit, cars were bumper to bumper for as far as I could see. I threw on 1010 WINS and had to wait until 6:38 to hear the traffic report. There was an accident on the Gowanus, so I got off at the Fort Hamilton Parkway, taking the side streets down until I could get back on the expressway past the accident. Since everyone else was doing the same thing, the streets were all backed up.

I wound up calling the precinct and telling the desk sergeant I'd be late because I hit traffic in the Brooklyn Battery Tunnel and all the way up the West Side Highway.

I got in at 7:20, and Joe was already dressed and drinking coffee. I signed in, changed into uniform, and Joe, Garcia, and I were walking up to the train by 7:40.

We had to testify in front of the grand jury for the geisha house robbery. Since Joe and I found the guns and Garcia interpreted both at the scene and for the detectives, we all had to be there. We stopped at the newsstand to get the paper and took the A train at 34th and 8th.

It was about 100 degrees as we walked down the steps from the entrance, and it stunk of urine. We had the subway clerk buzz us in. One of the few things the city does for us is let us ride the buses and trains for free. We waited about three minutes on the platform for the train and then packed ourselves into the third car.

We stood at the end of the car, Garcia and I at one set of doors, Joe across from us at the other. A group of three kids, two males and a female, got on with a boom box at 23rd Street. They never saw us; otherwise, they would never have made their "Ladies and gentlemen, can we have your attention, please?" spiel before they went into this rap/dance/gymnastics routine. They were actually pretty good and made a human wheel as they cartwheeled through the crowd that had stepped to the side to give them room. At one point the female did a jump and a back flip, and she jumped high enough that I thought she was gonna smash her head on the roof of the train. People were clapping as the kids made their way through the train, throwing dollar bills into a bucket as they passed. They cut it short when they saw us and got off the train at 14th Street.

We got off at Canal Street and headed east toward Lafayette Street and up to the courthouse. It was hot out, but there was no humidity in the air. We were sucking in the exhaust fumes from the traffic that spilled over from Canal to Lafayette. Trucks were double-parked, loading and unloading boxes onto handcarts and shuffling them into stores or sliding them down cellar doors.

I watched the Chinese in Columbus Park doing their tai chi moves and was impressed like I usually am by their age and agility. There are some Chinese in this area but not like in Chinatown. I read an article in the paper that said New York City has the largest China-town in the United States and the largest concentration of Chinese in the Western Hemisphere. The article estimated between 70,000 and 150,000 Chinese live on the Lower East Side. It's an estimate because a lot of them are illegal and we can only ballpark how many we've got.

The vendor truck was outside the courthouse, and we waited with the suits and ties for our coffee and buttered rolls.

We got our coffee and went into 80 Baxter Street and punched in with our ID cards before going across to the criminal court building.

ADA Katz's office is on the seventh floor. She's a special prosecutor that deals with felony arrests in robbery, burglary, gun possession, and assault one cases. Fiore and I both like her. She always tries to get us in and out of there without making us sit all day.

She lost some weight recently. The last time I was here she said she was on a no-carb diet. She said she hadn't had bread or macaroni in months. There had to be an easier way to do it. If I couldn't have bread or macaroni I'd shoot myself. Personally, I thought Katz looked better with the weight on. She didn't seem as happy now, and for some reason, losing the weight made her look older.

She smiled when she saw us. "Officer Cavalucci, how are you?"

"I'm good, Rachel, how've you been?" I said. "Still no maca-roni?"

"No, still no pasta. Hi, Officer Fiore, and you must be Officer Garcia. We've met before, haven't we?" she said as she shook Garcia's and Joe's hands.

"Yup, gun collar last June," Garcia said.

"The one in Times Square," she recalled with a nod.

"I'll be putting all three of you on. Officer Garcia, you interpreted for Officer Cavalucci and Officer Fiore?" she asked. "And for the spontaneous utterances at the scene?"

169

"Yeah, they started talking amongst themselves and didn't realize I spoke Spanish."

"Officer Cavalucci and Officer Fiore, you'll be testifying about the guns and the workers being duct taped at the scene. You found the videotape and the money that was taken, so we'll talk about all that." She smiled again. "Who did the lineups?"

"I was there for the lineups with Detective Sullivan," I said.

"I spoke to Detective Sullivan. He won't be here until about eleven, so I'll put the three of you on first."

We've done this enough times she doesn't have to walk us through it.

The grand jury is basically a preliminary hearing to see if the grand jury feels there's enough evidence to go to trial. It's similar to a trial; they swear you in and there's a jury, but we're usually not cross-examined by the defense attorney.

We had more than enough for a trial, and it's a lot easier to get an indictment than a conviction. I don't worry about testifying in the grand jury. The ADA is on the same team as us, and I know there are no trick questions, just straight questions about the arrest.

We sat in the witness waiting area, reading the papers.

Garcia asked us if we watched *The Sopranos*. He said he couldn't wait for the new season to start. The whole city was psyched; they loved *The Sopranos*.

"What about you, Tony, is your family like that?" Garcia asked, and Joe smirked.

I thought about that. There are only a couple of wannabes in the family, mostly my knucklehead uncle and his sons. But they're low-level goombahs, gum on the shoes of organized crime. The truth is, my father wouldn't watch *The Sopranos*. He loves Mario Puzo's *Godfather* trilogy, and I remember him reading the book before the movie ever came out. Plus, my father would never go to a shrink or move to Jersey.

But some of my uncles and cousins do wear track suits, velour in the winter and light-weight material in the spring. They eat gelato, drink cappuccino, eat macaroni on Sundays, cheat on their wives, and slap their children in the heads. My family is also run by my grandmother, and although I've only seen *The Sopranos* a couple of times, I think the grandmother runs the family there too.

We talked about *The Sopranos* until Garcia said, "You guys are crazy going fishing with Rooney. I'll never do nothing like that again with him."

"He'll be alright," I said.

"No, he won't. He was hammered out of his mind before we left the dock. He was so obnoxious the captain told him he'd never take him out again. Then Rooney started getting loud with the captain, and the first mate stood up to him. Rooney threatened to throw him overboard, and the captain wound up taking us back early."

"I never heard that part," I said, looking at Joe.

Nick Romano was gonna be out there with us, and the last time Nick and Rooney were drinking together they almost had a fight. Between the block party tomorrow and the fishing trip on Sunday, I was starting to get agita, and I could feel the acid in the back of my throat. I guess it could've been the buttered roll, but I didn't think so.

The court officer called me in first. The jurors were sitting along the far wall. I scanned them as I sat down, seeing everything from fascination to boredom to aggravation in their eyes.

After I was sworn in I gave my name, my command, and my shield number. Rachel asked me the basic questions about the date and time of the arrest. She asked questions like, "Did there come a time that you arrested so and so?" "Did there come a time that you found weapons on these individuals?" and "What were the weapons?" We went into it about the lookout, the money, the videotape, and the duct tape. I tried to keep my answers short and to the point so that when the defense attorneys looked over my grand jury testimony it was just the facts of the case. I was done within twenty minutes, and then Joe went on.

After Joe testified, Rachel told us Sullie would be going on next and we'd have to come back after lunch for Garcia to testify. I thought about going over to the federal court building to see my father, but with the way things have been between us, I didn't think it was a good idea. Garcia wanted to go over to City Hall Park. It had been closed for about six months while they redid it. They put in a fountain and new benches, but there's a lot of brass over there, and I didn't feel like getting hassled by them. We decided to go to a deli in Little Italy and walked two blocks up to Canal Street and across to Mulberry Street. Even without the humidity I was sweating in my uniform.

The deli always has a good lunch special and tables outside. Joe and I got the special of the day, a chicken cutlet hero with broccoli rabe sautéed in garlic and oil and a soda for seven bucks. Garcia didn't even know what broccoli rabe was and didn't like the look of it, so he got a meatball parm hero. Joe and I would never order meatballs while we're eating out. We're used to our own gravy and meatballs. Garcia probably never gets good meatballs at home, and he thought the sandwich was delicious.

We sat outside under the awning of the deli for half an hour, sucking exhaust and watching people talk on their cell phones as they walked by. Little Italy was gearing up for the San Gennaro feast that would start next week on the 13th and run for eleven days until September 23. This year would be the seventy-fifth anniversary of the feast, which started in 1926. They were calling it the diamond jubilee. I've been to the feast plenty of times, but I've never worked the detail. I guess the 5th precinct handles it.

When we walked back to the courthouse, Corrections had the street blocked off, and I knew they had a CMC, or centrally monitored case. The Department of Corrections is responsible for transporting prisoners from the jails to the courts. Corrections doesn't shut the streets down for the everyday perps, just for the high-profile cases. If it's a cop killer, a big enough drug dealer, a rapist, or any other lowlife that makes headlines, anything with a lot of media attention, they close it up like this.

We waited outside the perimeter that was closed to vehicular and pedestrian traffic. The bus to transport the prisoner was out front, and the area had Corrections officers stationed with machine guns. They do this to make sure no one tries to get in there and help the prisoner escape or kill the prisoner. I think a CMC is the only time Corrections has jurisdiction over the NYPD and they can keep us from crossing the line.

The Corrections officer closest to us, a female, made eye contact with us and waved us in. "Go ahead in before we move him," she said.

"Thanks," we said as we passed her.

We went back upstairs and waited another half hour before Garcia went in to testify.

"So is Pastor cheating on his wife?" I asked Joe once Garcia went inside.

Joe didn't seem surprised that I said it. He was quiet for a second before he said, "Not that I know of."

"But something's going on," I said. I could tell he knew something.

He took a deep breath and said, "I don't know, Tony."

I made a face and shook my head.

"Tony, Pastor is human just like everyone else—"

"Don't give me that crap," I said, disgusted. "Is he standing up there preaching to me, telling me how to run a marriage, and he's cheating on his wife?"

"Tony, I don't know if he's cheating on his wife. I know he's struggling," Joe said.

"Don't tell me he's struggling, he knows better. Is that why he's feeding us all that stuff about David getting in trouble? What a bunch of crap." I got up and started pacing. "And why didn't you tell me this if that's what you thought?"

"Because I don't know if it's true. I know they've been having some problems—"

"Yeah, the problem is he's got his eye on that singer," I said.

"And I didn't want you to fall away because of it," Joe finished.

"What's that supposed to mean?"

"I don't know, doubting God because Pastor let you down."

"Because I accepted Christ because of what he said?" I looked at him. "He's always telling us the way to stay out of trouble is to read the Bible and pray. Isn't that what he does all the time? How could he be reading the Bible and praying all the time and this happens?"

What I didn't say was that if someone like Pastor, who lives his life day and night for God, could want to cheat on his wife, how was I not supposed to do it? I also didn't understand why this was bothering me so much. Now I felt like I couldn't believe anything the guy said.

"If he's looking where he's not supposed to be looking, then he's being selfish and forgetting his covenant with his wife, Tony. It's a decision for him the same as it is for you and me," Joe said.

"No, it's not. I don't have all these people looking up to me. If you cheat on your wife, you're not letting down a whole church," I said.

"I'd affect a lot of people. My wife, my kids, our parents and friends, even people I work with. It would affect people that know I'm a Christian. When they see Christians sin like that, they think everything about God is a fraud, and it brings shame to the church.

That's why God doesn't want us committing adultery—it hurts so many people. This woman, Nicole, she's slick," Joe said, surprising me. He never says anything about anyone. "I don't know what her agenda is, but she's got one."

I almost laughed.

"I don't care what her agenda is. *He* knows he's married, and *he* knows he's the pastor. I don't go for that crap that she seduced him. It takes two to tango," I said, remembering what my mother always said about my father. "And you're the one that's always saying we're responsible for our own actions. You sound like my grandmother— 'Men fall because of women.'"

I saw him smirk. "You're right, Tony. Pastor is responsible for himself."

"What do you know about it? Tell me the truth," I said.

Joe ran his hands over his face. "Not much. I just know that they've been spending a lot of time together. My father saw them having lunch together at a restaurant in Patchogue, and he said it looked a little cozy. He approached them, and Pastor said they had been working out some kind of recording deal for the worship team and stopped after the meeting to have lunch."

"I saw them at the picnic," I said. "They were making goo-goo eyes at each other. Then the next Sunday when I went to church he was talking about how great she was. It made my stomach sick," I said as I waved my hand. "Please, his wife and kids were sitting there."

"I know," Joe said, sounding disappointed.

"It's just like these clowns preaching on TV. You find out they're sleeping around, stealing money, they're so full of it," I half yelled. "And he's scamming us, just like the rest of them."

"Tony, they're not all like that. There are some very good preachers on TV. But this isn't about them. Your relationship with God has nothing to do with what any of these people do," Joe said.

"Yes, it does. Because people give their lives to churches. They give their money, their time. I've worked all night and gone to church exhausted to hear what this guy says."

"No, you went to hear what God says."

I shook my head. "You know something, Joe, these people who supposedly work for God and they're so special because they preach or they wear robes, then do stuff like this, cheat on their wives, steal money, or molest kids—I don't see why they don't get struck by lightning or burst into flames or something."

"I guess for the same reason nobody else does. Because God is merciful and he wants them to repent," Joe said.

"Screw that. They should be held accountable for their actions. They should fear God. A few lightning bolts or heart attacks while they're preaching and I bet they wouldn't be so quick to pull this crap. He acts like he can do whatever he wants and we can't say anything about it because he's God's man. He should get over himself," I said.

"Tony, if Pastor is doing wrong, especially committing adultery, then he should step down."

"Yeah, well, I'm not sure he sees it that way," I said.

"If he's not obeying God's command to love his wife, then everything he's doing is off."

We stopped talking when we heard the door open and Garcia came out of the courtroom. Then it aggravated me that we stopped talking because Garcia was there, like we were covering something up.

We said good-bye to Katz and walked back up to Canal Street. The train was pretty empty on the ride back to Midtown, so we could actually feel the air conditioning in the cars.

We got back to the precinct at 2:30 and slept in the lounge for an hour before signing out at 3:30.

When we were walking out, Joe stopped on the steps of the precinct and tried to talk to me. "Tony, before we go jumping to conclusions, we need to pray for Pastor. I've known him a long time, and he's a good guy. If he's struggling with being tempted by this woman, he needs our prayers, he doesn't need us judging him."

"He needs a beating," I said, shaking my head, but then I lightened up a little because it wasn't Joe's fault. "I'll see you tomorrow, buddy," I said as I gave him a hug.

I drove my truck around to 8th Avenue and stopped across from Madison Square Garden to run into the pizzeria. The owner, Jay, wasn't there but had left orders to give me two commercial-size buckets of Italian ice. I got a cherry and a rainbow and tossed them forty bucks. They threw in about forty of the paper Italian ice cups and gave me a bag of ice to keep it cold while I drove home.

I was going to head downtown, but the entrance of the Lincoln Tunnel was clear enough, so I shot through Jersey. It was Friday, and the traffic through Staten Island to get down the shore would be horrendous. I took the Jersey Turnpike and got off in Bayonne, so when I got on the Staten Island Expressway I'd have only one exit till I got off.

I stopped home and threw the Italian ice in the freezer and drove into Great Kills to the hot dog store. It's the place that all the hot dog carts and concession stands buy from. I loaded up on hot dogs, frozen burgers, and rolls. I threw in a bag of knishes and some deli mustard.

Now that I don't drink anymore I hate being home alone on a Friday or Saturday night. All my old friends would be in the bars or down the shore, and I tried to think of something to do for the night.

When I got home the kid next door was outside shooting hoops with his face pulverized. He was a nice kid, maybe fifteen years old, and played a lot of sports. My first thought was that his father did it. I didn't like his father. He reminded me of my father with a lot of booze thrown in. He was quick to slap the kid in the head, and I'd see him sitting outside sucking down beers and trying to talk to women as they walked by.

Just to show you his mind-set, lately everyone in the neighborhood has these bumper stickers that say, "My child is an honor student at PS 30," or whatever school the kid goes to. This clown gets a bumper sticker that says, "My kid can beat up your honor roll student."

"Hey, what happened to you?" I said as I walked up on him.

"I got in a fight playing football," he said as he bounced twice and shot the ball through the net.

"Weren't you wearing equipment?"

"Yeah, but I was on the sidelines and my helmet was off."

"Was this the thing with the cheerleaders?" I asked.

There'd been a big fight at the fields down on Father Capodanno Boulevard—a bawl broke out between the two cheerleading squads, and it turned into a riot.

"Yeah."

"Did the cheerleaders do that to you?"

"One of them clocked me when I tried to break it up. After that it was the defensive line."

"It made the papers," I said.

"Don't remind me," he said, sounding miserable.

"I hear *Sports Illustrated* is featuring it in an article about violence at kids' sporting events," I threw in.

"Come on. Are you serious?"

"Nah, I'm just messing with you." I smiled.

He threw the ball at me, and I dropped my bags to catch it. I shot hoops with him for a couple of minutes before going inside.

I figured he was catching enough grief from his old man about getting hit by a bunch of cheerleaders. When I was a kid, if I came home after catching a beating, my father wouldn't let me in the house. One time when I was about eleven I came home all beat up by this kid Mark Russell. I don't even remember what the fight was over, but my father dragged me back to his house and stood there and made me fight him until I won. When Mark's father came out of the house to stop it, my father told him he'd kill him if he tried to break it up. Mark was upset and kept saying, "I give, forget about it." But my father wouldn't let me leave till he was bleeding. It was a stupid fight, and Mark and I would have forgotten about it the next day. But to this day he's never talked to me again.

I carried the food into my apartment and changed into shorts and a T-shirt. I called Michele before I went out for a run but got no answer. I took my truck over to Midland Avenue and parked by the beach. The boardwalk was full of joggers, walkers, and bike riders, and there was a good amount of people out on the beach. The tide was low, and I knew if I walked out on the sand I'd see the leftover bottles, needles, jellyfish, dead horseshoe crabs, sea glass, condoms, and seaweed that wash in with the tide.

I took it all in as I jogged along the cement part of the boardwalk. I didn't care if the place was a cesspool, I loved it.

The late day sun was shining off the water, and I could see Hoffman and Swinburne Islands as I ran. I could see clear across to Brooklyn. The old parachute drop on Coney Island was silhouetted against the sky just past Seagate.

The parachute drop, or Brooklyn's Eiffel Tower, as it's sometimes called, was originally designed for paratrooper training back in the 1930s. It was bought at the World's Fair and has spent the last sixty-some odd years in Steeplechase Park. It stopped running back in the sixties and was actually declared a landmark twice, in 1977 and again in 1988. I figure with the new Mets farm stadium and the area getting a face-lift, eventually someone will restore it and get it up and running again. My mother went on it once when she was about six years old, and she'd never go on again. She said she made it to the top but got so scared she blacked out and doesn't remember coming down.

The concession stands were closed, so I got off the boardwalk at Seaview Avenue, where the boardwalk is actually made of wood. I was sweating now, and I ran across to the deli for a bottle of water. Since I hadn't run in a week, I was sucking wind, and I slowed it down to a walk as I headed toward South Beach. I turned around when I ran out of boardwalk up by the boccie ball courts and did a slow jog back to my truck.

Alfonse was outside watering the garden when I pulled up. He'd cleared a lot of it, and it was mostly tomatoes at this point. I had about ten tomatoes sitting on my windowsill, and what I didn't eat, Michele would probably take home tomorrow. She kept asking me to bring her some, but I never knew which day I'd be out there.

"Tony, Julia made you some zucchini," he said, putting the hose down as he walked into the house.

Julia making zucchini could be anything. She fries them, stuffs the flowers, makes them parmigiana, or puts them in a stew. Alfonse brought out a bowl with foil over it and a piece of bread, so I was guessing stew. Julia makes it with tomatoes, potatoes, onions, garlic, and basil. I could tell she just made it; it was still warm.

It was 7:30 when I went down to my apartment and ate the stew, sopping up the juice with the bread. I took a shower and flipped through the channels on the TV while I waited for Michele to call back. I was bored out of my mind, so I went back outside to thank Julia for the stew. She shooed me away, saying I eat too much take-out.

"Tony, don't forget to move your truck off the block for tomorrow," Alfonse said.

"Thanks, I forgot about that." I went inside for my keys and parked my truck up on Greely Avenue. The sun was just about down now, and streaks of pink stretched across the dark blue sky.

When I walked back, Alfonse and Julia were talking to Sandy in the front yard.

"Hey, Sandy," I said, smiling.

She was looking better these days. Her husband was out on bail for when he stabbed her, but so far he hadn't bothered her. He was facing some serious time for assault and attempted murder, and if he messed with the restraining order now, he'd be in jail until trial.

"Hi, Tony," she said.

"Where's the kids?" I asked.

"In their pajamas, watching TV," she said.

She looked like she wanted to tell me something. "Everything alright?" I asked.

"Yeah." She nodded. "I talked to the ADA today. So far Ralph hasn't taken a plea. He said he'll take his chances at trial. He's probably gonna say I'm crazy, that I take antidepressants and stuff."

"Sandy, he stabbed you. And he assaulted you. He can't justify attempted murder, don't worry about it," I said.

"You're probably gonna have to testify. I'm sorry to drag you into all this." She was getting upset now, starting to cry.

"Don't worry about me, I testify all the time. In fact, I testified today for an armed robbery."

The truth was, this would be different. It was someone I knew, and an off-duty incident. If Ralph had a good enough lawyer, he'd make me look like a vigilante.

Julia had gone inside, and now she came back out with some salami and cheese, a bowl of figs, two bottles of wine, and four glasses. It was Chianti, the old man's kind with the straw going up the bottle.

"Come and sit," she said as she motioned us over to the picnic table. She lit a couple of citronella candles, and we all sat around the table.

"None for me, Julia." I held up my hand when she went to pour the fourth glass.

She looked at me and nodded. Alfonse and Julia never say anything about me always turning down a glass of wine. She went inside and got a bottle of Pellegrino and some lemon slices and poured it into my wine glass.

Joanne, Sandy's friend and our neighbor to the left of us, came over to schmooze with us. She has five daughters that all look alike to me, and she was telling us about some Irish step dance competition they were in. Neal from down the street was walking his dog and wound up sitting down. We talked about the weather, the Yankees, the next mayor, and Ralph. Sandy and her kids were in counseling. Her daughter seemed to be having the hardest time with it. She asked to see Ralph, and Sandy didn't want her to.

"I wouldn't let her," I said. "He'll play with her head."

"They won't let him see the kids," Alfonse said. "Look what he did to you."

I didn't want to tell Alfonse that there was a good chance the courts *would* let him see her, especially if she wanted to see him.

"But, Tony, they told me at court that I wasn't allowed to say anything bad about Ralph to my children. The judge said I'm not even supposed to talk to them about what happened." Her voice went up a notch on that.

"That's ridiculous," I said. "The kids are traumatized, and they can't talk to their mother about it?"

"They said that's what the counselor is for. So now whenever they want to talk about it I have to tell them to talk to Sylva, that's the counselor."

"Don't get me started with lawyers and judges," I said. Everyone knows that lawyers are sharks, but they forget that the judges are all lawyers.

After they finished the second bottle of wine and were opening up a third, Alfonse asked me, "You don't drink, Tony?"

"I used to," I said. "Then it got out of hand, and I try to stay away from it."

"But this is just wine, it's good for you," he said, looking confused. "The doctor tells me I should have a glass every day for cholesterol. But it's gotta be red wine." He pointed at me. "Even the Bible says to drink wine." His face lit up, like a lightbulb went on, and he said, "Jesus drank wine!"

"Yeah, I know," I said. "In fact, in Jesus's day, that area was the most wine-producing and wine-consuming region in the world. They drank it at every meal."

They looked impressed that I would know that. The only reason I knew was because Denise read it in a gourmet food and wine magazine and called me to tell me so I could drink wine and be healthy.

I was holding my wine glass full of Pellegrino, rolling the stem between two fingers, wishing so bad it was wine so I could bring it up to my face and breathe it in. I could almost taste the smoothness and warmth of it sliding down my throat. I envied them their easiness in being able to drink it, and I wanted to pick up the bottle and pour myself some. I wished for the thousandth time that there were a way I could learn how to drink socially. You know, just have a glass of wine like everyone else and leave it at that.

"You go to AA, Tony?" Sandy asked.

"No, nothing like that," I said.

"If you don't need to go to AA, then why can't you have a drink?"

New York logic. I almost said, "Yeah, you're right," and picked up the bottle to pour myself some. Then I thought about Michele.

She'd never know that I had a drink, and neither would Fiore. But they'd be here in the morning, and I'd have to face them. I thought about what Michele said last night about being honest with each other right from the beginning and about how I haven't been honest about a lot of things with her.

The truth was, I felt kind of like a fraud with Michele. Like maybe if she really knew me, she wouldn't be so quick to marry me. Here I was with everything going my way. I was getting married, getting a great kid, and I was sitting with my neighbors, wanting to drink so bad my eyeballs hurt. It was like I kept waiting for the hammer to hit me and things to crash and burn around me like they always did.

I felt a little detached, and I had to concentrate on what Alfonse was saying. He was talking about growing up in Italy until he was about fourteen, which made him younger than I thought. He came from farmers, poor as anything, who came here because they'd heard that in America the streets were paved with gold.

"The streets were paved with the sweat and blood of the Italians," he said, a little drunk and heated now.

It wasn't just the Italians, but you'd never convince him of that.

"I worked hard all my life here. I never took no help from nobody. My father died, and my mother sewed and cleaned houses to keep food on the table. There was no welfare; you worked if you wanted to eat. I started working when I was fourteen years old. I was a laborer, I worked on the docks. I knew how to work hard."

He's from the old school like my father and grandfather, hard-working men who respect a good work ethic over an education. It's funny, but sitting there I realized they have two separate sets of values. They believe in honesty and integrity in their work, but their principles are a lot different at home. They keep things from their wives, things like money and women. You wouldn't think it to look at Alfonse, but he still has something on the side. Every Thursday he dresses up nice and meets his girlfriend. He tells Julia he's going to the old neighborhood in Brooklyn, which he is, because that's where his thing on the side is. Part of me was thinking that he treats Julia good—she has a beautiful home and he loves her, so what she doesn't know won't hurt her. I realized I was stuck somewhere in between with two sets of values and that I used either one when it suited me.

I stood up and said I was tired and spent ten minutes talking them into letting me go to bed. I went downstairs and looked at the clock, surprised that it was 11:30. I saw the message light blinking on my answering machine and played the message from Michele asking me to call her.

"Hey, it's me," I said when she picked up on the third ring.

"Where were you?"

"I was sitting outside with Alfonse and Julia." I was gonna leave it at that, but I added, "Sandy was there with her friend Joanne and Neal from down the street."

"How is Sandy? She's the one you helped with the husband, right?"

I could hear her thinking. She'd never met Sandy, and I knew she was curious about her. She thought she had a thing for me, which in a way she did, but that was just because after my run-in with Ralph, he was gone and she thought I did it.

"Yeah, she's doing good." I paused and said, "Alfonse brought out a couple of bottles of wine and some food, so we were sitting around talking."

"Is that hard for you? I mean with everyone drinking wine like that." I noticed she didn't ask me if I was drinking, she just assumed I wasn't. "Did you want a drink?"

"Today I did. Lately I do."

She was quiet for a second and said, "Why didn't you tell me?"

"I don't know. I guess I should though. You should know things like that about a person before you marry them. In case you want to change your mind."

"No, Tony. You should know things like that about a person so you can help them through it. I appreciate you telling me. Is there anything else I should know?" She said it jokingly, but I knew she meant it.

"Yeah, actually there is," I said, wondering if this was the right thing to do. "A few months back my old girlfriend Kim came here. Nothing happened, but I never told you."

"Oh," she said. "What did she want? Never mind, stupid question." I could hear the anger in her voice. "I know what she wanted. Why didn't you tell me?"

"Because I didn't want to fight about it. I didn't ask her to come here—"

"How did she know where you live?"

"She said she ran into Mike Ellis's girlfriend on the boat." The boat is the Staten Island Ferry, but everyone just calls it the boat. "She was only here for five minutes, and when I told her I didn't want nothing to do with her, she left."

Now, this is the part where I learned why men never tell women anything.

"So why are you telling me now?"

"I guess because of what you were saying last night about being honest with each other right from the beginning. I'm trying to do that," I said. "Are you still there?" I didn't hear anything and thought she'd hung up.

"I'm here. I'm sorry. You surprised me with this, and I'm mad that you didn't tell me then, but I appreciate you telling me now. Did you think I would have blamed you for it if you told me when it happened?"

"No, but I didn't want you worrying that she'd be coming to the house. I don't know what I thought, but I thought it would be better if I kept my mouth shut about it."

"I'm glad you told me, Tony, about Kim and wanting a drink."

"Is this the part where you tell me you're glad but you're really mad and this really isn't over?"

"Only if it happens again," she said.

We talked for a while, and I put on ESPN to watch the game highlights. Both New York teams won. The Yankees beat Boston 3 to 2 up in the Bronx. The Mets were down in Florida and beat the Marlins 6 to 1. I sat there until my eyes were closing and finally went to bed around 1:00.

II

I woke up at 8:30 to the sound of kids playing. I had slept with the window open and wound up having to grab a blanket in the middle of the night. I heard what sounded like a skateboard on the sidewalk outside. I guess the block was already closed off for the party and the kids were taking advantage of playing in the street. The "No Parking Today" signs are posted the day before, so the kids are up at the crack of dawn to cross the street without hearing the screech of tires and having to run for their lives while they dodge cars.

I heard Alfonse calling for Julia to bring out the tablecloths, and I could hear the scrape of his picnic table against the concrete.

I put some coffee on and jumped in the shower. It was cool in my apartment, and I put on a pair of jeans and a T-shirt, but it'd probably be 80 degrees by noon and I'd have to change.

Someone knocked on my door at 9:00, and when I opened the door there were two foil-covered trays sitting outside it. I thought it was from Sandy across the street until I heard Denise talking to Alfonse.

"Oh, these are beautiful, I love figs!" she said. "Thank you. Should I rinse them?"

"Ah, just eat them, you'll be fine," he said.

I guess they were picking them right off the trees. He had two big trees with the purple figs, and they were perfect this time of year. He's been giving me figs for a couple of weeks now, but I never get sick of them.

"Wait till my grandmother sees these," Denise said. "Her and my grandfather always had fig trees. When he had a stroke they sold the house, and now she's in an apartment."

I couldn't hear what Alfonse said after that; they were walking toward the front of the house.

I was taking one of the trays in when Denise came back down the stairs. She was dressed in low-riding jean shorts that showed off her belly-button ring, black sandals, and a skimpy red shirt, and her hair was long and straight. She was carrying two glass-handled bottles of mudslide mix.

"Hey, Tony," she said as she kissed my cheek. "I'm glad you're up already."

"Mudslides?" I nodded at the bottles.

"Yeah," she said, daring me to say something.

"I don't remember asking you to bring any booze," I snapped.

"I'm glad you're in such a good mood. Hopefully, you'll cheer up by the time everyone gets here," she said.

"Who's everybody?" I asked. "I don't remember inviting everybody."

"Vinny, Christie, Dad, Marie, Mom, Ron—"

"Who's Ron?" I cut her off.

"I told you, the guy Mom's been seeing. Plus, you invited Aunt Rose, Aunt Elena, and the cousins.

"I didn't invite them, they invited themselves," I said.

"Either way, they're coming," Denise said as she put the mudslides on the counter and started out the door again. "Give me a hand with the food."

"What did you bring?" I asked.

"I made potato salad, the one with the scallions and bacon that you like. This tray is ribs, I marinated them. The other is Jell-O Jigglers for the kids. I made a tossed salad and a fruit salad."

The truth is, whenever we have a party or dinner Denise always comes early to help set up. She cooks food and then stays to clean up. I like that about her.

"Thanks, Denise, I appreciate it," I said.

She had to ruin it by saying, "And I brought a bunch of those test-tube tequila shots," when she was already halfway up the steps.

"Are you out of your mind?" I yelled at her. "Things are bad enough with everyone to begin with. Mom's bringing her new boy-friend, and you bring shots of tequila? You know better than that. Get rid of them."

"Excuse me? You're the one that decided to have a block party, Tony, not me," she said. "And then you go and invite the whole family, cousins, aunts, uncles, and expect me to get through it without alco-hol? You're the one that's out of your mind. The tequila stays."

"If anyone dies, remember who brought the tequila," I said, point-ing my finger at her.

We walked outside, and I saw the street cleared of cars. Kids were on their bikes and skateboards. Sandy's two kids were trying out their roller skates, and Chris and Joanne, a fireman and his wife who live two doors down from me, were out with their five daughters, who were writing on the street with chalk.

Up and down the street people were setting up their tables and chairs and barbeques. At the corner the police barriers were set up, closing off the street. The rides we rented for the day were there. A huge red blow-up slide that looked about twenty feet long was already inflated. They were working on the moon walk, which still had a ways to go. Some of the kids were standing around watching, and I was sure the rubber on the ride would probably stink of feet by this afternoon.

The way we do the block party is all the families chip in and pool their money. The money covers the permit, the rides, the face painters, a candy cart, and a DJ. Everyone is responsible for their own food and drinks, and the fire trucks show up for nothing.

The weather was perfect, clear and cool without a cloud in the sky.

"Tony, do you have a picnic table?" Denise asked.

"No, but Alfonse has two folding tables he said I can use. Joe's bringing chairs, and I told Paulie to bring chairs. If we run out, Alfonse said he's got a bunch in the garage."

"Is Romano coming?" I asked, thinking maybe he got called into work.

"Yeah, he's picking up his daughter. He'll be here about noon," Denise said.

"You brought booze and Romano's kid's gonna be here? What's wrong with you?"

"For your information, Mr. Twelve Stepper, she's only gonna be here for a couple of hours. The booze is for when she leaves. And before you get all high and mighty, I can remember plenty of parties where you were not only the one bringing the booze, but you were drinking most of it. Remember? BC?"

"What's BC?" I asked.

"Before Christ."

I closed my eyes and shook my head, a classic look I inherited from my father that says "You're a moron" without saying a word. I got the tables and chairs out of the garage. They were sturdy folding tables, kind of like the ones they use in the cafeterias at school. They were old and stained, and Julia brought me out white tablecloths to cover them. Denise made a couple of trips for the metal folding chairs while I helped Alfonse carry the barbeque out to the front of the house. He wanted me to help him put together a plastic canopy in case it got too hot in the sun for anyone. We wrestled with it for a half hour and just about had it together when a breeze hit it and sent it tumbling.

At around 10:30 Denise took a ride with me to the beer distributor on Hylan Boulevard where we picked up ice and soda. Denise had the kid that worked there pick up two cases of Budweiser and carry them to the counter for her.

"You're killin' me, Denise," I said. "I don't want any problems today, and you keep loading up the drinks."

"Tony, there's not enough liquor here to get *me* drunk, never mind fifty people."

"If that's not enough liquor to get you drunk, you've got problems," I said. "Plus, birdbrain, we can't drive down the street, we have to carry it from wherever we can get a parking spot."

We bickered back and forth until we got back. I had to park two blocks down from my corner. I saw Fiore and Donna and the three kids and hit the horn. When they turned around I realized Fiore's parents were with them. I forgot they were coming and was glad they were there. I love Joe's parents. His father, Lou, is big, round, and balding. His mother, Connie, is pretty, short, and round, with dark red hair and pretty green eyes.

"Tony Baloney," Lou said, shaking my hand and pulling me in for a hug.

"Big Lou, good to see ya. Hey, Connie, looking beautiful as always," I said, giving her a kiss.

"Here, Denise, let me help you with that," Lou said, taking a case of beer she was trying to lift out of the car while he carried three folding chairs with his other hand. If he disapproved of the beer he didn't say anything, and he and Joe helped us carry everything to my house.

I had bought a small charcoal grill, and Joe fired it up while I filled up two coolers with ice, one for soda and one for Denise's beer and the mudslide mix.

Michele and Stevie got there next, dressed in shorts and T-shirts. Michele had brought Stevie's bicycle, a little two-wheeler with the training wheels still on. She wanted Stevie to keep a hat on. His skin's pretty light and he burns easy, but he said it was too hot. We got some sunscreen on him, and Joe went back to his van for Josh and Joey's bikes. Little Gracie, Joe's daughter, was pushing a little pink stroller around. She smiled when she saw me and lifted her arms for me to pick her up. She was finally getting some hair, and it was dark and straight with a clip thing on top of it.

"Hey, Gracie, is your baby in there?" I asked her, kissing her cheek and pointing at the carriage.

She gave me a blank look.

"What's in the stroller?" I peeked in to see what she had, figuring it was a baby doll or something. The ugliest stuffed gorilla was in there, covered with a pink blanket.

"Is that your baby?" I asked her.

She looked at me like I was a moron and shook her head no.

Donna heard me and laughed. "Tony, I have no idea what it is with the gorilla, she loves it. Joey got it at the zoo, and we can't get it away from her."

"We have incoming," I heard Denise say, and I looked up the block to see my father, my grandmother, and Marie walking toward us. They had released Grandma from the hospital the morning after I was there, telling her she'd had an anxiety attack.

"I thought Dad wasn't talking to you," Denise said.

"He's not. I don't know why he's here," I said, shaking my head.

"Because I won't talk to him and you're not around a lot," she said. "He has no one to fight with."

I heard the pipes of a Harley and saw a motorcycle parking near the corner.

"Tell me that isn't Mom," I said.

"Trust me, Tony, you'll like Ron," Denise said.

My father was wearing jeans and a black T-shirt, with his hair slicked back DeNiro style. Marie was wearing white shorts small enough to be underwear, a little black shirt with plenty of cleavage showing, and black-heeled sandals. It's funny, no matter how much I go to church and want to serve God, I can't seem to get past how I feel about Marie. I don't hate her like I used to, but as much as I try, I still can't stomach her.

Grandma was wearing black shorts that came to her knobby knees, gold shoes, and a black T-shirt decorated with gold sparkles. After my grandfather died she went the way of her foremothers and dressed in all black mourning clothes, but her partiality for cheesy gold and sparkly materials won out, and it only lasted about a month. Either that or it was her way of spitting on my grandfather's grave, I couldn't tell.

Traditionally when in mourning, Italian men wear black ties and armbands for a year, while the women wear black for the rest of their lives. The tradition isn't practiced much now, but some of the old Italians still do it.

I eyed up Ron as he walked down the street holding hands with my mother. He looked about fifty, a little chubby, with dark brown hair and blue eyes. He looked like a nice guy in a jolly kind of way. My mother looked good. She was dressed in jeans and a white tank top. Her dark red hair was a little windblown, and when she got closer I could tell she was nervous. Ron was carrying a big bakery box tied up with red string.

"Grandma Marilyn," Stevie yelled as he rode over to her on his bike.

Her face lit up when she saw him, and she pulled something out of her pocket to give him as she gave him a kiss. It looked like candy from where I was standing, and I saw him unwrap it and put it in his mouth.

When we were kids and she pulled something out of her pocket, it was money to get her cigarettes or to stop at the liquor store. Believe it or not, back then she could call ahead to the deli or the liquor store and tell them what to give us.

My father held up a foil-covered tray. "Tony, where do you want this?"

"What is it?"

"Antipasti," he said. "Your grandmother made it even though she's supposed to be taking it easy."

"Put it on the table in the shade. How're you feeling, Grandma?" I asked as she kissed and hugged me.

"Well, I went to bingo last night at St. Michael's with Lucy Dellatore, but I got tired and had to leave early."

"You just got out of the hospital," my father said. "You shouldn't be going to bingo."

If Grandma went to bingo, then she was fine. She's been going to Friday night bingo at St. Michael's for as long as I can remember. But she doesn't go for the bingo, it's the side bets she loves. You'd be amazed at how much gambling goes on at St. Michael's on a Friday night. Kinda like offtrack betting, but with old Italian women in rolled-down stockings.

Denise hasn't spoken to my father since last Christmas, so she breezed past him and Marie and gave a hug and kiss to my mother and Ron. My father's face got red when she did it, but I didn't know if he was mad at her, Ron, or my mother.

I saw Marie look my mother up and down and then walk up to Ron with her hand out.

"Hi, I'm Marie Cavalucci, Vince's wife," she said and smiled.

"Ron Dumbrowski," he said, shaking her hand.

"Dumbrowski?" My father choked on a laugh. "Come on, Marilyn, a Pollack?"

Ron put his hand in his pocket and pulled out a twenty-dollar bill and handed it to my mother.

"I told ya," she said and smiled and passed the twenty bucks on to Denise.

Denise smiled and shook her head while she stuck the bill in her shorts. "So predictable."

My father looked confused for a second, but then Ron put his hand out to my father and said, "That's the thing about having a name like Dumbrowski, you learn how to fight young." He said it with a smile, but my father got the message. Not so stupid for a guy with a name like Dumbrowski.

"You're looking good, Marilyn," my father said and smiled.

We all stood there, shocked. I don't think anyone was as shocked as Marie, who looked like he'd bit her. It's not that my mother didn't look good, it's just that he's never had a nice thing to say about her.

I saw the uh-oh look on Michele's face and the wave of panic that came after it. She'd been around long enough that she knew what was gonna cause a fight. Marie hated my mother, so anyone, especially my father, saying anything nice to her was a declaration of war. Plus, Michele knew that whether or not she said hello to everyone was important. To give her credit, she sucked it up and smiled and said hello to everyone. My mother, Ron, and Denise all gave her a kiss and hug, but my father and Marie just gave her a nod, and when she tried to kiss Grandma, Grandma turned her face.

"Tough crowd," Lou Fiore said.

"You have no idea," Michele said.

I could feel the tension, and I guess Lou did too because he said to everyone in general, "How about those Mets last night, ha?" Baseball is Lou's answer to everything.

"We're Yankee fans," Grandma said.

"Yankee fans? How about some Yankee trivia?" Lou smiled and looked around.

"And you know so much about baseball?" my father asked.

I don't know why he's so obnoxious sometimes. Lou was just trying to be nice.

"I love the game," Lou said with a shrug. "I know a little about it."

"Okay, so ask me something, see if you can stump me," my father said as he smiled and lit a cigarette. It wasn't a happy smile; it was an arrogant smile. "But only about New York teams, they're the only ones I follow."

"Okay," Lou said, clapping twice and rubbing his hands together. "Let's see, you guys are Yankee fans. We'll start if off easy. What's the name of the song that is played at the end of the game when the Yankees win at home?"

"That's simple," my father said. "'New York, New York' by Frank Sinatra."

"That's right." Lou nodded. "What song is played at the end of the game when they lose at home?"

Of course nobody knew the song. I didn't even know the song even though I've been at Yankee Stadium when they lost.

"So what's the song?" This from my father.

"'New York, New York,' but the original version by Liza Minelli."

"Okay, you got me," my father said. "I have one for you. Only one player in baseball history has ever played on the winning team in the World Series ten times. Who was it?"

My father didn't realize Lou knew everything about baseball and he'd know this.

"That would be Yogi Berra," Lou said, which wasn't bad until he added, "Of course, he played for the Yankees. I'll even give you the years—1947 and 1949, 1950 through 1953 . . . let's see that's six"—he was counting on his hands—"1956, 1958, 1961, and 1962."

I saw how mad my father was getting.

"Dad, you'll never get him," I said, trying to laugh. "I've tried a lot of times. I even took books out of the library, and I couldn't stump him."

"Are you saying he's smarter than me?" His eyebrows shot up. "Who is this guy, anyway?" He nodded toward Lou.

"This is my father, Lou, Mr. Cavalucci. I thought I introduced you to him," Joe said, standing up. Joe may be the nicest guy I know, but don't ever mess with his family.

Lou realized what was going on and said, "We better stop talking about baseball anyway. If my wife hears me I'll never hear the end of it." Lou smiled at me, and I could see the concern in his face.

"But this is great," Lou went on. "I haven't been to a block party since we left Queens. I'll tell ya, I miss the old neighborhood."

"See what you have to look forward to," my father shot at me. "I don't know why you're moving all the way out to Long Island. You're gonna hate it."

"It's nice out there," I said. "It's quiet."

"Yeah, it's quiet. It's quiet sitting in traffic for three hours each way."

"Dad, it's not three hours, I'll be taking the train," I said.

"Plus, they did a beautiful job on the house," Lou threw in.

"Yeah, well, I've never seen the house. I've never been invited."

"Dad, you told me not to expect you to drive all the way out there."

"Come on, Tony, if you invited me I would have come out there."

I didn't get this. All he did was complain that he wasn't sitting in traffic all day to come visit me. I realized he was hurt that Lou had been to my house and he hadn't, and I wished for the thousandth time he would just say what was on his mind for once. I was tired of trying to figure him out.

"You could come to our house," Stevie said. I didn't realize he was standing there listening. "We could teach you to play stoop ball with us."

"And who do you think taught him how to play stoop ball?" my father asked Stevie, nodding at me.

"You?" Stevie looked surprised.

"Yeah, me. Where do you think he learned it?"

Actually, I learned to play it on the steps in the park where I also learned to play skelsie, strip poker, and quarters. I've never played stoop ball with him in my life, and I was surprised that he'd tell a flat-out lie like that.

My mother and Ron were watching the whole exchange, and I could see from my mother's face that she knew he was lying.

I saw Vinny and Christie walking down from the corner. Even from where I was standing I could see Vinny looked mad. What I didn't get was if everyone was so mad at me, why were they here?

"Hey, Vin," I said, but he just threw me a nod.

I caught the look on Michele's face.

"Are you all right?" I asked her quietly.

"This is so stressful, Tony. I'm so uncomfortable."

"What do you want to do? Do you want to leave?"

"I don't know."

"Here he is." My father's face lit up. He hugged Vinny and kissed his cheek.

Christie and Marie squealed and hugged each other, something I didn't get. They were pretty chummy lately; it was probably more that they'd teamed up with mutual dislike for Michele than that they actually liked each other.

"Vinny!" Grandma was out of the chair, throwing her arms around him.

I told myself it didn't make me feel bad, but it did. Grandma started bragging about Vinny to Ron and Lou, how he's a foreman now in the electricians' union. Marie was talking about Vinny's wedding hall and how beautiful it was.

Sure, Vinny was the golden boy now. Everyone seemed to forget what a psycho he was when he was little. Like when he put aspirin in the goldfish bowl at St. Michael's and killed all the fish, and that he didn't talk all through the fifth grade and the school wanted to call the shrinks in on him. Or that we used to find him standing in the middle of Bay Street dressed in army fatigues directing traffic with a whistle. I remember looking for him one night when my mother was passed out and my father was at work. He was standing in the middle of the street, serious as anything, holding his hands up to the cars, blowing his whistle. It was bizarre—he was ten years old and everyone did what he said. No one even hollered at him.

Michele was quiet, looking tense.

"I shouldn't have had the block party," I said. "I know better."

"I'm sorry, Tony. I feel like this is my fault, that if you were with someone else they wouldn't be giving you this kind of grief," she said.

"I don't know about that. I think the reality is we're probably not gonna see them much anymore."

It made me feel terrible, but it was true. I couldn't be doing this to Michele and Stevie, and I couldn't give up Michele and Stevie to make my family happy. I was reading something in Genesis that jumped off the page at me about a month ago. That never happened to me before, where I felt like something in the Bible was talking to me. It was when God called Abraham and told him he would make him into a great nation and bless those that blessed him. But that wasn't the part. It was the part that said, "Leave your country, your people and your father's household and go to the land I will show you." I wished my family could be like Fiore's and just love each other. Instead, we're so fractured and difficult.

Nick Romano got there next with his daughter. He looked good. He was wearing one of those black ribbed tank shirts that showed off his muscles. I guess he had a lot of time on his hands at FD, because he was tan and didn't have an ounce of fat on him. His hair was short and spiked with gel, and he had a gold cross around his neck. I'd never seen his daughter before, and I don't know what I expected, but she was adorable. She never stopped smiling. And she had long hair. Joe's daughter, Gracie, was practically bald, and I didn't know any other kids, but Romano's daughter had dark hair halfway down her back. You could tell she was a little Staten Island Italian. She already had jewelry on—a ring, a bracelet, and pierced ears. Every time Nick introduced her to someone she'd say "Hi!" with this big smile on her face. She was dark like Nick, but her eyes were blue. It was funny, but to look at her, she could be Denise's daughter.

"This is my friend Tony. Tony, this is my daughter, Alexa," Romano said.

"Hi!" She smiled, and her whole face lit up. Happy kid. She wasn't shy either. She went with Denise over to Stevie and Joe's kids, and I saw her looking in the little pink stroller at Gracie's gorilla. She reached in to pick up the gorilla, and Gracie stepped in front of her. I smiled, thinking Gracie was gonna be the one to give Fiore a run for his money. Then I saw him go over to talk to Gracie, and she took the gorilla out and handed it to Romano's daughter, so maybe not.

"How's it going, buddy?" I asked Romano. "You ready for to-morrow?"

"Yeah, can't wait. I miss you guys," he said. "What time are we leaving?"

"Are you driving out with me?"

"Yeah, I figured we'd leave straight from here."

"The boat leaves Montauk at two. I think Joe said it takes four hours to get out there so they do an overnight trip. We should be fishing by six tomorrow morning, so try not to get too hammered tonight. If we leave here by eleven, we'll get to Joe's by twelve fifteen with no traffic. We should be out in Montauk by one thirty, one forty-five the latest," I said.

Denise had gone inside and came out with her tray of Jell-O things. They were different colored Jell-O cut into stars and other shapes. She called the kids over and started giving them out. Romano's daughter wanted a red star. Stevie wanted green. Gracie didn't like the feel of hers and dropped it on the street.

"What is that, Denise?" Grandma asked, looking confused.

"It's Jell-O. Here," she said and handed one to her.

"I don't want that." Grandma waved it away. "Why would you make something like that, anyway?"

"Because the kids like it," Denise said.

"Kids shouldn't be eating junk like that. Give them some fruit or something," my father threw in.

Denise rolled her eyes and turned around, almost knocking over Gracie, who was watching the other kids with the Jell-O.

"Watch what you're doing!" my father yelled. "You almost knocked the kid over."

"She's fine, Dad," I said. "She's got two older brothers, she gets knocked down all the time."

"Denise has always been clumsy," Grandma said to Marie.

"Like a bull in a china shop," my father said, shaking his head.

"Hey, come here," my father said to Stevie, who was sucking on his Jell-O. "Give me that." My father took the Jell-O and put it on a paper plate.

"Why can't I have it?" Stevie asked me.

"Dad, what are you doing?" I said. "He was eating that."

"He can have it. I just want him to have something good for him first." He got a fork and grabbed some roasted peppers and a piece of salami off the antipasti dish. He put them on a roll and handed it to Stevie. "Here, eat this and then you can have dessert."

Michele saw Stevie with Grandma and my father and was practically knocking people out of the way to get over to the table. My mother moved in too, and Denise hovered, knowing what was coming.

Stevie took a bite and made a face. I grabbed a napkin and put my hand under his mouth because I knew he was gonna spit it out.

"Dad, he doesn't like stuff like that," I said, balling up the napkin and throwing it in the garbage.

Grandma made a *tut-tut* noise. "He's picky, huh?" She looked at Michele, disapproval showing on her face.

"No, he's not," Michele said, "he just doesn't eat a lot of the stuff you do."

"He won't eat anything!" Grandma said.

"He eats plenty," I said.

"You gotta make him eat right, Tony, even if he doesn't like it. We never let the kids get away with that, right, Marilyn?"

My mother's eyebrows shot up. "We? Speak for yourself, Vince. You're the one who ran the dinner table like the gestapo."

"Remember, we couldn't leave the table without finishing everything or he'd get nuts about it?" Denise threw in.

"Come on, Denise," Vinny said. "Dad just wanted us to eat right."

203

"Oh, please, you're such a suck-up, Vin," Denise said. "Dinners were horrible. Especially for Tony. Dad used to shove the food into his mouth and hold it shut until he swallowed it. It's a miracle he never choked."

"Tony didn't like peppers and salami back then either," my mother said to Stevie.

"Marilyn, weren't you usually drunk by dinnertime?" Marie asked, smiling like a snake.

"Only on the weekends," my mother said brightly.

"Yeah, there was only so much Sinatra we could take. If I was old enough, I'd have been drunk too," Denise added.

"Yeah, it was Frank Sinatra's fault," Marie said dryly.

I guess I'd forgotten about that. Saturday was the day we'd all be together, but my father wanted to be out with whoever he was sleeping with at the time. The tension was so thick you could cut it. My father would start yelling at my mother over something, and she'd yell back. He'd stomp to the living room and blast Sinatra until she exploded. He'd leave, she'd drink, and then Denise, Vinny, and I would sit there like zombies until we were old enough to go out and drink ourselves.

A lot of times I'd be mad at my mother. My father would say he worked all week and why did she have to start with him on his day off. One day he said he couldn't take it anymore and he was leaving. I got so upset I started crying. I must have been about nine or ten at the time, and I rode after him on my bike after he screeched his tires away from the curb. I saw his car parked at the bakery up on Bay Street and saw him talking on the phone. I don't know who I thought he was talking to, but when I saw the look on his face I realized he wasn't upset at all. At the time I was too young to realize what sexual banter was, and I heard him say something I shouldn't have. He must have sensed me behind him, and when he turned around and saw my face, he started yelling for me to go home.

"No, it wasn't Frank Sinatra's fault, Marie, it was my fault," my mother said. "I'm responsible for my drinking; it was my choice."

"Yeah, well your choices affected all of us," Vinny surprised me by saying.

"You drank to keep him with you," Marie said. "He wouldn't have stayed with you otherwise."

"She drank to survive," Denise said angrily. "Maybe if Dad didn't cheat on her, she wouldn't have drank."

"That's still not an excuse, Denise," my mother interrupted. "But I appreciate you sticking up for me. I wasn't the wife or mother I should have been because of it." I saw Ron smile at my mother, and she smiled back, but it was a sad smile. "And I owe all of you an apology."

"It doesn't matter now," my father shocked me again by saying. "We all make mistakes. It's all water under the bridge."

I wasn't sure if he meant it or if he did it because he knew it was getting to Marie.

"I don't want an apology," Vinny said. "I'll never forgive you for it."

My mother looked like she wanted to crawl under a rock.

"What's wrong with you?" I said. "Don't talk to her like that."

I didn't know what was up with Vinny. I felt like I didn't know him anymore and wondered if I really knew him to begin with. Last year after my mother came out of rehab she came to me, Denise, and Vinny to apologize for a lot of things, especially her drinking. I guess I expected Denise to be the one not to forgive her, but it was Vinny.

"Don't tell me what to do, Tony." Vinny got in my face. "You can't make me forgive her. And it's none of your business anyway."

Michele panicked and tried to put herself between us. She pointed toward the corner and said, "Hey! Look who's here!"

I looked up the street, and Vinny took a step back and picked up his beer, still glaring at me.

We turned to see the rest of my family bopping toward us. Aunts, cousins, and Uncle Mickey, complete with gold chains, toothpicks, and sunglasses, looking like mafioso famiglia.

"Will this make things better or worse?" Michele wanted to know.

"I don't know, babe, it could go either way," I said with a shrug.

12

My uncle Mickey, my aunt Elena, and their kids were there. There was my cousin Paulie, who we call Paulie Two Toes because of an incident involving fireworks and his mother's macaroni pot, and his wife, Josephine, who we call Pina. Then there was his brother, Gino, who we call Brother because he's Paulie's brother, and their sister, Gina, who we call Little Gina because she's the youngest, not because she's little. Aunt Rose was there too. She's Elena's mother and Grandma's sister, but there's more competition than love between them. Uncle Mickey and Brother were carrying folding chairs, and Aunt Elena and Little Gina were carrying trays of food.

They were all dressed in black, except Brother, who was wearing a T-shirt that said, "Remember my name. You'll be screaming it later."

We spent the next ten minutes hugging and kissing with hands flying and talking goombah talk. Paulie's the worst one. He can't get through a sentence without saying, "*capeesh,*" "*meengya,*" and "fugheddaboudit."

"Hey, Paulie." I shook his hand while he pulled me in and slammed on my back.

"How you doin', Tony?" He wiped the sweat off his forehead, his diamond pinky ring glinting in the sun. "*Meengya,* I need a drink."

See what I mean.

"We have beer, mudslides, and tequila," I said.

"How about we throw this in the freezer?" He held up a bottle of vodka. "And here's the steaks I promised."

"Toss it in the cooler." I sighed. "The blue one's for the booze."

"Hey, Pina," Denise said, kissing her. "Did you lose weight?"

"Please, from your mouth to God's ears," Pina said.

"Hi, Pina. Hi, Paulie," Michele said, smiling at them.

"You!" Pina said pretty loud as she pointed. "I need to talk to you."

"Me?" Michele asked, looking confused.

"Yeah you. What's this I hear you won't let Tony have a bachelor party?"

Now, Pina's a big Italian girl with a big Italian mouth to match. All of a sudden everyone got quiet and all eyes were on Michele. I saw Michele's brown eyes flash, and for a second I pictured the two of them rolling around on the ground duking it out.

"Pina, I really don't think—"

That was as far as Pina was gonna let Michele go. "Sweetheart," Pina said, shaking her head and pointing her index finger. "You need to learn how to handle this kind of thing and work it to your advantage. If you do this right, you'll get whatever you want out of Tony."

"Pina, mind your friggin' business," Paulie said.

"Now you want me to mind my friggin' business, Paulie?" Pina said, head bopping, fingers pointing. "You're the one who was so worried about Tony and said we should talk to him."

"*Meengya*, I shoulda stood in bed today," Paulie said. "Get me a drink."

Michele's stunned look was almost comical until I saw the cat smile on Marie's face. I should have realized that this little get-together was the family's way of showing strength in numbers and getting me to do what they wanted.

"We'll talk later," Pina said to Michele.

"I can't wait," Michele said, looking aggravated. "These people never stop," she said to me. "I'm going to find Donna." She started walking toward the swarm of people that were gathered around the face painter's table.

I threw Paulie's steaks, some burgers, and some hot dogs on the grill. I stood in front of the barbeque, keeping my eye on a fortyish-looking guy with gray hair and glasses who didn't seem to be at anyone's table. I'd noticed him earlier, over by the inflated slide, watching the kids going up and down the ride. I thought at first he was waiting for one of the kids, but none of them came over to him. Now he was standing by the face painter's table, and I saw him talk to one of the little girls getting her face painted. He was smiling at her, and it looked like he was helping her pick out whatever she wanted painted on her face. I saw he didn't leave with her, just stood there watching the kids. I didn't like the looks of him; something about him bothered me.

The moon walk was across the street from my apartment, maybe sixty feet up from us. I could see Josh, Joey, and Stevie take little Gracie and Romano's daughter and walk into the entrance to the moon walk. I saw the guy say something to the kids as they passed. Michele and Donna were behind the kids, walking over toward the ride. They stopped about ten feet from the entrance, talking to Sandy across the street. The kids disappeared into the moon walk, just a bunch of bouncing heads, and I couldn't see them from where I stood.

Michele and Donna looked deep in conversation as I watched the guy walk past them over to the moon walk, going behind it.

"Take this," I said, handing the spatula to Marie, who was the closest person to me.

"Where are you going?" she snapped.

"Just watch the burgers," I said, already walking away.

Romano must have been watching him too, because he was already walking toward the ride.

"You see that guy?" Romano asked.

"Yeah, he's up to something."

We caught him behind the ride, trying to talk to the kids through the netting.

"Can I help you?" Romano asked, stomping toward him.

"No," he said, starting to walk away.

"Hey," I said. "We're talking to you. Who are you here with?" I said it pretty loud, and he stopped.

"What?" he asked, trying to look nonchalant.

"Don't 'what' me," I said. "I asked you a question. Who are you here with?"

"No one, I just came to see what the party was for." Maybe it was me, but the closer I got to him, the more he looked like a perv.

"I think you should leave now," Romano said.

"I'm not doing anything wrong," he said.

"It's a private party," I said. "And I want you to leave, and I don't want to see you here again."

He walked slowly up the street, and when he got to the corner he turned around to see if we were still watching him. I noticed both Romano and I were standing the same way, feet apart, arms folded across our chests.

We stared at him until he turned around and kept walking.

"It's scary, Tony, there's so many nuts out there. Sometimes it keeps me up at night worrying about my daughter," he said.

"Nick, just do the best you can," I said. "You keep an eye on your daughter, teach her not to go near strangers, and pray for God to protect her."

"You sound like Joe," he chuckled.

"Yeah, well, you spend enough time with Joe, you start to sound like him," I said.

"I know. I pray that psalm he gave me." Romano pulled Joe's old mini Bible out of his back pocket.

"You carry that around?" That surprised me.

"Yup. I carry it everywhere I go. I even know the whole Psalm 91 by heart," he said.

"Joe would be proud—Hey!" I yelled at Stevie, Josh, and Joey when I looked into the moon walk. The three of them had put little Gracie in the middle of them and were slamming down on the moon walk and bouncing her up in the air.

"Cut it out, you're gonna hurt her."

"No, Tony," Joey said. "She loves it."

It was true. She squealed every time they catapulted her up into the air, laughing hysterically as she came back down.

We walked back over to the grill. Denise was cooking now, adding cheese to the burgers.

"Denise, you look good in red," Pina was saying.

"Red makes me bad," she said with a smile aimed at Romano.

He smiled back at her, then caught my father throwing him a death look and lost the smile.

Denise and my mother had brought out the rest of the food and set out the paper plates, napkins, and plastic forks and knives. We sat down to eat, squeezing chairs into every available space at the table. We had Gina's eggplant parmigiana, a tomato onion salad, Denise's bacon-and-scallion potato salad, and Aunt Rose's dill potato salad. Personally, I liked Denise's better. Fiore's mother had made sausage, peppers, and onions, and we had a table full of pastry. Michele made cookies, and there were a couple of trays of Italian cookies from the bakery.

Stevie sat on my lap, taking bites of a hamburger. He wasn't really a picky eater, but he liked what he liked. I was the same way when I was a kid.

"So, Brother, how's work?" my father asked.

"Why do they call him Brother?" Michele asked me.

"Because he's Paulie's brother," I said.

"Actually, Tony, it was Paulie that used to call Gino Brother when he was little, and it stuck," Aunt Elena said.

I liked Aunt Elena. When I was a kid I had a mad crush on her because she was gorgeous. She was still pretty and well kept in that married-to-the-Mob kind of way. She had the cars, the houses, and the hair, nails, and jewelry that Mob wives get. She was nice, though, and didn't butt in to anyone's business.

"What do you do for a living, Brother?" Michele asked.

"I'm a bond broker," he said.

Whatever that is. Brother was the only one of Elena and Mickey's kids that actually graduated high school. Paulie paid someone to take his GED for him, and Little Gina stopped going to school in the tenth grade. By some fluke of nature, Brother actually went on to college and now works on Wall Street.

"He's a financial whiz," Aunt Elena said.

Which means he finds inventive and lucrative ways to launder money for the family business.

"Hey, look who's here!" Grandma said, standing up.

I looked up to see her friend Lucy Dellatore approaching the table.

"Sit, sit," Lucy said to my father, who stood up to kiss her. "Oh, it's hot today." Lucy speaks broken English, so it sounded more like "Oh, itsahot todaya." She had her gray hair pulled back in a bun and was wearing black pants and a white sleeveless shirt.

Lucy sat next to Grandma and whispered something in her ear. Grandma nodded toward Michele, and Lucy gave Michele a calculating look. It's not like the family's never been with Lucy before, but never outside Grandma's apartment. I had a feeling why she was there, and I could feel the anger rising up inside me. Lucy said something again to Grandma, and she laughed and said, "*A mali estremi, estremi rimedi.*"

"What are the desperate times, Grandma?" I said.

"What?" Grandma said, embarrassed that I heard her.

"You said desperate times call for desperate measures. What's that supposed to mean?"

"You speak Italian?" Michele asked, shocked.

"Mostly curses," I said, distracted. "But I understand a lot of it."

"Say something in Italian," Michele said, looking thrilled. "But not a curse."

"What?" I asked. I couldn't believe Grandma would do this to me, and I was so mad at her I almost told her to leave right then and there.

"Say something for me in Italian," Michele said again. She realized I was upset and touched my arm. "What's wrong?"

"Nothing." I focused and smiled at her. "You want to hear something in Italian, huh? Um, how about, *E state amore a prima vista.*"

"Oh, please," my father said. "I'm gonna puke."

"Very nice," my mother said.

"What's it mean?" This was from Michele.

My mother smiled. "It means, 'It was love at first sight.'"

"Really? Oh, I love it." She hugged me and whispered in my ear, "I want you to talk to me in Italian on our honeymoon."

"I won't be talking on our honeymoon, babe," I whispered back, "and neither will you."

I went back to straining to hear what Grandma and Lucy were saying. I couldn't hear a lot of it, but I heard Lucy say "*Medegon,*" which is slang for American, and it's meant as a slur. They were probably calling Michele a *medegon*, meaning she's not Italian. Then I heard Grandma telling Lucy that she reads the obituaries every day looking for someone's name.

"Why, Grandma?" I asked, confused.

"Because she better be in the box first for what she did to me," Grandma spat. "I told God I don't care if it's only an hour. I want her dead first."

I wondered if all the years I thought she was a sweet old lady were an illusion or if she had dementia or something now.

I noticed Lou Fiore was watching them, and like me, he saw Lucy pull out a small vial and a little dish out of her pocketbook, like the ones they give you in the restaurant to dunk a piece of bread into olive oil. Grandma had a bottle of water, and I saw her pour some into the dish. When Lucy opened the vial to pour it in, I walked around the table and knelt down next to her.

"Listen," I said quietly, looking at her and Grandma. "You're not gonna do this here. Now give me the oil." I put my hand out in front of her. She looked at Grandma, and I said, "I'm not kidding. I'll take it out of your hands if I have to, now give me the oil." Lucy put the stopper in and handed it to me. I walked across the street and threw it down the sewer and went back over to the table.

"Were they doing what I think they were?" Lou asked me.

"Yup," I said, furious. "My grandmother thinks Michele is putting the horns on her, and since Lucy is psychotic enough to think she can heal the *malokya*, she was gonna put the olive oil in the water and do her Italian voodoo prayers to show someone here was giving her the evil eye," I said, disgusted. "And of course they were gonna say it's Michele."

I don't know if it bothered me more that Grandma would bring someone to my home to say my fiancée was putting the horns on her or that she actually believed Michele could do it.

"That beer looks good, huh?" my mother said as she saw me watching Vinny drink one.

"Oh yeah," I said. "How about to you, is it looking good to you too?"

"I went to a meeting yesterday, knowing I had to be here today. I guess it helped," she said. "I got to say I was sorry to a few people without running to the liquor store."

"Yeah, and had your apology thrown in your face," I said, fuming at Vinny and just about everyone else in my family.

"It's funny, I thought you and Denise would have been the ones to throw my apology in my face. But you can't hold it against Vinny. He has a right to feel how he feels."

"But you're his mother!"

It's funny, but Vinny used to be the nicest out of all of us. He was the peacemaker; he couldn't stand to see anyone mad. I don't even know him anymore.

"Tony, my part of this was to apologize. I'm not saying I'm happy about it. I would have liked to sit and talk to him the way I did with you and Denise, but he won't let me. I can't control how other people feel, I have to make amends and accept the consequences of my alcoholism. I apologized and cleaned up my side of the street as much as possible, the rest is up to him."

She put her arm around me and put her head on my shoulder. "But I'm concerned about you. You have a lot going on in your life right now, and the temptation is there."

"Michele told you I've been wanting to drink," I said.

"Yes, she did," she said with a nod. "I'm not going to lie to you. She wanted to know what she could do to help. Are you upset that she told me?"

"No. I know if I had said not to mention it she wouldn't have," I said. "I just don't want her worrying about it. I really haven't drank in over a year, Mom. I had a couple of beers last Christmas and didn't start drinking again. I think I could handle it now. You know, just have a beer every once in a while like a normal person."

"And how would that beer change anything?" she asked.

"It wouldn't be to change anything, just to have a nice cold beer. I didn't say I was gonna drink, I said I was thinking about it."

"Stinkin' thinking," she said. "Relapse always starts with thinking, not with drinking. Once you taste it again, it's like an old friend. Trust me, Tony, when I went into rehab wasn't the first time I quit."

"Really?"

"Sure. I tried plenty of times. I never got help, I just tried not to drink and drove myself insane thinking about it all the time. Now I get myself to a meeting every day if I have to."

"And what does that do?" I asked.

"Why don't you go to a meeting? If you want we could go together."

"Yeah, mother-and-son AA meetings. Just like the Cleavers," I said. "Should I get you a corsage?"

"Tony, I'm serious."

"So am I."

"I think you'll get a little more understanding about what people are feeling. What compels them to drink and what helps them stop. What about you? What is it that's making you feel like crawling into a bottle?"

I couldn't tell her that I felt like I didn't fit anywhere, that I wasn't good enough for Michele and Stevie, that I'd never be as good as Fiore, and that my family were a bunch of psychos—well, she knew that part. Work was on my mind too. I didn't know about going upstairs to get my shield. I mean, I knew I was a good cop, but maybe I wouldn't be a good detective, and I guess that was on my mind. Then I had the weddings coming up, and I didn't want to go to church. All this stuff was swirling around me, and all I wanted to do was get through today without a bloodbath.

But all I said was, "Maybe if the family wasn't this way. You know, like if we had a normal family that helped each other instead of all the crap that goes on, we wouldn't all be so screwed up."

She laughed. "I used to think that if your father wasn't the way he was I wouldn't have drank. And I'm not saying that wasn't part of it. I mean, I let him butcher my self-esteem. But I had to learn not to drink in spite of everything that happened and not use it as an excuse to drink."

I just shrugged because I didn't know what to say to that.

"A meeting might help. Go to one, see if you can relate to what they say."

"Mom, the last thing I need is to be in a room with a bunch of ex-alkies telling war stories about their drinking days. I'd probably hit the nearest bar once I got out of there."

We shut up because Romano was coming toward us with his daughter on his shoulders.

"Tony, I'm gonna drop Alexa off and come back," he said.

"It was nice meeting you, Alexa," I said.

"Bye, Alexa. Can I have a kiss?" my mother asked her.

Alexa nodded, and Romano leaned in so my mother could kiss her.

"How about me?" I asked, and Alexa kissed me too.

"She's adorable, Nick," my mother said.

"Yeah, what a little sweetheart," I said. "She's so friendly, Nick, where does she get that from?"

"I have no idea, definitely not her mother," Romano said and stopped when he saw my mother shaking her head no.

"What's the matter?" he asked.

"Don't talk about her mother in front of her, Nick. It'll only

217

confuse her." I guess my mother realized she was butting in, because she said, "I'm sorry, Nick. It's none of my business, but that's her mother, wrong or right, and you shouldn't do that. It undermines her feelings for her mother, and it's confusing to children. They love both their parents. The best thing you can do for your daughter is respect her mother."

"But she doesn't respect me," Nick said. "She always talks bad about me to Alexa."

"Two wrongs don't make a right. I'm sorry," she said again, putting her hands up and taking a step backwards.

"If you want we can talk about it later," I said, not wanting to add any more drama to the day.

"I shouldn't have said that," she said when he left.

"Why not? It's true. Dad used to do it all the time, and it messed with our heads," I said. "We didn't trust you because of it."

"My drinking also gave him a lot of ammunition, Tony. He was right about a lot of what he said."

When we walked back over to the table, my father and Lou Fiore were in the middle of a heated conversation.

I heard my father say, "Listen, buddy, the day you're born God stamps a date on your backside [he didn't say backside], and when that day comes, the jig is up."

Michele looked panicked and said lightly, "Come on, you know what they say, the two things we're never supposed to talk about are politics and religion."

"And why is that?" my father challenged.

I could see Michele's face getting red as she said, "Well, because everyone has a different opinion and we don't want an argument."

"Are you saying we like to argue?" Marie said as her eyebrows shot up. She turned to my father and nodded toward Michele. "She thinks who she is, this one."

"Why don't you stick up for me?" Michele said quietly, looking hurt.

I didn't know what to say, because I didn't understand it myself. It's just the way it is. You don't mess with the family, even if they're messing with your woman. This was new to me.

"Cut it out," I said to Marie. "She doesn't think who she is. She's trying to be nice, and you wanna fight."

"Tony, the kids wanted to get their faces painted," Michele said. "I'm taking them over."

"I'll go with you," I said.

"I'm sorry." I looked at Michele once we were out of earshot.

"Is this almost over?" Michele asked, half smiling.

"I wish they'd all leave," I said, meaning it. I was exhausted, and the day was already ruined. I was just waiting for the brawl that I knew was gonna come. My father and Vinny were both looking to start, and Marie's always ready.

I waited while the kids got their faces painted. Stevie and Josh got green camouflage, and Joey got a full-face tiger. Donna and little Gracie had ladybugs painted on their cheeks; Gracie wiped hers off before it was dry. And Michele got a butterfly.

The fire truck pulled in up at the corner, and the kids went running for it. We stayed there about a half hour, letting them climb on the truck and listen to the firemen talk about fire safety. They had the kids singing, "Stop, drop, and roll," while they snapped their fingers and showed them how to get out if there's a fire. It was nice. Plus, the kids were learning something. When cops meet kids, the parents always tell the kids if they're bad we're gonna put them in jail. Then they wonder why the kids grow up to hate cops. Aside from that, the kids always want to know if we ever shot anybody.

It was about 5:30 now and getting a little cooler, so they brought out the candy cart. It was done up nice with stacked rows of every candy imaginable. Within seconds the kids were killing each other to grab the candy, and you couldn't even see the cart.

"Get something for Gracie," Donna was yelling to the boys. "A lollipop or something. Tony, I can't see them!"

"They're fine," I said.

The bigger kids were walking away from the cart now, with the little ones picking up what they knocked on the ground. It looked like the locusts had gone through, and there were only scraps left behind.

From where I was standing I could hear how loud they were getting at the table. They'd been drinking steadily for a few hours now and were starting to really get hammered. Nick was back, and he and Denise were drinking their tequila shots, looping their arms through like you do with a champagne toast.

"I'm probably not going to stay too much longer," Michele said.

"I don't blame you," I said. "I'm sorry, babe."

"Not your fault. And thanks for yelling at Marie for me. I appreciate it. Uh-oh," Michele said, looking toward our table. "Something's going on."

That's the thing about walking away from the table—you never know what they'll be fighting about when you get back.

Denise was drinking a mudslide, yelling at my grandmother, "What did he do to the cat?"

"Cut it out, Denise," Grandma said. "You always have to start."

"Anna, she's asking a valid question, the least you could do is answer her, since you brought it up," said my mother, the only person who calls Grandma Anna.

"Marilyn, you knew Vincent hated cats and you let her have it," yelled Grandma, the only person who called my father Vincent.

"The cat stayed outside, he didn't bother anyone. You could have dropped it off somewhere or taken it to the ASPCA."

"What did they do to Snuggles?" Denise asked my mother this time.

"Ask your father, Denise. It had nothing to do with me."

"You hated that cat too, Marilyn," my father snapped. "You knew I was getting rid of it."

"I didn't tell you to throw it off the Verrazano Bridge, Vince. Don't you blame me for that! I almost killed you when I found out about it."

"You threw my cat off the Verrazano Bridge?" Denise asked, her voice dead calm.

"Mid span!" Vinny busted out laughing, drunker than I've ever seen him. "Meoooooooow!"

"You know something, Dad, there is really something wrong with you," Denise said. "You're sadistic."

"Oh, cut it out, Denise," Vinny said. "It happened twenty years ago. What difference does it make now?"

"You know what, Vin, congratulations, you're just like Dad. Take a good look at him and Marie and his life, because that's gonna be you someday," Denise said, her voice cracking like she was gonna cry.

"What are you looking at?" Vinny asked Nick, who was staring at him.

"I'm looking at you," Nick said.

"Wait a minute, we're getting off track here," Pina cut in. "We're supposed to talk about Vinny and Tony's bachelor party."

"Pina, this isn't a good idea," I said again.

"Tony, let me talk to her woman to woman," Pina said sweetly. "Michele, the way I do it is I let Paulie have his fun and then I make him pay for it later. You see this?" She held up a diamond-encrusted gold watch. "This cost Paulie two grand for a three-day trip to Atlantic city when John Miceli got married."

"Pina, that's not the way I want my marriage to be," Michele said.

I shook my head, "Please, Pina, not today."

"Forget it, Pina," Vinny said. "I don't want my party to be with him anyway."

"You see what you started?" Pina said to Michele. "Now there's bad blood between Tony and his brother."

I could see Fiore looked stumped. I guess me telling him and seeing this stuff up close were two different things. It's not that he hasn't seen my family before. He was at my engagement party, but that was in a catering hall, and being that it was a public place, everyone acted a little better. Donna took Fiore's mother and the kids and hightailed it out of there, but Joe and Lou stayed, I guess to make sure things didn't get out of hand.

"Wait a minute," Paulie said. "Just let me explain it to her. At least let her know exactly what goes on and let her decide from there. Okay?" He looked at Michele.

"Fine, go ahead," she said, mostly because everyone was staring her down.

I wish I could say that Paulie was tactful and left out most of the raunch, but he didn't. He described in detail to Michele the equivalent of a live sex show. I guess I never gave much thought to the bachelor parties. It was just a crazy night before someone got married, and for the most part you never told the women. I was surprised that he told Pina, but like she said, they had a deal. He was stupid enough to think Michele would find it funny. At one point he said, "But that's just for the party itself, the piece of resistance—"

"Piece of resistance?" Michele looked at me, her eyes colder than I've ever seen them.

"He means *pièce de résistance*," I said. "You know, like in French it means the icing on the cake, the grand finale."

Paulie always talked like that. He said things like "piece of resistance" and "for all intensive purposes" instead of "for all intents and purposes." He was an idiot, and right then I could have killed him.

"Okay, however you say it." And then he told her the piece of resistance, and I watched the color drain from her face.

"Come on, Michele, it's hysterical," Paulie said.

Michele looked sickened, and I wanted to crawl under a rock with her, knowing I actually used to go to stuff like this.

"I don't want my husband doing something like that before he marries me," Michele said, looking at me.

I know she was expecting me to say it wasn't what I wanted either, and even though it wasn't, I couldn't seem to get the words out in front of my family.

She looked at me with such disgust that I said, "I didn't even know you, and I was a different person back then."

"Is this the way you were raised?" She looked at my father. "To think that's what women were for? Or was it just women who were lost enough to think they were so worthless they had to sell themselves and guys like you took advantage of them? And you thought that was funny?"

"I did then. Now I don't," I said honestly, but it didn't look like she believed me.

Out of the corner of my eye I could see Stevie and Josh running over, red faced and sweating.

"You are so whipped, Tony," Marie said, shaking her head in disgust.

"Marie—" I started to say, but she cut me off.

"You know what, Tony," she sneered. "Why don't you pick up your dress and grab your—"

"You watch your filthy mouth around my son!" Michele half screamed at her.

223

"Who do you think you are?" Marie stood up and pointed her finger in Michele's face.

Michele grabbed the finger and said, "Get your finger out of my face!"

Denise was on them in a second. "Get away from her, Marie."

"Vince, do something," my mother said.

"What do you want me to do?"

"Something!"

"Sit down, Denise," Vinny said. "This has nothing to do with you." And he gave Denise a shove backwards.

"Alright, enough!" my father yelled.

But Romano had already dived at Vinny, knocking him into the table, which knocked half the food off the table and onto Grandma and Lucy Dellatore.

Vinny came back swinging and clocked Romano with a hard right.

"Get Stevie out of here!" I yelled at Michele, who was standing there in shock. She picked up her pocketbook and grabbed Stevie's hand.

"I want to stay with Tony," Stevie said, starting to cry.

"I'm okay, buddy," I said, furious at Vinny for doing this in front of Stevie.

Michele pulled Stevie with her, shaking her head as she walked away.

"Michele, tell Connie to keep Donna and the kids away," Lou Fiore called out. Michele threw up a wave without looking back.

Paulie grabbed Romano by the arms to hold him back, and Vinny took another shot at him, this time hitting him in the nose. I jumped in front of Romano, and Vinny hit me in the jaw. Joe was on his feet, and then it was a free-for-all, with my father, Brother, Paulie, Lou, and Ron all trying to break it up.

Christie, Vinny's fiancée, laughed when Vinny caught Romano in the face a third time while Paulie was holding Romano's arms behind his back to keep him from going at Vinny. Denise came up and slapped the smile off her face, leaving a red mark on her cheek. The next thing I knew, the two of them were doing a slapping, hair pulling, scratching thing until Pina broke it up.

Romano leaned back into Paulie and picked up both his legs and kicked Vinny in the chest, knocking him into a chair and onto the ground. Now it was one big pile of people with Vinny and Romano on the bottom of it.

Someone took a bat to the table, sending food and dishes crashing to the ground. We all stopped and looked to see Sandy and Alfonse standing there, with Alfonse holding the bat.

"Get your hands off of Tony," Alfonse said. I had no idea who had their hands on me, but they let go. "Break it up right now."

Vinny yelled something foul at him.

"Shut up, Vin, don't you yell at him," I said, going at him.

Everyone scrambled again to hold each of us back. We were breathing heavy, eyeing each other down.

"There are children here, what's wrong with you people?" Alfonse yelled.

"Good question," Lou said, looking like he was having a stroke. He looked at my father and Marie. "This is terrible what you do to each other."

"Mind your friggin' business," my father yelled at Lou. "Who do you think you are!"

"Don't yell at him, Dad. I'm sorry, Alfonse," I said.

"Don't you be sorry, Tony. I saw the whole thing." Alfonse was breathing heavy, still holding the bat suspended like he was gonna swing it.

"Are you alright, Tony?" Sandy asked. "Should I call the cops?"

"No, Sandy, it's alright," I said, feeling terrible that she had to see something like this again and humbled that she would put herself in the middle of it to help me.

"I can't take this family anymore," Marie said to my father. She threw a disgusted look to my mother and said, "You might have thought it was okay to raise your kids in this environment, but I'm not going to. And except for Vinny, look how they turned out."

"Don't talk about my kids, Marie. And it's not like you'll be raising any kids of your own," my mother said.

"That's what you think, Marilyn. It might have taken a while, but Vince and I are expecting our first child next May."

"Is that true, Vince?" my mother asked him, looking confused.

He shrugged. "It's news to me. Are you sure about this?" he asked Marie almost nonchalantly.

"I'm positive, honey." She smiled at my father, but he was giving my mother a funny look.

"Oh, Vince," my mother said, shaking her head.

"What's the matter, Marilyn? Your last hope of getting Vince back didn't work? I guess bringing your new boyfriend didn't get the reaction you expected, huh?" Marie's expression was pure evil.

I was too stunned to move, but Denise started laughing. She took big gulps of air and laughed until tears were running down her face.

"It's not funny, Denise," my mother said.

"Yes, it is," she said when she could finally talk. "It's the funniest thing I've ever heard."

Ron stood next to my mother. He was watching everyone, looking to make sure no one started up again.

"Are you alright?" Ron asked her.

"I'm fine. I think we should get going though."

"Vinny," my father said. "Take Marie and your grandmother home."

"Why?"

"Because I asked you to."

"Why aren't you taking me home, Vince?" Marie said, not so sure of herself now. She was watching Denise laugh, and I could tell she was wondering if the joke was on her.

"Because I don't feel like it." He wouldn't even look at her, and he walked away from us, down the street toward Greely Avenue.

Christie was staring Denise down. Her face was red, and her hair was sticking up in every direction, making her look like that statue from *Trilogy of Terror*.

Vinny shot me a dirty look, and then he and Christie left with Grandma, Lucy, and Marie without saying good-bye.

We were all quiet for a couple of minutes. Then Fiore said, "What was that all about?"

My mother and I looked at each other, and we both busted out laughing along with Denise.

"What?" Romano asked.

"My father . . ." Denise laughed hysterically, tears running down her face. "My father . . ."

"What?" Romano said louder.

"Marie deserves this," Denise said.

"I don't get it," Fiore said.

"Vince had a vasectomy in 1982," my mother said, holding her knuckle over her mouth, trying not to laugh. "And he obviously didn't tell Marie."

"Wow," Fiore said.

227

13

The sun was starting to go down when everybody left. Donna came back down the street with Fiore's mother and the kids, with Michele and Stevie nowhere in sight.

"Where's Michele?" I asked.

"She left," Donna said, looking worried. "She wanted to get home."

"Was she alright?"

"She was a little upset," Donna said with a nod.

I wasn't sure what to do now. I dialed her cell phone, but it went straight to her voice mail, so I left a message for her to call me to let me know she got home okay.

Denise and Romano had gone down into my apartment to clean themselves up. Sandy, Alfonse, and Julia had started cleaning up the mess, picking up the food and broken glass and putting everything into the garbage pail. Joe and Lou started folding up the chairs and stacking them against the table.

"I'll get that," I said to Sandy and Alfonse.

"Tony, let us help you," Sandy said.

"Listen, I'm sorry," I said to everyone in general, shaking my head in disgust.

"Tony, there's nothing to be sorry about," Sandy said. "After what you did for me with Ralph, it's the least I could do."

"I'm so embarrassed," I said.

They all chimed in at once:

"Come on, these things happen."

"Every family has something."

"Nothin' to be embarrassed about."

"After what you saw Ralph do, this is nothing."

Yeah, all the things people say when you're mortified and they're embarrassed for you.

I realized I was gonna miss Alfonse and Sandy and the rest of my neighbors when I moved. I was pretty lonely when I moved here, and they made me one of their own. A lot of it was after I got Sandy away from Ralph that day when he went psycho, and now these people would throw themselves in front of a truck for me.

I thought about the Scripture in Proverbs that says, "Better a neighbor nearby than a brother far away," and it reminded me of Sandy and Alfonse.

Fiore's father was so upset he almost started crying. He kept hugging me, which made me feel worse. I actually felt myself getting choked up and sucked it back down.

"Lou, I'm really sorry," I said.

"Tony, you got nothing to be sorry for. I'm sorry for you and Denise. And your mother," he said. "It's terrible."

"You still want to come to my wedding?" I half joked. "If there is a wedding?"

"Of course there'll be a wedding. And I wouldn't miss it for the world."

"You alright, buddy?" Joe asked, looking concerned.

"Yeah, I'm fine. Just embarrassed, like I said."

"You still up to going fishing?"

229

"Of course," I said.

"Good. I'm gonna head home. Make sure you and Nick are at my house by 12:30. If you want I'll drive out and you can get some sleep on the way," he said.

"Sounds good."

I was glad when they left so I didn't have to talk to anyone anymore. I cleaned up the rest of the stuff, salvaging whatever food I could. I had potato salad, tomato salad, and some steak that was still good. The sausage and peppers got destroyed along with what was left of the eggplant. I wrapped up some leftover steak and put it on ice in one of the coolers with the potato and tomato salads. The pastry was gone, but there was a semi-crushed tray of cookies that I could take to eat on the boat. I transferred what was left of the beer and soda into one cooler and left them on the side of the house.

I heard a roar as the DJ fired up his equipment. Things would really start cooking out there now, and I just wanted to get out of there. I went inside and found Denise and Romano sitting at my kitchen table drinking wine.

"What's that?" I nodded toward a tray in front of them.

"Figs. Julia made them," Denise said, eating another one. "She wrapped them in proscuitto and put shards of Parmigiano Reggiano on them and drizzled them with honey."

"Freakin' delicious," Romano mumbled around a mouthful.

At least the two of them weren't so upset they couldn't eat dessert. I picked up Denise's wineglass and almost took a sip before I put it back down and grabbed a fig instead.

"Y'alright, Ton?" she asked.

"Yeah, Denise, I'm fine," I said sarcastically. "What about you, Nick, what's the damage?" I took a look at his face.

"I'm gonna kill your brother," he said matter-of-factly. "He sucker punched me while your cousin was holding my arms. He'll pay for

230

that." His eye and nose were swollen. There was dried blood around his nose. He had a bloody towel filled with ice next to him.

"You kicked him with a nice shot," Denise said, kissing his cheek. "I know he's rotten, but he's still my brother. Plus, he was drunk, so don't hurt him too much when you kill him."

"Your family has issues," Romano said. "Makes my family look normal."

"We make everyone's family look normal," Denise said.

"Don't say I didn't warn you, Nick," I said.

"You think Dad's gonna get rid of Marie?" Denise asked me.

"I don't know," I said with a shrug. "I can't see him staying with her if she's pregnant with Bobby Egan's kid."

"She's such a *putana*," Denise said. "But Dad's an idiot too. How could he not tell her he had a vasectomy?"

"She probably wanted kids," Romano said. "So he probably figured he'd keep her busy trying to have them and let her think there was something wrong with her, right? I mean, he already had three kids, so she'd probably think it was her that couldn't have them."

"I don't know and I don't care," I said. "I got my own problems now that Paulie made Michele think I'm a pervert."

"You're not a pervert, Tony. Was she really that mad?" Denise asked. "She has no right to be. You're not doing anything like that when you get married, and she can't hold anything against you for things you did before you met her."

"I don't want to talk about it. So, Nick, you want to get going?" I asked, changing the subject.

"It's only nine o'clock. I thought we were leaving at eleven?"

"I know, but I gotta get outta here, Nick. I'm taking a shower. Did you bring clothes to change into?"

"Yeah, and I borrowed a set of rubber boots and some rain gear; it's in my car."

231

I showered and changed into sweatpants and a T-shirt and a pair of old sneakers. I packed shorts and a cut-off T-shirt and another set of dry clothes for the ride back home. My jaw was still sore from when Vinny hit me, but at least it wasn't throbbing anymore.

When we left, we had to walk through the crowd, which was bopping to some rap song with their glow-in-the-dark necklaces that the DJ gave out. Romano carried my bag, while I shouldered the cooler. He grabbed his clothes out of his car and put them in my truck, which was still parked up on Greely Avenue.

Romano stayed with Denise practically until we drove away. I tried Michele at home and on her cell phone, but she didn't pick up. Romano was leaning against my truck, glued to Denise.

"Get a room or get in the car, Nick," I finally had to yell at him when they stopped to make out in the street.

"Have fun, Tony." Denise leaned in and kissed my cheek. "When are you going back to work?"

"Late tomorrow night," I said.

"Wanna have lunch Monday? I'm off," she said.

"Sure, call me Monday."

Her and Romano were blowing kisses and waving as we drove away.

"Oh, gimme a break," I said.

We left the windows open on the ride out. The air was clear and warm, probably about 70 degrees. The roads were clear now that the summer was over and everybody's lease ended on their houses down the Jersey Shore.

"So how serious is this thing with you and my sister?" I asked Romano.

He shrugged. "Why, you afraid you're gonna be related to me?"

"No, but you got a firsthand look at what you're getting yourself into. I don't mind if you don't."

"Your father didn't like me to begin with. Now he really hates me."

"He doesn't even like Denise," I said. "They fight constantly."

"If I marry Denise there's no way I'm going to your grandmother's every Sunday for macaroni. Besides, we probably won't see them at all once you move out to Long Island. You're only there for holidays now, and Denise only goes for you," Nick said.

"Really?" I don't know why that surprised me. I guess I never looked at it that way.

I slammed on my brakes when a private sanitation truck came flying through the red light on Sand Lane and cutting across two lanes, almost hitting us.

"Look at this moron," I said.

"Hey!" Nick yelled, giving the driver the Italian salute and calling him a couple of choice names. "Go after him, Tony, he almost hit us."

"No, Nick," I said. "I don't need any more problems tonight."

There was a time I would have chased him down and tried to run him off the road, flipping him the bird and mouthing obscenities. I realized I hadn't felt the urge to do that in a long time. I'd like to think it's because I've changed enough over the past year and my fuse is much longer. Plus, Fiore used to drill into me "Better a patient man than a warrior, a man who controls his temper than one who takes a city," which I translated into "You're always sorry when you shoot your mouth off and converse with your fists."

Traffic was clear through the Belt Parkway and slowed down a little in Queens as we approached Kennedy Airport, but we still made it out to Fiore's by 11:40.

Donna was still up, packing sandwiches into a cooler. She was kissing Joe, telling him to be careful and have fun.

Joe offered to drive, but he always drives the speed limit, which

233

drives me nuts. This is why I always drive when he's in the car. Even if we're in a thirty-five mile an hour zone, he won't go over the limit, and I wind up grinding my teeth the whole time.

"So, Nick, it looks like things are getting serious with Denise," Joe said.

"Yeah, pretty much," Romano said. "I think this might be it for me."

"Good," Joe said, "I like Denise. She's good for you, and you look happy."

"I am," he said.

I was eyeing Romano in the rearview mirror and caught him looking at me.

"What?" he asked me.

"Nothing," I said, laughing. "I'm glad. I like you, Nick."

"I like you too, Tony."

"But if you mess with my sister, I'll kill you."

"Oh, here we go." He threw his hands up. "I knew you were gonna say that."

"Just so you know."

I took 27 out east toward Montauk. Both Romano and Joe fell asleep, leaving me to replay everything that happened over and over from the block party. I was thinking about Michele and Stevie, remembering Stevie crying when he left and how scared he looked. I didn't see any real options here. I couldn't expect Michele and Stevie to have to put up with all my family's crap every time we saw them. I thought about what Joe told me about how family disputes escalate until they get violent. Things got ugly last Christmas, but I never thought of us as violent. The truth is, it's exactly that kind of thing that cops get called for, drunk people beating the crap out of each other. Granted, this was the first time Vinny ever put his hands on me. Probably because he's younger, we never fought that way. But still, it never came to blows before.

I rolled the window down and lit a cigarette. Between being out in the sun all day and the crash from the adrenaline from the fight, I was exhausted. I put the radio on, but I was out of range for the city radio stations. Driving was different out here. There were no street lights and not a lot of traffic lights. The few cars I did see had their brights on, and every time a car passed I got blinded with the high beams. Even if I flicked my brights at them, they didn't dim theirs.

Fiore woke up as I was entering Montauk. He had directions printed off the computer, so he watched the road, telling me where to turn.

I could smell the ocean before we got to the marina, that mix of salt and fish that I'd recognize anywhere. It's like the smell of fresh-cut grass on the Little League field or my grandmother's meatballs frying. It could make you homesick and happy at the same time. Nostalgic, I guess, is what you'd call it.

Rooney, Galotti, and O'Brien were already at the dock when we got there. Rooney and O'Brien had beers in their hands and a cooler at their feet. I could tell Rooney was already lit. He started singing, "Hey, mambo, mambo Italiano. No, no, no, no more mozzarella," as soon as he saw us.

I just shook my head at him. He never heard the song until he went to my engagement party, so technically it's my fault he won't stop singing it. He didn't know all the words to the song and changed them around to sing, "All the Cavaluccis do the mambo like a crazy."

Joe went onto the boat to say hello to the captain. He'd gone out with him before, and the captain knew his father.

"Romano the rookie probee," Rooney said, grabbing Romano in a bear hug and rubbing his knuckle into his scalp. "Good to see you, buddy. How do you like cleaning them toilets at the firehouse?"

"I love it, Mike," Romano said.

"What happened to your face?" Rooney stepped back to get a look at it. Romano was already getting a black eye.

"Ah, nothin'," Romano said. "You should see the other guy."

I was glad Romano didn't tell him, it shows loyalty. Plus, he knows not to air your dirty laundry to someone like Rooney.

"The mate's a fireman," Rooney said, nodding toward the boat.

"Really?" Romano asked. "What house?"

"He's from out here," Rooney said. "You know, real firemen who love to fight fires so much they do it for free."

Outside the city all the fire departments are volunteers. I mean, I'm sure there's a lot of perks to it, but they don't get paid like FD.

"Hey, I would've volunteered before I went on," Romano said.

"Yeah, I know, kid. You love being a fireman." Rooney rubbed his head again and added, "You still wearing those pajamas with the fire trucks on them?"

"Mike, how do you know what kind of pajamas Romano wears?" O'Brien threw in.

"He bought them for me," Romano said.

The captain, who's name was Rich, came out to introduce himself and the mate, who was his son-in-law.

"You guys been out before?" he asked, shaking our hands.

"I've gone out twice for tuna," I said.

"Just once for me," Nick said.

"I think Bruno's the only one that's never been out before," Joe said. "Right, Bruno?"

"No, I've never even been on a boat before," Bruno said. "Unless you count the Staten Island Ferry."

"Just the boat that brought him to America," Rooney said.

"Once we're out, we're not coming back in," Captain Rich said. "So make sure you want to do this."

It's true. The first time I went out for tuna, Mike Ellis was sick as a dog and they wouldn't turn back. He was also wasted and spent the entire trip puking and passing out down on one of the beds.

"I think I'll be alright," Bruno said. "I took Dramamine."

Rooney was already getting obnoxious with the captain.

"Rich, come here," he said like they'd been friends for years.

"Yeah?"

"You're Irish, right?"

"Yeah," he said, skeptical.

"Look at the shirt he's wearing." He pointed at Romano's shirt. "What's it mean?"

Romano had on a T-shirt from the San Gennaro feast. It was faded enough to be a couple of years old, and it had a picture of the American flag and the Italian flag and said, "America. We discovered it. We built it. We feed it."

"You're an Irishman, tell them who discovered America."

The captain looked exactly like you'd think he would: tan, weathered face, sturdy and stocky, with a beard. He was wearing an old baseball hat, beige work pants, and a sweatshirt. He had no idea what Rooney was talking about, and he threw out, "Christopher Columbus?"

"No!" Rooney said. "If you were a real Irishman, you'd know this."

"As far as I know it was Christopher Columbus."

"You never heard about Saint Brendan the Abbot? He discovered America in the sixth century."

We all looked at him like he lost his mind.

"No, I'm serious. Back in the seventies someone even made the trip to prove it could be done. They made the same kind of boat, a curragh, just like the one he would have used and sailed to Canada."

"Mike, it's too early for this," I said.

Rooney is always telling us all this useless stuff about the Irish. He swears Hell's Kitchen got its name from Davy Crockett, something about the Irish in the old Lower East Side slums were too mean to swab hell's kitchen. How could that be true? I mean, why would Davy Crockett the wilderness guy name Hell's Kitchen? Another favorite of Rooney's is that *West Side Story* is about the Irish and Puerto Ricans in Hell's Kitchen. I guess that could be true, but Rooney says it like it has something to do with him.

The captain and the mate exchanged a look, probably wondering if Rooney was gonna get out of hand. I saw Joe give him a "He's alright" nod and say, "He'll pass out on the ride out, it'll give him time to sleep it off."

We were going out to the Hudson Canyon, which is about an eighty-mile run that would take between four and five hours. We would go out to water between seven hundred and three thousand feet, to the edge of the canyon where the Atlantic abyss, which is about five thousand feet, is. I didn't know all this off the top of my head, just bits and pieces of what Lou Fiore told me.

We left the marina at exactly 2:00, idling until we got past the jetty and the captain let it go. The wind picked up and a light spray hit us, making me cold enough to grab my sweatshirt. The night was clear, with a quarter moon.

When we were out far enough and you couldn't see land, it was hard to distinguish where the water ended and the sky started. It was so dark, and there were a million stars out. It was a little scary out on the water with everything looking the same in every direction. I was thinking we could get lost out here, but I guess with technology the way it is with the GPS, the radio, and the cell phones, somebody would find us.

It was a weird feeling, the water and the sky were so huge. It reminded me of the movie *Titanic* when they already hit the iceberg and were sending up flares. The ship seemed so huge throughout the whole movie, but then the camera pulled back and you saw the flares shooting up into the air over the massive ocean. The flares looked like fireworks overhead, and the ship looked so insignificant compared to the vastness of the ocean.

Denise loves that movie, and I'll admit I watched it with her a couple of times. Personally, I think the reason the ship sank was because of the knucklehead that said, "God himself couldn't sink this ship." Rule of thumb, you say something like that to God, you better duck.

At one point I actually saw a shooting star. I'd only seen that once before, when I was a kid, and I stood there staring at the sky, looking for it to happen again.

Rooney, O'Brien, and Romano fell asleep. Bruno was freezing in a T-shirt. Since this was his first time out fishing, he didn't realized it would get chilly. I gave him my sweatshirt and got a kick out of him trying not to get too close to the edge of the boat while he looked over the side.

I was waking up now from the cool, salty air. I started talking to the mate about TWA flight 800, which went down somewhere in these waters and is still a big thing to most of the people who live out this way.

Flight 800 was the Paris-bound plane that went down five years ago off Long Island, eleven minutes after taking off out of Kennedy Airport. Captain Rich and the mate were volunteers who went out of the Moriches Inlet to do rescue. Since there were no survivors, it was a recovery effort, and we started talking about it.

"That had to be horrendous," I said. "Did you find a lot of bodies?"

"There were some bodies floating," he said. "But it was mostly body parts that we put into those medical waste containers and loaded on the deck of the boat. I remember Texas Instruments overnighted

239

those FLIRs, the forward looking infrared that we used with the search. We picked up everything, luggage, clothes, sneakers."

"So what do you think happened?" I asked. "Are you buying the center fuel tank explosion theory?" There was a lot of controversy over the whole thing, and since he was there, I thought maybe he'd know something.

"I honestly don't know," he said. "There was a massive investigation. The place was swarming with feds, and they talked to anyone who saw anything. They interviewed me at my house, writing down everything I said, asking me if I had any pictures or video. The people that did the independent investigation were retired Navy and Air Force; some had retired from TWA." He shrugged. "I mean, they had credibility. They felt the plane was shot down by shoulder-fired missiles. They said the government rigged the lab tests and lied in their reports. There were also a lot of witnesses out that night, and they all said they saw something hit that plane. One guy had been a pilot in Vietnam. He saw the crash that night, and he said something definitely shot the aircraft down."

"I heard they thought maybe it was friendly fire."

There were a lot of witnesses who saw what happened that night. Later on they took out an ad in the *Washington Times*, demanding to be heard. Most of the witnesses reported seeing a flare, others said roman candles or other fireworks, some said shooting stars, and others said a meteor flare. They may have varied on whether it was a firework or a flare, but all of them saw something streak toward the plane and then it exploded. Some felt it was a heat-seeking missile because they saw it change course.

Most witnesses reported seeing an initial small explosion, followed by a larger one. Most said it looked like something was launched from the ground, probably off a boat. It was a clear night, probably a lot like it was tonight, and there was nothing to hinder visibility.

I know that most of the plane was retrieved from the water and reconstructed somewhere out in Calverton. But it was the kind of thing where there's almost too much information and no straight answers. I think the thing that flagged me was the Navy stepping in and tossing out the divers who had jurisdiction in the area.

The FBI, the National Transportation Safety Board, and CIA tried to say that what the witnesses saw streaking toward the aircraft was actually flaming debris moving away from it after the explosion, and they even made a video to tell the eyewitnesses exactly what they saw. The CIA's version was mostly used to discredit witnesses. It got ridiculous, to the point where the witnesses were all accused of being drunk and not knowing what they saw. Personally, I thought something was up.

"Were you out that night?" I asked.

"Not before the crash. Once I heard about it, I went out." He pulled his cap off and put it back on, and I wondered if it was a nervous gesture.

"What did everyone else think it was?" I asked, hoping I didn't sound like I was interrogating him. I was just interested.

"Initially everyone thought it was terrorists. Later on people were saying that there were warnings in the Arabic newspapers saying they were going to strike us. I had also heard that an Israeli airplane was supposed to be in that flight path at the same time, but I wouldn't know about that. Personally, I'm not sure it was a center fuel tank explosion. Jet fuel isn't nearly as volatile as gasoline. Jet fuel's a lot more stable. Plus, you have to think how many planes have empty center fuel tanks and they never explode."

"So what *do* you think?" I asked.

"I think no one knows what happened, and the center fuel tank explosion is the best they can come up with."

Personally, I thought the whole thing stunk. Plus, I've been a cop long enough to know how much the higher-ups get away with lying.

Romano woke up around 4:30 and started talking shop with the mate, who was setting up the poles and cutting bait on a wooden table next to the big rubber bins that would later hold the fish. They were talking equipment and telling their fireman war stories. The mate couldn't keep up with Romano. I guess there's not a lot that burns out here. Rooney, Joe, and O'Brien woke up around 5:00, just as we could see the sky brightening on the horizon.

The sunrise is incredible in New York. Whether you're on the beach or out on a boat, there's nothing like it. It was still dark along the water but lighter above it. The sun sent a stream of light along the water, with streaks of orange, pink, white, and blue behind it.

Within a couple of hours we started to see other boats, and like us, they were putting out their chum lines. We were going out for bigeye, albacore, and yellowfin. What happens is each boat has a chum line, and the tuna make their rounds, feeding through all the chum lines and swinging back around. Chum lines are small pieces of cut-up fish, with the heads, the tails, the body, and blood all thrown together in a bucket. The mate uses a ladle and scoops out chum every thirty seconds, leaving a trail of blood and guts.

The mate set up six lines, three on each side of the boat. That's the nice thing about a trip like this; the mate does all the work for us, and we just have to worry about catching fish.

Romano, Joe, and I took one side of the boat, while Rooney, O'Brien, and Galotti took the other.

"If something comes up on this side, we'll take it," Rooney said, opening a beer. "If something comes up on that side of the boat, you three WOPS take it. I'll just plan out my week of free lunches that Joe's gonna buy me when I whup him in fishing."

"We're not WOPS, Mike," Joe said. "And you better get your

suit cleaned, you're gonna need it to go to church with me next Sunday."

"Mike, you don't even know what a WOP is," I said.

"Sure I do, it's an Italian," he said, guzzling half the can. "And we got the baby WOP over here with us." He nodded toward Bruno. "Right, Bruno? Do you know what a WOP is?"

"No idea, but I know it has something to do with Italians."

"WOP means 'without papers,' an illegal," I said.

"Really?" This from Romano. "I never knew that."

"Okay," the mate cut in, "I know the rest of you have been out fishing before, but I want to go over a couple of things with . . ." He pointed at Bruno.

"Bruno."

"Right. First, if you get something, yell 'Fish on' and I'll know you got something on your line. Put the pole in your belt, lock your reel, and pull." The belt is like a workout belt with a notch to put the pole into. He showed Bruno the stance, legs bent and locked.

"The fish is gonna pull, so use your body weight to counter it. Also, don't lose the reel and the rod. They cost a lot of money, and I'd hate to see you ruin your trip because you lose one and have to pay for it." He was talking to Bruno, but he looked at us all on that one.

"Don't go behind anybody when you got a fish on, go to the edge of the boat." He was saying that because tuna are the third fastest fish in the ocean, and if they take off and you're fishing behind someone, that person could get tangled in your line and get pulled into the water or cut by the line slashing into their skin.

He finished with, "And whatever you do, don't touch the line with your hands." That's so the line doesn't get caught around a finger and rip it off.

Then the mate started telling us a story about someone who went

243

sail fishing who had wrapped his hand around the line and pulled. The fish jerked and snapped the line and dove deep in the water, taking the guy with him.

"Was he alright?" Bruno asked, his eyes wide.

"No, he died. And they never found his body. Lots of sharks," the mate said, using his two hands to make a set of jaws.

14

The first hit we got was an eight-foot blue shark. Actually, Rooney got it. The chum lines attract more than the tuna. I guess the sharks can smell the blood, and pretty soon we had a few of them circling the boat. It was creepy being out in the water with no land in sight with the fins of the sharks circling the boat.

"How do we get rid of them?" Bruno asked, moving away from the side of the boat.

"I'm gonna catch one," Rooney said, then started imitating the theme from *Jaws*.

The shark took his bait and sat about six feet down in the water.

"If you reel him in real slow, he won't even know he's hooked," the mate said.

"We don't want sharks," Romano said. "We're here to catch tuna, Mike."

"I want that shark," Rooney said, bending his pole as he brought him up. "This thing is dead weight."

"It's like pulling up a Volkswagen," the mate said, waiting until it was a couple of feet below the surface. "Go ahead and jerk it hard."

Rooney jerked the line, and the shark went nuts, shooting water all over the boat.

"I can't hold it," Rooney said, his face red, the veins standing out in his neck. He buckled his knees into the side of the boat.

245

He struggled with it for about ten minutes before the mate finally said, "Are you done?"

Rooney was sweating now, with the bushy hair that stuck out of his hat plastered to his head. "Yeah." He blew out a breath as the mate cut the line.

We slowed down the chum line so the sharks would go away. The tuna were moving in schools, making the rounds on the chum lines of the other boats in the area. As they made their way back to us we started helping the mate cut up the bait and kept the chum line heavy so the tuna would stay around the boat.

Joe bagged the first tuna. We heard the *zzzttt* of his line going out, and he grabbed the pole and put it in his belt. He yelled "Fish on" and locked his reel, pulling back on the pole while he reeled it in, moving forward so the line didn't get loose.

Joe got the tuna up to the side of the boat. We could see the metal leader, so we knew he was close. I could see the fish's head was pointed down, with his tail up, as he tried to swim downward. Once the tuna saw the bottom of the boat, he gave it all he had and went wild. We heard the *zzzztttt, zzztttt* of the line pulling out even though it was locked. He went about thirty feet down, and Joe had to pull him up all over again.

When he got the tuna up to the boat again Joe put his left hand in the middle of the pole and kept his right hand ready on the reel. The pole was bent all the way down, and Joe pulled back to keep him at the surface.

The fish was tired now, and Joe called to the mate, who was still keeping the chum line going.

The mate came over with his gloves on and a gaff in his hand. He leaned over the boat, grabbed the metal leader, and gaffed the tuna in the gill. He yanked the exhausted fish up real quick, pulling the line and gaff and plopping him on the deck.

There was blood everywhere. You wouldn't know it, but tuna is a bloody fish.

It was a yellowfin, probably about sixty pounds. These tuna are built for speed, and they remind me of a torpedo. His tail was going a mile a minute, and the blood was spilling all over the boat, making it slippery. The mate threw him in the bin and grabbed the hose to rinse off the blood.

"Nice," the mate said.

"It was okay," Rooney said, sucking on a beer. "You almost lost him, Joe. Let's get that chum line going again, and I'll show you how it's really done."

Joe just smiled at him.

I hit next with another yellowfin, and then Joe hit again. Next was Romano and then back to Joe and me again.

After bagging my second tuna I sat down and lit a cigarette. I was tired from grappling with the fish, and I felt my face and arms stinging from the sun. I was already a little sunburned from yesterday, and I guess with the water around us the sun reflected more.

"So what's the score now, Mike?" I asked.

"WOPS 6, Rooney 0," Romano hooted.

"Yeah, you guys have the lucky side of the boat," Rooney complained.

"Then let's switch sides," Joe said.

"No way," Romano said. "This side is where the fish are."

"I wouldn't give up that side," the captain said.

Joe smiled. "We'll be fine."

Rooney practically ran over to our side of the boat, elbowing us out of the way.

An hour and a half later it was WOPS 11, Rooney 0, and by 12:00 we had caught twenty-two yellowfin tuna.

Bruno was looking bored with the whole thing, and it took him a minute when he heard the *zzzttt* of his line going out.

"Fish on!" he yelled, excited, clamping the pole in his belt and locking the reel just before he almost went over the side of the boat. He caught his knees under the lip of the side of the boat to keep him from going over.

"Help me!" he yelled as we all ran over to help him. He almost got the fish to the boat twice, and after the second time he said, "Someone else take it."

"No!" I yelled at him. "You do it. Come on, be a man and pull it in!" I guess he got psyched after that, because he let out a roar as he reeled it back up.

"This is a big one," the mate said.

And it was, it looked about a hundred pounds. Once the mate gaffed it and we got it in the boat, Bruno practically strutted over to the cooler and cracked open a beer. He put his head back to chug but slipped and went flying, landing on his backside, sending the beer flying and getting his white sweats covered in blood and water.

"What is this, dago day?" O'Brien growled. "They're like the friggin' apostles."

"It's because Joe's God's golden boy," Rooney said, aggravated.

"You could be God's golden boy too, Mike," Joe said with a smile. "He doesn't play favorites."

"I don't know," the captain cut in. "Whatever side of the boat these guys are on, they're catching fish."

We took a break and had some sandwiches and potato salad before going back to fishing again. Joe and I drank bottles of water, and the rest of them had beers.

When we started fishing again, Romano caught the next one; then Bruno caught a second. O'Brien finally hit, and then Rooney hit the mother lode.

"Fish on!" he yelled.

It was huge, a good two hundred pounds, and Rooney was whooping it up as he reeled it in. Then Rooney made the mistake of bending over to see the fish, letting his line get slack. As the mate went to gaff it, the fish started moving down, and it snapped the slack line as it dove down into the deep water.

After that things got into a frenzy. As soon as the bait hit the water, tuna would come out of the water and strike it. They reminded me of dolphins the way they were moving to the surface and then swimming down as if rotating in a circle. Romano was exhausted, pleading with us not to catch any more.

"This never happens," I said.

"I've never seen anything like it," the mate agreed.

"Good fish," the captain said with a nod. "Good fish."

About 2:00 we headed home. We were happy and exhausted, with our arms aching and our skin burned. The mate was busy with the tuna, steaking them for us, knowing he'd get a great tip for the amount of fish we brought in. The way it's done is we all chip in three hundred bucks apiece for the trip, so the catch is ours. There was a lot of fish, so we'd throw some to the mate and the captain, but the bulk of it would be ours. Out of the eighteen hundred bucks we paid for the trip, only three hundred of it would go to the mate.

Rooney, O'Brien, Bruno, and Romano were all drinking beers. I wanted to have just one, and I knew I could do it and walk away, but something was stopping me. Maybe it was Michele, and I found myself thinking that if Michele dumped me, then I'd go on a bender. Then I pictured myself going to Narcotics or the CAGE unit that works with the gangs, working the most dangerous thing I could and spending my off-duty time drinking myself into oblivion.

I was working myself into a state when Joe grabbed us each a soda and said, "Here, Tony, have a cold one."

"Thanks, buddy," I said.

Rooney was bragging how he had the biggest fish.

"And the biggest mouth," I said. "And it doesn't count unless you get him in the boat."

"So, Mike," Joe said. "You didn't forget our bet, did you? Be at my house at nine o'clock next Sunday. Donna will make you a nice breakfast before we go to church."

"I'll be there," Rooney said. "I'd never welch on a bet. They're not gonna be doing any weird stuff, right?"

"No," Joe said, confused. "Like what?"

"I don't know, screaming about the devil and all that other crap they say."

"Nobody's gonna be screaming, Mike. You'll enjoy it."

I wasn't sure it was a good idea. Rooney's not as stupid as he looks, he's pretty sharp. If I picked up that Pastor was doing something wrong, he might too. He already thought a lot of these preachers were shady, and if he sensed something was up, it might turn him off to God.

We were all tired, and Joe and I passed out on the ride back while the four of them were still drinking.

When I woke up about two hours later they were all asleep and didn't wake up until 6:30 when we slowed down at the marina.

I called Michele as soon as I hit the dock and got the answering machine again. I left a message telling her I'd be stopping by to see her and Stevie. We divied up the tuna, thanked the captain and mate, and said good-bye to Rooney, O'Brien, and Bruno.

I took 27 back, turning off at 111, and headed north.

"You stopping by the house?" Joe asked.

"Yeah, I'm not staying long," I said.

When I got to the house her car was gone. I went inside to see if she left me a note or something, which she didn't. I was getting

250

mad now along with that sick feeling in my stomach that was telling me she was leaving. I left a note saying I stopped by and to call me when she got in.

We dropped Joe off at home. I would have gone in if I saw Michele's car, but it wasn't there. The traffic going into the city was heavy but moving on the Long Island Distressway, but once I cut over to the Southern State it slowed down.

I dropped Romano off at his truck and helped him with his gear.

"Great time, Tony," he said, shaking my hand and slapping my back. "Fish on, buddy."

I let myself in and checked my answering machine. There were three messages—one from my mother asking if I was okay and if I would call her, one from Grandma asking where I was and that I better call her, and one from Sandy asking how I was and if I needed anything.

I called Michele again as I wrapped up the tuna steaks six at a time in plastic and foil. I tasted a piece of one. It reminded me of sushi, only it needed a little wasabi. She didn't answer again, and I didn't leave a message this time. I put the phone down instead of smashing it into the wall when someone knocked on the door.

I thought for a second it was Michele, then I thought it was my father or brother looking for a fight. It turned out it was Alfonse, checking on me and giving me a bowl of rice with peas and proscuitto.

"You okay, Tony?"

"Yeah, I'm fine. Anything happen after I was gone?"

"Yeah, the cops had to come for that kid on the corner, the one on drugs that's always fighting with his girlfriend. Did you know she was pregnant?"

"The blonde? No," I said when he nodded.

He was talking about a couple of crackheads that rented one of the tiny condos on Greely Avenue. Every time they got a new tenant it was the same thing, they got high and they fought. In June someone got shot over there. Supposedly it was gang related, but the neighbors were fed up with the two of them. I hated to say it, but what kind of life were those two gonna give a kid? They didn't think about anything but getting high, and the kids always suffer.

"We caught a lot of tuna," I said, taking a stack of them out of the freezer and handing them to him.

"Oh, Julia will love this, look how fresh," Alfonse said. "Come have dinner with us tomorrow before you go to work."

"Sure," I said. "Thanks, Alfonse."

I heated up the rice and peas and ate it while I watched the 10:00 news. I was sick of hearing about the mayoral race, so I shut it off and collapsed into bed. I didn't set my clock or read my Bible and was asleep almost immediately.

I woke up to the sound of the phone ringing and bolted to the kitchen to grab it, catching my knee on the corner of the cabinet.

"Hello," I said, groggy.

"Hi, it's me," Denise said. "You ready to go to lunch?"

"What time is it?" I yawned and looked at the clock. It was 11:10. "Wow, did I sleep that long?"

"I guess so. How about we go to St. George to that little place across from the ballpark."

"The ballpark? Oh, right, the bar there."

"It's a restaurant, Tony, it just happens to have a bar. Plus, you loved the zucchini there, remember?"

"No, that sounds good. What time?"

"Pick me up on your way down. How about twelve o'clock?"

"Yeah, I can be to you by twelve," I said.

I showered and shaved and changed into jeans and an Urban Pest Control T-shirt that's about a hundred years old.

When I pulled up, Denise was waiting outside her apartment, dressed in faded jean shorts and a black tank top, talking on her cell phone.

"Heard you caught a lot of fish," she said, kissing my cheek. "How about you come for dinner this week. I've got a bunch of tuna in my freezer."

I looked at her. "What'd Romano go to your house last night?"

"Yeah, so?"

"Is he living with you?" I thought he might be. He's there every time I call.

"Not really. He needs a room for when his daughter's at his apartment. I live in a studio. I don't even have a bedroom."

Parking was crazy in St. George. Between the courts, the DA's office, central booking, and all the other local agencies, you never get a spot. I parked at the 120, the St. George precinct, and threw my plaque in the windshield. The plaque was for my precinct, but I doubted anyone would bother me.

The restaurant was tucked into a side street between Richmond Terrace and St. Mark's Place, and if you got a table by the window, you had a view of the harbor and the Verrazano Bridge. The view always makes me a little homesick. Growing up we had the same view off our deck, just a couple of miles closer to the bridge.

"Pretty soon you won't be seeing this anymore," Denise said, reading my mind.

"Yeah, I know. The beaches are beautiful in Long Island too," I said. "But you can't get this view anywhere else."

"I'm thinking about moving," Denise said.

"Where?" I asked, surprised.

"I don't know. Once you go, there'll be no one else here for me."

I almost said, "What about Dad and Grandma?" but she barely talks to them now.

"Mom's in Pennsylvania, Vinny's moving to Jersey next month, not that he's talking to me anyway since I beat up his girlfriend. Sorry, his fiancée," she corrected, rolling her eyes. "You'll be moving out east in November, and Carla's all involved with Benny, so aside from Nick, why would I stay?"

"Who's Benny?" Carla was Denise's best friend since they were kids. Personally, I thought she was a bigmouth who slept around too much, but Denise was always with her.

"Benny works for her father, collecting vig," Denise said.

Vig is the interest payment on a loan from a loan shark. Carla's father is probably somewhere in the middle range with the Mob. I think his specialty is loan sharking, and if Benny collects vig for him, he's a moron with a lot of muscle.

"What does her father say?" I couldn't picture her father liking one of his workers sleeping with his daughter.

"He doesn't know. Neither does Benny's wife," Denise said.

"Good way to get dead," I said. "She's out of her mind."

"I know, that's what I told her," Denise said. "But she won't listen to me. We're not even talking."

"So where are you thinking of moving?"

If she was gonna stay with Romano, she couldn't go far. I was hoping she wouldn't say upstate, because then I'd hardly ever see her. Once I lived in Long Island it would be easy enough for me to stop in Staten Island on my way home, but if she went upstate it was too far.

She shrugged. "Nick was talking about transferring to one of the houses in the Bronx and moving upstate. The houses are cheaper up there, and he could stop in Staten Island and get Alexa every other weekend and then bring her back when he comes back in before work."

"He's gonna leave his mother and grandmother?" His mother never remarried after his father was killed, and the grandmother was his father's mother. I couldn't see Nick just leaving them alone.

"His brother took the upstairs apartment, so he's right there," Denise said, reminding me that Romano's mother owned a two-family house.

"Is this what you want, Denise?"

"Yeah, I think it is," she said, nodding.

We ordered the fried zucchini and a couple of burgers and watched the water traffic. It was a beautiful, clear day without a cloud in the sky. I watched the tankers as they came in and went out of the harbor and saw a couple of tugs and smaller boats.

"What do you think is in this?" I asked, dipping zucchini in the creamy garlic sauce. It was thick, and I didn't taste sour cream, so I was guessing it was mayo, but there were a lot of spices in it.

"I have no idea. The chef wouldn't tell me, and I couldn't find anything like it on the Internet," Denise said. "If I knew how, I'd get it analyzed so I could figure it out."

I paid the bill, and we started walking down toward Richmond Terrace. Instead of turning left at the corner, Denise grabbed my hand to pull me across the street.

"What are you doing?"

"Come on, let's take the boat like when we were little," she said, dragging me across the street.

"Denise, I don't want to go into the city, I have to be there tonight."

"We won't get off the boat, just turn around and come right back. It'll only be an hour."

"I had enough boat yesterday, I was on the water for sixteen hours."

"Please, Tony, when's the next time we'll get to do something like this? You'll be married soon, and you'll never come back here."

"I'll come back."

"Not like this." She looked like she was gonna cry. "Not just me and you."

I waited a beat. "Sure," I said. "Let's take the boat."

When we were kids we'd cut out of school and wait till after rush hour so nobody's parents would see us, and we'd take the boat and hang out in the city. We'd make fun of the old guy who walked around with his wooden box saying, "Shine, shoe shine," with an accent I probably still couldn't place. Sometimes on the weekend if our parents were going at it, we'd take the boat back and forth to pass the time, sometimes hopping on the 1 train to go up to Midtown to walk around.

We waited ten minutes for the 1:30 boat, sitting on the hard wooden benches that have been here since before I was born. The terminal is dusty and the bathrooms are filthy, and most people sit and read the paper, with a few congregating by the doors leading outside with their eyes on the overhead clock. At 1:29 we walked toward the doors. If this were rush hour we'd be smashed in the crowd of people and pushed out once the doors opened. We walked through the boat to the front deck, facing downtown, looking for the shoe shine guy as we went.

The boat blew its horn as we left St. George and headed toward lower Manhattan. From the ferry you get a great view of the Statue of Liberty, Ellis Island, and Governor's Island, with the Twin Towers shooting up into the sky. Denise threw money in the two-eyed telescope thing as we passed the Statue of Liberty and let me look through it after a couple of minutes.

"Are you gonna miss Staten Island?" she asked.

"I don't know," I said with a shrug. "My life is different now. I don't hang out with any of the guys anymore."

256

"That's a good thing," Denise said. "Your friends were sick, sadistic perverts."

I laughed. "No, they weren't."

"Yes, they were, Tony, and so were you when you were with them. Don't you remember what you did to me that Halloween when you took me to Ichabod Crane's grave and left me in the cemetery in the middle of the night? I almost died of fright."

I'd forgotten about that. Denise must have been about fourteen years old. I told her we found Ichabod Crane's grave, and she wanted to see it. I don't know if that's where the writer got the name, but there's an actual Ichabod Crane buried in the cemetery on Richmond Avenue near the old Henny's Steak House. I remember it said on his tombstone that he was born in 1787 and died in 1857 and that he served his country for forty-eight years. Mike Ellis, Marty Burns, and I took Denise to the cemetery at midnight on Halloween, brought her to Ichabod Crane's grave, and tore out of there, leaving her screaming.

"I guess there's some stuff I'll miss about living here," I said. "Mostly the food, you can't get good bread like here. And I'll miss the neighborhood, even the one I live in now."

"I think the family's pretty much done now," Denise said. "Do you think anyone will come to your wedding?"

"I don't know that I want them to. If Michele ever talks to me again, we'll see what we want to do. I don't want them there if they're gonna ruin my wedding."

"What a mess," she said.

The thing about the ferry is that as it approaches the dock, Manhattan sucks you in. Especially at night when the water is black and the lights of the city seem to swallow you up and pull you into the middle of it. No matter where in the world you come from, everyone recognizes New York. Most of the time the city's just part of the scenery, but when you're coming in on the boat, you always look at it in awe.

We stayed on the boat as it docked at South Ferry. Actually, we held on to the side of the boat as it smashed into the pilings. Aside from smashing as you dock, the ferry is pretty safe. The only accidents happened when ferries got hit by tankers in the fog a couple of times. One ferry was sunk that way about a hundred years ago.

The boat ride is probably twenty-five minutes each way, and we got back to Staten Island at 2:25.

Denise didn't want to go home, so we drove down to South Beach and walked the boardwalk and then went to the arcade on Sand Lane and played skeeball for an hour. We had a bunch of tickets for the high scores, but not enough to win any of the good prizes, just the cheap plastic stuff.

I dropped her back at her apartment at 5:00 and got home in time to eat dinner with Alfonse and Julia at 5:30.

I checked my machine when I got home. Both my mother and grandmother called again, but no Michele. I called my mother back and almost hung up before she answered on the fourth ring.

"I was outside with Aunt Patty," she said.

"Tell her I said hello."

"I will when I go back outside. Are you okay?"

"Yeah, I'm fine," I said. "How 'bout you? You recovered from the block party yet?"

She laughed. "It was interesting. I thought it'd be the last time I saw Ron, but he came back yesterday to have dinner with me."

"He seems like a nice guy," I said. I liked the way he looked after my mother, making sure no one got near her during the fight.

"He is. I'd love for you and Michele to come up with Stevie and have dinner with us. Next weekend is the hot air balloon festival, and for the last two years a hot air balloon landed in the field behind my house."

Stevie would go nuts if he saw that.

"I'm off next weekend. But I haven't talked to Michele since Saturday, so I don't know what's going on there. I left her about five messages and stopped by the house, but she hasn't called me."

"Give her time to cool down. She loves you, she isn't going anywhere."

We talked for a couple of minutes about school. My mother is taking her general courses for the nursing program at the community college near her house. One of the classes is psychology, so I guess she can get an understanding about all the family pathology.

Alfonse was grilling the tuna went I went outside. Julia had set the picnic table with real dishes and was pouring Pellegrino.

"This is good, what's on it?" I asked when I tasted the tuna.

"Basil, olive oil, garlic, balsamic vinegar, and pignoli nuts. They've been marinating all day," Julia said.

I was glad that the block party never came up in conversation. They told me about their daughter, Tina, who told them over the weekend she was getting a divorce. It was pretty quick, they'd only been married about a year. Apparently, the husband had been cheating on her with his secretary since before they were married and she just found out about it.

"At least they didn't have kids," Julia said. "It's hard for kids."

"She's young, she'll get married again," I said.

"Please, twenty-five thousand dollars for a wedding that didn't even last a year," Alfonse said. "Don't talk to me about another wedding."

I went back downstairs at 7:00 and set my clock for 9:00. I was tired and knew if I didn't get some sleep I'd be shot tonight.

I showered again before I left. I probably could've shaved too but didn't see the point.

I called Michele again even though I'd told myself I wouldn't.

"It's me," I said when the machine picked up. "You know, for all your talk about wanting to be honest right from the start, you're not doing such a good job. Why don't you pick up the phone, and let's be honest here." I waited another ten seconds to see if she'd pick up. I pictured her standing there smirking at the phone.

The roads were clear through to Midtown, and the air was nice and cool, around 70 degrees.

I got to the precinct early enough to change and talked to Vince Puletti for a few minutes before roll call. He said his daughter got engaged to some shem, which is short for *shemanooda*, which means he's an idiot.

I told him about Alfonse's daughter not even being married a year and they're already getting a divorce and how the wedding cost twenty-five grand.

"I know! How am I gonna pay for this? I can't retire now. At this rate the undertakers'll take me out of here," Vince said, hoisting up his pants and shaking his head.

O'Brien and Rooney were talking to Terri Marks over at the desk, telling her about the fishing trip. Rooney was yapping about the now 250-pound tuna that got away.

Joe came upstairs with Bruno, and Bruno threw in, "Terr, wherever Tony and Joe fished, that's where the fish were."

"Even the fish can't resist you, Joe." She sighed. "When are you gonna leave your wife and marry me?"

Joe shook his head and changed the subject. "Hey, Terr, did Mike tell you his uncle Brendan discovered America in a rubber boat?"

"Oh, come on," Rooney said, shaking his head. "That's not what I said."

"Tony, Joe." Hanrahan gave me and Joe a "Come here" signal as he headed into the muster room.

"Hey, boss."

"Roll call screwed up notifying the day tour to come in early for the election duty tomorrow. There's about an hour OT, and I figured I'd throw it to you and Joe first."

"I'll stay, boss," I said. "What about you, buddy?" I said to Joe. "I'm driving out after work anyway, I'll drop you off."

I figure if I'm sleeping in her bed, the future Mrs. Cavalucci will have no choice but to talk to me. The way I see it is that to have a good fight, you need good strategy, and I was already thinking of all the Scriptures I could throw in her face, like "Do not let the sun go down while you are still angry," and "Love keeps no record of wrongs." Plus, I'll pick up some flowers and a box of Godiva. She loves the truffles. Michele may be smart, but I'm much less principled. I'll fight dirty if I have to.

"Sure, I'll stay, boss," Joe said.

"Okay, take a four thirty meal. The polls open up at six o'clock. You'll be over at Norman Thomas High School on 33rd Street. The day tour should relieve you by eight thirty," Hanrahan said before he gave the attention to the roll call order.

"The color of the day is yellow," he said. He gave out the sectors and foot posts and the return date for C-summonses and finished it up with, "There's a couple of openings for about an hour of OT for the morning. If anyone wants to take it, see me after the roll call. After that it's mandatory."

15

We stopped at the deli on the corner and threw Bruno out of the car for coffee and the papers. We drove up to 44th and 8th, across from the Milford Plaza, and sat with Bruno until we finished our coffee.

"We got a four thirty meal, so you're gonna have to get yourself back to the house later," I told Bruno.

I made a left on West 45th Street, and Central came over with "South David."

"South David," Fiore answered.

"We got a person harassing passersby at three-one and eight."

"10-4," Fiore said.

Technically, 31st and 8th is South Charlie's sector, but we heard them answer a job at 34th and 7th for a pedestrian struck.

We drove down 30th Street, past the French apartments and up 8th Avenue. I rolled along the row of parked cars on my left, and we could see a drunk sitting on the southeast corner of 31st and 8th, next to the pizzeria where I got the Italian ice for the block party.

Something was going on across the street. I saw people coming out of the Garden. I read that the Rangers were gonna be holding training camp there, so maybe that was it.

The drunk was sitting on the corner, leaning up against a chain-link fence with a parking lot behind it. He was wearing a button-down shirt opened to the waist, dirty shorts, black socks, and sneakers. He was pacing back and forth, almost getting in front of people as they walked by while he yelled and made kissing sounds to the women as they walked past him.

A woman who looked about thirty, wearing jeans and a white shirt with those thin straps, walked by talking on her cell phone, and he started with the kissing sounds again. She threw him a nasty look, and he yelled, "Hey, I might not be the best looking guy here, but I'm the only one talking to you, baby." He slapped his leg and cracked up while she rolled her eyes.

He was drinking out of a paper bag, probably Thunderbird, the drink of choice for skells. I guess at three bucks a pint you can't go wrong.

We got out of the car and walked up on him. He was busy yapping at a woman who told him where to go in a West Indian accent. I guess he had a line for everyone, because he said, "You must be Jamaican, 'cause Jamaican me crazy," and cracked up again.

He didn't see Joe and me until we were about five feet away. When he caught us out of the corner of his eye, he sat down by the fence and hid the bottle behind his leg and tried to pretend he didn't see us.

"Hey, buddy, what are you doing?" Joe asked him.

He acted like he just noticed us. "Hey, hayadoon, officers," he slurred.

"What are you doing here, buddy?" Joe asked again.

"Nothin'," he said with a shrug. "Just hanging out, not bothering nobody." He knocked the bottle over, and I heard the *clank* when it hit the sidewalk.

"What's that?" I pointed to the bottle. "Are you drinking here?"

"Noooooo, I don't drink. No way. I don't know whose that is." He was shaking his head no.

"Listen, you can't stay here," Joe said.

"Ah, c'mon. I'm not botherin' nobody."

"We're getting calls, buddy, you're bothering everybody," I said.

"I'm not bothering them, they're bothering me!"

"Listen," Joe said. "Why don't you pick up your bag and let's call it a night over here. Go up the block toward 9th Avenue. This way no one can bother you there."

He waved us away, but he picked up his stuff and walked down toward 9th Avenue.

Joe and I patrolled our sector, driving east to west and back then north to south. It was quiet, probably because it was a Monday night and all the summer tourists were gone. We parked on 37th Street and read the paper and looked at the Empire State Building.

I was reading an article about the Gowanus Canal. A couple of years ago a propeller was put in to force fresh water through the tunnel connecting the Buttermilk Channel and the Gowanus Canal. The Gowanus Canal was disgusting, full of raw sewage and probably the filthiest water in the city. The water was stagnant and had been that way for thirty years. The article said that since they put the propeller in, there were blue crabs, jellyfish, and schools of fish there.

I went on to read about the Ronaldo Paulino All Stars from the South Bronx, who lost the U.S. final in the Little League World Series a couple a weeks ago. It turns out their star pitcher, a kid from the Dominican Republic, was really fourteen years old and not qualified to play. Supposedly, the kid and nobody else knew how old he actually was, which was a lie. How could you say nobody knew how old the kid was?

"How many bridges do you think there are in the city?" Joe asked.

I mentally counted off the GWB, the Queensboro, the Triboro, the Willis Avenue, the Third Avenue, the Brooklyn, and the Manhattan bridges.

"Seven?"

"No, in the whole five boroughs."

"I have no idea," I said.

"Fifty-seven," Joe said.

"Really? I guess I could see that. Staten Island alone has four bridges, and it's the smallest borough."

"South David," Central came over the air.

"South David," Fiore responded.

"We have an aided case, person not breathing at 250 West 37th Street."

"10-4."

We drove over to 250, where a well-dressed male Korean, maybe five foot ten or five foot eleven, who looked to be in his thirties waved us down in front of a ten-story building. There were a lot of sweatshops in the area, this building being one of them.

Joe radioed Central to tell them we were 84, on the scene.

"Is the person breathing?" Joe asked as we got out of the car.

"No."

"How long is he not breathing?"

"Not long, maybe five minutes."

I'm thinking five minutes is a long time. We followed him through the door and across to a flight of stairs next to the elevator.

"You live here?" Joe asked.

"No, our business is here." He named a clothing manufacturer. "My mother is downstairs with the super, he's unconscious."

Down the hallway to the right there was a middle-aged Korean woman standing outside a doorway. When we walked into what looked like a break room with two couches and a TV, we saw a white male, about fifty years old, lying faceup on the floor next to the couch.

He had that ashy death pallor that they get from no oxygen, and he stunk of booze. He was wearing work greens with "250 West 37th Street" embroidered on his breast pocket. His pants and shirt were unbuttoned, and his work boots were unlaced.

Joe radioed Central and told them to put a rush on the bus.

"Two minutes out," Central said.

The woman was crying, saying something to the son in Korean that sounded like, "*Mar hoge mar seo!*"

Whenever people are speaking Korean around me I always think of that *Seinfeld* episode where Elaine brings George's father to the nail salon with her because she thinks the manicurists are talking about her in Korean.

The son shooed her away, and she said it again while Joe knelt down and felt for a pulse and shook his head no at me.

He started doing chest compressions to keep the blood moving and gave me a look.

"No way," I said. There was no way I was doing mouth-to-mouth. This guy stunk and could have AIDS for all I knew. If I had an airbag I would have used it, but I didn't.

The mother and son were going back and forth in Korean. The woman looked over at the son and said, "*Fa rasio?*"

"I don't know," the son said.

"What?" I asked.

"She asked if he's dead."

"It's not looking too good," I said. "How do you know him?"

The dead guy was wearing a wedding ring, and I was guessing he was the super of the building.

"Are they married?"

"Uh, no," the son said with a funny look. "He's the super."

The son went back upstairs to wait for EMS, when all of a sudden I heard a gurgling sound and saw yellow fluid coming out of

266

the guy's mouth. I flipped him on his side to let the fluid out while holding my head away 'cause it smelled nasty and I didn't want to get any of it on my uniform.

We couldn't do compressions with him on his side, and we didn't want him choking on his own vomit, so we just crouched there waiting for EMS.

The mother was still standing outside in the hallway, taking a peek in every couple of seconds and crying all over again, putting her face in her hands. Something was going on here. Nobody gets this upset when the super dies.

We heard footsteps and the jingle of equipment as two paramedics came down the hall and into the room.

Joe and I stepped back and let them take over. One started doing chest compressions, and the other put his finger in the guy's mouth to see if he was choking on something before putting on an airbag.

"We did chest compressions," Joe said.

"Any mouth-to-mouth?" He must've known from our expressions that we didn't.

I walked out into the hallway to talk to the son, who came back down with EMS.

"How'd your mother know he was down here?" I asked him.

He walked me away from her, and she yelled something in Korean, and he yelled back.

"Listen," he said, talking low. "They were down here having sex, and he had a heart attack."

"Is he married?"

"Yeah, he's married."

I nodded. That explains why the clothes were half off.

"*Can chen io?*" the mother yelled.

"Do you think he'll be okay?" the son asked.

"I have no idea," I said, thinking he was probably gone already.

Then I realized what I was thinking and started praying for the guy. I didn't want him meeting God in the middle of committing adultery.

I took the son's info for the aided card, writing down his name, address, and home and cell phone numbers. I got a brief statement, leaving out the sex part, and walked back into the room.

EMS was rushing to pack up their stuff.

"They got a pulse," Joe said, excited.

"Is that from us, with the chest compressions?"

"They shot him up with something," Joe said.

"Are you coming with him?" they asked the mother.

"My mother will go," the son said. "I'll follow in the car. Where are you taking him?"

"Bellevue."

I thought it was pretty messed up that this guy was married and his wife was home, oblivious, thinking he was working, and meanwhile he had a heart attack while having sex with a woman who owned a sweatshop in his building.

We had no jobs other than an alarm at 48 West 39th Street, which we gave back 90 U, unable to gain entrance. We couldn't get in to check, but the ground level was secure.

We went back in for our meal at 4:30 and slept for an hour down in the lounge.

◆

After our meal, we stopped for coffee on the corner of 9th and 35th and went up to Dyer to make the right at 36th Street to go across town.

Some nut job was standing on the cement island outside the Lincoln Tunnel where the hot dog vendor usually sits in the afternoon, flashing the cars coming out of the tunnel.

"It's that drunk from last night," I said as we got closer.

He would wave at the cars and then drop his pants, cracking up at people's faces when he flashed them. People were screaming out their car windows at him, and the driver of a silver Suburban rolled down his window to throw something at him but changed his mind when he saw us. He pointed at the guy, giving us a "Go get him" look instead.

I pulled over on 36th Street and saw the drunk's uh-oh face when he saw us and scrambled to pull up his pants.

"Hey, didn't I tell you to behave?" Joe said as we crossed the street to him.

"I went to 9th Avenue, it's right there," he pointed toward 9th.

"Listen," Joe said. "We don't got time for this."

"I'm sorry," he stammered, trying to look remorseful.

"Where's your belt?" I asked him.

"I don't know," he said with an exaggerated shrug.

"Listen," I said. "This is what I want you to do. Go over to the precinct on 35th." I pointed toward the precinct. "Tell them at the desk you want to turn yourself in, and they'll give you a belt."

He held his pants with one hand and saluted us with the other. "Okay, Sarge."

He started walking up 36th toward 9th Avenue when I called after him, "And if anyone gives you a problem, tell them Officer Rooney sent you."

He threw us another salute.

Our election duty started at 6 a.m., we went to Norman Thomas High School on East 33rd between Park and Lexington. This would be my first time there. Usually I wind up in the 13th precinct. I parked across from the school, outside a deli. I looked up at the sign that read, "High class deli, we accept food stamps and WIC checks."

The election detail is boring to begin with, and the morning's pretty slow. A few people come in before work to vote, but most go on their way home. Plus, this was the primary and there wouldn't be as big a turnout.

Joe and I were basically there to make sure the "No Parking," "No Campaigning Beyond This Point," "Vote Here," and "*Vote Aqui*" signs were up. One of us would be outside; the other would be inside with the retirees from the League of Women Voters and other volunteers who work the elections making sure no one tries to interrupt the voting or influence anybody.

A group of people jabbering away in Spanish walked in together, and I saw a Pakistani-looking woman shaking her head at them as she came out of the school. I didn't know why she was looking at them like that, and I almost busted out laughing when she said, "These foreigners can't even speak English." I didn't know what to say to her, so I just nodded and tried not to laugh.

The day tour relieved us at around 8:30, and we talked to Carl Beers for a couple of minutes before we left.

Joe's cell phone rang as we walked to the RMP. "Hey, babe," he said and listened for a second. "I grabbed an hour OT. Tony's driving out anyway, so he'll drop me off. Sure, I'll pick it up. Love you too." He closed the phone. "Gotta stop for milk."

"No problem, buddy."

"I'm hungry," Joe said. "You hungry? Forget it, you're always hungry."

"Let's get a good bagel," I said. "We'll stop on three-one and five."

"Yeah, I love their bagels," Joe said.

I drove up 33rd Street and made a left onto 5th. I drove two blocks south and parked outside the bagel store, smelling the bagels before we got in the door.

"Are the everythings hot?" I asked the guy behind the counter.

"They just came out ten minutes ago."

"Great," I said. "Give me an everything with butter and a regular coffee."

Joe was getting an egg sandwich, so I went outside to have a cigarette with my coffee. I put the coffee and bagel on the trunk of the RMP, lit my cigarette, and pulled back the plastic tab on the Styrofoam cup to blow on the coffee. Something caught the corner of my eye, and I looked straight down 5th Avenue and saw smoke coming from one of the towers of the World Trade Center.

I stood there looking at it when I heard over the radio that a plane just crashed into the Twin Towers.

I put the coffee down and switched over to the citywide channel on my radio and heard,

"Large explosion . . ."

"Plane hit the Trade Center . . ."

"We got debris everywhere . . ."

"North Tower approximately 85th floor . . ."

"The building's on fire . . ."

Joe ran out of the deli with the guy from behind the counter and looked down 5th Avenue. "Was it a big plane or a small plane?" Joe asked.

"I don't know," I said, watching the plume of smoke rise from the building.

"What difference does it make?" the guy asked.

The difference is a small plane could mean that an inexperienced pilot veered off into the no-fly zone and lost control of the plane. A large passenger jet wouldn't hit the building by accident.

The radio got wild now with 10-13s, with officers needing assistance being called all over the place. I heard a lieutenant call Central and say there was a big explosion at the World Trade Center and to call for a level four mobilization.

"Lieutenant, you don't have the authority to call a level four mobilization," Central said.

Then reports started coming in that it was a commercial aircraft. We kept our radios on the citywide channel as we jumped in the car and headed back to the precinct.

I heard Central say, "Lieutenant, can you confirm if it was a big plane or a small plane?"

"It was a big plane, Central."

"I'm going down there," I said.

Joe paused for a second, then nodded. "I'm going too."

People were coming outside and looking down the avenues as we made our way back to the precinct. The precinct was busier than usual for the day tour, and we saw Hanrahan on the phone at the desk when we came in. He was supposed to be working OT, scratching our memo books at the election detail.

"Hey, boss, we got a detail going downtown?"

"Yeah, they're mobilizing us."

"Joe and I are going," I said.

"Alright, get your helmets and meet me up here. We're taking van 4553."

Joe and I were the last two cops to get in the van. We had two sergeants, Hanrahan and Charlie Bishop. Bishop pulled a few of his angels off their foot posts—John Bertram and Ernie Jones, who we call Bert and Ernie, and Paddy Fitzgerald, who was six foot six and skinny, with glasses, and might as well have been Big Bird.

From the midnights there was me, Joe, Walsh, Rooney, who finished up his collar and wanted to come with us, and Noreen, Hanrahan's driver.

We stacked our helmets behind the back bench. That way if we needed them later all we had to do was open the back door so we wouldn't be climbing over the seats to get them.

Noreen took 34th Street to the West Side Highway and headed downtown. We were quiet on the way down. We all had our radios on the citywide channel and listened to the fractured transmissions over the air.

"Mobile command center to Manhattan mobile command center, stand by . . ."

"Be advised the FEMA equipment from the Brooklyn Navy Yard will be unloaded on Chambers and West . . ."

"Smoke too heavy . . ."

"Citywide . . . on the air . . ."

"Staten Island Ferry . . ."

"New citywide mobilization point for all citywide task force is . . ."

"26 Federal Plaza evacuated . . ."

"Bomb threat . . ."

"We're trying to ascertain right now, gonna get a head count . . ."

"In building, can't be moved . . ."

"Be advised Brooklyn Bridge is open from Manhattan into Brooklyn . . ."

"Pier 40. . . . spare millennium gas masks . . ."

I heard a loud rumble when we were at about Houston Street and leaned my head down to look through the windshield.

Hanrahan yelled, pointing, "There's another plane," and for a split second we saw the commercial jet before it slammed into the south side of the South Tower, sending up a fireball that swallowed up the top of the building.

People that were standing along the West Side Highway started screaming, their faces frozen in horror as they watched the smoke pour out of the South Tower.

"We're being attacked," Joe said.

My first thought was that someone was doing this on purpose, something I never thought I'd see. It felt surreal, like this couldn't be happening, but it was happening.

"Okay, listen up, boys and girls," Hanrahan ordered as he turned around and looked at us. "This is the real deal here, no screwing around."

We all looked at Rooney.

"This is serious," Rooney said. "We gotta help these people."

"I want ya's to stick together, no joke," Hanrahan said.

Yeah, like any of us thought it was funny.

Walsh leaned down to look out the windshield and said, "Where'd the plane go?"

I looked at him. "It's in the building," I said. But he looked like he didn't get it.

The radio was chaotic now, with everybody getting stepped on, making the radios basically useless.

The West Side Highway was clogged to Canal Street, so Noreen cut over to Broadway and got as far as Chambers Street before the street was crammed with emergency vehicles. People were running up Broadway away from us, while others stood in the street looking at the buildings. Some were crying with their hands over their mouths; others were pointing at the buildings as they talked on their cell phones. There were papers everywhere, floating down out of the sky, almost like a ticker tape parade.

A black male flagged us down as we got to Chambers Street. His leg was ripped open, and his head was burnt. His hair looked like burnt plastic glued to his head.

"Nor, take him over to Beekman," Hanrahan said, talking about Beekman Downtown Hospital. "Then meet us back at the command post at Church and Vesey."

"Easy, buddy," I said as Joe and I put him in the van.

We ran the five blocks down Broadway with people running past us in a panic now. Everyone was out on the sidewalks, standing in the street and talking on their cell phones, looking up at the towers in horror. As we got closer I could see the orange glow of the fire inside the tower and the thick black smoke as it poured out.

We saw an airplane wheel the size of a table lying in the street, and there was debris everywhere. It was falling from the buildings onto cars, the street, and the sidewalk. We could hear things hitting the ground around us, and I realized our helmets were on their way to Beekman Hospital with Noreen. If something was to hit us from one of those buildings, we'd be dead.

When we got to the corner of Church and Vesey, Hanrahan and Bishop went over to talk to the brass. They were all business, with their radios in their hands, pointing toward West Street and methodically pointing at each sergeant, letting them know where to mobilize on West Street and then putting their radios to their ears before pointing again. I heard what I thought was the chief of the fire department yelling into his radio saying, "New York City is under attack, the Air Force must be notified immediately."

We stood there trying to take in everything around us with our hats in our hands. People were holding bags, pocketbooks, or their hands over their heads to protect themselves from the falling debris as they ran. Some were holding hands as they walked. Others looked dazed.

An older guy who looked about sixty years old was stumbling toward us as he crossed Vesey Street. He had a nice gash on his forehead, his shirt was ripped, and he was bleeding from his shoulder.

"Easy, buddy," I said as I crossed toward him. He started to collapse on me, and Joe grabbed his other side.

I could tell he was Italian; he was heavy around the middle, had a roman nose, and wore a button-down silk shirt.

"Thank you, officers," he said as he leaned on us.

275

Joe and I looked around for an ambulance and spotted one on Church about half a block up from Vesey. We steered him that way while he told us as he sucked in air that he'd just walked down almost thirty flights of stairs.

"How'd you get banged up?" I asked.

"Fell in the stairwell," he gasped. "Thank God no one trampled me, they picked me up."

The paramedics were bandaging burns and cuts, taking the most serious first.

"Whaddaya got?" a stressed-out looking paramedic barked to us.

"He fell on the stairs coming out of the building," Joe said. "He seems okay, he was able to walk down thirty flights of stairs."

"You're gonna be okay, buddy," I told him.

"Thank you, officers." He hugged both Joe and me, thanking us over and over.

As we walked back down Vesey we saw a group of people with injured among them that were more serious. They were helping each other out of the area instead of standing around watching like people usually do when someone gets hurt. They were half carrying each other and half holding on to each other. We saw a woman who had burns on her arms and back; half of her shirt was burned off her back. A man had burns on his hands and along his arms. I thought the fabric of his shirt was hanging off his arm until he got closer and I realized it was his skin. Paramedics were coming down into the area now, setting up a triage and moving out the worst of the injuries to the ambulances to transport to the hospitals. The noise was insane. There were sirens, people screaming, and horns from emergency vehicles, plus the static of the radios.

I saw chunks of concrete and pieces of metal on the street and cars with broken windshields and dented roofs from falling debris.

When we got back to the mobilization point our guys were directing people out of the area and pushing back the onlookers to keep the street clear. Joe and I joined in, telling them, "Come on people, you gotta get moving, you can't stand here." They would look at us for a second and then go back to staring at the buildings as they walked away.

I saw Aviation circling the towers from a distance. At one point they came in closer, I guess to see if they could land.

"That's a bad idea," Joe said, looking up at them.

"There's too much smoke up there, they'll never be able to land," I said, wondering if they were attempting a rooftop rescue.

I know there's a helipad up there and that some people were rescued when the tower was bombed back in 1993. But the tops of the buildings were so thick with smoke, I couldn't see anyone being able to stand out there in it, never mind risking getting smoke and debris in the engine of the helicopter.

All of a sudden it felt like everything around me was coming from a distance. The sound dulled, and I felt a little dizzy. I took a couple of steps away from Joe to clear my head, looking at the ground to compose myself. I noticed there were bonds and memos and paperweights, papers that were burnt, and paper that you'd never know was blown out of the building. I saw a check for seventy-six thousand dollars made out to a phone company; part of the name was singed black. It was mindboggling that up until a little while ago, this stuff was just sitting harmlessly on someone's desk.

"A plane hit the Pentagon," I heard Big Bird say. He looked shaken.

"Who told you that?" I asked, looking up at him.

"That reporter right there," he said and pointed to a woman with a press tag around her neck.

"She said she heard planes were hijacked in Washington, DC, and Philly too," he said.

"This is bad," I said, wondering how many other planes were out there. "This is really bad."

"Our country is under attack," Joe said like he couldn't believe it. He rubbed his hand over his face and put his head down.

"Okay," Hanrahan said when he and Bishop walked back over. "The command post has been moved over to West and Vesey, we're gonna muster up over there."

We hurried down the north side of Vesey toward West Street. People were running past us toward the East Side. I could tell they were coming from their offices; they were dressed in suits, some were rumpled, some looked fine, some had briefcases and pocketbooks, and others looked like they just ran out of the building.

The closer we got to West Street, the worse it looked. I had to step over a woman's leg; I could tell by the size and shape of it that it was a woman's. It had no shoe on, and I could see the bone sticking out of it.

Rooney made the sign of the cross as he stepped over it, but Walsh stopped, staring at it.

"Come on, buddy," I said, giving his arm a tug. "We gotta keep moving."

I looked up at the building as if I could see where the leg had come from, and I saw people trapped above the fire in the North Tower standing on the window sills, close to the edge. They would disappear into the smoke and emerge again as the smoke swirled around them. The windows were broken. I don't know if they knocked them out or the explosion did; they aren't easy windows to break. Then I saw someone jump from the building, suspended in a free fall, and land with a sound that I'll never forget.

"Did you see that?" I asked Joe.

"I saw it. Someone just jumped," Rooney said.

I got confused all of a sudden and felt like I didn't know what was happening around me. Then the realization that someone did this on purpose hit me again, and I got scared, wondering how many more planes were coming.

I was thinking this was not a good place to be, so close to the North Tower. There were building materials like metal, glass, and insulation all over the street and sidewalk, and we were stepping over body parts that looked almost fake to me. I felt my body jerk at the bang of another body hitting as it slammed onto the roof of the customs building, the six-story building adjacent to the North Tower.

I was walking, looking up at the building and the jumpers, looking down at the ground every couple of seconds to watch where I was stepping. I was thinking one of these bodies could get close enough to hit us and we'd never survive it.

I was glad when Rooney said, "Boss, can't we go up a couple of blocks and come down West Street? I don't want to get hit with a jumper."

Bishop whirled around at him and yelled, "Why is your hat off? Why are all your hats off?"

Hanrahan looked at Bishop like he was crazy. Bishop always takes the easy gigs, and I'm sure he was scared out of his mind to be here. He was known for taking his temper out on whoever was closest to him at the time. We all looked at each other, and Rooney's eyebrows shot up. We were stepping over body parts and he was worried about our hats.

"C'mon, we gotta get over there. Everybody put your hats on," Hanrahan said in a no-nonsense, "I don't have time for this" tone of voice.

When we got to West and Vesey the whole area was jammed with fire trucks, police cars, ambulances, and city vehicles. There were cops and firemen everywhere, some being mustered up, some running toward the towers. The brass were back to talking into their radios, barking out orders while they pointed at the sergeants and pointed to the direction they wanted us to go.

They posted us on the corner of West and Vesey, right across from the North Tower, with instructions to evacuate all civilians out of the area and not let anyone back in.

Over the next few minutes I saw more people start jumping to their deaths from what looked like about the ninetieth floor on the north side of the North Tower. They jumped head first, with their arms and legs out and their feet up in the air like a free fall. I saw what looked to be two people holding hands.

Every time someone jumped, the crowd would let out a frightened scream, and I could see the terror on their faces as they watched with their hands over their mouths. The sound was so loud that my whole body jerked every time someone hit. Rooney and Walsh made the sign of the cross every time someone jumped, and Joe would run his hand over his face and put his head down.

I watched in horror as they smashed into the roof of the Customs House or onto the ground. When they hit, a red mist came up from where their bodies landed.

After about ten people jumped, Walsh said, "Oh, come on," as he started to cry. "Why doesn't Aviation land on the roof and get these people out of here?"

The helicopters were still in the area, but they made no attempt to approach the rooftop.

"Because the smoke would get sucked into the engine and it would seize," Joe said before he turned around and threw up.

"You okay, buddy?" I asked him, rubbing his back.

"I'm fine," he said. He spit and wiped his mouth.

"There's got to be something they can do," Walsh said.

"If they could land, they'd land," Joe said, looking up.

I had to turn around. I didn't want to see it anymore. I don't know how, but I managed to compose myself. I started praying for each person that jumped from the building. I remembered what Joe said about going into God's throne room, and I asked God if I could come in and talk to him. On the inside of me I felt like he told me yes, to come in and pray for these people. I prayed to him to help these people jumping, to take them before they felt the pain of hitting the ground. I prayed for their parents, their wives and husbands, their children and grandchildren, for God to help them through this. I prayed for my family too, and for everyone else dead or alive that was in those buildings.

"Alright," Hanrahan barked. "No one is allowed in the area. We are directing the evacuations of civilians uptown, and under *no* circumstances does anyone get in."

"What about the press?" I asked. There were already a ton of reporters here.

"We were told nobody," Hanrahan said. "If they want to get in, they'll have to get in someplace else."

We started moving people out of the area. We'd point up West Street and say, "Go, go, go," as we waved them on their way.

For the most part, people would listen, but you always get people who just don't listen.

"I need to get in there—"

"Uptown! Move it, don't you see what's going on? No one's going in there."

"Officer, you don't understand—"

"Go! Go!" we'd tell them, waving them up West Street. "Move uptown, come on, out of the area."

"Why won't you listen to me?" one woman started crying.

"Nobody's going in," I yelled at her. "You have to leave the area *now*."

"But—"

"No but, just go!"

They would walk away, looking back at the tower as they walked.

A guy walked toward us, a suit-and-tie type with half a smile on his face. "Do you think a lot of people are dead?" he asked Rooney.

"Are you kidding me? Get out of here!" Rooney screamed at him.

We had a steady stream of people now, and for the most part, we stood there pointing and saying, "Go, go uptown, let's go, move it."

There was a cameraman standing with us, filming as we moved people out.

"I need to get my daughter out of school," some guy said, trying to get past us.

"No way," I said, putting my arms out to block him as I shook my head. "Everyone is out of the buildings and uptown."

"Please, I need to get in there. I don't know if my wife got my daughter and got out," he pleaded.

"Everyone's already been evacuated from the area," I said, hoping it was true. "I'm sure you'll meet up with your wife and daughter further uptown."

Bert and Ernie told the cameraman to move it uptown now. He walked about three-quarters of the way up to Barcley Street and continued filming.

Walsh was still green enough to fall for a sob story and a pretty face. He walked a female about twenty years old over to Hanrahan and said, "She was supposed to meet her sister—"

"No! Everyone out of the area! Let's go!" he yelled at Walsh.

We were hearing more things hit the ground now. Bodies and chunks of debris were falling with more frequency now, and every time we heard something hit, our bodies did an involuntary jerk.

Rooney was staring at the FD and ESU trucks parked on West

Street and said, "If anything big comes down, we'll dive under the fire truck and we'll be safe."

We had been there probably close to an hour when pedestrian traffic started to slow down. The area was filling up with firefighters getting their equipment out of their trucks and heading right into the towers. Civilians that either had been on their way to work or had made it out of the buildings after the first plane hit were crying, breathing heavily, holding hands, or looking back in shock with their hands over their mouths as we sent them uptown.

The buildings seemed to be burning out of control now, with a lot more people jumping to their deaths. Then the ground started to shake, and I heard a sound like a thousand trains pulling into the station all at once.

16

The sound of the trains was coming from the South Tower, and we looked up to see the top floors of the tower give way and start collapsing one at a time onto the floors below. It reminded me of a building being demolished, and it almost looked as if explosives were being set off seconds apart on each floor.

"It's coming down, run, come on!" Hanrahan yelled.

The cameraman was now directly behind us, still filming as the building started to collapse.

"Let's go, shut the camera off!"

As the top floors started to slide down we ran north on West Street, yelling, "Come on, come on, let's go!" as we grabbed people, dragging them with us as we ran.

I could feel the dirt and dust on me within seconds, and when I turned back I saw the rest of the building crumble to the ground.

Then I saw the smoke, coming toward us like a wave of death.

Everyone on the street was now screaming and running in all directions. Some ran across West Street toward the water, some uptown, others toward the East Side.

"Move, now. Move it, let's go!" Hanrahan and Bishop were waving their arms and pushing people with frenzied moves. I was grabbing people's arms, dragging them with me as I ran, yelling, "Come on, come on, don't stop, keep moving!"

The cameraman stood there filming until he saw the smoke coming, and then he turned so quick he tripped and dropped his camera.

I started running again, thinking whatever was in that smoke was gonna hurt us. I could feel debris hitting my hands and flecking off the skin on my arms. I looked back, wondering if we could outrun the cloud, but it was coming too fast. The smoke was huge as it chased us, and just as I was about to reach Chambers Street I took a deep breath as it overtook us.

The smoke enveloped us, and we were getting hit with bigger things now. I don't know if the wind was on our side or if it was God helping us, but as soon as I was into it, it was almost like the smoke retracted back and I was out of it.

While the cloud itself seemed to have pulled back, the whole area was consumed with white dust from the collapse. It was getting dark now, almost impossible to see, and with each breath I took, my mouth and nose filled with grit and powder.

We ran as far as the Chambers Street footbridge to catch our breath. I saw that, like me, Joe was trying to tuck his chin into his shirt. We were all covering our faces so we weren't breathing in the dust. I can't really write down a lot of what everyone was saying—I'd be bleeping out every other word—but they kept saying the same things over and over as we stood there in shock, sweating and breathing heavily.

"All those people just died," Walsh said.

"They did this on purpose," Rooney kept saying. "They did this on purpose."

"It came down," I said. "I can't believe it came down." All those people, they must have been so terrified.

For the first time in my life my knees actually got weak. I felt nauseous and shaky knowing that all those cops and firemen had that building come down on top of them, all those people.

"They're gone," Hanrahan said. "They're all gone. All those people are dead."

Hanrahan was right. All those people were dead. There was no way anyone could have survived a hundred-story building coming down on top of them. There was no way.

More people were reaching us now, holding their chests and bending over from running. A gray-haired man sat down on the curb, looking to be having trouble breathing. He was covered in dust; I guess he didn't outrun the cloud. He pulled a shoe out of his shirt, stared at it, and then looked down at his own feet. He had shoes on. I guess it got stuck in there with the debris. He started to take deep, gulping breaths, and I was afraid he was gonna have a heart attack.

He looked up at Joe and me and put out his hand with the shoe in it. "It's not my shoe," he said, looking confused.

"Come on, buddy," I said, taking the shoe from him as Joe and I grabbed either side of him. I dropped the shoe behind my back into the street as we brought him over to an FD ambulance that was parked in the middle of West Street.

"He's having trouble breathing," I told the EMTs.

They must have been there awhile. They were washing out eyes, cleaning out gashes, giving oxygen, and dressing burns. I thought they seemed almost oblivious to the fact that the South Tower had just disintegrated, but then I saw that the EMT working on the guy with the shoe was crying, making tracks down the dust on his face with his tears.

I looked around at the dusty crowd around me and realized I didn't know where everyone else was. Rooney, Walsh, Joe, Hanrahan, and I were together, but somehow we got separated from Bishop and his guys.

"Where'd they go?" I asked Hanrahan.

"I don't know. But we're together and we're going back," Hanrahan said. "We need to see what we can do to help."

"Boss, if we go back, the North Tower'll be closer, and we barely got away from this one," Rooney said.

"Alright, here's the plan," Hanrahan said. "If the North Tower goes, we'll run north along the building line on the east side of the street. This way, at least we'll have some protection from the buildings."

I thought about it, and it made sense. The buildings would give us some cover as long as the top section of the tower didn't fall off and land on the buildings.

I tried to hear the transmissions on my radio, and I could hear calls for help and 10-13s that sounded frantic. Someone was screaming, but the battery on my radio was dying. I could hear static and pieces of transmissions but nothing clear to give me a location.

I pulled my cell phone out and saw that I was down to one bar. I wanted to call Michele just to hear her voice, but I got an "All circuits are busy" recording. I tried it twice more and shut the phone off to save the battery, since I forgot to charge it before I left for work.

Fiore tried using his cell phone but flipped it shut and said, "It says all the circuits are busy."

"That's what I got," I said.

"I need to let Donna know I'm alright," he said.

Visibility was almost zero as we started to walk back toward the command post. The air was thick, clogging my nose and my eyes. With each breath, I could feel my mouth and nose fill with grit from the chalky powder. We were disoriented as we walked; at one point we walked into scaffolding that was in front of a building because we didn't see it until we were right on it. We went into the building to try to use the phone. The air in the lobby of the building wasn't much better than outside. People were crowded in, and I could hear moans and crying. I tried to use the phone at the security desk but got the "All circuits are busy" message again.

People were crowding into the building now, crushing into each other, and I knew we had to get out of that building.

"Everyone remain calm," Hanrahan ordered the crowd. "Don't push and don't crowd each other. You're far enough away that you can safely walk uptown."

"Let's get everyone moving uptown," Hanrahan told the four of us.

We made our way to the doorway and started taking them outside and directing them uptown. They were too stunned to argue with us and moved uptown like blind cattle, holding on to the buildings as they walked.

It took maybe five or ten minutes to clear the lobby. We walked back out to West Street and almost felt our way down toward Vesey with our arms stretched out in front of us. The closer we got to the corner of Vesey Street, the thicker the dust became. I felt like I was walking in half a foot of dust, conscious of the powder being kicked up with each step I took. I could feel the dust caking around my neck and getting underneath my vest as it went down my back as I walked. My feet were crunching over fragments of whatever there was under there.

People were crawling out from under parked cars, almost appearing out of nowhere, covered in so much dust you couldn't tell they were people.

The dust was so bad I untucked my shirt and used the corner of it to wipe my eyes. My eyelids felt like they were filled with sand, and I felt them scratching my eyes every time I blinked.

"Can you believe this?" Rooney asked when we got to Vesey.

From the limited visibility we had we could see that cars were on fire, moved, and smashed in at odd angles. The fire truck that Rooney had talked about running under was smashed beyond recognition. If we had jumped under it, we'd all be dead right now.

When we got to within about fifty feet of the command post, a lieutenant was waving us over as the brass started to straggle back to the post. He was a task force lieutenant, mustering up his guys in hats and bats. The task force is who we use for crowd control. They respond at a moment's notice in vans to help beef up our numbers in crowds. The lieutenant was pumping them up, saying, "We gotta get in there, and we gotta get everyone out of that building before it comes down."

"Come on!" He waved us to move as we got closer. "You're coming with us, we're gonna get everyone out of that building before it collapses."

Now, here's the thing. Task force is mostly for crowd control, like in riots, protests, parades, anything where you have a ton of people you don't want getting out of hand, and when they're not looking all tough, they're usually out writing summonses. The patrol cop answers jobs for disputes, drugs, robberies, and street crime. We're not rescue workers. The only time we rescue people is when they're stuck in elevators, and even then we don't have the equipment for it and wind up calling ESU half the time anyway. When we have a rescue situation, we call ESU.

We had no idea what the conditions were inside that building, and it was wrong for him to send us in there without oxygen, protective gear, and radios. We had no communication equipment; we didn't even have helmets.

The cops from task force weren't standing in their usual helmets-on, bats-held-up, don't-mess-with-us stance. Their bats were down by their ankles, and they didn't have that confident look on their faces; like us, they didn't want to go in there.

Hanrahan surprised me by saying, "With all due respect, Lou, our inspector gave us a command to stay on this post and make sure nobody gets into that area."

Technically, the lou is a higher rank and we'd have to follow his command, but the truth is, we're not rescue workers and he was putting us in harm's way.

"Sergeant, we are going into that building," the lou said, dead serious. "And we are getting as many people out as we can before it comes down."

A chief who was walking up behind him caught what he said and started yelling, "Are you crazy? I'll take your bars from you right now!" The chief got in the lou's face. "I'll suspend you right now. *Nobody* is going in that building. It's unsafe, and I'm not losing any more men. If you listen to your radio, you'll hear we're calling everyone out of the North Tower."

I couldn't help but think that if we were out here and we couldn't hear them ordering everyone out of the building, how were they gonna hear it in there?

Both sides of West Street were now jammed with fire trucks, police cars, and ambulances. I spotted a "pumpkin" on the helmet of a young firefighter rushing past us. They call it a pumpkin because probees wear an orange patch on the front of their helmets instead of the black and white or red and white insignia that has the engine or ladder company they're assigned to. I should have realized there'd be probees here. They love something like this when they're new. Nick Romano was here. I don't know how I knew, I just did. There may be almost forty thousand cops in New York City, but there were only about eight thousand firefighters. I remembered when the Oklahoma City bombings took place, our FD went all the way there to help out. If something this catastrophic happened in their own city, they'd be here even more so.

I prayed again, this time for Nick, asking God to get him out alive. I didn't want his daughter to have to grow up like he did, to have her father die a hero for reasons she could never understand. And I didn't want Denise to have to lose him, to finally find something good only to have it snatched away from her.

There were firefighters everywhere, and I watched, fascinated, as they ran from their fire apparatus toward the North Tower. They never slowed down, they just ran right into that building. They knew the other tower had fallen, but they ran anyway, like it didn't even matter to them that the building was unsafe, they were going in. We could hear the jangling of the fire equipment as they ran past us kicking up dust as they went.

The radios were frenzied now, and I could hear this one cop screaming for help from inside the tower. Someone was trying to get his location, but they didn't know where he was.

There were still a lot of civilians in the area, and we went back to moving them uptown.

"Keep moving north," we told them. "Everybody head uptown."

I realized that this would be all over the news by now. I thought about Michele, Denise, and Grandma. They would be worried about me, and I needed to call them. I turned my cell phone back on and tried to call Michele but got the "All circuits are busy" recording again.

I heard the sound of the trains again and everyone started running for their lives again. I looked up and saw that the North Tower had started to collapse. The ground shook, and the world went insane as the North Tower crumbled to the ground. The smoke curled around the buildings and snaked through the streets, filling the crevices of the city blocks as it chased us.

We ran toward the river this time, completely forgetting our plan. We passed a bunch of firemen who had kicked open the door of a city bus and piled into it on top of each other. We almost jumped in the bus with them, but Hanrahan yelled, "This way." We were running as fast as we could, and just before we reached the water, we jumped over a six-foot ledge and backed up against the cement wall as the wave passed over us.

I could feel the dirt and debris as it washed over me. I covered my face with my shirt and arms. We were closer to the building this time and got caught in more of the fallout, and my shirt was already full of dust, so it was pretty much useless. I could feel the dirt in my hair and on my skin and seeping through my clothes.

I looked down at my radio and realized it was silent now, and so was everyone else's. Whoever had been calling for help never made it out of the building.

I don't know how long it was until we moved, probably only a couple of minutes. I had no idea how many people were dead, but I knew the casualties were massive.

It was like being in a bad dream that you can't wake up from. Visibility was worse than when the first tower fell. We may as well have been blind as we walked back to West Street. Even through the smoke I could see that there was nothing left of the towers but massive piles of twisted steel sticking out in every direction. I didn't see any movement coming out of the piles, no signs of life.

One of the pedestrian bridges that crosses West Street had collapsed to the street and was lying twisted on its side.

The buildings that were still standing in the Trade Center were all on fire, it looked like every floor was on fire. Even the Customs House was burning.

West Street was filled with piles of steel and impossible to get through in places. The buildings on the west side of the street, including the World Financial Center, had sustained a large amount of structural damage. Huge I beams had fallen and crashed through the side of one of the buildings and were hanging dangerously from about thirty floors up.

Fire trucks, RMPs, ambulances, and other vehicles were either destroyed by the falling steel or engulfed in flames.

The cars in the outdoor parking garage across from the World Financial Center were completely destroyed, with a lot of them still on fire.

I'd never seen anything like this in all my years as a cop, and nothing could have ever prepared me for this. The whole area looked like those pictures you'd see on the news of Beirut and Israel, places where these psychos usually have their fun.

As we crossed the street and headed back toward the collapse, we heard a sickening sound that got louder as we got closer.

"What is that?" Walsh asked.

We all stopped and listened.

"It's the alarms," I said, looking at Joe and watching his face as he realized what it was.

"Oh, Jesus, help us," Joe said, his voice cracking.

"Oh no," Hanrahan said, choking up.

"What is it?" Walsh asked. "What alarms?"

"It's the pass alarms," I said. FD wears them so they can locate someone if they're not moving.

I listened as the sound of beeping alarms swept over the whole area like a field full of chirping birds that were really dead firemen.

"We gotta get over there," Joe said, and all of us started toward the area of the towers.

"We gotta get a land line and call the house," Hanrahan said. "Then we'll go over. I want us to stay together."

I was ankle deep in powder and building debris that had fallen from the towers. We held on to the buildings as we made our way north up West Street, bumping into each other as we fumbled our way along. The further we got from the site, the better the visibility was. We stopped in the first building we came to once we could see, a school on the corner of Murray Street, a couple of blocks up from the towers, and got a land line.

I caught the one side of Hanrahan's conversation as he called the precinct.

"We were? . . . Yeah, he was a moron standing there filming. I didn't realize it was live. We got separated from Bishop and his guys after the South Tower fell. . . . You did? Oh, thank God. What about Noreen, we sent her over to Beekman. . . . She did? Okay, good. Yeah, get him for me. Hey, boss. . . . Yeah, thank God. Listen, we're gonna head back there and see if we can help looking for survivors. . . . What? Are you serious?" I didn't like the look on Hanrahan's face. "Okay, boss. Will do. Thanks, boss." He hung up and turned to us.

"That guy that was filming showed us live," Hanrahan said. "Coughlin said they saw us just as the building fell, and I guess it looked like the building caught us when the guy dropped the camera and everything went black." He looked down for a second and said, "They hijacked another plane, it crashed somewhere in Pennsylvania."

This was too much. I wondered how many planes were out there and who they'd be hitting next.

"How many planes did they hijack?" Rooney roared. "They put two in the towers, one at the Pentagon, and now one crashed in Pennsylvania? How are they getting all these planes?"

Good question.

Fiore used the phone next, and I could hear Donna screaming and Joe trying to calm her down.

"It's alright. I'm alright. I didn't lie to you, we saw the plane hit on our way back to the precinct. I've been trying to call you. Donna. Donna." He looked at me and shook his head. "Donna, you're gonna scare the kids, calm down."

She screamed loud enough for us to hear her say, "Don't you tell me to calm down, Joseph, your face was the last thing I saw on television before that building fell!"

"Don, I can't do this with you now. What? Is she there? Okay, I'll tell him. I have to get back down there. No, I'm fine," he said, trying to calm her down and get off the phone at the same time.

"Wait," I said. "Is Michele there?"

He shook his no. "I gotta go, babe. If I can get to another phone I'll call you. I love you too, more and more every day." Joe always tells her that.

"Wait," I said. "Let me talk to Donna."

"We gotta get back down there," Hanrahan said.

"Boss, give me a second, I want to make sure Michele knows I'm okay," I said taking the phone from Joe.

"Donna, it's Tony," I said. "Did you talk to Michele?"

"Yeah, she said to tell you to get home now."

I almost smiled. "Where is she?"

"She was still at school and called me when she heard the towers were hit. She said when she didn't hear from you she got worried. I told her I saw you on TV, and she lost it."

"I gotta get in touch with my family," I said. "They probably all saw it."

"Give me someone's number, and I'll keep trying," Donna said, her voice shaking.

I gave her Denise's and Grandma's numbers. "Get a message to Michele," I said. "Tell her I'm okay and I love her and I'll keep trying her cell."

"I will. Tony, be careful and make sure Joe comes home safe," she said, starting to cry.

"He'll be fine," I said.

As we walked back down, I started to feel disoriented. West Street was unrecognizable, and if it wasn't for the water, I wouldn't be able to figure out where the towers used to be.

Cops and firemen were pouring back into the area, and Bishop and Noreen were back at West and Vesey, with Bert, Ernie, and Big Bird with them. Noreen looked shell-shocked. She said the first building fell when she got out of the van up on Chambers Street. She got stuck in the smoke and was holding on to buildings, trying to make her way out of the area. She said she had to go step-by-step along fences and buildings, and when she could finally see a little, she realized she was back on Vesey, and then the second building went down.

"I went into a building, and the next thing I know, the smoke is so thick in there, everyone started to panic, trying to get back outside. We could hear people were screaming as they ran past the building. It was so dark it looked like nighttime outside," she said. "I had to feel around for the door handle to get out of the building. It was so much worse outside I didn't know what to do." She put her hand over her mouth. "I tripped over a body," she said, choking up. "And when I tried to reach down and help them, I realized they were dead. The crowd almost trampled me, and I had to leave them there. I don't even know where I was, or I'd go back and get them."

"Nor," Hanrahan started to say, but we heard fighter jets over-head. I wondered if they were ours or if this nightmare was just beginning.

People started to run in every direction again. They ran about ten feet before someone yelled, "Why are you running? They're our jets." Everyone slowed down. When no bombs dropped from the planes and they didn't kamikaze into a building, I actually felt safer, knowing our boys were in the air, watching over us.

I looked around at the devastation and the piles of steel girders and twisted metal. There was no Sheetrock, no desks, no computers or fax machines lying on the ground. If all these tons of concrete and steel couldn't survive the collapse, what chance would a human have?

"Come on, let's get in there," Hanrahan said, and I realized that the cops, firefighters, and EMS workers had already started spreading out, picking through the debris. The pass alarms the firemen wore were still going off, but not as many as before, and I realized that once the batteries went dead on the alarms we'd have no way to know where they were.

"Pete, listen," Bishop said to Hanrahan. "We're gonna stay on post."

"Alright, Charlie, we're gonna go in and see if we can find anyone."

"Listen up," Hanrahan told us. "Stick together and be careful everywhere you step. If you're not sure it's safe, test it first. I don't want any of ya's falling in."

The scene was surreal, and as we picked through the rubble, I looked around. We looked so insignificant crawling around in the massive piles. I heard the alarms, but they were buried beneath the rubble where we couldn't get them. We were quiet as we took tentative steps, checking for solid footing before we put our weight down. It was difficult walking, and the pieces of steel were jagged in places. There were a lot of ways to get hurt here.

"There's nothing left here," I said to Joe. "How are we gonna find anyone in this?"

We were making slow progress, concentrating on not falling, when Walsh called out, "Can anybody hear me?" breaking the silence. I jumped a little, not expecting it. No one answered him, but it was a good place to start.

"Don't go in there," Hanrahan barked at Rooney, who was trying to shimmy into a hole in the debris. "We don't know how deep this stuff is, Mike. We don't know how deep it is, and we don't know how secure it is."

"Boss, then what's the sense of being here if we're not gonna look for anybody?" Rooney said, frustrated.

"Mike, we don't have any lifelines, and I don't want anybody falling into any crevices. If we hear anybody, we'll take it from there. There's no reason to take chances unless we got somebody alive in there."

I felt so frustrated, we needed to get them out *now*. Any real search would be useless without heavy equipment to move the debris. The beams and pieces of building were just too heavy to move by hand, and they'd have to be moved to do any real search.

We must have been there about an hour, and I realized we'd only gone maybe fifty feet. As we got further into the debris we saw pieces of humans. I stared at a bloody, torn-off torso. It was a man, but that's all there was to him. I saw shoulders and the back of a man's head with short, dark hair covered in gray soot. We caught up with a couple of guys from FD who were already picking up pieces of people and putting them in body bags. I was thinking this wasn't what I was here for. Wasn't there someone alive in all of this?

"What are you doing with the body bags?" Hanrahan asked a fire captain.

"We got an impromptu morgue set up by the Winter Garden," he said. "They're stacking the bodies and the parts over there.

We heard someone yell, "Hats off," and we stopped, taken aback for a second. Then we took our hats off and knelt down as a couple of firemen passed with a body. "Hats off" meant the body was a member of service, either PD or FD.

We came up on an assembly line. FD had found a body in a crevice of the rubble. It was a whole body, and there were what looked like three more pinned beneath her. She looked like a doll, lifeless but surprisingly intact. Then I realized the bodies beneath her were just body parts.

I heard someone say, "I got something here," and we scrambled, tripping and falling as we converged to the spot. Body parts were being put in body bags for the last guy on the line to take over to the morgue. We stopped to help them, moving what we could by hand, but it seemed futile.

I kept praying for someone to be found alive, and I wondered how sick and evil someone had to be to do this to innocent people. These people weren't doing anything, they just went to work and were doing their jobs.

It's different for us cops and firemen. It's part of our job. We could get shot or killed in a fire, and we know that when we show up to work. But these were office workers, stockbrokers, janitors, and maintenance people. They showed up downtown on a beautiful Tuesday morning and got incinerated because some psycho thought they'd score some points with Allah if they went down in a fireball, taking us with them. I knew it was them, and I don't care how politically incorrect it is to say it.

A retired fire chief who now worked for OEM, or the Office of Emergency Management, who introduced himself as Frank, was working through the debris with us. He must have been right here when the building went down, because he was covered head to toe in soot, like someone dumped bags of flour on his head.

"I was a firefighter for thirty years," he said, tearing up. "And I never dreamed I'd see anything like this." He put his hands out as he looked around. "I feel so helpless."

"I know," I said. "I don't even know where to start."

We were looking around at the size of the massive steel beams.

"We need equipment in here, heavy machinery. Dogs." He looked over at 7 World Trade Center and said dully, "My office is on fire."

"That's right, you're in the Trade Center now," Joe said. "You guys used to be over on Church Street."

"Yeah, we moved here in 1999."

"You're in the bunker?" Joe asked.

"We were," he said.

Not doing much good on fire, I thought. The EOC, or the Emergency Operations Center, was supposed to be the place where the city government operated during a time of crisis. They called it the bunker because that's what it was built to be.

"Didn't I read somewhere that in an emergency that's where the mayor's supposed to go?"

"It was too dangerous, they moved him up to Barcley Street."

"I thought the bunker was supposed to withstand anything," I said, watching it burn.

He wiped the dust from the corners of his eyes and rubbed his hands on his dusty pants. "It was built to withstand two-hundred-mile-an-hour winds in the event of a hurricane." He started rattling off the perks. "The exterior walls have steel framing. They're bombproof and bulletproof. They have three generators independent from the building's backup generators, a six-thousand-gallon fuel tank, an eleven-thousand-gallon potable water supply, and a backup system for heating and air conditioning." He shrugged. "It even has a pressroom."

It's got more than that. I remember reading about it, one of those "Big Brother is watching" articles that the liberals write when they're up in arms about privacy. It said that the Coast Guard allowed the EOC to monitor all of the city's major waterways by video and they can rotate and zoom in and out. They can also feed off the metro traffic cameras to look at the major roadways in all five boroughs. They have direct weather feeds, Doppler radar, and satellite that the National Weather Service feeds every hour.

I guess they never thought to watch the airports.

We heard "Hats off" again and knelt again as they brought the body past. It was a fireman. I could see the sleeve of his turnout coat as his arm hung lifelessly. I prayed for him and his family and again for Nick and to find someone alive here.

"The irony," Frank continued a couple of minutes later, "is that today the office was pretty quiet because we were doing a drill for weapons of mass destruction up at Pier 94," he said, talking about the passenger ship terminal. "I was supposed to be there at ten o'clock." He shook his head. "In the exercise, we were simulating the distribution of medication to about a thousand people who were exposed to a biological agent."

"Who does the drill?" I asked as I sifted. I knew the city did drills like that and other drills for catastrophes. I would have never thought someone would do something like this with the planes, and it was hard to comprehend that someone could be that evil.

"Most of the staff does something in the exercise, and we were using fire and police cadets from the police and fire academies."

"I didn't realize the city was doing stuff like that," Joe said. "Was something up?"

I knew from working New Year's Eve in Times Square that the city got threats, and we were concerned about this in crowds of almost a million people. But never something like this.

"Nothing specific," Frank said. "It's not like they haven't tried to hit these buildings before. Plus, recently, with the embassy bombings, we have to be ready for stuff like this." He paused. "But I never thought I'd see something like this."

We looked up as the Air Force jets crisscrossed over Manhattan. The sound was amplified now, and we could feel the force of the jets in our bodies as they roared overhead.

Once they were gone there was an eerie, menacing silence. I'm not saying there wasn't noise. People were yelling, and there was some machinery noise. But this was a different kind of silence. Manhattan is never quiet. I realized that all the ambient sounds of the city were gone. There were none of the usual sounds: no cars or buses, no horns, no sirens, and no people. It seemed as though the aura of the city was gone and all that was left were these mountains of rubble.

We heard the "Hats off" call again. It was a cop this time, and Joe and I knelt in the dust for our fallen brother.

There were more cops and firemen here now, sifting through the wreckage.

"They're saying we have an estimated two hundred firefighters missing," Frank said.

"And the 1st Precinct lost their whole day squad."

"Where did you hear that?" I asked. A day squad would be at least twenty-five to thirty cops.

"Someone from the mayor's detail," he said.

That didn't mean it was necessarily true, but the mayor's office would probably have more information than most.

As more people joined in the search, the "Hats off" calls became more and more frequent.

I saw someone I went to the Academy with, and we both started crying. I couldn't even remember his first name, but I was so happy to see he was okay.

"Thank God you're alive, buddy," I said. I didn't shake his hand. It was unspoken—I grabbed him and held on.

"This is unbelievable," he said, crying. "I can't believe this is happening."

"Tony," Joe interrupted me and nodded toward a fireman in a helmet and turnout coat. He was scanning the area with a telephoto lens, taking pictures of the devastation in and around the site.

"Boss." I motioned to Hanrahan.

Rooney and Walsh caught it and were half stomping, half stumbling over to the guy.

"Get Rooney," Hanrahan said.

Joe and I stumbled through the debris to keep up with them before either of the two muscleheads lost it and killed the guy.

"Hey!" Rooney yelled. "What are you doing?"

I saw the guy scramble for the lie as he hid his camera. "I'm going down here," he said as he pointed. "I'm looking for my company."

"What house you in?" I asked, almost friendly, as I reached him.

I pulled open the turnout coat and saw his clothes and press ID. Joe caught Rooney as he lunged.

"Give me the camera," I said, my voice shaking with rage.

Hanrahan turned to the guy I knew from the Academy. "Go get me someone from FD. See if you can get a chief or a marshal."

He looked at the reporter with disgust before he went.

"Give me the camera," I said again.

"I'll sue you if you break my camera," he said. I guess he knew by my face I was about to smash it into a million pieces.

"I'll kill you," Rooney roared. "You sick piece of garbage, you're stepping over dead bodies so you can sell your pictures."

It took Walsh and Joe to pull Rooney off. He was still screaming, "You animal, I'm gonna find you! Get his name, Tony"—he pulled away from them, and the photographer stepped back, scared now—"because I'm coming back to kill him."

"What'd you do? Did you take that coat off a dead fireman?" I asked.

"No," he said, "I got it off one of the trucks."

"Either way, you stole it," I said.

I grabbed the camera and tried to figure out how to open it. I saw him staring at the camera like he had gold in there, which infuriated me more.

"Give me the camera," Hanrahan said. He turned it over a couple of times, opened it up, and ripped the film out, exposing it.

"Check his pockets," Hanrahan said.

I found two rolls already used and a bunch he hadn't shot yet.

"You can't take that!" he said. "You can't search me."

"Buddy, this is not the day to tell me something like that," I said.

"Shut up," Hanrahan yelled at him. "You're in enough trouble."

We held him until we got a chief and then turned him over to the fire marshals.

FD was all over now, their movements looking strange as they crawled through the maze of twisted metal and steel. I kept looking for the pumpkins on the fire helmets of the rookies, hoping to see Romano. There were so many cops and firefighters there that as I looked around this hell I thought, *If everyone is downtown, who's watching the city?* I was thinking that this wasn't over and while we were all down here stuff was gonna blow up all over the city. Our guard was down, and the city was completely vulnerable to attack now.

The radios were starting to chatter up again, and I heard, "Sergeant Hanrahan from the South on the air?" coming from Hanrahan's radio. Mine was dead, and so were Joe's, Walsh's, and Rooney's. Hanrahan must have grabbed a new battery before we left the precinct. He was kneeling down, trying to move a piece of metal framing with insulation in it, and I guess he didn't hear the radio.

"Boss, they're calling you on the radio," I said.

"Oh," he said, pulling it out of his back pocket.

"Sergeant Hanrahan on the air."

"10-2 your post."

"10-4," Hanrahan said and sighed. "Time to head back."

When we got back to West and Vesey, we were mustered up in small groups.

Some of us would be establishing a perimeter now and screening everyone who was trying to get into the collapse site. We started allowing store owners in to the area to open their doors, but they weren't allowed near the collapse site. Others would be searching the buildings, making sure there were no injured and the buildings were evacuated.

Help was pouring in to West and Vesey now. Water and shovels and buckets were being passed out, along with masks for us to breathe through. They were the paper ones but still better than nothing. Stores and restaurants in the area were opening their doors with food, water, and whatever they had to give out.

We rinsed the dry, gritty dust from our mouths and poured the water over our eyes.

Big Bird waved us over to him. "I hear we got estimates that between five and ten thousand civilians and five hundred cops and firefighters were lost in the collapse," he said quietly, looking around as he said it.

"How many people did the buildings hold?" Joe asked him.

"I think fifty thousand," Big Bird said.

That meant a lot got out, but the numbers were staggering. I couldn't even imagine that many people being dead.

"Listen up," Hanrahan said. "We'll be searching the buildings just outside the Trade Center, across from 1 World Financial Center. We're going in with a team of cops and firefighters. We're gonna search twenty floors of the building and mark off each floor once we establish there's no one in there."

We crossed West Street and walked south. I noticed no one was talking, just looking around in shock, not believing that we were actually in downtown Manhattan. It looked like a war zone. We got a closer look at the piece of the Trade Center that was imbedded in the building next to us.

The building was hot and dusty. I took off my paper mask. Some of the cops had them on, but the masks were so full of dust now they were useless anyway. All they did was make your face sweat so that you were tasting the dust in your sweat, and there was so much dust seeping through the mask, clogging it up on us. FD had long abandoned their Scott Packs, which only gave them about forty-five minutes of air. After that they were deadweight.

We used flashlights to see our way up the flights of stairs and got off at each floor to search. The building had been evacuated, but it had explosion damage and was filled with debris. The windows had imploded from the collapse, and parts of the building were crushed.

We searched each room, looking under desks and in closets, calling out to see if anyone was in there. As we finished each floor we marked it off with a big *X* in orange spray paint, closed it off with caution tape, and went up to the next one.

It was almost 4:00 in the afternoon now, and we were exhausted. I'd been up for over twenty-four hours and on my feet for close to seventeen hours, but I didn't want to stop. I wanted them to get the backhoes in here and start digging it out. We had such a small window of opportunity to find someone alive here, and so far I hadn't seen anyone survive this. I think deep down I knew the search was futile. I hoped it wasn't, but I thought it was.

I was having trouble handling all this, and I was a little concerned about Walsh and Rooney. Walsh looked dazed and Rooney had been trying to get through to someone on his cell phone, I guess his wife. I wondered if the antenna on top of the tower being gone was interrupting all the communications. Rooney dialed the number again. Then he went nuts, screaming and yelling about the phone as he smashed it on the ground. Then it hit me. Rooney's wife was a stewardess.

"Mike, was Jodi working today?" I asked him. I saw it dawn on Joe.

"That's right, she's a stewardess," Joe said.

"She's a flight attendant, Joe. They don't call them stewardesses anymore, Jodi gets mad when I call them stewardesses," Rooney said. "And yes, she was working. She was on standby at Newark."

"Who does she work for?" I asked, thinking maybe someone saw what kind of plane went in.

"Continental," he said.

I know Joe well enough to know he was praying without letting anyone know; he nods his head slightly as he focuses his eyes on something.

We finished searching the building, giving a yell again as we passed the floors we already searched.

I lit a cigarette when I got back outside. The fog from the smoke was in the air, and visibility was probably only about fifty feet, so we didn't see a chief as he approached us.

"Where you from?" he asked. He was making the rounds, taking inventory of who was missing and who was accounted for.

We all gave our commands and our sergeants. Hanrahan told him we had worked a midnight and we'd been here since the second plane hit. He asked if we'd been in touch with our command, and Hanrahan said, "Yeah, everyone's accounted for."

He told us about the businesses in the area that were opening their doors with food and water. Also, showers were available at Manhattan Community College, and Verizon was giving out working cell phones over at St. Andrews Church.

We heard a rumble, and I thought it was the fighter jets again until someone yelled, "It's coming down, it's coming down!" Someone grabbed my arm and pulled as we ran for our lives again.

When we were far enough away I turned to see 7 World Trade Center, where the bunker was, collapsing. I knew the building had been evacuated—the whole area was evacuated—so at least no one died there. The building had been burning without any kind of extinguishment for hours.

I watched as the plumes of smoke and dust belched out where the almost-fifty-story building once stood. It was supposed to be indestructible, the city's nerve center in case anything catastrophic ever happened to New York.

Now it just looked like every other pile of crap here.

17

As the sun went down, the whole area was enveloped with a sense of doom. There were massive piles of rubble, some as many as twenty stories high. Sections of the buildings that had fallen were embedded in the ground, and the lights hooked up to the portable generators cast ugly shadows on the skeletal remains.

The embedded pieces actually confused me, some stood straight up and I couldn't tell if they were part of the original building or if that was how it fell. I tried to picture the towers the way they looked before.

A lot of people don't realize it, but the Trade Center complex is like a small city. It's got four subway stations, TV and radio stations, banks, a mall, parking garages, hundreds of businesses, bars, and restaurants. It's even got a drug store open twenty-four hours a day, or at least it did until this morning.

I was just here a few weeks ago with Denise. She called me on a Tuesday morning when I had collared up to meet her for lunch. Over the summer there are free concerts for lunch and dinner at the plaza that separates the two towers. They'd recently renovated it, and there was a huge gold-and-black ball fountain in the center of the plaza. I forget the name of the band we saw, but I know they sang the song "Wild Thing."

We'd been coming here since we were kids, cutting out of school and taking the ferry downtown. When I was in high school I got an A in photography for a black-and-white picture I took of the towers. I remember lying on the ground to get the whole thing in one shot. The teacher loved it; he even made a copy for himself. In fact, I still have the picture. I found it awhile back when I was going through some boxes.

As kids we loved to watch the window-washing machine go up and down, thinking what a cool job that must be. The towers stretched so far up into the sky that on a cloudy day, the tops of the buildings would disappear. And in the winter it was so cold up there that snowfall would turn into rain before it hit the street.

The day I met Denise for the concert, I finished with the ADA around 10:30 and took the train downtown. She brought us sandwiches, and I remember how packed it was with people for the concert in spite of the heat.

Now I watched as groups of workers, mostly firefighters with cops mixed in, were spread throughout the site, picking through whatever they could lift, searching for survivors, and I realized I'd never see those towers again. It was all gone. And I knew nothing was ever gonna be the same again.

We joined back in with the search, plugging away as we prayed for a moan or cry that would signal someone was alive.

EMS had set up a triage on Chambers and West streets, and the paramedics were assisting people. We stopped and had a paramedic help wash out our eyes. He gave us a bottle of wash to take with us.

We were starting to hear bits and pieces of what happened from people who had talked to their families. We now knew that a total of four planes had been hijacked, the two that hit the Trade Center, one that hit the Pentagon, and one that crashed somewhere in Pennsylvania. I tried not to think about the fact that my mother lives in Pennsylvania, and no one seemed to know where the plane crashed.

We were beyond exhaustion now as we made our way over to Manhattan Community College to take showers. I tried Michele again, getting the "All circuits are busy" line again. It was hit or miss with the phones, so I figured I'd try again after I took a shower.

There wasn't much we could do about our clothes, so we clapped them and shook them to get the dust off. I could feel the stinging of cuts on my arms and hands as I showered off, and my eyes burned as I let the water run on them. It felt like I had sand in them, and every time I rubbed them they would tear.

After drying off and putting my filthy clothes back on, I used the phone at the college and finally got in touch with Michele.

"Oh, thank God," she sobbed. "Are you okay? Where are you?"

"I'm still downtown. We're taking showers at Manhattan College, and I was actually able to get through. I've been trying on and off all day," I said. "Did you talk to anyone?"

"I talked to your mother, and I told her Donna talked to Joe, but she wants me to call her as soon as I talk to you. I talked to Denise a few times . . ."

"Did she hear from Nick?"

I heard her pause. "No. At least, the last time I talked to her she hadn't spoken to him."

"What about my brother?" Vinny was an electrician, and he worked jobs all around the city, so he could've been anywhere.

"I know Denise talked to him. He's worried about you."

"How's Stevie handling all this?" I asked, worried about him being scared.

"He doesn't really understand it. He seems to be taking his cues

311

from me. He asked if I was scared, and I said no but that we need to be praying right now. And he did, he prayed for you and Joe and everyone else in the world." She paused. "He was more worried that I was mad at you and he wouldn't see you anymore."

"And what did you tell him?"

"I told him that just because I was mad it didn't mean we wouldn't see you anymore."

"Good to know," I said.

"I'm so sorry, Tony. I shouldn't have done that to you. You were trying to call and work this out, and I was purposely ignoring you. If you had died there, that's the last memory I would have of you, and I realized how horrible I've been."

If I wasn't so exhausted and this wasn't so serious, I probably would have enjoyed seeing her grovel a little. Instead, I said. "I love you, and I'm sorry. You come first from here on in, babe, before the family, before everything," I said.

"You too," she said.

"Tell Stevie that I called and that I love him."

"I will."

"Did anybody hear from my father?" My father worked over in the federal court building, and as far as I knew they were safe over there.

"Denise heard from him this afternoon. As far as I know he was fine. I think she said he was staying at work, that they were locking down the building." When I didn't say anything, she said, "He's worried about you. Denise said he called the precinct and found out they sent people down."

"But as far as you know everyone's okay, right?" I asked.

When she didn't answer me right away I knew something had happened. "Who's not okay?" I asked.

"I don't know, Tony. Denise said something about your cousin Gino, the one you call Brother."

"He works on Wall Street," I said dismissively. "As far as I know they were fine over there. He probably just couldn't get in touch with anyone yet."

"Denise said he worked in the Trade Center," she said quietly. "Denise was at their house today when she called here, she said he worked in the South Tower."

"I thought he worked on Wall Street," I said, feeling dread seep into me. "What floor was he on?"

"I think the eighty-eighth or eighty-ninth," she said.

"Do you have their number?" I asked. I wanted to call my aunt and see if maybe they got their information mixed up.

"No, but if you want to call me right back, I'll call Denise on her cell phone."

"Yeah, I'll call you right back."

"Joe," I called and waved him over. "My cousin Gino worked in the South Tower," I said, starting to panic. "And Denise hasn't heard from Nick."

"Nick may not have been able to get to a phone yet," he said.

"We did," I said. I noticed he didn't say anything about Gino. If he worked on the eighty-eighth or eighty-ninth floor, he was probably dead.

"Who are you calling?" he asked as I dialed again.

"Michele. She's getting my aunt's number from Denise."

I wrote the number on my hand and talked to Michele for a few minutes. I didn't want to hang up. The sound of her voice was the best thing about this day, but I knew I had to get back out there.

I called my aunt's house, and my cousin Paulie picked up. "Paulie, it's Tony," I said.

"Tony," he said and started to cry. "Brother was in the South Tower."

"Are you sure?" I asked.

"Yeah, my mother called him when the first plane hit."

"Did he get out?" If he knew the first plane hit, he had time to get out.

"I don't think so, Tony. He told my mother his building was okay. He didn't realize what was going on. He said some friggin' moron flew his plane into the other building, he figured it was an accident. He would have been right where the second plane hit."

"Can I talk to Aunt Elena?" I asked.

"She's not good, Tony, they had to give her something," he said. "Little Gina too. Hold on, Grandma's here, she wants to talk to you."

"Tony, thank God you're safe." I could hear her start to cry, but she couldn't talk, and she gave the phone back to Paulie.

"Tony, how could this happen?" Paulie said, still crying. He went into a tirade and said he was going to hunt down whoever did this. This was too much for me to deal with right now and I told him I had to go and I'd get over there as soon as I could.

When I got off the phone, Joe was talking to a cop from the North precinct whose brother was a Jersey state trooper. He said he finally got in touch with his brother, who told him that supposedly a truck full of explosives was stopped trying to go over the George Washington Bridge from Jersey into Manhattan. He said the feds swooped in and took the passengers and the truck.

"Can you believe that?" Joe asked, throwing his arms up in the air.

"What else are they looking to do?" I asked, shaking my head.

Another cop, a female, was telling us that a panel truck had been parked about a block down from the firehouse in the West Village with a mural painted on it of a city with a plane about to crash into one of the buildings. He said two men, the driver and the passenger, were detained and the truck was checked for explosives.

I listened as I taped up a gash on my thumb, not knowing whether any of this was true and if it was true, how long was something like this planned without us knowing?

Within minutes of going back outside we were full of dust and soot, but at least the shower woke us up. We went back to sifting through the debris, with the smoke and the darkness working against us and the smell of burnt cement stuck in our throats. The sound of generators filled the air and hummed as they lit up the perimeter.

Around 1:00 in the morning we made our way back to the van, not talking, just trudging through, with our footsteps sending up small puffs of dust as we walked. The van was still parked with the swarm of emergency vehicles on Chambers and Broadway and was covered with a couple inches of dust, paper, and bits and pieces of debris.

The mood was somber on the ride back to the precinct. Everyone was quiet and either leaned back against the seat or had their head down as they rested their arms on their knees.

Walsh was sitting next to me, and he started to lose it, taking deep breaths as he fought back sobs. I looked at him and saw that he had turned around and was looking back toward the Trade Center. I looked back with him, seeing the entire tip of Manhattan consumed in smoke, with the buildings obscured by the thick clouds, as if all of downtown were burning.

"It's all right, buddy," Joe said. "We got through this, and you're gonna sign out tonight." But that seemed to make it worse, and Walsh's shoulders shook as he heaved big sobs.

I turned my head back and looked at the familiar sights of the West Side Highway, and except for the fact that the streets were empty and there wasn't a soul in sight, everything looked the same. Even though it wasn't. There were no towers to light up the sky, just generator-powered spotlights that got lost in the dust and the smoke.

We parked the van on the corner of 9th Avenue and walked up 35th Street. When we opened the doors I was surprised in a detached way at the amount of hustle in the precinct. The midnights are pretty quiet, and it seemed as busy as the day tour. The phones were ringing and people were moving, but when they realized we were standing there the whole area by the desk got quiet.

They were staring at us, and I saw Terri Marks's eyes fill up with tears.

"You okay, Joe?" she asked.

He looked like she was interrupting wherever his mind was and nodded yes, kind of like when you don't understand someone and just nod to let them think you do.

I didn't understand why everyone was staring, and then I realized how we must have looked to them. We were filthy, and our rumpled clothes were covered in dust. The showers we took down at the college had long worn off. Our hair was messed from being dried with a towel and sooty from the ash sticking to our damp heads. We had five o'clock shadows, me and Joe more than anyone, but I think it was the vacant stare that I noticed the most. We looked shocked and worn out as we tried to get our thoughts together to deal with everyone. I looked over at Walsh to see if he was okay, and he looked so much older to me than he did this morning.

Then they seemed to converge on us all at once, hugging us and slapping our backs. They were telling us how they saw us on TV right as the South Tower was falling. They said that it looked like the tower fell on us and they all thought we were dead.

"Good man," Vince Puletti said as he hugged me. "Ya's are good men. And women," he added for Noreen.

I heard someone yelling in the room down the hallway past the desk. It was an angry yell, and it took me a minute to realize that the voice belonged to my father. I looked at Terri, and I guess she could see the confusion on my face.

"He got here a few hours ago," she said. "We told him you were okay, but he didn't believe us. He went down to the Trade Center to look for you."

"He never would have found me there," I said as I walked around the desk, and I heard him more clearly now.

"I want to know where my son is!" he yelled. "I don't want to hear any more of this. Don't tell me he's fine, that you talked to his sergeant, I want to see my son. If he's fine then why isn't he here? Why hasn't he called back?"

"Mr. Cavalucci, we have no way of getting in touch with him," I heard someone say.

"Listen, I was a cop in this city for twenty-two years. If something happened to my son I want to know about it. If he's hurt or dead down there I want to know, because I'm gonna go get him!" he yelled.

I could hear how upset he was, and I called out, "Dad?"

"Tony," he said as he grabbed me. He was dressed for work, dusty in his blue jacket. The stuff he uses to slick back his hair was gone, and clumps of his hair fell on his forehead.

"Hey, Tony," Goldberg said. "Good to see you."

I nodded. "Hey, Whoopie," I said as I hugged my father, surprised at how glad I was to see him. I could feel myself choking up, and I didn't want to lose it in front of Goldberg. It's not that I didn't like Goldberg, we're just not close.

"Denise called and said she saw your partner on TV as the building fell," he said. "We locked down the courthouse, and then I went over to the mobile command center and asked what precincts responded and where the South was. I told them my kid responded, but everything was all over the place and they didn't know where you were."

"It was a madhouse, Dad," I said. "You never would have found us."

"I didn't want to go there, Tony, I saw enough in the service. I didn't need to see more dead people." He held up his hand as his eyes filled up, and his voice cracked as he tried to talk. "But I want you to know, if you were hurt, or dead, I wasn't gonna leave you down there all alone. I would have found you and got you out of there."

"I know. It's alright, Dad. I'm alright," I said, hugging him.

"No," he held up his hand, "I want you to understand, I wouldn't have left you there."

"I know, Dad," I said. I knew there were a lot of things about him that I didn't like, but I couldn't think of any just then.

"I love you, Tony," he said, crushing me with each word.

"I know you do, Dad, I love you," I said as I tried not to think about all the people who wouldn't get to say that tonight.

"Your sister is . . ." He looked for a word. "Inconsolable," he said, wiping his eyes. "She still hasn't heard from Nick."

"When was the last time you talked to her?"

"I don't know. My cell phone's dead. But call your mother, she needs to hear from you," he said.

"I don't have her number on me," I said.

"I have it. I wrote it down, she called me, hysterical, and said she wants to hear from you herself and not have someone else call her." He fished a piece of paper out of his pocket and handed it to me.

"Did you hear about Gino?" I asked.

"Yeah," he said. "Maybe he got out, Tony, and he just hasn't gotten in touch with anyone. All the phones downtown are out, I heard the junction box for Verizon was in the explosion site. Look how long it took me to get in touch with you," he pointed out.

We both knew he was dead, but we weren't ready to say it out loud yet.

We walked back out by the desk, and my father surprised me by hugging Fiore.

"What are you gonna do now?" I asked him.

"I'm going back to the federal building. They locked the building down as soon as the second plane hit and they realized it was sabatoge. I'm gonna go back and relieve Pete," he said. "We've been there since six o'clock this morning."

"Hang on, let me get someone to take you back down," I said.

We walked back out to the desk, and I waited for Terri to get off the phone.

"Terr, can you get someone to give my dad a ride down to the federal building?"

"Sure, Tony," she said without a smirk or wisecrack for once.

Rice and Beans wound up taking him downtown. They wanted to get a look at what was going on down there. I walked my father out to the RMP, letting him hug me in front of Rice and Beans without being embarrassed. When he drove away I realized that was the first time in my life I'd ever seen him cry.

I went back in and called my mother. Because it was an out-of-state call, I needed to get clearance. A while back the department got fed up with cops waiting till they were at work to make their long distance calls, and now we can only call certain areas.

"Hey, Mom," I said when she picked up.

"You sound exhausted," she said. "And I won't keep you. I just wanted to hear your voice. I'm very emotional right now, and I don't want to make this worse for you."

"Thanks, Mom, I appreciate it," I said, not having it in me to deal with one more thing. "I'll call you as soon as I can."

"I love you," she said, choking up.

"I love you too."

Hanrahan was at the desk, talking to Coughlin, who for once wasn't wearing his wise guy smirk.

"Hey, boss," I said to Coughlin.

"Good job, Tony," he said, nodding.

"What was it like down there?" Terri asked Walsh.

"It was horrible," Walsh said.

"We can't talk about it yet, Terr, give us a little time to get through this," Joe added.

"Sure," she said. "I'm just glad everybody's okay."

I was catching bits and pieces of the conversations around the desk. Vince Puletti was talking to Rooney about the plane that went down in Pennsylvania.

"Mark my words, Mike," he said as he pointed at Rooney. "We shot it down ourselves. Either that, or the people on that plane took it over. They should just line 'em up and shoot 'em. No more playing games with these animals, that's the only thing they understand."

I'm sure everyone was throwing their opinion in, and I just didn't have the energy to get into it with anyone.

Hanrahan and Coughlin still had their heads together at the desk, and they called Bishop over. When they finished talking, Hanrahan gave me, Joe, Rooney, and Walsh a "Come here" signal with his hand.

"Okay, here's the deal," he said. "We're doing twelve-hour tours until further notice and no days off." We nodded, exhausted. "The day tour is four in the morning till four in the afternoon. The four to twelves will do four in the afternoon until four in the morning, and the midnight tour is split, half to the day, half to the night. They decided we're the detail to the Trade Center, I guess 'cause we were there already."

I was glad we were going back. As tired as I was, I needed to get back there.

"You okay to go back?" Hanrahan asked Walsh.

"Yeah, I wanna go back," Walsh said.

"You sure? Because there's enough to do up here if you think it's too much."

"I'm sure, boss. I'm not saying I'm not upset, but I still want to go back."

They must have been working on this all day, because they had all the posts in place for the day. Even though our command is only about one square mile in size, we're one of the largest, if not the largest, in the city, with over three hundred cops.

We would be guarding every government building, especially the post office on 33rd and 8th, which is the largest in the world, open twenty-four hours a day. We'd have details at the Empire State Building, Madison Square Garden, Port Authority, Grand Central, Penn Station, and all the subway stations. There were posts at the synagogues; at El Al, the Israeli airline; up and down every corner of 42nd Street; and all through Times Square. Any place that was considered a target would have a detail.

The streets would be closed south of 42nd Street with nothing but emergency vehicles allowed through. Coughlin told us that no one but emergency personnel was allowed into the city, and even then only with ID. He told us the Staten Island Ferry would only be running for emergency personnel, and ID had to be shown and bags would be searched.

Since we'd only be getting a couple of hours sleep, Joe and I headed down to the lounge. Walsh and Rooney went upstairs to sleep in the dorm, which was probably better. The TV was on in the lounge, and we saw for the first time the images of the planes hitting the buildings.

They had the film of the first plane hitting, which a lot of the guys said they were seeing for the first time. The images were being played over and over, and while seeing the first plane hit was horrendous, the second plane hitting seemed so much more vicious to me. I could hear the plane accelerate as it approached, something I hadn't noticed from the van. The fireball was huge, and the flames glowed inside the building. I got so angry as I watched it, I wanted to find whoever did this, like Paulie said.

The cameras zoomed in, and I could clearly see the people up in the windows, waving pieces of clothes as they were enveloped in smoke. I just hoped none of their families could recognize any of them and know it was them who jumped and died that way. As I watched them jump I could still remember the sound they made when they hit the ground. They actually showed the clip from the cameraman who was with us. Out of all of us, you could see Joe the most clearly, and the horror showed on his face when the building started to come down.

When the smoke churned out when the building collapsed, it almost looked like a tornado spinning, with pieces of paper and debris flying out of it. I was looking at it, stunned that this could happen. It was like I couldn't believe this happened. I was there, and I still couldn't believe it happened.

I saw for the first time the carnage at the Pentagon. They didn't have any film of the plane hitting the Pentagon, but I could see where it hit and the people being evacuated. Without the smoke and debris like we saw downtown it looked almost mild compared to the Trade Center. Then I saw the hole in the ground with smoke coming out of it where the plane went down in Pennsylvania, and I hoped to God those people never knew what hit them.

I watched the replay of the president's address to the nation. I was glad to see that he quoted the Twenty-third Psalm, and I knew without a doubt he was going after whoever did this.

I closed my eyes and tried to sleep, but my mind was still awake. I didn't think it was physically possible for me to be awake, but I was.

I heard the guys talking and found out that people walked from all over the city downtown to the Brooklyn Bridge to get out of

Manhattan. They said all public transportation had been shut down since this morning, and the only way to get home was on foot.

"Come on, guys," I heard Joe mumble. "We gotta get up in a couple of hours."

"Sorry, buddy," someone said.

I guess I fell asleep. The last thing I remember was the flickering of the TV and the sound of the fighter jets circling Manhattan.

18

I woke up stiff and groggy to the sight of the second plane hitting the South Tower on the TV screen. I didn't know what woke me until I heard Joe's watch beep. I picked up Joe's cell phone, which was charging on the table, and saw that it was 4:00 a.m. I had only slept for probably two hours, and I was heading out for a twelve-hour tour.

"C'mon Joe." I shook him as I flipped through the channels on the TV. It was one after the other with the planes hitting the towers, the buildings falling, the blizzard of smoke that followed, the Pentagon, and the crash in Pennsylvania. I don't know why I sat there looking at it, but I couldn't turn away. I finally hit a station that had arrows and planes, outlining where the planes took off from and where they crashed.

The plane that hit the North Tower was American Airlines, hijacked out of Logan Airport in Boston, and the one that hit the South Tower was a United Airlines flight hijacked out of Newark. The one that struck the Pentagon was American Airlines, hijacked out of Dulles, and the one that went down in Pennsylvania was United, also hijacked out of Newark. I wondered if Rooney knew yet that none of the hijacked planes were Continental, even though two of them were out of Newark. I went to use the bathroom and brush my teeth so I could go tell him.

"Joe, c'mon," I said again as I returned from the bathroom. He was sitting up now, looking like a zombie with his eyes wide and his hair flattened to his head.

"I'm up," he said with a nod. "Go head up, I'll be there in a couple of minutes."

I stopped to watch the local news giving a rundown on the damage to the downtown train stations. The 1 and 9 lines at Cortland Street were destroyed, with structural damage to the tunnel, and the station was buried in debris. The 1 and 9 and the N and R at Rector Street were buried in debris, and the 2 and 3 lines at Park Place were underwater.

The muster room was packed, with all of the day tour cops and half the midnight cops present for duty. They spilled out of the room and were lined up outside it, all the way to the desk.

Everyone had been ordered into uniform — detectives, plainclothes, undercover, it didn't matter. I saw Sullie and Eileen Toomey and almost didn't recognize them dressed like cops.

"I heard you were down there," Sullie said.

"Yeah." I nodded.

"Y'alright?"

"Yeah," I said with a shrug. "I want to get back down there."

"So does everyone else. I don't know why they're sending you guys back down, you're exhausted," Sullie said. "And you look shell-shocked."

I guess that was it, then. The city probably figures if they send the same cops back down, it'll cost less later on with the shrinks because not as many will be shell-shocked and the three-quarters pay if we get hurt down there.

Everyone was talking at once, and I was catching bits and pieces of the conversations:

"So I hear my wife yelling at the TV, saying, 'What's the matter, you didn't see the building in front of you? . . .'"

"And I hear him say this moron flies his plane into the Trade Center . . ."

"I had no idea, my mother called me from Florida . . ."

"He was on the ferry when it hit . . ."

"No, I was on the Belt Parkway, listening to Howard Stern . . ."

"My brother-in-law works in that house, their entire company is missing . . ."

I caught a few people looking me up and down, and I realized I was still in my clothes from yesterday.

"Tony, we're gonna stop for coffee and head down there," I heard Hanrahan say.

I turned around and saw that, like me, he was still in the same clothes. No sense in changing them. They were just gonna get filthy again anyway.

"Hey, boss, did you see Rooney?"

"Yeah, he's out in the van already."

"Do you know if he talked to his wife?"

"Yeah, she called the house while we were down there. He got in touch with her last night."

We all piled in the van at 4:30 and stopped for coffee on 35th and 9th. Everyone but Noreen and Big Bird wanted bacon, egg, and cheese on a roll. Noreen wanted a blueberry muffin, and Big Bird wanted a buttered roll.

Joe, Walsh, Rooney, and I went in to get the coffee and breakfast.

Geri started cursing us out the minute we walked in the deli.

"Don't ever do that to me again," she said, coming around the counter, looking mad and kinda messy.

I thought she was gonna hug us, but she gave me and Joe a whack on the head, slapped Rooney on the backside, and kissed Walsh on the lips. Then she hugged us.

"You know, I thought I meant more to you than that," she said. "I see you guys as the building's coming down, I think you're dead, and nobody comes in to tell me you're okay."

"We just got back here a couple of hours ago, we were exhausted," I said. "How'd you get back into the city? I thought everything was shut down."

"It is," Geri half yelled. "I've been here for two days already. I was supposed to go home eight o'clock yesterday morning, and my brother-in-law's backing out of his driveway, and some old man plows into him. He winds up in the hospital with thirty stitches in the head. The next thing I know they're flying planes into the Trade Center, and I see you guys in the middle of it and the camera goes blank." She put her head down, and I could see her shoulders start shaking.

"It's alright, Ger," Joe said.

"No, it's not," she said. "Nothing's alright." She went behind the counter and got a napkin, wiping her eyes while she was talking. "I went over to the precinct, and they hadn't heard from you yet. O'Brien came in for coffee and said you called, but that was the last thing anybody told me."

"Sorry, Ger," Walsh said.

She looked us over and smirked. "I thought I looked bad, you guys look like a truck hit you," she said.

"Thanks," Joe said and smiled at her. "We're on our way back down, so I hope you got some coffee for us, and maybe even some bacon and egg on a roll."

"I got coffee. I didn't get rolls delivered, so the ones I got are stale. If you want I can make the eggs on bread."

"We don't care," I said. "The rolls are fine."

"You guys get the coffee." She nodded me and Joe toward the coffee machines. "I made up some sandwiches to send over to the precinct, you can take some with you."

She pointed to about a hundred sandwiches made up and wrapped in white paper.

"What's that for?" I asked.

"My brother-in-law was too cheap to close the store down so I could walk the ten miles home like everyone else. He said all the cops would be here and he could make money on the sandwiches. I told him I was making three hundred sandwiches and donating them or I was gonna quit and leave the store open with a sign that said, 'Going out of business, take what ya need.'"

I smiled, because she would actually do it too.

"Come on, Walsh and Mike can help me make the egg sandwiches."

"Ger," Joe said. "We appreciate it, but we can't carry the stuff around."

"Then I'll give you a bag of ice, and you can leave it in the van. This way at least you'll have something to eat down there."

She had a point. Yesterday the stores downtown were donating food, but there's been no power for almost twenty-four hours, and there might be nothing for the whole twelve-hour tour. This way at least we could walk over to the van and grab a sandwich.

Geri had some bacon made on the grill, and she had Walsh cutting the rolls and Rooney helping her fry the eggs.

I made the coffees, using the biggest cups she had and adding milk and sugar all around.

Since she didn't get rolls delivered, the hundred sandwiches were on regular white bread and rye.

She had them marked "turkey and cheese," "roast beef and muenster," "baloney and cheese," and "ham and cheese."

"Ger, can I get a pack of Marlboro Lights?" I said.

"Me too," Rooney said.

She took a cardboard box, stuffed in the egg sandwiches and about ten cold-cut sandwiches, and threw in six packs of cigarettes, gum, and candy bars. She put the coffee in carry trays and filled up another box with bottles of water, juice, and soda. She went into the freezer and threw a bag of ice over the drinks and added a bunch of napkins to the sandwiches.

"What do we owe you?" I asked, too out of it to even try to calculate it. Even if the sandwiches were free, there was a lot of stuff here.

She shook her head. "Don't insult me. Your money's no good here."

When we started to argue she started yelling, "Don't try to argue with me, and just take the stuff. It's the least I can do. If anybody comes in here saying you're taking stuff for nothing, they can deal with me."

We thanked her while she told us to be careful and we better stop on our way back to let her know we were okay.

On the ride downtown it looked pretty much the same as it did yesterday, covered in smoke. There was a light wind blowing, sending the smoke toward Brooklyn. The strangest thing was there was no one on the streets, making the whole area seem abandoned. I started to panic for a second, thinking yesterday was the warm-up and they'd be moving in for the kill today while we were reeling from this.

The closer we got to the Trade Center, we could see the buildings and sidewalks covered with powder. The streets were still clogged with vehicles, some abandoned, others destroyed.

We parked on Chambers, closer to the water, and walked over toward West and Vesey again, reliving everything we saw yesterday.

When we got to West and Vesey, we saw that the different city agencies were already arriving. There were payloaders and backhoes, as well as flatbeds from Sanitation, the Department of Traffic, and the DEP to move the vehicles blocking the roads out of the outer perimeter and clear the roadways as much as they could for the heavy equipment we'd need for rescue.

"Look," I said to Joe, nodding toward a ladder company from the Weehawken Fire Department in New Jersey.

"Wow. I never thought I'd see that," he said.

"Home of the Indians," I said.

"What?"

"Right before you go into the Lincoln Tunnel you can see the Weehawken Little League fields. There's a sign that says, 'Welcome to Weehawken Stadium, Home of the Indians.'"

I've lived in New York all my life, and I've never seen another fire department backing up FDNY. They've gone out to other departments that didn't have the resources they did, but they've never needed help before. I felt touched that the guys from Weehawken came to help us, and I guess in a way stronger, like we weren't alone in this.

When we got to the command post, we found out that teams were working from Liberty and West and Vesey and West, with the two locations separated by one block, a mountain of debris, and a portion of the South Tower that was impaled in the ground and bowed over West Street, making it impossible to see up or down it.

Joe's cell phone rang about 6:00 a.m., and I could tell by his face he didn't recognize the number. He was saying, "What? On West and Vesey, who's this?" He squinted as he tried to hear.

"Who was that?"

"I don't know, I couldn't hear them."

"What was the number?"

He read it off. Somewhere downtown.

About ten minutes later I heard Romano calling mine and Joe's names. He looked banged up and worn out, and his eyes had that haunted look everyone down here had. He choked up when he saw us, like when you're a kid and you fall down and hurt yourself but you hold it in until you see your mother. We all lost it then. I was so happy to see him I couldn't hold it in, and Joe and I went to grab for him at the same time.

"Come here, I'll kiss your dirty face, you scungili," Joe was saying, crying and hugging him. "Oh, it's good to see you, buddy. Thank God. Thank God."

"Did you let my sister know you're alive?" I asked, hugging him.

"Yeah, I finally talked to her about two o'clock."

"Hey, boss," Romano said as Hanrahan grabbed him.

"We thought you were dead, you rookie," Rooney said, tearing up.

"I almost was," he said. "You have no idea how close I was."

"Where were you?" This from Joe.

"The North Tower. I would have been in there when it fell too. I was on my way in, and a chief stopped me and made me help someone out of the building. I wanted to be in there with everyone else." He had to stop for a second, and he looked at Joe. "But then I was thinking about my daughter and my mother, and Denise," he added as he looked at me. "On the way in from Brooklyn I was reading that Psalm 91 you told me about." He pulled Joe's old little black Bible out of his pants pocket. "I said that prayer you told me to say, about giving his angels charge over me, that no evil will befall me. And when I was helping this woman out of the building I was praying it again, this time that a thousand will fall at my side, and ten thousand at my right hand, and it won't come near me. I told God I didn't want to die here and hurt everyone that way. And I made him a promise," he said, having a hard time talking now. "I told him if he let me make it out, I'd never doubt him again. I said that prayer you told me, the one where I said I know that Jesus died for me and he's the Son of God and that he's it for me now." It was funny how he explained it, but I think he got it right. "And, Joe, we were barely out of the building when it came down, it was like something pushed me from behind." He locked eyes with Joe. "And the next thing I know, I'm on Church Street in the middle of all that smoke. I know everyone's gonna think it was the force from the building coming down, but it wasn't. Someone pushed me."

"I believe you," Noreen surprised me by saying.

"So do I," Hanrahan said.

"Excuse me," someone said, and we all turned to see four men dressed in jeans, T-shirts, and baseball hats. Two were stocky, maybe five foot ten or five foot eleven, and one was blond and about six foot two, with a marine hair cut. The fourth guy was Hispanic, tall and thin.

"Can I help you?" Hanrahan said, a little sharp. There were no civilians allowed in the area, and I didn't know how they got down this far.

They pulled out their shields, the four of them at once. "They told us the command post was here. We drove up from Miami when we saw the buildings fall," the blonde said.

I looked at their shirts and hats again and saw that their PD logo was on the shirts.

"You got here that fast?" I asked. I knew it was less than twenty-four hours ago, but my mind couldn't calculate the hours.

"We grabbed some clothes and money and drove straight through," the Hispanic cop said. "We only stopped for gas, peed in bottles all the way up."

"Does the department know you're here?" Hanrahan asked, still not getting it.

"Of course," the blonde said. I could hear a Southern accent. "What do you need us to do, sir?"

We all looked at each other, dumbfounded that these guys drove all the way here to help us.

"Hang on," Hanrahan said. "Let me talk to the lieutenant."

Romano and the Florida cops stayed with us as we worked on the bucket brigade, working in line, digging what we could and passing the bodies or the parts of them to the next person. The Miami cops had to be as exhausted as we were, but they worked like animals, moving what they could to search, sweating in their now dust-filled clothes.

Help was coming from people in the area now. Store owners filled up shopping carts with bottles of water, granola bars, cookies, soda, and whatever else they had. Someone actually showed up with a cart full of cigarettes and cigars.

People were starting to pour into the site now, and everyone worked intensely to look for survivors. We had no idea how many were dead and missing and were still working on the number between five and ten thousand people. Every once in a while all the machinery would be shut down, and we'd call for complete silence to listen for anything beneath the pile that would let us know someone was alive. It was becoming more and more frequent for someone to yell for silence, and within seconds hundreds of people would stop whatever they were doing and give the whole area complete silence. We hadn't found anyone alive yet, but there was so much to go through.

We were working in a mixed group—cops and firemen, the Miami boys, Frank from OEM again, and a couple of Port Authority cops. When we found the body of a firefighter, we stepped aside and let FD do the honor of carrying it out.

We heard "Hats off" again and again, and we stopped what we were doing to kneel in the dust each time a body passed by us. The Miami cops looked confused the first time it happened, but now every time they heard it they put their hats over their chests and knelt down with us.

Firefighters were coming now from all over Long Island and New Jersey. Romano told us that they had relocated to firehouses throughout the city and were responding to structural alarms for us. By now there were hundreds of volunteers helping out, searching by hand, digging, or working on the bucket brigades.

Private contractors from around the city were arriving with excavating equipment and machinery. Port-a-Potties were set up, and there was a makeshift mess area with the food from the stores and restaurants.

We stopped for a smoke and a coffee at the mess area. My feet were swollen in my shoes, and while my feet screamed to get out of my boots, I knew if I took them off I'd never get them back on. I used Joe's phone to call Michele. I was guessing she was at school. I didn't ask her, and I had no idea if the schools were even open.

"Tony, this is so horrible," she said. "I'm still in shock, I can't believe this happened."

"I know, babe, but it did," I said, looking around at it. "I'm standing here looking at it, and I can't believe it happened."

"I wish you weren't there."

"I know. I wish I could see you. Ya know, you're the best part of my life," I said. "But right now I need to be here."

"I know you do," she said, and I could hear her smile. "I just want to see you."

"I have no idea when I can get out there. We're doing twelve-hour tours with no days off indefinitely," I said, wondering if I could make it that long without seeing her.

"Can I come in to see you?"

"Everything's closed. Only emergency personnel can get into the city."

"Can they do that? How are people supposed to work?"

"I don't know, babe," I said, too tired to have to think that much. "I gotta get back to this. I'll call you when I get back to the precinct. I love you."

"I love you too. Be careful."

As soon as I disconnected, the phone rang. I saw the 631 number, showing it was Long Island, so I handed Joe his phone.

I heard Joe say, "Hey, Dad," and then walk away from us with the phone.

"Hey, Miami Vice, you okay there?" I asked. They were starting to look like us now, full of dirt and vacant stares as the reality of it seeped in and became surreal at the same time.

"This is unbelievable," the blond marine-looking one said. I know they told us their names, but for the life of me I couldn't remember them. "I don't understand how someone could be this evil. What are they getting out of this?"

"Oh, they'll be getting plenty," Rooney said. "Trust me. We won't lay down for this."

"I hope we bomb these frigging lowlife scums," Romano said, at least that's what he said after I cleaned it up a little. "I hope we get every last one of them."

"We have to figure out who they are first," Noreen said.

"Please, it's the same nut jobs that did it last time. Trust me, they're bragging about it already," Hanrahan said. "You ready?" he asked Joe as he walked back over to us.

At around 2:00 in the afternoon we were working closer to Church Street. Romano was doing a recap of how he was blown away from the building, showing us where he wound up after the building fell.

I thanked God again for saving Nick. It didn't matter to me if he was blown away from the building or if an angel pushed him. He was alive and I was thankful.

Hanrahan got a call on the radio to move us over to Liberty and West Street. We saw the Winter Garden, seeing for the first time the massive damage done to it. The side of the glass dome that faces the North Tower was completely destroyed in the collapse. We heard someone call out, "I think I got something here," and silence fell over the area.

A pane of glass fell from about five stories up from one of the surrounding buildings and smashed into a ledge, shattering into pieces. Someone yelled, "It's coming down," and we took off running in every direction. One of the Miami cops slipped and fell, dropping his bucket while he looked behind him and ran. Rooney picked him up by the arm and kept running.

We stood there for a couple of minutes, wondering if it was gonna fall, when from inside the Winter Garden we heard people laughing and yelling and the sound of bottles clanging. The laughing sounded strange, like we hadn't heard anyone laugh in a long time, and we walked toward it, mesmerized.

Inside the Winter Garden a bunch of cops had taken over a bar. The place was a shell, with the windows blown out and debris and soot all over the place. There must have been about thirty cops and firemen standing around the bar like it was happy hour.

The bar had once been either circular or half round, I couldn't tell. The firemen were in T-shirts and the pants from their gear. They were sweaty and dirty like we were, with their hair dusted white. The cops were in uniform, and like us, they looked like they'd been up for the better part of two days.

We stood there watching them talk and drink like none of this was going on. There was a chaplain there too, standing there drinking a Heineken.

"Jim, these men look like they could use a drink," the chaplain said, giving us a nod.

"What can I get ya, brother?" the cop behind the bar said.

Brother. We were all brothers now.

"I'll take a beer," Hanrahan said as we went inside, glass crackling under our feet as we walked.

"Me too," Romano said.

"One for the lady? How about you, sis?" Jim the bartender asked, nodding toward Noreen. It was funny in a way, but when he said that, Noreen tried to tuck her hair back into the clip.

I saw by Jim's collar brass he was from the 17th precinct. He wasn't an old-timer, but he wasn't a rookie either.

"I'll take a beer, thanks," Noreen said.

"I'll have a beer," Walsh said.

"Do you boys have any good Irish whiskey?" Rooney asked.

Jim found an unbroken bottle of whiskey covered with dust. He blew into a dirty shot glass and wiped it on the filthy apron he had tied around his waist. He poured Rooney the shot and wiped the bar, smearing the dirt around before he placed the shot.

Bishop, Bert, Ernie, and Big Bird all had ice-cold Heinekens, and I was amazed that with the planes crashing and the buildings collapsing there was still ice in that chest keeping the beers cold.

Jim nodded at Joe and me. "What about you, brothers?"

"I'll take a beer," Joe said.

"Yeah, me too," I said, looking at Joe, giving him a nod. He seemed to understand I didn't need the drink, that it made sense right here and I was okay.

"And I'd like everyone to meet our brothers here from Miami. John"— Joe motioned toward the blond marine-looking cop— "Rob and Eric"—he pointed at the two stocky cops—"and Herman"—he finished by pointing at the Hispanic cop. "When the towers fell they left Miami and drove all night to come here and help us."

337

A cheer went up in the bar, and everyone came over to the Miami cops and shook their hands and hugged them. Jim the bartender was wiping his eye and shaking his head.

Jim raised his bottle. "To the Miami PD."

"Miami PD," everyone cheered.

"And to better days," the chaplain said. "And the grace and strength of our Lord to get us through these days."

"Here, here," Rooney said, downing his shot.

The beer was ice cold and tasted delicious. I didn't wait for the rush to come, for some reason I knew it wouldn't. I can't explain it, but I knew I wasn't gonna struggle with this anymore. These last two days had been the hardest of my life, and I hadn't stopped once to think of having a drink. The only reason I drank that beer was the same reason Joe and the chaplain did: to let these people escape the death and destruction that was right outside this door. As I watched the chaplain I was thinking, *This guy knows Jesus.* He wasn't down here to make himself look good or to try to take advantage of the fear everyone was feeling to get his religious point across. There was no talk of wrath or judgment or the end of the world. He came down here to roll up his sleeves and get his hands dirty. He wasn't weak or frail like Hollywood would like to portray a man of God. He was strong enough to stay here all day and all night, sweating and filthy, so he could bless the bodies as they brought them to him and encourage the people digging for them.

For a little while we pretended the bar wasn't a blown-out shell and that the smell of death wasn't hidden in those piles of pulverized rubble. We were running on heart now, hoping against everything that we'd get someone out of here alive. If it wasn't for that, then we had nothing left to give.

The chaplain didn't try to help us make sense of it, he just drank his beer with us and prayed for God to bless us and keep us. It was funny, but as he talked to us about how God was gonna help us get through this, I pictured Jesus in the garden when he was on his knees, praying and sweating blood, refusing to give in to his emotions and let fear and dread keep him from the cross. I made a decision right then that I wouldn't be moved by whatever was around me and that I would do God's will for me in this place.

We heard a "Hats off" call as a body was carried past outside the bar. It was draped in a flag, another fireman. We put our drinks down and knelt on the ground as the chaplain went over to bless the body. We lifted our bottles to the body on its way out and finished our drinks before heading back to reality.

Romano left after that. He was going over to Liberty and West to try to meet up with guys from his house. At this point the cops and firemen weren't separated, but I could tell by the amount of people coming in that we would probably start being posted around the whole perimeter of the site to keep people out. It was dangerous here, and even though no civilians were supposed to be here, I could see them threaded in with us.

We were getting used to the fighter jets flying overhead, and we barely looked up anymore when they passed.

The day wore on as we searched through the rubble. I tried not to stop too long on the personal items we came across. A shoe or an interoffice memo could be dismissed as anyone's, but when I came across a school picture of a little girl who looked about ten years old, my mind stayed on it. I wondered if it was on her mother or father's desk and if they were alive or buried under here somewhere. Or if the glass paperweight that had starfish and seashells inside it was from someone's family vacation or a souvenir someone brought them. I thought about my cousin Gino buried under all of this and prayed for my aunt and uncle and Paulie and Gina and for the rest of my family, for God to help get us through this.

As I looked around I realized there were probably about five hundred people searching the area with us. There were a lot of members from different departments that had family members missing. I could see the horror and panic on their faces when they realized that their children or brothers or sisters could be trapped in this. I'd been here over thirty hours now, and I still hadn't seen anyone come out of this alive.

As the sun went down we started seeing new faces come in, and while the tours were 4:00 a.m. to 4:00 p.m., no one seemed to be relieving us, just adding to us. We could tell who the first timers were when the new cops came in with their clean uniforms and the looks on their faces when they saw this up close for the first time.

At 9:00 p.m. Hanrahan got the call for all day tour posts to 10-2 the command post, which meant to go back to West and Vesey.

"What are you guys gonna do?" I asked the Miami cops, wondering if they had a place to stay.

"Someone made arrangements for us," John said. "We have a hotel on 42nd and 10th, they said there was free parking there."

"We'll stay a little more," Herman said. "What time will you be here tomorrow?"

"Same time," Hanrahan said. "If you want, you can meet us at the command post around five or five thirty."

We shook hands and thanked them, telling them we'd meet them in the morning.

It took us awhile to get back to the mobile command center. The city was quiet again except for the sounds of machinery and the hum of the lights from the generators.

The command post was lit up, with a lot of movement, people going in and out and handing the brass papers and them barking out orders into their radios.

We were shuffling now, with barely enough energy to pick up our feet as we walked. I pulled off the leather work gloves that some-

340

one had donated earlier in the day and stuffed them in my back pocket.

The lieutenant talked to Hanrahan and told us, "You're out at nine fifteen, your tour is over at twenty-two hundred hours," giving us forty-five minutes of travel time that we wouldn't need to get back to the precinct.

Walsh was a little better today as we made our way back to the van. We were torn between not having the energy to stand anymore and not wanting to leave the site.

The van was covered in a couple of inches of dust and from a distance almost looked like your car does when you come outside after a snowfall.

Our mood was somber, and the streets were empty again as we drove, but I noticed traffic was down as far as Canal Street now. Noreen would beep the horn as we passed cops or other emergency vehicles as we drove up West Street.

Walsh broke the silence by saying, "Do you think anyone's still alive?"

No one answered at first, and then Rooney said, "I hope so."

"I know you hope so, Mike, but in reality, is anyone alive?" Walsh sounded agitated. "I mean, half the stuff is still on fire. Can somebody be alive buried under all that stuff, breathing in the smoke?"

"I don't know," Rooney said. "But I hope so."

My mind was wandering as we drove up West Street. I thought about Romano and my cousin Gino, and about my father coming to look for me yesterday when he thought I got caught in the building coming down. He'd never been a protective father. When I was a kid he used to throw me to the wolves, trying to make a man out of me. When I saw him at the precinct he was like a thousand other fathers I've met, beside himself that his kid was hurt and scared that he was dead. I guess in a way I've always seen him as so strong and

341

tough, and it was strange to realize he was just like everyone else. I got a glimpse of how he really feels about me, and I wondered how it would play out from here.

I thought about Michele and Stevie, and I realized they were my real family now. I felt like I was starting to get this love thing with Michele, and over the past few days I'd started to let her see me for who I am, all the good and bad, strengths and weaknesses. When those buildings came down and all those people died I felt like God spared me, and I didn't want to take that lightly. And in the middle of all that horror I thought about her and Stevie out in Long Island safe at home waiting for me. And I wasn't gonna screw it up.

About a hundred yards south of Christopher Street we heard a commotion, with a crowd yelling as we approached. I was in no mood to deal with anything right now, and I hoped whatever it was, they didn't need cops for it.

There was a crowd of people facing the northbound traffic on West Street. They separated into two groups, one on the east side of West Street and the other on the island in the middle of the street. We all sat up to look at them and saw they were waving and holding up signs and yelling.

We couldn't see what they were doing until we got right up to them. They were jumping up and down, waving the signs at us. They didn't look like protesters, and then we heard them.

"You guys are heroes . . ."

"We love you . . ."

"God bless you . . ."

The signs said, "New York loves NYPD," and "Our Heroes," and "God Bless America."

The "New York loves FDNY" sign didn't surprise me, everyone loves them. I was more shocked that they were cheering for us; usually they spit and throw bottles.

The light was red, and we actually stopped. There were no cars on the road and we didn't have to, but I guess we wanted to hear them.

We must have been a sight, because I saw some people start crying when they looked at us.

"We love you," they yelled. "You're our heroes."

We all leaned forward, staring at them as they yelled and cheered, touched and encouraged that they came out here to do this for us.

We waited for the light to change, waving at them as we drove past. I sat back, still amazed at the cheering crowd. Tomorrow morning when I had to go back down and sift through that rubble, I'd pass this corner and think about them cheering us on. And I'd be able to do it again.

ACKNOWLEDGMENTS

We found that as we wrote this book we had to keep a running tab on everyone we want to acknowledge for their input along the way.

First and foremost Mike Valentino, our agent. This is the fourth book and we never stop being grateful for you taking us on in the first place. We're glad the curse of the Babe is finally broken and you got to see Boston win a series in your lifetime. We hope you took pictures, it may not happen again.

Lonnie Hull DuPont, the more we do this, the more we love you. Opa baby, bada bing.

Sal Ventimiglia, thank you for sharing your experiences at the Trade Center on that day and about FDNY. Thanks, bro, you're still our favorite hosehead.

Joe Folino, retired FDNY and OEM. Thank you so much for letting us read your personal account of 9/11 and afterwards, we were riveted by your story.

Al O'Leary again for his friendship and endless connections. You're a great guy.

Sandy Pedersen, the second born like me. Thank you for all your years of friendship and for really understanding the alcoholic family. Thanks for all your input, especially on step 4.

Richie Henberry, thanks for reliving the horror to give us your perspective of the towers when they fell. We hope we did it justice.

Scott Hennessy for sharing his story about that day before Frank got there.

Everyone at Baker Books.

Ben Laura and Pure publicity for all their hard work.

And Kathy Lione for her nursing experience, love, and support. I love you, Mom.

Olivia Mierzwa for her help with *Español*.

Dave Jones's mother for her help with Korean. Connie and Dave, we love you, man.

As always, Georgie and Frankie for their love and support, we love you more every day.

And P. O. Stephen Driscoll and Cira Patti, two of the many who lost their lives that day. May you rest in peace, old friends.

F. P. Lione is actually two people—a married couple by the name of Frank and Pam Lione. They are both Italian-American and the offspring of NYPD detectives. Frank Lione is a veteran of the NYPD, and Pam recently left her job as a medical sonographer in vascular ultrasound to stay home with their two sons. They divide their time between New York City and Pennsylvania, in the Poconos. They are also the authors of the Midtown Blue series. To contact the authors, log on to their website at www.midtownblue.com.